EPITAPH
for an ANGEL

EPITAPH
for an ANGEL

A CONNOR HAWTHORNE MYSTERY

BY LAUREN MADDISON

alyson books
los angeles

© 2003 BY LAUREN MADDISON. ALL RIGHTS RESERVED.

MANUFACTURED IN THE UNITED STATES OF AMERICA.

THIS TRADE PAPERBACK ORIGINAL IS PUBLISHED BY ALYSON PUBLICATIONS,
P.O. BOX 4371, LOS ANGELES, CA 90078-4371.
DISTRIBUTION IN THE UNITED KINGDOM BY TURNAROUND PUBLISHER SERVICES LTD.,
UNIT 3, OLYMPIA TRADING ESTATE, COBURG ROAD, WOOD GREEN,
LONDON N22 6TZ ENGLAND.

FIRST EDITION: NOVEMBER 2003

03 04 05 06 07 **a** 10 9 8 7 6 5 4 3 2 1

ISBN 1-55583-812-X

LIBRARY OF CONGRESS CATALOGING-IN-PUBLICATION DATA
MADDISON, LAUREN.
EPITAPH FOR AN ANGEL : A CONNOR HAWTHORNE MYSTERY / BY LAUREN MADDISON—1ST ED.
ISBN 1-55583-812-X
1. HAWTHORNE, CONNOR (FICTITIOUS CHARACTER)—FICTION. 2. WOMEN
NOVELISTS—FICTION. 3. BOSTON (MASS.)—FICTION. 4. LESBIANS—FICTION. I. TITLE.
PS3563.A33942E65 2003
813'.54—DC21   2003052402

CREDITS
COVER PHOTOGRAPHY FROM STONE/JONATHAN MORGAN.
COVER DESIGN BY MATT SAMS.

For Sandra,
loving companion,
wise friend,
and a light in the world

ACKNOWLEDGMENTS

How would I ever manage without my friends? They brainstorm, proofread, critique, make me a little crazy with sweating the details, and it's all good. Thank you, Sandra, always my number-one collaborator. And I'm blessed with good, good people in my life who love me and inspire me and restore my optimism when it flags a little. They are my own Circle of Light—Katherine Missell, Debbie Elston, Judy and Dennis DePrete, Alys Sullivan, Debra Jordan, Marj Britt, Karen Epps, Glenda Knox, Maggie Bell and her brother, Jeffrey, Shaun Field, Debra Baker Cullen, Amy Jahn, Billy Carter, Vicki Stephenson, Carolyne Mathlin and her mom, Barbara Mathlin, Russell Burns, Shirley Martin, Gloria Maddock, and so many others. Thank you all for your love.

A high five to my nephew, Devin Elston, for tips on the performance and sheer good looks of the BMW featured in this story. He also wanted to have a character named after him, so I obliged. And my other nephew, Teal Elston, as my technical advisor, carried out serious scientific research using model cars to determine whether a limousine can fly, and how far.

Once again, my editor, Angela Brown, demonstrated her ability to really understand the heart of a book and then used her considerable talent to make it better. Thank you. (It's okay if we don't always agree on commas.)

AUTHOR'S NOTE

We writers love to take liberties, so if you Hingham folks think my rendering of your fair village is not quite accurate, you're right. I've plonked down a church where there isn't one, and swapped around a street or two. But not out of disrespect. After all, I have my very own ancestor, one John Leavitt, a-moldering in a grave in Old Ship Churchyard since the 17th century.

So, to all of you who find a little bending of reality here and there, please forgive me. Remember, it's only fiction...or is it?

Prologue

There be none of Beauty's daughters
With a magic like thee.
—George Gordon Byron, Lord Byron, *Stanzas for Music*

In the year of our Lord,
Eighteen Hundred and One
In the Southwest of England

"Why can't we stay here, Mama?" Receiving no response, the little blonde girl stamped a slippered foot. "Why do you keep looking out that window?"

"I'm watching for your Uncle Fitz," the woman replied wearily, letting the heavy curtain drop into place over the set of French doors. "He should have been here by now."

"But why must we leave, Mama?" the child persisted. "You said on Easter Sunday that we might live here forever and ever. Papa said this would always be our home. And Jack was going to teach me how to ride a pony."

"I'm sorry, Eliza, but we have no choice. Your papa has gone away, and Uncle Fitz's friend has a lovely big house with acres of gardens and a stable."

"But Jack won't be there." The child pouted, more for dramatic effect than out of misery, her mother thought. "Why can't he come along?"

Lady Genevieve Fitzhugh smiled at her daughter. "I don't know how you've gotten so attached to that foolish stable lad, but he simply can't come with us. You know that. And you know that where we're going is a secret."

"I'm tired of secrets. I never get to have any friends because of secrets."

Genevieve sat down in the dark-red horsehair-covered armchair near the window. "Come here, my love." Reluctantly, Eliza came to stand in front of her mother. Genevieve tugged at the ribbon ties of her high-necked dress and carefully extricated a pendant that had been concealed beneath the fabric of her bodice. "Do you remember what I told you about the story of our family?"

Eliza frowned for a moment. "Yes," she finally muttered. She was an exceptionally intelligent little girl, far wiser than her years, but when she was in a rebellious mood, as now, she didn't want to be reasoned with. Her seven-year-old self wanted motherly indulgence, not logical explanations.

"Then you remember what I said about us, that some of those in our family receive a special kind of talent, a gift. And we have to protect that gift or some people might abuse it."

"I don't see why it's so important, knowing things before they happen. What difference does it make?"

"Well, that isn't quite all that it does. Do you recall on Wednesday last, when you ran to tell Jack not to take the coach horses out into the pasture because there was going to be a thunderstorm with lightning?"

"Yes, and I was right," Eliza said with a triumphant grin.

"Indeed," her mother replied. "Jack kept the horses in the stable just to humor you, but imagine his surprise when there was a storm."

"That's not like telling the secret, is it?" Eliza asked, a trace of worry in her bright blue eyes.

"No, my little angel, not really. But if you did it often enough, people would start to talk, and eventually there would be rumors."

"You said only ignorant people like the publican in the village listen to rumors."

Genevieve laughed softly. "True. And you do seem to remember almost everything I say, at least when it suits you."

"I can't help it. I can always think of exactly what everyone said, all the time. I couldn't forget if I tried."

"I know. Someday you may find that helpful, but it has its disadvantages as well. Now, look, you've gotten me completely away from the subject. You said just now that it didn't matter if you knew things before they happened. But it does matter."

"Because I saved the horses from being out in the storm," said Eliza hopefully.

"You kept them in," Genevieve nodded, "but you didn't stop to think if you ought to have done it."

"Well, of course, I thought about it," replied Eliza, annoyed at her mother's failure to understand. "That's why I warned Jack."

"But you only saw a small part of the picture. You saw the storm raging over the pasture, and you assumed the horses would come to harm. But what you don't know is that because Jack kept them in the stable, Highboy got into a bushel basket of apples and ate so many he's terribly ill."

Eliza's hand flew to her mouth. "He's not going to die, is he?"

Her mother started to answer, then paused. "Don't you know the answer to that?"

Eliza's face twisted with concentration, but after a few moments, she looked up, tears in her eyes. "No, there's only a big white cloud when I try to think of Highboy."

Genevieve took the child into her arms. "Don't cry, my love, the horse will be fine in a few days. But remember that you can't rely on the gift, especially when you're worried about someone or something you love. And you must always be careful about telling people the future. When you're older, it will be easier to know what to do."

"I don't want to be older," the girl said with a shrug. "I've seen people's faces change sometimes when I look at them. It's as if they get all wrinkled right while I'm watching. Then I look away, and when I look back, they're the way they are in the Really Real."

Genevieve smiled gently at Eliza's way of putting things. The child had come to define her experiences as either part of the Really Real (what other people saw) or Dream Pictures (the things other people apparently couldn't see). Her mother wondered whether her daughter might one day come to understand that she had the definitions backward.

Eliza gripped tight to her mother's hand. "That never happens to you, you know."

"What doesn't, sweetheart?" said Genevieve absently, her ears straining to hear the sound of her brother-in-law's coach-and-four.

"Your face never gets wrinkly, even when I squint my eyes and look at the edges of you, the way you taught me."

Genevieve, startled, looked at Eliza closely to see if she were being sincere, or only wanting to be kind.

"Never? Not even once?" asked Genevieve, breathing deeply to keep the tremor from her voice. Eliza was acutely sensitive to the emotions of those around her.

"Honestly, Mama, not even one time. You always look like..." The child paused for a moment and regarded her mother with ultimate seriousness. "You always look the way you do right now. Soft, and..." She struggled for the words. "A little cloudy and beautiful, like an angel."

Genevieve swallowed the lump that had risen in her throat

and blinked back the tears that itched behind her eyes. "That's lovely, my darling. Thank you. Now, you'd better go and tell Margretta to make sure all our luggage is in the foyer. And don't forget your hat and gloves. The night air is cold."

Eliza hesitated. Her perfectly elfin face, under its halo of golden hair, tilted up to gaze at her mother. "What's wrong, Mama?"

"Nothing at all, child. Now go along and do as I told you."

Genevieve waited until Eliza had darted out of the drawing room and her small footsteps had retreated to the rear of the house before letting her guard down. Standing once more by the window, she parted the drapes and let her forehead rest against the smooth, cold, wavy surface of hand-blown glass. Her teardrops fell silently to the thick carpet. *No, please,* her mind reached out. *She needs me, my daughter needs me.* Genevieve knew there could only be one explanation for Eliza's inability to "see" her mother's countenance aging.

A sharp clatter of hooves and the rumble of carriage wheels alerted her to an arrival. She strained to make out the shapes in the darkness. With a sigh of gratitude, she saw the familiar white blaze on the forelock of her brother-in-law's lead offside coach horse. She rushed to the foyer and pulled back the heavy bolts, tugging at the massive oak. Within moments, Fitz flung his arms around her. "I'm not a moment too soon," he said quietly. "That fool, Dorrance, has got the old duke in a lather about Eliza. witchcraft and all that utter nonsense."

Genevieve took a step back to better see his face. "Surely not. This is 1801, Fitz, not the Dark Ages. It's been almost a century since—"

"Yes, but the Duke of Crevier hasn't let go of the family obsession. You know his father was still trying to hunt down healers and midwives and have them imprisoned in madhouses right up until the day he died. And the son is just as insane. He's whipped some of the village folk into a frenzy, telling them Eliza is some seed of Satan. And he's paid that senile vicar and some greedy sheriff to agree with him. I think the two of you are in danger. At the very least, he's coming to confront you, and you could lose your freedom. It's high time we were on the road."

"Crevier is coming here?"

"Yes, and we haven't time to spare. He may only be an hour behind me. Eliza certainly wouldn't benefit from that kind of confrontation."

Genevieve turned quickly back toward the hall. "Margretta! Eliza! Come here at once!"

In less than a minute, Eliza emerged, tugging the young lady's maid by the hand. "Uncle Fitz!" Eliza crowed, flinging herself toward him.

He scooped her up and whirled her around once. "Ready to go on a new adventure, my little elf?"

"Mama said they'd have horses. They *will* have horses, won't they?"

"You know your Mama only tells you the truth," he smiled, putting her down. "I've heard they have ponies, too, just right for little legs to straddle. Now find your cloak." Fitz quickly hefted the valises and strode outside with them.

Genevieve helped her daughter wrap up against the cold, then told Margretta to take the small items of hand luggage and help Eliza into the coach. Fitz returned a minute later, and beckoned. The look in his eyes spoke volumes. He wanted them gone long before Crevier showed up with some ragtag delegation of drunken village folk.

"What will happen if he arrives here shortly after we're gone?" asked Genevieve. "Won't he follow?"

"Perhaps, but it's more likely he'll go home."

"Not him," she replied. "He's more than obsessed, Fitz. He's driven by something we hardly understand, something very dark and very dreadful. And if the thinks he has the law on his side..."

"He won't be able to catch us up," Fitz insisted. "My team is barely winded. We'll make excellent time to the docks at Chillwater. And once we've sailed—"

"The ship doesn't sail until the late tide. That leaves a couple of hours for Crevier to follow us once he finds us gone."

"It will be safe there," he insisted.

"Not at that hour. You don't know what we're dealing with. I do, I'm afraid. Crevier's driven to destroy me and Eliza, whether or not he knows why. And can you imagine what would happen to her in one of those horrible asylums? Those who aren't already insane become mad anyway."

"When my brother died, I swore that I would protect you," Fitz declared, his jaw muscles rippling with anger.

Genevieve put her hand on his arm. "I know you'd give your life to keep us safe, my dear brother, but what about Jack and the others?"

Fitz snorted. "The stable boy? Send him away. The grooms and house staff, too."

"But then all of them would know we were going, and Crevier could easily frighten them into talking. He might even harm someone. And you know I can't allow that."

Fitz looked at her, horrified. "You don't mean you'd stay behind. You can't. Eliza needs you...all of us need you. Genevieve, please, think about what you're risking. If Francis were alive, he would never countenance such a decision."

"But he's gone, Fitz, these four months now. I'll follow when it's safe. But I can hold Crevier here as long as he thinks Eliza is here, too. By the time he knows the truth, the ship will have sailed and it will be too late."

"The man is unbalanced! He may not even act rationally

toward you. And there is no one left here who can protect you against him."

"Fitz," she said, squeezing his strong hand between her two much smaller ones, "I am never alone. None of us is ever alone. She is always here."

He sighed. "The Holy Mother helps those who help themselves. This is foolhardy, Genevieve!"

"No, it is my duty, Fitz. The gift is strong in Eliza. There are those who would destroy her, and those who would exploit what she knows. Both are dangerous! I'm entrusting my daughter to you. Promise me you will keep her safe. "

Fitz looked down at her, tears glistening in his eyes. "I swear to you by all that is holy, I will let no harm come to her."

She smiled. "Good, because I will soon have another little one for you to look after. And I think it will be a boy."

Fitz gaped. "You are with child?"

"Yes, and I will take no unnecessary risks. But some are necessary."

"Genevieve, please, don't do this!"

"Don't do what, Mama?"

Fitz and Genevieve turned to the open door. Eliza stood there, a puzzled look on her face. "Why is Uncle Fitz angry?"

Genevieve hurried to her child and knelt in front of her. "He isn't angry, my love. We were having a little disagreement. You see, I want to stay here and explain to Jack and the others why we're leaving. Then I'll meet you and Uncle Fitz at the ship in a little while. And if I'm late, I shall sail on a different ship. So you see, everything will be fine."

Eliza flung her arms around Genevieve's neck. "No! I want you to come with us now. Please, Mama, please."

Genevieve squeezed her eyes tightly together to hold back her tears. Her arms trembled as she held her precious little girl, whose tiny heart beat in rhythm with her own. "Remember what I've taught you? That sometimes we must be braver than we feel? This is one of those times, my darling, and I need for you to go with Uncle Fitz without delay." She pulled back and looked at the child's tear-stained face. "There's something I'd like you to take care of for me, though."

Genevieve reached behind her back and unclasped the chain from which dangled the pendant she'd worn since she was barely Eliza's age. It was hand-carved and appeared to be solid, a stylized image of two figures intertwined as lovers—one rendered in gold, the other silver. Yet when she twisted the carving a certain way, the figures separated. She slid the gold figure off the chain and pressed it into Eliza's hand. "You know how important this is. It belonged to my mother and her mother before her, and…well, the women of our family have worn this for a very long time. I'll keep one half, and you keep the other safe until I see you again." She pressed the small figure into Eliza's hand. "Your uncle will find you a chain for it later." She smiled. "You'll not lose it, now?"

Eliza's lips trembled with the effort not to cry. "No, Mama, I shan't lose it."

"Good, I knew you'd be the perfect keeper." Genevieve refastened the chain with the remaining silver figure around her neck and tucked it beneath her dress. Smoothing a lock of Eliza's hair, she pulled the ties of her daughter's cloak together more securely, then looked over her shoulder at Fitz, a question in her eyes.

He nodded, and rearranged his stricken countenance into a tight smile, then stepped forward and scooped up his little niece. "Mama will be fine, pumpkin. But you know it's always best if we do as she asks. She's a very wise lady, isn't she?"

Eliza didn't answer, merely stared hard at her mother, as if seeing her differently. "I love you, Mama," she whispered, then buried her head in Fitz's shoulder.

"I love you, too, Eliza Miranda," Genevieve whispered, her hand pressed against her heart as if she might somehow ease the pain in her chest. "Now go quickly!"

With a last appeal in his eyes, Fitz backed toward the open door. Genevieve answered with a shake of her head. In seconds, Eliza was inside the coach, in Margretta's arms, and Fitz leaped to the driver's seat. The sound of the whip cracking above the heads of the horses rent the air like a pistol shot. And they were gone.

Genevieve watched until the sidelights of the coach disappeared into the distance, until she could no longer hear the horses' hooves. From force of habit, she felt for the pendant. She knew its power to protect her had been profoundly diminished because it was no longer whole. She would gladly have given both halves to Eliza, but for the new life that grew within Genevieve. Somehow, the unborn child must be protected, too. *Let it keep her safe,* she thought, *until the light and dark are reunited in one.*

She went back to the drawing room, and built up a roaring fire. Then she lit lamps, both downstairs and up. Retrieving one of Eliza's old cloaks and an outgrown pair of shoes from a bedroom closet, she took it downstairs and draped it over an oak settle. Finally, she crept up the back stairs to the servants' quarters. Tapping on the door, she awoke the two housemaids and quietly and firmly instructed them to dress, go to the stables, and tell the others that the mistress was expecting trouble and they should all leave at once and not return until the next day. She waited until they were out of the house before locking the rear doors and bolting the front.

Seating herself before the fire, she waited. And never saw the wide-eyed stable boy, Jack, hunkered down in the shadows, peering in through the French doors. But what he saw that night would haunt him to the end of his days.

CHAPTER ONE

In sure and certain hope of the resurrection to eternal life
through our Lord, Jesus Christ,
we commit to Almighty God our sister,
and we commit her body to the ground;
earth to earth, ashes to ashes, dust to dust.
—The Book of Common Prayer

Massachusetts, The South Shore

Connor Hawthorne yanked on the lapels of her jacket. "I don't like funerals."

"There can't be many people in the world who actually do like them, sweetheart, and if you do that to your collar one more time, you'll tear it off," replied Laura patiently.

"All right, let me be more specific. I positively, without a doubt, hate funerals."

"If you don't finish getting dressed, I won't get a chance to find out just how much you hate them. And we'll be the center of attention when we walk in late."

Connor ran a wide-tooth comb through her hair and regarded the skillfully trimmed brush cut with moderate satisfaction. "I really like how Angel does my hair," she commented. "Do you think it's too long in the back?"

"Darling, it's just touching your collar." Laura gently brushed a lock of Connor's black hair to one side. "But the front is starting to get acquainted with your eyebrows."

"Too late now."

Laura touched Connor's cheek. "Why are you so nervous about this funeral? And don't tell me it's because you don't like being around dead people."

"Well, I don't. Especially the kind who refuse to die and remain silent."

"I don't think there's much risk of your friend's mother coming to visit us-in the Dreamtime, or any other time."

"You can't know that for sure."

"True, but since neither of us has a connection with her family."

"Except for me...and Grace," Connor mumbled, her back to Laura.

"You know, it's okay to say her name out loud. Surely you don't think I'm jealous of someone you knew back in college."

"That's 'knew' in the biblical sense," Connor reminded her, blushing slightly.

"I figured that out, sweetie. And since both of us had a life before we met each other, I think it's safe to assume we weren't virgins."

"Hardly," Connor nodded, reaching for her raincoat. "I just want to be sure you're okay with going to this thing."

"If I weren't, I'd tell you. When have you known me to be less than frank?"

"There have been a few occasions when you've thought I didn't need to know something."

"Maybe. But we have a deal now," said Laura, hands on hips. "Truth, no matter what."

"Yeah, I know. But I've been meaning to ask you if we could modify that slightly."

"Why?"

"So, for instance, when I ask you if you like my green chile stew, you could fib just a little bit."

Laura laughed. "But honey, your stew isn't all that bad."

"Damned with faint praise," Connor shook her head. "See what I mean?"

"Not all that faint. Considering I'm a Navajo whose grandmother is the best cook on the Rez…"

"Okay, you're right. I'll have to choose my battles more carefully. I'll wager your grandmother can't make jambalaya."

"Probably not, and you're just stalling. We have to go."

Connor sighed. "I'm not looking forward to any of this."

"Especially not since you found out your mother will be there."

"Yep."

Laura put her arms around Connor from behind and rested her head between Connor's shoulder blades. "Just keep breathing and maintaining that neutral expression you use for dithering fans at your book signings."

"Inane questions just annoy me. My mother, on the other hand, pisses me right off."

"I know. But for Grace's sake, don't let your mother get under your skin."

"She hates Grace, too. I can't imagine why she'd come to this."

Laura let go of Connor and reached for her coat. "Didn't you say your mother and Grace's mother were friends?"

"More like teammates in a self-pity marathon. As in, 'How could people like us have daughters like that?'"

Laura opened the door and shoved the old-fashioned key into the lock. "Personally, I'm pretty happy Amanda Hawthorne had a 'daughter like that.'"

Connor followed her through the door, shut it, and locked it. "Thank you. I'm glad someone is."

"Oh, stop it! You're loved, and you know it. There's me, of course. Your dad and Malcolm and your daughter and your Aunt Jess and—"

"All right. I give. Just trying on a little martyrdom."

"Well it doesn't fit."

"Damn. I was hoping for sympathy."

"Only when you deserve it. Today all sympathy is reserved for people in need. Like your friend Grace."

They stepped out onto the porch of the bed-and-breakfast that perched on a cliff. The ocean lay beneath them harsh and gray in the tepid light of an overcast morning. Swirls of fog floated close to the ground, and a cool mist seeped from the clouds so that every shrub and flower dripped. They crunched over the gravel to the parking lot where they'd left their rental car and climbed in.

"Perfect weather for a funeral."

"Maybe this particular one," replied Laura, pulling the end of her raincoat in before slamming the door. "Since I imagine everyone will be mourning and nobody celebrating the transition to the next life."

"WASPs don't really celebrate," said Connor as she started the car. "We try to avoid excessive displays of emotion."

"That doesn't exactly describe *you*, sweetheart."

"No, that's because lesbians are disqualified from full-fledged WASP membership."

"You didn't want to be one, did you?"

"A WASP or a lesbian?"

Laura smacked Connor's arm. "Oh, stop!"

Connor grinned. "I tried the Junior League lifestyle when I got married. But I just couldn't get the hang of it. You know, what color pumps to wear with the frilly apron."

"No one does that, you goof."

"I beg your pardon," said Connor, signaling a left turn onto Jerusalem Road. "Have you never sat in awe of Donna Reed? Jane Wyman? Beaver's mom?"

"I wouldn't call it awe. More like deep puzzlement."

"Me, too."

Connor glanced at a street sign. "You've got the directions?"

Laura slid the folded paper out of the side pocket of her shoulder bag. "Let's see. We stay on this road for a couple of miles. As soon as we cross over Hull Street, we continue straight ahead, but it's then Rockland Street."

"Check. And then?"

"Then it becomes Summer Street."

"They can't settle on one name for the same road," Connor muttered.

"This is Massachusetts, dear. An old friend of mine is from this area. She says you get used to it."

"That and rotaries," sighed Connor.

"According to this map and the directions Grace sent us, we'll get to one of those before long. Right around Hingham Harbor. Then we go straight through the rotary, past the Fruit Basket, whatever that is, and bear left at Star's Restaurant onto North Street. Left at a fork onto South Street, left on Main, and we're there. You going to remember all that?"

"Probably not," replied Connor. "You'll have to remind me as we go."

A few minutes later, they saw the tips of masts sprouting from the harbor. "There's just something about New England," murmured Laura.

"I know. Much as I hate clichés, I can't stop the word 'quaint' from rolling around in my head."

"Quaint in a good way?"

"Sure. How can you not get a little moony over a picture like this? Seagulls, the smell of briny water. Even the clouds and the gray sky are perfect. None of that California-sparkly, movie-set feel to it. You know?"

Laura smiled and laid a hand on Connor's arm. "Did you realize you tend to think of the world in terms of settings for a novel?"

"Perils of being a writer, I suppose. But now that I come to think of it...hmm." Connor slowed for the rotary.

"Got an idea cooking?"

"I'm thinking of a murder in a little seaside village. Something involving boat hooks or—what do you call those things, gaffs?"

Laura laughed. "You'll have to brush up on your nautical knowledge before you tackle the next book."

Connor glanced over at Laura. "I like your hair down like that."

"I know you like it, sweetheart, but you don't have to deal with it getting in your way all the time."

"So why no long braid today?"

Laura shrugged. "A little cliché-conscious myself, I suppose."

Connor frowned. "What?"

"Something that woman at the restaurant said last night while you were in the ladies room."

"What woman? The hostess?"

"She said, 'Oh, that braid is so Indian—I love it.'"

Connor shook her head. "Some people are incredibly stupid."

"I know. And I've never been anything but proud of my heritage, even if I'm a little bit of a mutt. It's just that...okay, I'm a little nervous about all these D.A.R. types who'll show up for the funeral today. And your friend Grace...well, they'll all be checking us out, I imagine..." Laura trailed off, as if unwilling to finish her thought, then grabbed for the dashboard as Connor hit the brakes, skidded onto the shoulder of the narrow road, and slammed the gearshift into park.

"What?!"

"Don't *ever* sell yourself short, and don't ever think for a moment you're not every bit as good…make that *better* than a bunch of self-proclaimed blue-blooded snobs who still live in the 19th century. Grace's mother was a bigoted pain in the ass, just like my mother. That's why I didn't even want to come to this damn funeral."

"Because you'd be with me?"

Connor slapped the gearshift. "No! Because I'd be reminded of all the crap I've had to put up with all my life. All the sneers and icy glares and tight-lipped murmurs about Amanda Hawthorne's daughter…" Connor screwed up her face into a mask of disapproval and shifted her usually low-timbred voice into a shrill falsetto: " 'What a shame'… 'And she seemed like such a nice girl'… 'Thank goodness her ex-husband found a nice woman'… 'Her poor daughter must be so mortified to have a mother like that. No wonder she moved to England.' "

Laura reached for Connor's hand. "Oh, sweetheart, I'm sorry. Has it always been that bad?"

"Ever since I divorced Alex and began living with Ariana." Connor was quiet for a moment, and Laura let her be. Even after several years, Connor still felt partly to blame for Ariana's murder. "I've gotten used to it, more or less. But I hate the thought of you being subjected to it."

"Been there, done that, honey. You seem to keep forgetting I'm a person of color."

"I do keep forgetting. To me, you're just…you. The woman I love. The woman I want to spend the rest of my life with. I don't give a tinker's damn for what anyone else on earth thinks."

"I don't doubt that for a moment."

"So what's with the self-doubt? I've never known you to be anything but supremely confident. Hell, I've seen you field-strip an assault rifle, fix it, reassemble it, and put twenty rounds in the middle of a target at fifty yards. You're not exactly a shrinking violet."

"I don't think that particular skill set would endear me to many Boston socialites. And I'm *not* doubting myself. I was just worried about making things more difficult for you with your mother and her cronies."

"So here we are trying to protect each other from ignorance. How absurd is that?"

"Moderately to extremely."

Connor leaned over and put her arms around Laura. "So, what say we knock it off? Deal?"

"Deal." Laura nestled her cheek against Connor's neck and inhaled the scent of Opium perfume. "I love you."

"Love you, too, darling," said Connor, gently kissing Laura's hair.

"But I think what we're doing may be illegal in this town."

Connor sat back and looked around. "Probably. We're a long way from gay old Somerville."

"True."

"We could turn around and drive to Hull, and then try public displays of affection."

"Hull?"

"Never mind," said Connor, as she put the car in gear. "Long story. And we have a funeral to attend."

Without any reminders, Connor negotiated the series of twists, turns, forks in the road and streets that arbitrarily changed their names in midstream until they arrived at the 250-year-old beige clapboard village church.

"It's beautiful," said Laura as they got out of the car. "It's so…"

"New England?"

"Definitely."

Connor joined Laura on the sidewalk, but made no move toward the church.

"We don't really have to go in. We could wait out here and follow the procession to the cemetery," suggested Connor.

"No, your friend is expecting us. And…" Her voice trailed off as a black limousine rolled to a stop on the other side of the street closest to the church. The driver hopped out and trotted around the car to open the curbside doors. The first figure to emerge was a tall, almost willowy woman wearing dark glasses. Her shoulder-length hair, tucked behind her ears, glittered with blonde highlights, stark against the black jacket and skirt she wore.

"That's Grace," said Connor. "I wonder why she was in the front seat with the driver."

"Maybe there wasn't room in the back," Laura replied. "You didn't tell me she was a such a knockout."

"What? Oh. I guess she's good-looking." Connor suddenly turned. "Wait a minute. Is that jealousy rearing its ugly head?"

"Well…maybe just a teensy bit." Laura shrugged.

"What happened to 'We both had lives before we met'?"

"I was feeling very mature about it until I actually *saw* her. And as I recall, Ariana was a fashion model. Now I'm starting to feel kind of short."

"Oh, for heaven's sake," Connor said, about to become exasperated until she saw the glint of humor in Laura's eyes. "You're yanking my chain, aren't you?"

"Maybe a little," Laura chuckled. "Sometimes you get so serious."

Connor sighed. "I do, don't I?"

"Yes, and I like it lots better when you smile."

They watched as a figure finally emerged from the rear compartment of the limousine. One older woman, not as tall as

Grace, yet slightly hunched as she leaned on a thick cane. The chauffeur closed the doors. No one else got out.

"Seems those two don't get along," commented Laura. "Or they've started making those limos with only one seat in the back."

"That must be Grace's aunt, Florence Gardner."

"Ah, one of the aforementioned snarling bigots."

"In spades, sweetheart. She seems to have made a lifelong career out of hating people for one reason or another. Let's wait until they get inside."

"Didn't you say Grace also called you for legal advice? Is that the woman Grace is fighting because of Catherine's will?"

"She surely is."

"But you said the will hasn't been read yet."

"It hasn't. But Florence says she already knows what's in it, and that Grace won't be getting much at all. The old lady says she's the chief beneficiary."

"That sounds pretty harsh, disinheriting a daughter. Is the aunt hard up for money?"

"Only if you call owning a brownstone on Beacon Hill and a house in Chatham poor."

"So what gives?"

"I don't know all the details. Grace was pretty upset when she called, and her letter wasn't much more coherent. We'll have to find an opportunity to talk to her alone, maybe after the service."

With Grace and her aunt safely in the door of the church, Connor and Laura crossed the street. They stepped inside the vestibule and the sound of the pipe organ grew louder. The small church was packed, and they chose to stay by the door in consideration of Connor's claustrophobic reaction to crowds and small spaces. It was just as well, as it gave them plenty of opportunity to size up the goodly crop of mourners. The color of the day was black, with no variation other than a bit of white trim here, or a tasteful piece of jewelry there.

"You know," whispered Laura. "Even if someone wasn't particularly sad when they came to this funeral, they'd be damn depressed when they left."

"I believe, in this instance, that's what people like Aunt Florence have in mind."

The minister rose and began to speak. After almost half an hour, the air in the church grew hot and stale. Finally, Connor nudged Laura's arm. "I need an air break."

"Me, too."

They crept out a side door, though not quietly enough to avoid disapproving glances from the back pews at their early exit.

The path led around to the churchyard in the rear, and beyond that stood a small cemetery. The chauffeur they'd seen earlier was leaning against a tombstone smoking a cigarette. He smiled when he saw them, then quickly rearranged his face into a more suitably somber expression and stuck out his hand "We haven't met," he said. "I'm Billy Dagle." He paused. "Dagle & Sons Mortuary—I inherited it, you know, though I don't think I was exactly Dad's favorite son...for obvious reasons. But his Dad gave the business to him, and I was the only one left after my sister took off for parts unknown." He dropped his cigarette and stamped it out, then peered at Connor and Laura from under the hat brim. "Is it the chauffeur getup? Thought I was just the hired help, naturally." He giggled. "That's okay. I like this outfit: satin lapels and white gloves, though you've got to admit, the whole solid-black thing is kind of out these days. But the shoulders of the jacket make all those gym workouts worthwhile. And when you're stuck at five foot nine, black looks taller, don't you think? Of course, with a little more trim, a few rhinestones..." He suddenly stopped. "I hope I haven't made a serious mistake."

Connor laughed out loud. "No, Billy. You're among family. Are we that obvious?"

He smirked. "Compared to that crowd of stuck-up shrews and shrewettes in there, yes. But don't worry. Neither of you is exactly bucking for superdyke of the year or anything. Now I, on the other hand, couldn't pass if I tried. But then I'd much rather camp it up until Judy comes back from the dead." Laura looked at him blankly. He frowned. "Judy *Garland!*"

"Ah," said Laura. "Sorry."

"So, is the Right Reverend Blowhard almost done in there?"

"I hope he's winding things down."

"Good, because the traffic is going to majorly suck. I can't believe the family *insisted* on having the funeral at this time of day. So, did you two know the deceased?" he asked, straightening his lapels.

"I was a friend of her daughter, Grace."

"Friends, hmm. She's lovely to look at." Billy regarded Connor with curiosity. "But not much for talking. She declined to give a eulogy, you know."

"No, I didn't know that."

"Some people can't do it, get up in front of the house and let it all hang out. Just as well. Some of those scenes are right out of a Tennessee Williams play." He stepped a little closer to Connor, and she saw that he might be a little nearsighted. "You seem awfully familiar to me. Like I've seen your picture or something."

Connor smiled at him. "You know how it is, Billy. All us lesbians look alike."

He roared with laughter, showing off a row of perfect white teeth, then clapped his hand over his mouth in alarm. "Now look what you've made me do. What if someone heard? I'll never hear the end of it. Oh well, my business partner, Devin Underwood, says I'm a complete failure at the funeral gig. But what does he know? He's so-o-o-o *straight,* for crying out loud. I'd like to see *him* decorate a visitation room in mauves and saffron. Can you imagine someone *picked* that? Oh well, if you're rich enough, bad taste is no obstacle." He sighed, and picked at imaginary lint on his sleeve. "I don't usually end up wearing the boy-toy suit, but Devin said our usual driver called in sick. And it's so beneath the ever-so-dignified Mr. Underwood to actually *wait* on anyone. Then he tells me he's sick, too, and can't be here. I've never quite gotten it across to him that this is a service industry—you know, grieving people pay us good money to help them get through the aftermath of death. You see, I do have some business sense." His grin was so genuine, Connor and Laura both smiled.

"So why is your partner in the business?" asked Connor. "I take it he's not one of the '& Sons' part."

"He bought into the business about a year ago. We needed an infusion of cash." He leaned forward to whisper. "I'm all for cremation, frankly, but there's, like, no profit in it, and now everyone's doing it." He glanced toward the church. "Not this family, of course. No way. This is a top-drawer—you should pardon the expression—funeral." Connor and Laura exchanged puzzled glances, so he added. "Top-drawer: you know, morgue, drawers and trays…oh, well. Guess you have to be in the biz. So, where was I? This funeral—now, this will help the numbers this month, at least so says the great Devin. He tells me things are definitely looking up for Dagle & Sons. Best casket we sell, the Olympus, solid thirty-two-ounce brass, hermetically sealed." He shook his head. "Still don't know why people get so worked up about a body when the soul's gone."

"So why be in the funeral business at all?" asked Laura with a smile. "Sounds like you don't put much stock in all this." She waved her hand at the cemetery.

"Family tradition, I suppose. It's what Dad left me. Funny, he never liked me very much, but we're a lot alike in some ways. He always cared about 'his families'—that's what he called them. 'My families,' he'd say, 'need someone to see them through.' That's how I feel about it. You know, they're usually so sad and lost when they come in. I just sit and listen, and when they're ready I help them plan every little detail. I'd probably have been a better party planner, you know, than a funeral director. But I just think of funerals as the last party the deceased is ever going to have." He paused for a breath, something Laura and Connor noticed he didn't do often.

"Now, Devin on the other hand—well, I needed someone who could actually decipher the reams of paper our doddering old CPA sends me. He was my father's accountant, so I kept him. Anyway, I handle the people part as a rule, and Devin does the detail work. He seems to like it, though I wonder he didn't pick something else to invest in. Not exactly a booming business, what with the big funeral home chains snatching up all the independents." He looked back toward the church where the doors still remained closed, and then leaned back against a headstone. "Guess he's giving the Wainwrights all the piety money will buy… Are you sure I don't know you?" he asked Connor. "All kidding aside."

Laura poked Connor gently. "Give him a break, sweetheart."

"I'm an author," said Connor.

Billy's eyes lit up. "I knew it. You write those mysteries with all the courtroom drama. Oh, my God. Wait till Chris hears about this. Chris is my *amour*. We've been together four years, and we're planning a big anniversary bash for next week. I can't wait to tell him I met you! Hey, maybe you'd like to come to the party. It'll be wild."

"I'm glad you like my books," said Connor politely.

"Oh, honey. I don't *read* them."

Connor looked so completely disconcerted, it was all Laura could do to keep from laughing.

"Excuse me," said Connor. "I…um…"

"Oh, no, I didn't mean to offend you, darling," Billy burbled. "No, no, no. It's just that I don't really *read* books, you know. It's so…time-consuming. Not that I didn't try. When I heard you were one of us, dear, I tried. But such long sentences and so many pages—couldn't do it. Love your photo on the back, though. So strong and elegant. You must have a great photographer. Anyway, I give your books to all my friends—you know, lots of them really do read…*all the time.* Amazing. Of course, Chris is a professor at B.U., so he kind of has to read. I've accused him of liking his books more than he does me—"

They all turned at the creak of the side door opening, and Billy straightened up from his slouch. "Well, I suppose I'd better stand by. That old battle-ax told me I'm"—he raised his voice even higher to a raspy falsetto—"'insufficiently prompt in my door-opening.'" He slipped on his gloves and examined them closely. "Damn, a spot. Nice talking to you two girls. Have fun—oops, not a good line for the next act in our little drama today: the graveside service. Ta!"

He strode quickly down the walk toward the front of the church, and Connor and Laura followed more slowly. "Do you suppose he talks that much all the time?" said Laura.

"If he does, his friend Chris must wear headphones while he reads."

"Ever met a fan who doesn't read your books?"

Connor smiled ruefully. "Not anyone who's admitted it so easily. Though I imagine my novels are holding up uneven table legs and propping open doors in many places throughout the world. That knowledge alone keeps me humble."

"I'm not exactly worried about you turning egomaniacal on me, darling."

They rounded the corner in time to see their new acquaintance, Billy, in a heated discussion with Grace Wainwright.

"But I thought this was the time of day you *wanted* the graveside service to take place, ma'am. Otherwise, we would have done it earlier in the day."

"Mr. Underwood informed me this was the *only* time we'd be able to use the church and get into the cemetery in Quincy immediately afterward. And I've just found out that a wedding was pushed back two hours, and their guests are already arriving." She pointed to a clump of people gathering on the sidewalk. "How do you suppose they feel about seeing a hearse out in front when they're coming for a marriage ceremony? And now the weather is turning bad. We should have done this in the morning!"

"But we *could* have," Billy protested. "Ordinarily we schedule for 10 o'clock."

"Then why did Mr. Underwood tell me otherwise?" Between her anger and the cold wind, Grace's cheeks were mottled crimson and white.

"I...I don't know," said Billy, obviously confused and embarrassed. "I'm sorry if there was some sort of miscommunication. But he's out sick today and—"

"Miscommunication, my ass!" said Grace, drawing the attention of the mourners who were filing out of the church. "You're going to be—" She stopped abruptly as she caught sight of Connor and Laura, and her expression changed, the anger draining out of her. "Oh...never mind." She dismissed him with a wave, and he shrugged helplessly before trotting over to the limousine.

"Connor!" said Grace, moving quickly to cover the few yards between them. She started to open her arms, as if to hug Connor, then appeared to change her mind in mid-stride. Instead, she put out her hand.

"Hello, Grace." Connor took the slim, cold fingers between her own. "I'm so sorry about your mom."

Grace trembled slightly. "Thank you for coming. I still can't quite believe it myself." Her eyes strayed to Laura, and Connor immediately stepped back slightly and placed her left palm gently against the small of Laura's back. "Grace, I'd like you to meet my partner, Laura Nez. Laura, this is Grace Wainwright."

Laura extended her hand. "It's a pleasure to meet you, Grace. I'm sorry about the circumstances, though."

Grace studied Laura for a moment. "Yes, the circumstances are—"

A voice registering somewhere between a shriek and a gargle erupted a few feet from them. "Grace! As long as you're standing around, you should be standing here to greet people as they come out."

Connor and Laura peered past Grace to the elderly woman standing behind her. Up close, they saw a stony countenance glaring back at them. Pale gray eyes, with a spot of black at the center, narrowed in disapproval. Grace turned hurriedly to the older woman. "Aunt Florence, I *am* greeting people. This is Connor Hawthorne, an old friend from college, and her friend Laura Nez."

"Hmmph! I can just imagine what kind of friends."

Grace reddened. "That's quite enough, Aunt Florence."

"I'll decide what's enough," she snapped. "And as for you, young lady, I suggest you see to your duties. There are people already leaving for the cemetery. And I won't keep the car waiting for you, so come along."

Connor observed the fury on her friend's face and sensed that if Grace lost control of that much anger, Aunt Florence would be blasted into ashes and vapor, along with anyone else in the vicinity. A scene would hardly help the situation. Just as she was about to attempt a polite intervention, her hopes for a quick exit were dashed. There was Amanda Hawthorne closing the distance between them at an alarming pace.

Connor stiffened. "Hello, Mother," she said, her face expressionless.

The elegantly coiffed, perfectly coutured Mrs. Hawthorne, slid an icy gaze over her daughter, then Laura, and finally Grace. "Lydia," she sniffed, using Connor's given name, rather than the middle one her daughter so adamantly preferred. "I didn't see you and your…friend…inside."

Connor bristled. "I'm happy to introduce my 'friend,' mother. This is Laura N—"

Amanda interrupted. "Florence, I believe the hearse is ready. Perhaps I could get you settled in the limousine before I go in search of my driver. These rental agencies are so unreliable." Amanda craned her neck looking over the crowd.

"Mother, I…" Connor tried one more time. She felt the vein in her temple pounding with the effort to control her temper. *Not here,* she told herself. *We don't need a confrontation here.*

This time it was Aunt Florence whose utter rudeness took the three younger women aback. "How kind of you, Amanda. It's sad when one's own family can't be relied upon to show any sort of attention to duty, or respect for their elders. Perhaps you would care to accompany me in the car. And Grace, if you're quite finished here, let's get on with it."

Grace blanched, as if horrified that she might have to endure the company of these two venomous old women. "I'm *not* finished, Aunt Florence," she snapped.

Laura, the ignored party in this poisonous gathering, leaped into the fray. "Grace, why don't you ride with us? We're not very familiar with the area. It would be a help if you came along to navigate."

Aunt Florence huffed into her handkerchief. "Do as you wish. We're leaving." She ostentatiously took Amanda's arm, her demeanor transforming from iron-fisted harridan to frail and elderly mourner. The tactic was so blatant that Connor would have laughed out loud, were she not so angry. They watched as the two women processed grandly to the car, where Billy stood at attention. Amanda's voice was barely audible except for the stray phrase that the shifting breeze happened to amplify. "...a bit of brandy perhaps, to brace you."

Connor shook her head. "If there's anything left in the limo bar by the time they get to Quincy, I'd be surprised."

"Aunt Florence hardly touches liquor," said Grace.

"There's hardly a time when my mother *doesn't* touch it."

"I'm sorry" said Grace, laying a hand on Connor's arm. "I thought maybe she'd have, um...changed by now."

"I've always hoped, but never really expected," replied Connor. "Dad has footed the bill for so many trips to Betty Ford, I think they now have a Hawthorne wing. She's okay for a few weeks, then she finds a reason to start in again." She paused, her eyes on the limousine. Billy was trotting around the side. He gave them a wide grin and jaunty wave before sliding into the driver's seat. "Of course, she always says I'm the reason."

Laura put her arm around Connor's waist. "Don't go there, hon. You know it isn't true. You aren't the source of her pain. She is."

Connor forced a half-smile, and flung her arm around Laura's shoulders. "I know, honey, I know. But logic and feel-ings...there's a gap there. I've always wanted to like my mother, and I've always wanted her to like me. It just never happened." Laura's head was tilted toward her, and Connor rested her chin on top of it for a moment.

Grace watched the intimate interaction, an odd expression playing across her face.

"What?" asked Connor, remembering that look from years earlier. A memory surfaced of a night at a women's nightclub in Boston. Connor had been dancing with another friend. Nothing serious, no flirtation, just a dance. But Grace had had that look, and the argument they'd had later proved to be the beginning of the end of their relationship. Grace was jealous, pure and simple, and Connor, who had never been fickle or dishonest, had shown little patience for it. Grace wanted more reassurance than Connor had been willing to provide.

"Nothing," said Grace. "I'm just relieved they're gone. And thanks for the offer of a lift to the cemetery. My cousin Henry asked me in the church if I'd ride with him. He's an incredible bore, but then I thought about putting up with my aunt for another hour." She glanced around at the thinning crowd. "I suppose I should try and find him and tell him I've changed my mind—wait, there he is." Connor and Laura followed her gaze to a dazzlingly blond young man with the build of a wrestler, though his fairly short stature, perhaps five foot seven or so, made him look more squat than strong. Grace walked quickly to where he waited at the foot of the church steps.

"He doesn't appear happy about her change of plan," said Laura, a consistent student of human behavior and body language.

Connor turned her attention to Grace and Henry. "Hmm. He looks as if he's pouting. So unattractive in a grown-up."

A few moments later, Grace rejoined them, shaking her head. "What is up with that guy? You'd think I'd turned down an offer of marriage just because I said I was riding with you."

"Maybe he's got a crush," said Laura.

"He'd have to be a complete idiot. He knows men are not my partners of choice, and even if they were, I'd hope I could do better than squatty little toad like him. He must be getting desperate if he's hitting on cousins." Her moue of distaste instantly shifted to a smile as she reached for Connor's arm. "So, shall we be off?"

Connor saw Laura's puzzlement, and she herself wondered what had gotten into Grace. She'd never have described the woman as mercurial, and yet…

"Our car's over here," said Connor, casually disengaging herself from Grace's hand as she led the way down the walk where only a few guests lingered. When they reached it, Connor pressed the door lock button and swung open the driver's door. Grace walked around the car in front of Laura, and they both reached for the front passenger door at the same moment.

"Oh, I'm sorry," said Grace. "Just habit. Of course, you'll sit up front."

Laura, whose expression indicated that her own renowned patience might be eroding, offered to sit in the back so that it would be easier for Grace to direct their trip to the cemetery.

Grace moved toward the door, as if she would accept, but something in her face shifted as she looked at Laura's calm expression. She sighed heavily. "No, I'm…no, I can see fine from the backseat. Forgive me. I'm acting like an idiot. I don't know what I'm even thinking." She quickly opened the rear door and got in.

Connor watched the whole exchange over the roof of the car, and began to wonder if this whole trip hadn't been a particularly bad idea.

*

"They must have been late leaving the church."

"Why?"

"I wasn't there. I don't know."

"You guaranteed us that you would stay with them." The faraway voice spoke with stiff formality, as if unused to the rhythms of the English language.

"I couldn't hang around near the church. It's a small town, and people notice. And if I'd been recognized—"

"Enough of your excuses! I simply require your assurance that everything is in proper order—that it will happen as planned."

"Can't miss. Our man is in place, and I'm at the observation point so I can confirm." There was silence on the line. "Here it comes now. I can see the hearse and the family limousine is right behind it. They're only a few minutes behind schedule."

"You are sure she's inside?"

"Of course."

"But you weren't at the church. How do you know?"

"Because she was in it on the way to the church, and it's reserved for the family. How else would she get to the cemetery? Look, this is my project, my strategy. I don't like being second-guessed."

"That's one of the perils of being second-in-command. Telephone me at the other number after everything is concluded."

"But with the time difference, that will be the middle of the night, maybe later."

"I've waited sixty years to reach this point, and we're finally close. Do you imagine I will be sleeping?"

"No, I suppose not."

"Good supposition. Report to me when you have solid confirmation." The voice paused. "And Devin, don't disappoint your brothers."

*

Connor slipped back into line, only two cars behind the hearse and the lead limousine. The funeral procession snaked out behind them, still moving at a crawl, and snarling traffic from Hingham to Quincy.

Laura smiled. "I don't think you're supposed to jockey for a better place in a funeral procession, darlin'."

"I'm not, well…not exactly. But I *am* going to find the best parking place at the cemetery."

"Best, as in easiest to get out of."

"You'd better believe it. Do you realize how many cars are following? Must be more than fifty of them."

"A lot of people knew my mom," said Grace, who'd been silent other than providing concise directions. "She was involved in a lot of charity work and headed up committees—things like that. I don't really know all the details. We didn't talk a lot."

"You and your mom didn't get along?" asked Laura

"We might have had a chance, except for Aunt Florence. She's my mother's twin sister. Looks ten years older, but always reminded us she's the younger of the two. The old biddy never stopped carping at Mom because of my 'lifestyle,' though I doubt she put it that euphemistically. Not that she always approved of Mom either. Said she wasn't sufficiently conventional, or something like that."

"Now there's one old lady with a stick up her—"

"Connor!" said Laura with a definitive flick to the back of Connor's head.

"Sorry. Tasteless of me, but—"

"But it describes my dear Aunt Florence to a tee," said Grace, laughing for the first time since Laura had met her. "She's like the whole Moral Majority, the Christian Coalition, and every single right-wing bigoted Bible-thumper all wrapped up in one vicious little package. She makes Strom Thurmond look like a liberal."

"Really?" said Laura, smiling. "And she seems like such a nice old lady."

It took Grace an extra beat to realize Laura was joking. Then she snorted. "She loves to shake that silver-headed walking stick in your face when she's telling you off. I've often been tempted to tell her what she can do with that stupid thing."

"But being well brought up," said Connor, "you didn't."

"Too well brought up, I suppose. All those stupid rules and expectations. But then you had to go through it, too. Those horrid debutante balls and freakish dresses and those slick-haired bachelors they line you up with. Thank God I never made the mistake of marrying one of them. That would have been so—" Grace stopped abruptly. "I'm sorry, Connor. I wasn't even thinking."

"It's all right, I did make the mistake. But at least one good thing came out of it—Katy."

"How's she doing?"

"Happy, as far as I can tell. She's still in England. Finished up at Oxford, but she's working in London now."

"And what about Alex?"

"He married a nice woman and settled down…again…not long after we divorced."

"You ever talk to him?"

"Not for years. He didn't do much fathering either where Katy was concerned. But she doesn't seem any the worse for it."

Grace seemed about to ask more, to the point where Laura, with her natural Navajo distaste for prying into the private affairs of others, was thinking of changing the subject when Connor said, "Would you believe it? They're going to raise the damn drawbridge, and only the hearse got through."

Laura peered through the windshield. The family limousine had been forced to stop on the Fore River Bridge. Warning lights flashed, and the heavy barrier began to descend.

"I can just imagine what Aunt Florence has to say about this," said Grace. "Poor Billy must be getting an earful."

"As if it's his fault," said Laura.

"According to Devin Underwood," said Grace, "they schedule these processions when no river traffic is expected. As a matter of fact, that's why we had to have the funeral at this time of day. I wanted to have it much earlier. But he insisted on later."

"The funeral director?" said Connor idly, as she watched the steel bars of the barrier stop abruptly in a downward arc. "Looks like the barrier's stuck. That should hold us up a little more. And now they're raising the bridge. They need to get their equipment synchronized."

"The bridge is old," Grace commented, looking behind her at the endless line of cars. "And Devin insisted we had to have the funeral at this time of day, though I knew the traffic would be horrible. Something to do with the cemetery schedule of interments, I guess."

Laura, whose attention was also fixed on the metal gate that appeared to be stuck, and the bridge section slowly rising, suddenly grabbed Connor's arm. "Can you see the back of the limo?"

Connor craned her head, but only Laura, on the passenger side, could see past the two cars in front of them. "No, what's wrong?"

"There's smoke coming out of it. The tires are…" She rolled down her window and they could hear it, the squeal of rubber against pavement. "What the hell is he doing?"

In the limousine, Billy was wondering the same thing. He was horrified when he felt the car lurch forward. He jammed his foot down hard on the brake pedal, but the car kept surging like a mad dog straining at a leash. He grabbed the gearshift lever and slammed it up into "park," but nothing changed.

The partition between the compartments was winding down.

"What is going on, young man?" a shrill voice inquired. "Why is this car jerking around like this? And why are we stopped? You assured me this procession wouldn't be interrupted. I hope you don't think the estate is going to pay you for this kind of service."

"Lady, will you please shut up!" Billy shouted, his legs trembling with fear as he put his whole weight on the brake pedal. But he caught a whiff of a tangy mechanical burn—something that he dimly recalled meant the brakes were failing. The pedal suddenly had no tension at all. It rested on the floor.

"How dare you speak to…" Aunt Florence began, her voice even more abrasive.

"Just shut the fuck up!" screamed Billy, frantically jiggling the ignition key, trying to turn off the engine. But the car had a mind of its own.

Almost a hundred feet back, Laura had flung her car door open and was running toward the limousine. Connor, still not comprehending the problem, was a little behind her. But before either of them could get near the car, it took off as if launched from a rocket. They watched in sheer horror as the lower end of the metal barrier scraped across the roof of the limo on one side of the car.

By now the bridge was passing a thirty-degree slant, and the opening was more than forty feet across. Despite its length and weight, the limousine's enormous V-8 engine propelled it up the slanted bridge section, even picking up speed over the short distance. To their horror, they heard screams from the occupants as the car went over the edge, fast enough so that it was past the point of balance long before the rear tires lost their grip on the asphalt. It tipped, stood on its nose…then for a moment the trunk end swayed toward the opposite piece of bridge. For the tiniest fraction of a second, it appeared to be suspended in air like some sort of far-fetched Calder mobile. And then gravity won. Grille first, the car plunged toward the river, more than sixty feet below. Connor and Laura reached the railing in time to see the car plow into the river, its entry launching spouts of water as high as the bridge. The entire vehicle disappeared completely.

Connor was already climbing the railing, with every intention of making the absurdly high dive into the water, when Laura grabbed her arm. "No! Don't even think it! You'll break your neck." Connor tried to shake off the arm. "But my mom, she's…"

"I know. But stop and think! You can't help them by getting killed. We'll call 911, they can scramble a rescue team."

"My God, what happened?" Grace panted, as she appeared suddenly behind them.

"Some kind of malfunction," said Laura, punching numbers on her cell phone, "but we need to call emergency services right now. They'll have…" She stopped speaking as they all felt the rumbling beneath the bridge. The decking trembled. Then an enormous spout of water shot skyward, and they were all drenched in freezing water.

Grace grabbed Connor's arm and screamed. "What was that?

But Connor was speechless. Laura's shoulders slumped as she said, "I think it was an underwater explosion."

CHAPTER TWO

Tantaene animus caelestibus irae?
(Can heavenly spirits cherish resentment so dire?)
—Virgil, *Aeneid*

The Boston Globe, in its dignified yet bold style, carried a front-page story about the freak accident on the Fore River Bridge, and numerous sidebar articles about the historic bridge, the three victims, and tidbits about the surviving family members of each. The *Herald* took a rather more sensational approach, though staying generally within the limits of reasonably good taste. *Newsday of America,* which picked up the story the next day, was much less reserved. A reporter, citing the ubiquitous "confidential sources" who materialize during sensational events, speculated that this had perhaps been a sort of suicide/double homicide—the gay funeral director decides to off himself in a spectacular fashion and take two clients with him. None of the stories, even the most accurate ones, could begin to capture the experience of the three women who stood on the bridge and watched the tragedy unfold.

"Your dad's on his way from the airport," said Laura, snapping shut her cell phone. "He'll be here in less than an hour."

Connor didn't answer, though she nodded almost imperceptibly.

She'd spent most of the night sitting in a chair in their room at the tiny bed-and-breakfast, looking out into the darkness. Laura had mostly just let her be. Whatever the tension and anger between Connor and Amanda, they had been daughter and mother, and that physical link had been severed forever. Worse, it had been a violent death, perhaps intentionally caused, though by whom was still unclear. Connor had talked half the night, about the past, about what might have been in the future, before insisting that Laura retire. At least one of them should have a clear head, she maintained. But Laura only napped, occasionally opening her eyes to see Connor's head bent to her chest, her shoulders heaving with almost, but not quite, silent sobs. This was a misery Laura couldn't prevent or even completely share, and she knew it. Yet she enfolded Connor in as much healing energy as she could muster, if only to take the edge off the pain.

"I'll go downstairs and get us some coffee, sweetheart."

Connor looked up, focused on Laura. "I'll go, too. I need to get out of this room."

One of the owners of the B&B, Tracy (whose partner also happened to be named Laura), was already in the small, cozy dining room checking the coffee urn and turning up the warmer under the hot water for tea.

"I thought you might need this earlier than usual," Tracy said. "I'm so sorry about your loss."

"Thank you," replied Connor, her voice rusty with the night's tears and sleeplessness.

"There's a basket of warm muffins in case you're hungry. And some sesame bagels by the toaster. You probably need to eat something."

"Maybe later, but I appreciate it. Just coffee for now."

"Suit yourself, hon. Call us if you need anything."

Laura reached for one of the sturdy mugs hand-painted with the B&B's logo. "We will. And, Tracy, I thought I'd let you know that Connor's dad is on his way here. I hope that's all right."

Tracy looked momentarily puzzled. "Oh, you mean because we advertise this place as a women's retreat. No, we're not rabid separatists, just women innkeepers who prefer to cater to other women. That's our personal choice. Any guest of a guest is welcome here, especially with…I mean…under these circumstances. Hey, some of my best friends are guys." She smiled a little, winked at Laura, and pushed through the swinging door into the kitchen.

"Nice lady," commented Laura, filling her coffee cup, and then another for Connor, who was standing near the window that looked out on the ocean, where the sun was making a spectacular entrance. "What say we take the coffee outside?"

They sat in the well-worn Adirondack chairs on the veranda, and cautiously sipped the stalwart espresso blend. Laura shivered a little. Fall had arrived, and with it a sharply cool breeze coming off the water.

"I'm going to find out what happened," said Connor.

Laura thought for a while before answering. "I know."

Connor turned her head slightly toward Laura. "What? No argument? No lectures about this being too close, too personal, letting the authorities handle it?"

Laura shook her head and smiled a little. "As if you'd listen if I tried to keep you out of it. Besides, I feel the same way, though for different reasons."

"What do you mean?"

"I can't say exactly why, but I have a strong feeling we're the only ones who can actually get to the bottom of this—I mean, beyond the usual investigative procedures the local cops will employ. And the FBI."

"Why the FBI? This was a local homicide."

"Can you imagine that the Feds aren't going to jump all over your mom's murder? She was Amanda Hawthorne, mother of a celebrity author, ex-wife of a former U.S. Senator who was a former national security adviser to the president, etc. etc. And Benjamin still has his hand in things. I don't do as much work for him anymore"—she paused and smiled at Connor—"since I've developed other interests. But I keep up-to-date. And the Feds aren't going to stay out of this one."

Connor sighed. "I imagine you're right, but I hate the thought of this turning into a three-ring circus."

"Can't be helped."

"Yep." She stared out at the water. "You know what's ironic?"

"What, sweetheart?"

"She always wanted so badly to be the center of attention. Wanted people to know who she was. And…and now she is, and now they will." Connor cleared her throat a couple of times. "Of course, she would have hated being involved in something as tawdry as murder."

"I'm willing to bet her perspective has changed somewhat," said Laura.

"I hope so. I hate to think of her as a troubled soul, wandering around confused about being dead."

"Some are, some aren't. But you never really know unless…"

"You're asking me if I want you to try and reach her in the Dreamtime?"

"I wouldn't unless you asked."

A long silence stretched between them, broken only by the sound of the gulls screeching over the rights to edible tidbits.

"Not yet," said Connor. "I don't think I'm ready for that. Besides…" she left the thought unfinished, but Laura knew her well enough by now to hear the unspoken part.

"Besides, your personal jury is still out on the woo-woo stuff."

"No," said Connor. "I don't mean it like that…well, maybe a part of me does. I can't deny what we've both seen and felt and experienced. It's impossible to pretend all that weird stuff didn't happen. But it makes me kind of nauseous, you know. Every time I think about what went on when I first met you in New Mexico and then what happened with my grandmother and the Carlisles in England…"

"Not forgetting Father Angelico out in California, and the disappearing mural at the old mission."

"Yeah," Connor sighed. "That, too. I keep wishing the world could just go back to being simple and understandable."

"You mean go back to the way you *thought* it was."

"Hmm. Something like that. I guess these grand mysteries of life were always there, but I didn't see the need to decipher them."

"I don't think your destiny could have been avoided, darling," said Laura. "Delayed, maybe, but not avoided altogether."

"Ah, yes. Here I am," she cupped her hands around her mouth to create a melodramatic echo effect, "in the long line of Celtic priestesses." She paused, shaking her head. "And I don't really know jack about any of it. All hail the powerful idiot priestess."

"And denial is a river in Egypt," said Laura with a smile. "But we're making progress."

They both turned at the sound of gravel crunching beneath tires. A black sedan drew up near the side of the house and the back door flew open. A trim silver-haired man, over six feet and broad in the shoulder, emerged quickly, an overnight case in hand. "Don't wait," he said. "I'll make other arrangements." He turned, saw the two women on the porch and hastened toward them.

"Connor!" he exclaimed and pulled her into his embrace. "Oh, honey, I'm so sorry about your mother. Are you all right?"

Her voice muffled in his lapel, Connor murmured, "Yeah, I'm okay, Dad." But he continued to hold her, and Laura felt a pang of empathy and maybe even a little envy in her heart. To still have a father who'd hold you, let you be his little girl for a few moments when the need was great. She retreated slightly and stood by the railing, not wanting to intrude on the reunion. But she was prevented from any forays into mild self-pity by Benjamin himself. "Come here, you," he said to Laura, as Connor stepped back from their embrace. "I hardly ever hug people who work for me, but you're the definite exception." He gave Laura a strong, almost fierce bear hug. "I'm so grateful you're both all right."

"We weren't in any danger, Dad," said Connor. "Only Mom, and Florence Gardner. And that guy Billy."

"We don't know that yet," he replied. "We don't even know what the motive behind this was. And we don't have any details of how the car was rigged, why the bridge barrier didn't drop all the way, and most of all, why the bridge was raised in the first place. I've already been told there was no river traffic at that hour large enough to require the bridge to be raised."

"So it was all a setup?" asked Laura. She noted the extra lines of fatigue around his eyes, and a whole new crop of near-white sprinkled generously through his thick, dark hair. He was handsome man still, but clearly exhausted.

"Seems so. I know the police already asked you a thousand questions, but did either of you see the bridge operator in his booth?"

"I wasn't paying attention to that," Connor admitted. "All I was focusing on was the car going over the edge."

"There was someone inside it," said Laura. "I told the cops that when I was running toward the back of the limousine, the glass booth was in my direct line of sight. I know there was movement, but it's just an impression."

"The regular bridge technician was found at his house, overdosed on heroin. Problem is, the man never used drugs in his life."

"Pretty sloppy way to make his death look accidental, then," commented Connor. "Someone's not too bright."

"I don't know," Benjamin frowned. "Maybe. But then maybe they don't really care whether we know the man was murdered. They certainly didn't worry about whether the bridge going up partway and the barrier not dropping would seem accidental."

"Or maybe they did want it to seem that way," suggested Laura. "But the plan didn't work right. Maybe we're supposed to blame Billy. And assume that it was all a horrifying coincidence—mechanical failure of the car and the bridge machinery."

"If that was the intention, it failed, and someone's going to pay for this." Benjamin's voice had taken on a tight, angry edge. "I may not have loved Amanda anymore, and she—well, she was pretty damn difficult to deal with, but she didn't deserve to die."

"Same thing goes for Grace's aunt," offered Laura. "She was a mean old biddy, if our brief acquaintance was any indication, but death is a harsh sentence for sheer meanness."

"How's Grace doing? Is she at home?" asked Benjamin, his voice neutral. Yet Laura caught something in his demeanor that made the question more than casual inquiry.

"I guess so," said Connor. "I haven't talked to her since last night."

"I, well, I don't want to sound overly suspicious, but I've thought about this a lot in the past eighteen hours or so, and I do have to wonder how this affects Grace from a legal standpoint—I mean, her inheritance. Was her aunt expecting part of the estate?"

Connor frowned. "I don't know the details. Grace may have

said something about her Aunt Florence gloating over something she was getting, but come on, Dad. Surely you aren't thinking Grace engineered all this. You actually think she'd kill my mother?"

Benjamin shook his head. "I'm sorry, hon. But from what Laura said to me on the phone last night, Amanda wasn't supposed to be in the car. That was just a last-minute change. Maybe this plan couldn't have been called off, even if someone had wanted to do so."

Laura noticed he took care not to name Grace as the "someone" in question.

"But Grace herself was supposed to be in the car," Connor protested.

"That may be true, and it was only pure coincidence that saved her life. But, on the other hand, she may have been planning to ask you, or someone else, for a ride to the cemetery all along. If her Aunt's temperament were well-known among their friends, who would find it surprising that Grace had had enough of sharing the same car with the woman?"

"Dad, it's not that she and I are close, but I've known her for over twenty years. This is pretty hard to swallow. Some cousin offered her a ride at the church. Up till then she'd planned to be riding in the limo."

"I'm only speculating, But I do think you need to be circumspect in what you say to Grace until we get a better idea of who's behind this."

"He's right," said Laura. "Though I really don't think she's involved, either. But my hunches aren't always reliable, and there's no sense jeopardizing any potential investigation. Speaking of which, I believe we're about to have more company." She alone had heard the slight squeal of brakes on the road that lay between them and the beach area, and seen the back end of a dark car. Sure enough, the gravel once again heralded another arrival, and a dusty four-door sedan of the "official" variety, rounded the high rhododendron shrubs and came to a halt at the end of the sidewalk.

"Well, I'll be," said Connor, instantly recognizing the slender, statuesque African-American woman who emerged from the driver's side. "The Feebs have arrived."

Benjamin shook his head, as if resigned to the impending conflict.

Laura poked Connor in the ribs. "Shush. Don't get off on the wrong foot with Ayalla again, okay? You know she and Malcolm are getting kind of serious."

"And I can't imagine what he's thinking," hissed Connor. "She's a royal pain in the ass."

"Who just happened to have averted a nuclear disaster in California, darling, and got shot in the process. So let's cut her some slack."

"As long as she does the same for us. I wonder if she's gotten over her homophobia yet."

"She isn't really that way," whispered Laura, "and you know it. She's just confused about what she doesn't understand. So let it go, please. For the sake of cooperation."

Connor sighed. "All right, but one crack out of her and..."

Benjamin was now walking beside Special Agent Ayalla Franklin as they approached the veranda. Connor and Laura couldn't catch what was being said, but Ayalla was nodding as Benjamin spoke. Laura thought that a good sign. In her estimation, Ayalla looked wonderful, even in her conservative dark skirt, jacket, and white blouse—the "uniform" of female federal agents. The boxy cut of the blazer almost concealed the weapon she wore, and yet still managed to enhance her unmistakably female physique. Laura had little difficulty understanding at least one aspect of their friend Malcolm's attraction to the woman. But with him being a cop in D.C. and her an agent in Boston, she figured the commute must be getting expensive.

At the top of the steps, Ayalla paused. "Connor, please accept my condolences. I'm sorry about your mother."

"Thank you," Connor replied somewhat stiffly, and Laura realized these two women were still a long way from being comfortable with each other.

"I don't like having to bother you right now, but—"

"But you're just doing your job," Connor finished.

It was Ayalla's turn to stiffen. "Yes, as a matter of fact, I am. But I'll try to keep the visit short. I know you have things to do, arrangements to make, um, that is…"

"No, you're right. We do have arrangements to make. I just wasn't ready to think about them yet."

An awkward silence could have stretched on forever, had Laura not chosen to intervene. "We'll tell you all we can, Ayalla. Although I don't think there's much that will help you. Why don't we sit down over here?"

Point by point, the FBI agent took them over the events, beginning with Grace's note to Connor about Catherine Wainwright's unexpected death in an auto accident and ending with the funeral limousine careening off the Fore River Bridge. Then she flipped back in her notes.

"Did she say why she wanted you to come to the funeral? I mean, you were a couple thousand miles away."

Connor bristled. "I think it's because we used to be friends in college." She stopped as if waiting for Ayalla to make something of that, but the agent continued in a mild tone. "So she didn't mention anything about being concerned over the circumstances of her mother's death?"

"Not really," frowned Connor.

"Not really?" Ayalla raised one interrogative eyebrow. Laura had forgotten how aristocratic the woman looked—and how autocratic she could sound.

"I only mean she didn't say anything specific about being suspicious. But she called the day before we flew to Boston and asked me if I could spare some time after the funeral. Said she was—I don't remember exactly the words she used, but she sounded...maybe as if she were holding something back, something she wanted to tell me." Connor shrugged. "I'm only guessing. Why are you asking?"

Ayalla nodded, still squinting at her small leather notebook. "Just the routine round of questions."

"No, it isn't!" snapped Connor, and Ayalla's head shot up, her eyes locking with Connor's. "You seem to forget how many years I spent as a prosecutor and how many interrogations I've seen. There's nothing routine about any of what happened, and your questions reflect that. So why don't you stop stonewalling and try a little give-and-take."

Anger blazed in Ayalla's remarkable eyes. "This is a homicide investigation, and I don't *have* to tell *you* anything," she began, and then her gaze shifted to Laura, who sat quietly with her hand on Connor's arm. Laura shook her head ever so slightly, conveying a simple message: *Don't make this any worse.* Ayalla blew out a long breath through her mouth. "All right. I *will* tell you that Grace Wainwright insists her mother's death cannot have been accidental."

"Why?"

"The whole idea is pretty thin on logic, really. She's decided that since someone killed her aunt with a car, and her mother died in a car, the events are related, and there is a common denominator."

"Aside from the fact that they're part of the same family."

"Yes, aside from that. But Ms. Wainwright can't say what other factors there might be."

"I imagine you'll be looking into the inheritance issues," said Benjamin softly.

"Yes. And in the meantime, we're having the car fished out of the river so we can recover…" She stopped abruptly, her eyes aimed somewhere over Connor's shoulder.

"Recover the bodies," Connor finished for her. "That's all right. You don't need to shield me from unpleasantness. I saw my mother die. It doesn't get much more unpleasant than that."

Ayalla nodded and closed her notebook. "Obviously, our lab techs are going to go over the limo with a fine-toothed comb. We need to figure out if it was sabotaged. Then there's the bridge mechanism itself, which—"

Connor interrupted her. "What you do you mean, 'if it was sabotaged'? What other possibility is there?"

"I guess you haven't seen the more lurid scandal sheets. There's some speculation that the driver," she flipped open a page of her notebook again. "Billy Dagle, took that car over the edge of the bridge on purpose."

"You mean a suicide to commit homicide." said Laura incredulously. "That's absurd."

"Why?" asked Ayalla, turning to Laura.

"Sorry. I can't say that I have direct evidence. But we talked to that young man for a while at the church, while he was waiting for the funeral service to be over. Granted, we didn't exactly get to know him, but you get a feel for people, for who they are. He was the epitome of happy-go-lucky, more excited about wearing the fancy suit than anything else."

"Well, maybe," said Ayalla with only a hint of her usual skepticism. "But it bears looking into. I'll be talking to his business partner, Devin Underwood."

"There's something…" Laura began.

"What?"

"I had a thought there for a moment, but it escapes me. Something about that Underwood fellow. Maybe it'll come back if I leave it alone."

"Then I'll be going," said Ayalla, and Benjamin rose along with her.

"I'll walk you to your car," he said, and started down the steps, leaving no opportunity for her to protest without seeming ungracious.

As soon as they were out of earshot, Laura squeezed Connor's arm. "I imagine Benjamin's gently but firmly letting her know that he wants to be kept apprised of all developments."

"That's my dad," Connor smiled. "He usually gets his way, especially when he's feeling protective."

"For all that urbane, dapper demeanor, he's really a big papa bear," said Laura. "I've never known anyone so concerned about the safety of the people who've worked for him, so it only follows he'd be even more so with his family."

"He is, which sometimes makes it a little hard for him to let me take any risks."

"I'd say he's getting used to it. Kind of has to under the circumstances."

Connor waited for her father to return. "So what's our next step?"

"Our next step?" he frowned.

"I want to start with the funeral director, this Devin Underwood."

"Connor, wait a second. We have a lot to do, but I was thinking more in terms of making arrangements for your mother. Once they finish the autopsy, she can be flown back to D.C. We have to choose a funeral home and a church for the service and—well, there's a lot to do."

"You just said they have to do an autopsy. That'll hold things up for a while. The medical examiner's office won't release her right away."

"Yes," said Benjamin slowly. "But that doesn't mean we should be involved in an active ongoing investigation. You know as well as I do, that—"

"Are you trying to tell me you had no intention of looking into this? I know you, Dad, and that's not how you operate."

He sighed. "I couldn't honestly say I was going to leave it alone completely, but—"

"But what?"

"It isn't a good idea to poke around something like this when you're so emotionally involved."

Connor turned to Laura. "So…will you keep an eye on me? Make sure I don't go running around like a crazy person?"

Laura smiled. "I think I could guarantee her behavior, Benjamin, more or less. And maybe it would be better if we stayed a team. We've done pretty well in the past."

"I suppose," said Benjamin, still not looking convinced.

"Good, I'm going to go get our jackets and we'll head for Hingham and the Dagle & Sons Funeral Home." Connor was moving so quickly the screen door didn't have time to swing closed before she hit the first step of the stairs in the front hall.

Laura stared after her. "I know you're worried about this, Benjamin. But she has to be doing something, or she really will go a little crazy."

"I don't doubt it. But I'm just afraid there's so much anger and guilt that she's built up inside because of her mother. And now she's going to move heaven and earth to find the truth. She won't be careful about it, either."

"But I will. You've known me a long time, Benjamin. Back when I used to be so awestruck and thought you were the most brilliant intelligence officer on earth, a man who could do no wrong."

He grinned. "Gee, and now you know I've got the same feet of clay as everyone else."

"No," she said. "You're still damn near perfect at most things. But you've got a blind spot, too. You'd go out on any limb on earth for your daughter."

"And you wouldn't?" he asked, a tiny smile curling the edges of his mouth.

"I would. But all I'm saying is that even before I fell in love with her, I wouldn't have let anything happen to her, just because she was your daughter. Now I have an even bigger stake. But I'm not going to act foolish in the process. You trained me, and you're the best there is. I daresay this is going to come down to either a freak accident, or just maybe Amanda inadvertently got caught up in some sort of conspiracy. But I'll wait to see what we find out."

"What about this friend of hers, this Grace?"

"Don't know much, and I've spent maybe an hour with the woman. She seems a little off to me, somehow, but that may only be the stress of her mother dying, and now this. Still…" Laura stopped, her brow creased in thought.

"Still what?"

"One minute she's, I guess you'd say, acting normal, Connor's her old friend, etcetera. And then she's—this sounds silly—but kind of jealous."

"Of you and Connor?"

Laura shook her head. "Maybe I was only imagining it, but there's something about the way her personality swings back and forth, sort of from real to mildly phony."

"I've already initiated a background check—the works. On her as well as her family."

"Can't hurt. And we'll have better intel than the local cops."

"So we'll share if need be. And speaking of cops, I think one will be descending on us, probably tonight."

"Malcolm's coming," said Laura, her face lighting up.

"Malcolm's coming?" echoed a voice from the vestibule.

"He's trying to get the time off and he's been trying to call you all afternoon, but there was no answer here, and both of your cell phones have been turned off until late this morning."

"I think the regular phones are working here," said Connor frowning as she opened the screen door and handed Laura her well-worn leather jacket. "Knowing him, he must be frantic."

"He was. I called him after I got hold of Laura. He's trying to juggle some stuff and get a few days off. I'll check in with him in a little while. See how its going."

"I think the only time that poor man ever gets a vacation is when he thinks you need him," said Laura.

"I'm one of the few people on earth with a six-foot-six, 240-pound, gun-toting guardian angel."

"Honey, you have a whole committee of guardian angels, and I'm counting the ones you can't see, too."

"Oh, yeah," said Connor, shrugging. "There is that."

*

"This doesn't seem to be proceeding according to your plan, Mr. Underwood."

"There were complications. How was I to know she'd offer a ride to one of the guests? She was an obnoxious old bat. And she should have been in the car alone. I made sure that Grace's cousin Henry would insist on driving her."

"And yet he didn't, did he?"

"I couldn't have anticipated she'd choose someone else. I had Henry primed for that part of it."

"And did your stellar research indicate that she had invited an old college friend to the funeral, someone who would turn out to have extremely strong connections to the U.S. government?"

"I did see the name in one of the phone-tap transcripts, but there wasn't time to pursue it."

"I suggest you should have taken the time. This woman's father is a highly respected and well-connected individual. He has the resources to put us in jeopardy."

"You're the one who insisted we move ahead quickly."

"Yes, but with care and precision. Precision is imperative. That's what turned decades of research into a more than viable plan."

"I'm aware of that. My grandfather…"

"Karl would be most disappointed in you."

"Don't you dare say that!"

"And don't you dare raise your voice to a superior. When we talk again, I want to hear that this mess has been cleaned up and the final preparations made for the conversion. Without the heir, without her capabilities, we will fail."

Devin mumbled something.

"Speak up!"

"I still don't know why you're so hell-bent on believing that old idiot, Schumann. He could be completely wrong. All this mumbo-jumbo about second sight."

"Enough!" the voice roared, and then the sound of a deep hacking cough came over the line. Devin waited, but within moments he heard a double click. The old man had hung up.

The funeral director swore under his breath before pressing the cradle switch for a dial tone. "Get me Gerhard," he snapped at the person who answered. As he waited, he tapped his gold pen on the blotter. When his impatience was finally assuaged, he didn't take any time for pointless pleasantries. "I want a full workup on these names: Connor Hawthorne, Benjamin Hawthorne, and…" He opened his top desk drawer and pulled out a sheet of paper filled with handwritten notes. "Laura Nez... No, I don't know where they live right now, but the two women flew here from New Mexico... What? The first one's a woman, too!... Yes, Connor! And there will be more names to come, but get started on that. You know what I want—all the dirt you can find. We need some leverage and we need it fast."

*

Police Captain Malcolm Jefferson would never have been mistaken for a particularly patient man. He had pursued every responsibility in his life and his career with the intensity of a long-distance runner, something else for which he would not have been mistaken, given his physique. Weight lifter, defensive tackle, boxer—any of those would fit. But he'd been a cop for more than twenty years. His rise through the ranks of the department had hardly been meteoric, given his outspokenness and the insidious racism, even in a city whose inhabitants were predominantly black. But Malcolm's determination had paid off. He'd earned his stripes, his commendations, even a medal or two, and passed every exam with high marks. Even the entrenched system couldn't shut him out forever.

Now, though, he more and more often regretted the bureaucrat's job that kept him behind a desk, and rarely in the field. He had begun to doubt whether he accomplished anything meaningful besides pushing piles of paper around his desk. And even though the promotion gave him more free time with the kids, and a lot less risk to his life than a shift patrolling the streets, his heart sometimes ached for the old days. It was the cops on the street who in his estimation did the real work of policing the District of Columbia. These days, the only times he'd felt really alive were those he spent in the company of his old friend Connor Hawthorne, her father, Benjamin, and her lover, Laura Nez. Then there was Ayalla, though he often found himself at a loss to deal with her sheer prickliness.

Malcolm and Connor went back a long way, from the time he'd collared the scumbag who'd snatched her purse. The unlikely friendship between a black cop and a white gay prosecutor blossomed into something unexpectedly profound that expanded to include their respective spouses. They'd seen each other through a lot of heartache—the death of Malcolm's wife, the abduction and murder of Connor's partner, Ariana, and much more in the years that followed. They'd saved each other's lives, something that tends to cement a friendship.

Malcolm still remained uncomfortable with all the crazy spiritual stuff that seemed to go on around Connor and Laura, because he'd seen things he knew shouldn't be possible. But he kept an open mind, because as his sister, Eve, the angel with an iron hand who'd helped raise his children, would say, "There's more magic in the world than you'd think."

At this moment, magic was not apparently working for him. He slapped the top of his desk in frustration over the delay in getting approval for a temporary leave of absence. The last time he'd been away for any length of time, was to accompany Benjamin to California, where Connor and Laura had gotten themselves embroiled in a murder and the pursuit of a sociopath. True, Benjamin had pulled a few strings, and the trip had been legitimized by his acting as liaison to the FBI agent who'd been assigned to the case. The perp they wanted had been a D.C. felon. But this time around he didn't have any good excuses for official involvement. His interest was personal, and the bureaucracy dictated that even police captains did not take vacation time without advance notice and official approval.

He wished for the twentieth time that he didn't have to fall back on Benjamin's connections. That tended to annoy Malcolm, not being able to reach a goal on his own efforts. On the other hand, he knew that was simply a matter of pride, and he couldn't let it stand in the way of his being on hand to help Connor. Her mother had been killed...murdered...and who knew what Connor might get involved in. He'd just have to cave in and call Benjamin. That would incur the wrath of some higher-up bureaucrat who would remember being strong-armed by one of the federal big shots and gladly take it out on Malcolm somewhere down the line. What the hell!

His hand was hovering above the phone when it rang. "Jefferson!" he snapped.

"Bad day, Captain?" said a familiar voice.

"Worse than usual, Benjamin. I was just thinking about trying to get in touch with you."

"Life is one cosmic coincidence."

"You've been hanging around Laura too long," sighed Malcolm. "And in answer to your question, none of my calls to Deputy Chief Rensaleer have been returned in the past several hours."

"Do you suppose he's been busy?"

"Busy screwing up my life, which is one of his favorite hobbies as far as I can tell."

"Ah, so outspoken on a department telephone."

Malcolm paused. He ought to know better. Watching your mouth on the phones here was basic CYA.

"Hmm," he said.

"Don't sweat it, my friend. I imagine everything will work out, sooner rather than later."

"You sound better informed than I am," said Malcolm.

"Sometimes. We'll talk again soon. In the meantime, try

cultivating patience, or…" There was a long pause. "…a reasonable *facsimile.*" And he was gone. Malcolm sat there holding the receiver. Why did Benjamin always sound cryptic? Must have something to do with his former spy business. Maybe once you got in the habit of that "need to know" bullshit, you never got out of it. And what was all that crap about patience? Since when did Benjamin start handing out stupid advice? A few seconds later the fax machine beside his desk chirped to announce an incoming transmission. *Ah,* thought Malcolm, smiling. *A reasonable facsimile.*

The first page was in Benjamin's tidy printing.

"Everything's taken care of. The FBI has requested your presence in Boston to facilitate the reopening of an old investigation related to a case you solved about eight years ago. Even your deputy chief can't complain someone's greasing the way for you to take time off."

Page two of the fax was a blurry but legible copy of an itinerary: Flight 113 out of DCA (known as National Airport for decades and Malcolm couldn't stand calling it Reagan National) at 7:05 P.M. Seat 3-A: first-class. Malcolm grinned. He wouldn't have to sit for an hour with his knees tucked under his chin. There was a time when he'd have been annoyed that Benjamin had bought him a plane ticket. With years of effort, he'd finally gotten over the pride issue and admitted that some people had more money than he did and however they wanted to spend it was their business.

He phoned home and asked Eve if she would mind packing him a suit and a couple of shirts in his overnighter. "It's already done, sweetie," she replied in her deep-voiced drawl. "Soon as I heard about Connor's momma, I knew you'd be off up north. Now you come on home so I can feed you a decent supper before you go. Probably starve yourself while you're gone."

"Eve, I never starve myself."

"Honey, if you ain't eatin' my cookin', you starvin'." He could hear her rumbly laugh as she hung up the phone, and he smiled. Even though it still hurt every time he thought of his wife, and he still had nightmares about her death, he knew he was a lucky man to have a kind, loving, down-to-earth sister like Eve to keep his life together and his kids on the right track. She was very good at "keepin' it real."

CHAPTER THREE

Here we may reign secure, and in my choice
To reign is worth ambition though in hell:
Better to reign in hell, than serve in heav'n.
—John Milton, *Paradise Lost*

Somewhere beneath the frail, time-worn façade of the elderly Herr Doktor, given name Friedrich (he no longer used his
true surname), still lay the handsome, virile warrior of his rem-
iniscences. And who could blame him, really, that he still lived
much in the past? There he had been honored, or at least
scrupulously obeyed. His memories of glory and conquest, of
power over life and death—these had never dimmed; in fact,
they loomed larger than cold reality. Had he been an American,
he would have called them the "good old days." The present was
cold and inhospitable to those who'd come so close to master-
ing the world, yet failed…but only by what Friedrich estimated
as the slimmest of margins, only by a few turns of fate's wheel.
That wasn't how it was written in later years, but he reminded
himself of the oft-proven adage that it is the winners of wars
who write the history books.

The capture of the U-505 and its code books, logs, charts,
and the two Enigma Code machines had been the first near-

fatal blow. And the high command had not known of the U-boat's fate until their strongholds in Europe had crumbled one by one and their once-feared fleet of German submarines was decimated. They hadn't known, because the one person who should have been able to at least partly foresee that disaster, or at least sense it after the fact, had been utterly blind. But for the failure of one individual, the civilized world would be speaking German, not English. And that failure could now, after almost sixty years, be rectified. He believed destiny, in the end, was stronger than all the machinations of man, and his destiny was clear to him.

Scores of others had made futile and foolish attempts to reclaim the glory of the past, but their reasoning had been fallacious, their strategies doomed from the start. The restoration of the Fatherland to its rightful place could no longer be achieved by force of arms. The world had changed too much, weapons abounded, most of them in the hands of the mentally unfit. No, the Führer himself had understood there was more to achieving one's destiny than Panzer divisions and U-boats, just as there was more to this world than what a pair of human eyes could see. The tools of war were just that—tools. The secret to victory was something far less tangible, and immeasurably more powerful than even the most horrendous weapons of mass destruction.

As was his habit each evening before retiring, Friedrich made a tour of his cozy, softly lit library. His hands brushed lovingly across the spines of leather-bound books collected by his own father and grandfather, the crystal decanters of whiskey and brandy, the old-fashioned globe of the world on a pedestal. He paused beside it, spun it slowly. His wrinkled, spotted hands came to rest on either side of the orb, one palm over Africa, the other in the middle of the Pacific Ocean. Holding the world in his hands. The symbolism was hardly subtle, but it pleased him enormously. He smiled—thin dry lips pulled back over yellowing teeth, the loose skin of his elongated face sinking into deep furrows. An observer might have likened the end result to a particularly unpleasant Halloween mask perched atop a gangly, slightly hunched scarecrow. Not a pretty sight. Still, for a man of eighty-seven years, he was well preserved. Were it not for the cancer eating at his insides, he might well have been able to last another ten or fifteen years.

He crossed the room to a tall cabinet some four feet wide with glass doors. Within, the black wool uniform still hung, neatly pressed, carefully preserved. The silver aluminum trim, the stiff shoulder boards. The lightning runes, the black swastika on a field of red, the insignia of his rank. He raised his eyes to the shelf where the black field cap rested, its death's head insignia glittering beneath the eagle crest of the nation. He had always favored the death's head, even when he had transferred from the Totenkopf Division to the Leibstandarte Adolf Hitler in Berlin. It had struck fear and loathing even in the hearts of those innocent of treason. Those who were not innocent—the men or women who dared even the slightest lapse in loyalty— knew that an impending visit from the SS-VT or its police arm, the Gestapo, could have only one conclusion too horrifying to contemplate. Any number of traitors had swallowed the barrel of a Luger, or endured the bitter taste of cyanide rather than face the Doktor's interrogation. That had been his specialty, and the title was neither honorary nor an attempt at dark humor. After attending a military academy for young Nazi men from good families, he'd received a degree in medicine. He'd ranked at the very top of his class, and his blond good looks, the fine aquiline nose, firm chin, the ramrod straight spine, made him the envy of other men and the subject of much female interest which he generally ignored. He had achieved leadership in the Hitler Youth, and he was destined for greatness. He didn't need any encumbrances.

The day rolled around when his destiny was shown to him. An officer of the SS came to his small apartment in Berlin. Friedrich's academic record had caught the attention of those in authority (which is to say that the government had ordered all universities to report the names of their top students). Himmler's aides, in their quest for pure Aryan officers, had liked the looks of this young man. Once singled out, he had been carefully watched, his political leanings evaluated, his entire background thoroughly investigated.

So, the officer concluded in his monologue to Friedrich, after a succinct summary of their findings, the newly minted physician was to be offered a commission. The Fatherland needed him; Heinrich Himmler had personally selected him. The answer, of course, was a foregone conclusion. Even before he learned the inner workings of the elite military cadre that would become his family and home, he knew instinctively that had he refused, he would have been a dead man. By 1941, the power of the SS was absolute. Even if there were grumblings in Hitler's inner circle that the war was not going as well as the Führer claimed, to the SS divisions fighting all over Europe, the Third Reich was invincible. And its death camps were running at full capacity, slaughtering thousands of "undesirables" a day—mostly Jews, but also Gypsies, blacks, gays, prisoners shipped from all over the continent, common criminals, political enemies—they were all fodder for the factories, work farms, and eventually for the firing squads, gas chambers, and the so-called scientists.

Thus, at the age of twenty-five, he became one of the youngest officers in the SS-Totenkopf division. His intellectual brilliance was never once put to use in the saving of lives. Quite the opposite. He threw himself body and soul into his work, which was primarily interrogation. He used drugs on occasion, but he considered himself a scientist, and thus coldly rationalized an array of ghastly experiments in the limits of human tolerance for pain. When time permitted, he was methodically thorough in eliciting the truth. If his prisoners weren't actually dead by the time they were taken from his custody, they were generally insane.

Friedrich, however, had been even more interested in the research program carried out by Hitler and his most rabid racial profiler, Himmler. They had for years been passionately devoted to the goal of procreating a race of "pure" Aryans. Admission to the officer ranks of the SS had been limited to those who could demonstrate so-called untainted ancestry for at least three generations before them. Later, Himmler's ancestral researches went back even further. In their zeal, they had established the Lebensborn homes, where "racially" selected young women, impregnated by selected soldiers, spent their maternity in confinement. This new crop of babies was to be the future of the Reich.

As the Nazis overwhelmed country after country in their quest for expansion, Himmler's minions continued to search for what they considered perfect specimens of Aryan manhood among the sympathizers and collaborators (of which there were many). It was in one such French town, in the once Germanic province of Alsace-Lorraine that a young man of extraordinary beauty and physical strength was found. His name was Guillaume de L'Aigle, and he was the twenty-eight-year-old son of a wealthy French industrialist who fervently supported whichever side in a conflict would yield the greatest profit to his company. He had opted to align with the Nazis, even before they began flooding into France, and for a while at any rate, it seemed he had chosen well. Thus, when one of Himmler's aides invited Guillaume to attend the training school for officers, M. de L'Aigle was more than happy to consent.

Friedrich, because of his growing friendship with Heinrich Himmler, had been transferred from his duty at the camps to the Leibstandarte Adolf Hitler in Berlin. He was intrigued by the genetic researches and the tests performed on the young candidates for admission to officer training. He volunteered to perform the initial physicals on particularly promising specimens, and one day in the examination room he met the young man, Guillaume. Friedrich had been impressed by the young man from the instant he removed his clothing. Here was a model for a Greek statue extolling the beauty of the male animal: broad in the shoulders, narrow in the waist and hips, ridges of muscle in the biceps, calves, and thighs. He stood peacefully, yet proudly as the doctor listened to his heart and lungs. When the knock came at the door, Friedrich was almost annoyed to be interrupted. But the protest died on his lips when he recognized the slight figure with the round glasses. Reichsführer Himmler had come to call.

"Doktor," he smiled. "How is it coming? Jürgen told me you were seeing a particularly promising candidate today." His eyes came to rest on the handsome young man, and his expression was one of appreciation. "Ah, yes. Jürgen was quite right." He came to stand in front of Guillaume. "You are from one of our patron families in Alsace-Lorraine, is that right?" he questioned in passable French. To his surprise, the young man answered in more than passable German. "Yes, sir. My father has permitted me to join you if I am worthy."

Friedrich, who had turned away to prepare the needle for drawing blood, became aware that an awkward silence filled the room. He swung back and found Himmler staring fixedly at the silver pendant that glittered in the young man's light golden chest hair. Friedrich could not imagine what was wrong.

"Reichsführer," he said. "Is there something I—"

"Where did you get that?" Himmler hissed, ignoring Friedrich.

"What, sir?"

"That," said Himmler, pointing at the pendant. "Where did you get it?"

The youth looked puzzled. "From my father, sir," he replied. "I've had it since I came of age. He gave it to me as a gift."

"Where did *he* get it?"

Now the boy was truly baffled. He knew who Himmler was, and it seemed he had somehow managed to get on the wrong side of the man who commanded the most feared organizations in Germany. "I…that is…from his father before him. He tells me it is of some importance, that it has been in our family for many years. Other than that, I do not know anything about it, or even what it is supposed to be."

Himmler closed his eyes for a moment. Friedrich could see his hands were trembling, and the man's usually ruddy countenance was deathly pale. "No, I suppose you wouldn't." He took a piece of paper and pen from the desk. "Report to this address in one hour." He pressed the paper into the Guillaume's hand. "Do not be late, and bring that"—Himmler pointed at the pendant—"with you."

"Yes, sir," said Guillaume, now thoroughly bewildered as Himmler stalked from the room.

"I don't understand," Guillaume looked at Friedrich pleadingly.

"Nor do I," admitted the Doktor. "What is that thing anyway?"

Guillaume rubbed the pendant between the thumb and forefinger of his right hand and shrugged in that eloquent Gallic way. "I think it looks sort of like a person, but there's no significance to it, no real value. I only wear it because my father was most insistent."

"Well, clearly the Reichsführer considers it significant for some reason. If I were you, I'd do as he instructed. Here, let me see that paper."

Friedrich looked at the address—Hitler's headquarters. He didn't know exactly what was going on, but he made it his business to find out. Within a few days, he finally understood what Hitler was looking for and why. Friedrich, sensing the potential enormity of Himmler's discovery, determined that he, himself, would become a mentor to Guillaume. It was, in fact, Friedrich who later stood beside him as he received his commission and his officer's saber. And it was he who suggested Guillaume receive a new name in keeping with his destiny. It resonated with the name given him at his christening, for the meaning was essentially the same. But as the brightest star in the constellation of occultists around the Führer, and the one who could hold the key to a victorious future, the young man must assume a Germanic identity. Thus Guillaume de L'Aigle became Wilhelm von Adler. Until January, 1945, he was always within call of the Führer's voice. And then he disappeared.

*

Friedrich peered intently at the black uniform. True, he couldn't discern every detail of the decorations—for valor, loyalty, and sometimes simply for surviving when others did not—that hung from the chest pocket, for Friedrich's eyesight had degenerated more than he'd admit. And their colorful contrast to the black uniform was lost on him. Since childhood he'd hidden the shameful genetic defect of his color blindness. The pure Aryan race tolerated no such deviations from perfection, and during every day of his all too brief service to the

Reich, the fear lurked that his deficiency might be discovered, his superiority questioned. And then the Reich had fallen, the Führer had died, and being color-blind no longer seemed to matter quite so much.

He took one last look into the corner of the cupboard at the shiny, knee-high jackboots that had once goose-stepped to the cadence of war. Those, for him, were not only the good old days, but the days that would be again.

He returned to the bookshelves and removed three books. Then he felt behind them for three tiny depressions—barely visible to the naked eye—in the surface of the shelf. When he was confident his fingers were properly aligned within the hollows, he began to press with gradually increasing force. The once-simple task had grown more difficult over the years for his arthritic fingers. One of the security features of the hidden lock was the time needed to activate the mechanism, and this mere fifteen seconds had come to feel like an eternity. Yet, with all the security his villa boasted, he did not dare leave his most precious possessions in a more accessible place. He sometimes suspected that his greatest fear was not that they would be stolen, but that he would die, and someone else would stumble across them, someone who would usurp the role Friedrich reserved to himself alone. He couldn't bear the thought.

Finally, a series of three clicks signaled the rotation of the tumblers. Nothing happened to the shelf or the bookcase. No visible panel slid open, no hidden compartment was instantly revealed. This was yet another security feature. Should someone, through cleverness or sheer good luck, find and activate this switch, it would lead them nowhere. They would also be locked in. The switch locked dead bolts on both the interior door and the French doors leading the terrace, themselves deceptively delicate in design, yet constructed completely of steel and bullet-proof flexglass, an invention of Friedrich's own company.

He crossed the room to the cabinet where his uniform was displayed. Inside, on the left wall, hung his ceremonial sword in its engraved sheath. The sword pointed downward at an angle toward the rear of the cabinet. He opened one of the glass doors and quickly shifted the hilt of the sword so that it was precisely parallel to the back wall. Had he not done so within five seconds of opening the door, the next line of defense—a concealed canister of gas—would have been activated. At the moment, it was charged only with an odorless anesthetic that would render an intruder unconscious while simultaneously setting off alarms in the guards' rooms. On those rare occasions when Friedrich was away from the villa, the canister was exchanged for one with far more deadly consequences—a form of Sarin nerve gas that killed in mere seconds, even before the victim was fully aware he was dying.

Friedrich could have disconnected the canister completely, but there was something about the small element of risk in being knocked out that delighted him. He didn't take many chances nowadays, surely none that could set his blood to surging through his veins as it once had. And he certainly wouldn't be foolish enough risk the nerve gas. But even a tiny illusion of danger was welcome in these endless years of colorless existence.

He got down on his knees and moved the boots to reveal a five-by-ten-inch horizontal wood panel in the back of the cabinet that was now slightly ajar, just enough that he could grip it with his fingernails. It slid open from left to right on carefully oiled tracks. Conscious of the pain in his joints, he nonetheless took his time in gently removing the cloth-bound package lying in the reinforced, airtight, fireproof safe. He rose with difficulty and carried it across to his desk, the same ornate Louis XIV gilded piece, looted from a museum in Paris, that had stood in his office in the Leibstandarte headquarters. On a whim he'd had his bodyguards carry it from the building during the bombing of Berlin. They'd almost balked, fearing that one of the Allied shells would hit them at any moment. But their brainwashing held true. They were the chosen, Hitler's Valkyries, immune to defeat. Ten minutes after they'd loaded the desk into a small truck, Friedrich raised the machine gun he'd slung over his shoulder and shot all eight of them. He felt some sorrow at their death, but he could leave no one behind who knew with any certainty that he was escaping Berlin. He'd sent his wife and children to Hitler's bunker, but he knew what would happen there, and he had no intention of tasting cyanide himself. He'd been shown a different future.

He fled in the truck with only one trusted ally—a twenty-one-year-old rank lieutenant named Karl Unterholz. Other than the ornate desk, his uniforms and regalia, personal files, and the objects that lay wrapped in this bundle, he had nothing left of those times…except money, of course. And even the large sums of stolen money he'd deposited in various European banks during the last year of the war would have run out in the last sixty years had he not built up a substantial engineering firm near Munich. In the '70s and '80s, the firm opened branches in London, Tokyo, and Sydney, his influence spread, and his supply of ready cash flowed like water. He kept a low profile, but not because he had to. While so many of his former brothers in arms had fled Germany, only to be relentlessly pursued for decades by the Nazi hunters like Wiesenthal and Klarsfeld, Friedrich and his aide went only as far as Austria, to a tiny mountain cabin fully stocked with supplies for many months. When they emerged in the year following the fall of Berlin, they were entirely different people—pale, dark-haired, rail-thin, and, because of Friedrich's meticulous contingency plan, their perfectly authentic papers identified them as Jewish: Friedrich and Ernst Kesselberg, two brothers who had escaped the persecution. The irony of hiding in plain sight at one time had amused him. But now he rankled more and more under the false label of Jew. Within the cloth bundle, though, lay the truth.

He unbound the gold cord, pulled back the fabric, and laid each item reverently on his desk. In sleeves composed of a special plastic compound, he had sealed the evidence of his true identity, preserving it against the ravages of time. He looked longingly at the picture of himself (eyes glowering under the black uniform cap) affixed to his SS identification booklet, before laying it aside. Next, a sheet of writing paper covered in a faded scrawl. At the bottom, he traced the unmistakable signature of his Führer—Adolf Hitler.

Two weeks before the Allies—Americans and Russians closing in from opposite directions—Hitler's personal courier had delivered this note to him. It was brief, yet powerful. The Führer was issuing final orders. Friedrich was still following them. With the note had come a tiny clothbound book, not quite a personal diary, more of a record of the single-minded pursuit of a goal the dictator found more imperative than anything else. Even during the dates of the buildup to Operation Overlord, the failed plan to invade England, Hitler's entries were about something else entirely, something Hitler and his closest occult adviser desperately needed, but had been unable to find. Now the information in the book was known only to Friedrich, and so far he had used it well.

Lastly, he patted a tattered leather-bound journal, its pages roughly three by five inches in size and its hand-sewn binding barely intact. He unsealed the special bag and pulled out the book. With utmost care, he slowly opened the cover. On the first page, he read again the words, "The Personal Diary of Jack Fortis." He turned to the second page, and ran his fingertips over rough foolscap covered with careful handwriting. "When I was but a lad of twelve, and a stable boy on a large estate, I saw things I never told anyone about, but now I must put them down before death claims me. Thanks to the kindness of the Lady Eliza, I learned to read and write, and for all these years I have kept from her the truth of what happened. Perhaps she will read it for herself."

Friedrich sat back in his chair and closed his eyes. This was the key for which he'd spent years searching, and one day, only a few years earlier and by sheer good fortune, it had come into his hands. The gods of war had smiled upon him. These two books, one written by one of history's most successful conquerors, and the other by a mere servant, couldn't have been more different. Yet with both of them, Friedrich was assured (whether or not he lived to see it) that the Fourth Reich would not fail.

Chapter Four

And all my mother came into mine eyes,
and gave me up to tears.
—William Shakespeare, *King Henry V,* act IV, scene 6

"I don't think it would be appropriate for us to handle the arrangements," said Devin Underwood, his expression as unreadably neutral as any Connor had ever seen.

"Why do you say that?" she asked, flicking a quick glance - at Laura.

"Well, under the circumstances, with the police making certain allegations about my business partner, I don't see—"

"I don't believe the police have made any allegations at all," Connor interrupted. "Granted, the press has been extremely busy with unfounded speculation, but that doesn't make it official."

The funeral director pursed his lips and straightened a handful of gray folders on his desk that didn't need straightening. "Perhaps if I were completely candid," he paused, "you might agree that Dagle & Sons is hardly the most suitable choice."

Connor raised an eyebrow. "Candid would be good."

He squirmed in his chair. "Mr. Dagle, that is, Billy…how can I phrase this delicately? He was—"

"If you're trying to tell us your partner was gay, Mr.

Underwood, that's hardly a surprising revelation," Laura said.

He colored slightly, scowled at her, then smoothed his tanned face with one hand as if troweling his countenance back into its proper blandness.

"What I intended to say was that Billy had been extremely depressed of late. The business has been on very shaky ground—we've had very few cases. And I believe there may have been some sort of falling out between Billy and his, er, love interest…a separation or something. He was moping about the place."

It was Connor's turn to frown. "Really, he didn't seem that way."

"You spoke to him?" Underwood barked the question, leaning forward in his chair.

Connor, startled by his vehemence, was about to answer, but Laura beat her to it. "We saw him standing by the car at the church, chatting and laughing with one of the other drivers. He seemed pretty cheerful, though we didn't actually have a chance to speak to him."

Underwood settled in his chair. His relief was obvious. "At any rate, given the possibility that Billy did have some active role in this tragedy, I hardly think it would behoove any of us to have your mother or Ms. Wainwright's aunt here." He reached into his desk and removed a business card. "Ms. Hawthorne, I recommend you call Cheri Marshall at Westmoreland. She's extremely professional. I'm sure you'll be more than satisfied with the service there. Now, if you'll excuse me, I have a great many things to attend to." He was on his feet and opening the office door before either of them could get out of their seats.

"But you just mentioned you have very few cases," said Connor.

Underwood looked momentarily nonplused. "I wasn't referring to clients," he snapped, his thin veneer of civility slipping. "The accident—I have claims to file and other matters." He stood rigidly beside the door as they gathered up their coats. The door closed none too gently behind them. Within a few moments they were standing on the sidewalk.

"I believe that's referred to as the bum's rush," said Laura.

"Preceded by a pack of lies, to borrow yet another cliché," said Connor.

"Obviously. And you couldn't help baiting him a little, I see."

"You mean about being so 'busy.'"

"I know. It was a cheap shot, but he left me an easy target. Oh, and thanks for stepping in before I said something about Billy that I'd have regretted. My reflexes are getting slow."

"Not a problem. I just had this instant hunch that we didn't want him to know we had that little chat with his former partner."

"Glad we did. Mr. Underwood is doing everything possible to point the finger of blame at his own business partner. If we hadn't talked to Billy in the cemetery, we might have believed that bunch of crap about him having broken up with his lover and being depressed and worried about impending bankruptcy."

Laura shook her head. "Underwood's incredibly stupid if he thinks he can sell that to the cops without them doing anything to corroborate it. All they'd have to do is talk to,—what was the guy's name? Billy's 'amour' as he called him?"

"Craig? No, Chris, I think. But there's something about Underwood that makes me think he's not really foolish enough to try that story on anyone he thinks would actually check up on it. That was probably for our benefit, something to stifle our curiosity and get us out of his office."

"But why?" asked Laura. "And why drive away business? If he really was afraid that Billy had anything to do with this, what better way to alleviate public suspicion than to have the families of the victims come to Dagle & Sons for the funeral arrangements? It's profit and good PR."

"I have a feeling Mr. Underwood isn't all that interested in the funeral business."

They walked down the sidewalk to where they'd parked.

"Seems that way to me, too. He's a little too slick."

Connor smiled. "And what is your definition of slick?"

"Armani suit, silk shirt, $75 haircut, handmade Italian shoes, diamond cuff links."

"My, my, you are the noticing type."

"And he never looks you right in the eye."

"I noticed, but I thought he was simply so taken with you…"

Laura laughed out loud. "Get serious. He couldn't wait to see us gone."

"True. But what's so scary about little old us?"

"You don't suppose your reputation precedes you," said Laura, a smile playing over her lips.

"Which reputation? The gay one?"

"Well, I don't think *that* would make him nervous, you goof. But your former life as a rabid district attorney might have him in a sweat."

"You mean he's worried I might suddenly come out of retirement and threaten to bean him with a thick law book."

Laura lightly punched Connor's arm. "Be serious. I mean he could assume you have connections."

"Maybe."

"Or he could be worried because your father's a 'someone,' as they say."

"Also a maybe. But except for a very few of us, everyone assumes my dad is completely out of the government, out of the 'game.' Which makes me wonder—"

"How a funeral director would be so anxious about dealing with the Hawthornes that he'd turn down business, and lie about material facts."

"You're finishing my sentences again, darling."

"Sorry. That must be bothersome, you being a famous writer and all."

It was Connor's turn. She gently poked Laura's waist, a slightly ticklish spot.

"Hey! Just tell me that isn't what you were going to say and I'll apologize for real."

"What I was going to say was…" Connor shook her head. "All right, that *is* what I was going to say: Damn, you're tough."

"You'd better believe it." Laura unlocked the doors, and got in. Connor followed suit. Just as Laura started the car, they heard a slight squeal of tires. In the rearview mirror, Laura saw a car turning hard and fast out of the funeral home driveway. It accelerated past them—a black BMW M5 —Devin Underwood at the wheel.

"Guess he wasn't so buried in paperwork after all," said Laura, as she shifted into gear. "Want to see where he's headed?"

"Follow him in a rental car?" Connor snorted. "Please. That was an M5."

"So what's a struggling funeral director doing driving a $90,000 car and wearing ten grand worth of clothes and jewelry?"

"And if he does have money, what's he doing at Dagle & Sons?"

"Why don't I give your dad a call and have him do a little data run on Mr. Underwood?"

"You mean snooping," said Connor.

"We veterans of the spook business really prefer euphemisms. Most branches have a whole department devoted to euphemism development."

"You mean like 'terminate with extreme prejudice,' for example?"

"Oh, please. That's so Cold War."

"Rub out?"

"That's more Al Capone."

"Okay, so how does the modern-day intelligence operative communicate?"

"We gather information, acquire assets, identify threats, neutralize targets—all very civilized, don't you think?"

"No, it still means snooping, bribing, making potentially faulty assessments, and then killing people. But I imagine our stellar legislators on the Hill like the euphemisms a lot better."

"Does this mean you do or do not want me to check up on Mr. Underwood?"

Connor sighed. "I do, but I'm having a little crisis of conscience about it. Personal privacy and constitutional rights are taking a bad beating these days."

Laura patted her arm. "When we move to a perfect world, honey, where no one is sneaky, venal, or murderous, we'll do away with Big Brother entirely."

"I wish."

"In the meantime, we'll just walk softly among the databases and peer only where necessary. If we're going to find out why your mom died..." Laura left the sentence unfinished, not knowing if they'd ever be able to learn the truth.

"I'm almost afraid we will."

Laura shook her head. "I don't believe for a moment that your mother was involved in anything underhanded. She was just at the wrong place at the wrong time."

"I hope you're right. Somehow, though, I think there's more to it."

*

Devin drove as fast as he dared. He was late meeting Arthur, and it wasn't a good idea to keep Arthur waiting. He was too damn weird for words, and there was something about his eyes—colorless, clear, and without any discernible expression when he looked right at you—that raised the hairs on the back of Devin's neck. The man never looked angry, happy, puzzled, or excited. His expression was blank. Yet Arthur was certainly not blind. He was, according to a loan shark of Devin's acquaintance, the most brilliant demolition expert, electrical engineer, and hit man working the East Coast, maybe the whole country. Thus Devin had, with the hesitant approval of his superiors in Europe, contracted with Arthur to take out the occupants of the limousine. But the plan had been to make it look like a freak accident. So far as Devin could tell, though, the police were not treating it like any such thing. And the balance of the fee had not been transferred to Arthur's Cayman Islands account. Friedrich had refused. Now Devin was caught squarely in the middle between an obsessed Nazi and a certifiable killer. But he thought he had a plan, and although it would mean divulging something of utmost secrecy, he'd decided he would rather offer Arthur a share in the spoils. Otherwise the police might one day soon be scraping up small pieces of Devin and his cherished BMW.

*

When Malcolm emerged from the Jetway into the boarding area, he was slightly disappointed to find no familiar faces. He'd half expected that Connor and Laura, maybe even Benjamin, would be there to meet him. Then he grimaced at his own foolishness. Like they didn't have better things to do at the moment. Of course, he'd also wondered if just maybe Ayalla would show up. But she had her hands full with what the press was calling the Fore River Bridge murders. The FBI office in Boston was no doubt seething with activity, much of which she would be overseeing. He wondered how she was dealing with the pressure of being a woman in what stubbornly remained at its heart a thoroughly entrenched boys club. He suspected that even Ayalla's sixteen years of sweat and dedication, a brilliant mind for investigation, and her heroism in the line of duty would have not have justified her promotion in the minds of those agents who would have been happier in the FBI of the 1960s. To them, she probably wasn't simply the assistant special agent in charge of the Boston field office. No, she was a black woman giving them orders. And J. Edgar was probably twirling in his grave.

He gripped his overnighter and headed for the main airport concourse at Logan's Terminal B to find the car rental counter. He'd just reached the main lobby and joined a long line at CarsQuick—a new company that promised to be cheap, if ungrammatical—when he heard his name over the loudspeaker. *"Attention, please. Will arriving passenger Malcolm Jefferson please report to the curbside baggage stand for East Coast ShuttleAir."* It was repeated twice. Malcolm frowned. He hadn't flown on that airline. So why would they page him? But he might as well double-check.

Beneath the airline marquis at the curb, where porters were busily loading bags onto trolleys, a nondescript government sedan idled. Standing on the driver's side, looking over the car's roof toward the terminal building was Ayalla Franklin. Malcolm couldn't help himself. He grinned. Every time her saw her, he thought her even more beautiful. But he had to ration the number of times he told her so; she didn't take compliments well.

He waved and she waved back, her lips forming the merest presumption of a smile. "Hey, cop!" she said.

"Hey, Feeb," he teased. He slung his bag into the backseat, and didn't even think about going around the car and sweeping her into his arms, though he would sorely liked to have done just that. For Ayalla, public displays of affection were anathema. Being seen as one iota less than perfectly professional had made her a good agent, but a rather frustratingly guarded and temperamental lover.

Malcolm climbed into the passenger seat and looked at her for a long moment. Ayalla's skin was only a shade or two lighter than Malcolm's own deep mahogany hue, but where his eyes were a soft brown, hers were a stunning crystal blue, and her high cheekbones seemed to imply a more exotic heritage than his own. He loved her tallness. She was very near six feet in her low-heeled shoes, and the money she spent on having her jackets tailored was well spent. It enhanced but didn't flaunt her curves, and almost completely disguised her holstered weapon. Her brown hair, flecked with blonde highlights, was swept back from her face the way he most liked it. But he also didn't mention that very often. Ayalla shied away from catering to the likes and dislikes of men. Malcolm figured that had a lot to do with her work.

With a quick but thorough circuit of the rearview mirrors and a glance over her left shoulder, Ayalla pulled out into the challenging evening traffic of one of the busiest airports in the country. As she merged into an exit lane, a cab blared its horn. She hadn't actually cut him off, but she had delayed him perhaps a second and a half. She had also gotten in front of him. Boston drivers, especially cabbies, took everything personally, including their individual share of the pavement and their timetables. Horn usage was common, a great deal more common, in fact, than turn-signal usage…which might have explained the prevalence of hand gestures in rush hour.

Ayalla didn't respond to the horn, or the barely comprehensible imprecations of the cabbie as he changed lanes to get around her again.

"So, you like Boston?" asked Malcolm, waving in a friendly fashion at the cabbie to annoy him even further.

"I don't like it, I don't hate it," she said, accelerating smoothly. He liked the way she handled a car—firmly but gently. "I haven't had time to buy enough furniture for my apartment, let alone sightsee. But my cousin's kids visited. Said Boston was educational."

"Assuming you're real interested in elitist white guys and religious fanatics," said Malcolm.

"Exactly," she nodded. "The people history makes heroes of, even the phony ones. I don't think heroes always live up to their P.R."

He started to answer, then paused. "You talking about our founding fathers, or about yourself?"

"What?!"

"Hey, don't get all bent out of shape. It just sounded kind of personal. And I know you didn't want to come up here with all that above-and-beyond the call of duty stuff fresh in everyone's mind."

"No, I didn't. So half the guys here think I got a citation because I got wounded and was lucky enough not to die, and the other half think it's all hype to keep the Black Congressional Caucus happy."

"Half and half? Hmm. So you're saying every agent in the field office resents you?"

She shook her head. "Of course not!"

"But you said—"

"I know what I said, but…" She stopped and glanced at him, and the tiny smile playing around his lips. "You're baiting me, aren't you? Trying to make me realize I sound paranoid and ridiculous."

He allowed himself a real smile. "You're not ridiculous, not ever." He gently rested his hand on her shoulder. "But as for paranoid, well…"

Ayalla laughed out loud. "You're right. I take myself way too seriously sometimes."

"Only because you're afraid other people won't."

"Yeah. Probably."

"So, is it all business tonight, or could we maybe have some dinner and spend a little quality time?"

"You want to skip dinner?" she said. "And go right to the quality time?"

"Seriously?" Malcolm's jaw dropped open. Under the circumstances, he hardly dared hope she'd take any time out from the investigation at all.

Ayalla grinned. "I'm full of surprises, Captain. All avenues of pursuit are being handled by other agents. I'm learning to delegate. And besides," she added, reaching for his hand, "I've been thinking about quality time all day."

★

"I wonder where Malcolm got to," said Connor, after she spit out the toothpaste, and wiped her face with one of the thick, soft towels the owners of the bed-and-breakfast provided in generous quantities. "He should have been in Boston by now."

"Your dad called while you were in the shower," replied Laura. "He said Malcolm's flight got in earlier this evening, but Benjamin hadn't heard from him either. He had a feeling maybe Ayalla showed up at the airport, since Malcolm didn't pick up his rental car."

Connor strolled out of the bathroom, tying the belt of her navy blue chenille robe. "Oh, well, I guess that would explain it."

"What's the matter, sweetheart? You almost sound peeved."

"I'm not. I mean, I want whatever makes him happy. But that woman just plain annoys me. Why did he have to pick an overzealous, judgmental FBI agent to hang out with?"

Laura smiled. "I don't know if you actually pick the people you fall for. I didn't exactly plan on getting involved with my boss's daughter, you know. But here we are."

"And it was a good career move," said Connor, flopping down on the bed beside Laura. "Plus my dad already liked you a lot, and this way he gets to keep you as a daughter-in-law, sort of."

"You make it sound as if he was matchmaking when he sent me to New Mexico to look out for you."

Connor looked thoughtful as she stroked her index finger along Laura's jawline. "I don't know if he's quite that devious, but on the other hand, he probably wasn't opposed to the idea either. At the time I think he was mostly interested in making sure I didn't have any more "accidents."

"You know, when you come right down to it, I didn't do all that good a job. If it weren't for your big guardian angel cop, we'd both be dead."

"Hey, you did just fine up to the part where you got shot. And if I hadn't been so damned uncooperative in the first place. God, I was being such a pain in the ass."

"Yeah," said Laura, "you kind of were."

"Hey! You don't have to *agree*."

Laura laughed. "You are so easy to 'get' my darling. I'm only kidding."

"Good, because otherwise I wouldn't want to kiss you."

"Well, what's keeping you?"

"Nothing at all," said Connor, turning out the lamp.

Her visits to the Dreamtime had been few. Unlike Laura, who regularly, and at will, walked the pathways through other realms,

Connor was only drawn there through need or by summons from her Grandmother Broadhurst, who had passed beyond the earth plane a few years earlier. But tonight, Connor felt herself awaken, sat up abruptly, and then realized with some consternation that her body still slept peacefully beside Laura in the warm, cozy bed. The act of sitting up was all in her mind, so to speak. And around her the features of the room—the love seat, the chintz-covered chairs, the fluffy curtains at the windows overlooking the ocean—faded, like the images in an ink drawing left out in the rain. "Gray," she thought. "Why does it always seem gray?"

Connor didn't like the sense of separation from the solid and familiar world in which she lived. It still made her nauseous. She felt herself rising from the bed. This was the time, if she were going to turn back. Laura had taught her how to stay anchored. She could refuse to leave and simply drift back to sleep. But something had summoned her. It apparently wasn't Gwendolyn. The old lady was always clearly present…when she was present. So what was pulling, tugging at Connor?

The room faded away completely. Now there was only a soft grayish cloud of undifferentiated matter all around her, drifting in wisps. This was the 'in-between' place, Laura had explained. If you really weren't supposed to be here, you wouldn't be able to pass through. You'd simply bounce off an invisible barrier and end up firmly back in your body. This, Connor figured, was the cosmic version of a home security system.

The fog cleared. She was standing on the edge of a highway in the desert. She turned slightly and saw a ramshackle roadside diner with a few cars parked beside it. The land around her felt familiar, some place she'd seen in New Mexico perhaps, on the Rez. She walked toward the diner and glanced in the open door. To her dismay, she recognized the woman perched on one of the red leatherette and chrome counter stools. It was her mother, Amanda, yet…not Amanda. This woman was much younger. Her clothes were from the '50s maybe—a rose-colored shirtwaist dress, pumps. The figure that was so like her mother began to turn toward Connor, and Connor fled to the parking lot, embarrassed to find herself hiding behind a car. She heard the click of high heels on the pavement, the same click she'd heard the day her mother walked down the hall of Connor's prep school dorm and announced she was going into therapy for her "problem." Pain knifed through her heart as she felt once more the anger and humiliation of being sent to that Freudian moron who'd tried to resurrect her "normal" feelings for the opposite sex. That might have been the day she hated her mother the most.

Connor's dream self turned and ran, rushing up a gentle slope and down into a narrow defile. In the near distance, she saw a group of people gathered atop a small mesa. Their voices came to her over the clear air. They were chanting something. With but a thought of curiosity, she was instantly standing directly behind them. They were Native American, though not of a tribe she recognized. And their attention was on something within their circle. She rose up to see what it was, and the circle suddenly parted to admit her. In the center she saw a mound covered with colorful blankets. She knew it was a grave, and she didn't like graves. But she knelt beside it anyway and began to pull back the layers of blankets. Beneath that were layers of newspaper, copies of the Washington Post society pages, the same papers her mother saved in box after box, stored away in the attic in Potomac. And finally, she pulled back the last one, and there lay an old Indian woman—ancient and wizened, and seeming more asleep than dead. These people were mourning the passage of their shaman, their medicine woman, their matriarch. And Connor knew, though it seemed absolutely impossible, that this was also her mother, Amanda.

The grave site melted away and Connor was looking at a more familiar scene—the Sangre de Cristo mountains near Santa Fe. She looked out at the sunrise in silence. But she was not alone. The old medicine woman was beside her. And the woman's voice was in her head, just as when Gwendolyn Broadhurst chose to communicate with Connor.

"I'm sorry, my child. So very sorry you were hurt."

"Who are you?" said Connor, aloud…at least she thought she was talking out loud.

"Don't you know?" said the old woman softly.

"You're…it's really you?"

"Yes."

"But I don't understand."

"We look different here. Your grandmother must have told you that."

"She did, and I know we do. But this is so much more vivid, and really different."

"When I was your mother, I didn't strike you as very wise, did I?"

"Well, no."

"That's because I wasn't. But now when I see all the pain I caused you, all the ways I chose that brought you unhappiness, my heart feels like it's breaking."

"Why did you—I mean, why did it have to be like that? I only wanted you to love me the way I was." Connor could feel the tears coursing down her face, even though she wasn't sure there was such a thing as tears (or faces) in the Dreamtime.

"Oh, my dear child," said the elderly woman, reaching for Connor's hand. "I'm so sorry. I did love you, you know. But the trials I set for myself in that lifetime—they were so terrible. The addictions, the anger, the loneliness, the confusion, the pain. I needed to know those things, and I don't regret learning them. But I still regret that it hurt you so much, that it made you close up inside and *pull away from me. I didn't know how to reach you anymore, and after a while, I didn't even want to try. All I thought of was my own pain. Now that we're here, I can see a great deal more."*

"I didn't think a lot about your pain," admitted Connor, still staring at the peaks of the mountains in the distance. "I got so accustomed to you hating me, and that hurt so much I tried to forget about it entirely."

"The being I truly am never hated you. Never! But the frail human whose life I lived for a brief moment in time, she was a sad, angry person and she hated herself most of all. Can you forgive me?"

"Forgive you?" said Connor in wonderment. "But you just said you didn't mean to hurt me."

"Forgiveness is divine," said the shaman, her eyes twinkling a little. "I'm sure you must have heard that somewhere."

"Yes, I suppose so. But it feels kind of weird—I mean, forgiving someone who's already gone."

"None of us is ever 'gone,' Connor."

"That's the first time you've ever called me that. You always insisted on 'Lydia.'"

"We try to control other people when we're only focused on our own fears. That was just my way of trying to make you into something I thought would make me feel better, more useful, more valuable perhaps. But it didn't work. Not with you or with your father. At the end, I thought I was completely alone. Then I died and found out I'd never been alone, not really." She squeezed Connor's hand. "So, will you forgive me?"

Connor couldn't speak. She looked into the deep dark eyes of the old woman and saw, as if on a movie screen, the lives she'd lived, the faces of women and warriors and queens and peasants, the pageant of reincarnations right up until…the familiar visage of Amanda Hawthorne. Connor's tears poured out; she couldn't stop them. A dam had broken, and years of hurt feelings and dashed hopes and desperate needs gushed into the light of day. The old woman stood there and held her hand until the flood abated. For a long time they remained that way, side by side, in the full light of the morning sun.

"I forgive you," said Connor. "I really do." And she meant it from her heart and soul. She'd been given a gift of understanding.

"Thank you," said the old woman. "And everything is going to be all right now, especially for you two." Connor glanced to the side and now the Indian woman stood slightly behind her. She felt a different touch on her wrist, and Laura was right there. The shaman held both the women's hands and brought them together, her own leathery palms pressing them together. "I'm glad you found each other. The dark places of your lives were painful, my daughters, but they brought you together. Be at peace. It's time for me to go now." She laid one hand against Connor's cheek, and an instant later her tiny figure receded into the distance.

"Goodbye…Mom," said Connor. And she closed her eyes.

"Honey, are you all right?" Laura's warm breath tickled her ear. Tickled. *Hmm,* thought Connor. *I'm back.*

"Yeah, I think so." Connor's hands went to her cheeks and felt the wetness there. She'd been crying in every dimension apparently. She turned to look at Laura, barely visible in the first light of dawn. "Did you, I mean, were you there? Really there? Or did I just dream you there?"

"I was called," said Laura, "and I found you standing on that hilltop with the old woman."

"That was my mother!" said Connor.

"I know. But before she was your mother, she was a very wise woman. And now she is again. I got the impression she took on a very limited consciousness to live out the life of Amanda Hawthorne."

"That's what she said. But I never thought of her as anything more than, well, than what I saw every day."

"And you found out there was?"

"Yeah, I did. And…"

"And what?"

"I think I could have loved her more…if only I'd known." After several moments of silence, Connor's head dropped to her hands. "My mom's dead," she choked out the words. "She's really dead." Her shoulders heaved with almost silent sobs.

Laura wrapped her arms around Connor. "I know, sweetheart, I know."

Chapter Five

Underneath this stone doth lie
As much beauty as could die;
Which in life did harbour give
To more virtue than doth live.
—Ben Jonson, *Epigrams: Epitaph on Elizabeth*

From the Personal Journal of Jack Fortis

I was so young then, I couldn't imagine what was going to happen in the drawing room that night. At first, when I saw the coach on the road in the distance, I thought they'd gone, the Lady Genevieve and Mistress Eliza. But the lamps were lit in the house and I crept to the edge of the light to see why. Lady Genevieve was moving about in the room, straightening little figurines on the table, moving a cushion here or there. Then she sat in a chair by the fire and I couldn't see her face, only the skirts of her gown. Even though it's been more than forty years, I can still remember so many details. I shivered in the damp cold, but something held me to the spot. I wondered what the lady was doing at that hour.

I don't know how much time passed, but I heard a commotion out on the road and saw torches through the trees along the drive to the house. Men were shouting and I was very afraid because they sounded angry and drunken. Soon, a coach and pair followed by a procession of perhaps a score of men passed by my hiding place and I recognized from the markings on the coach who it was that led them. He was the Duke of Crevier, a man my uncle said was to be much feared for his ill-temper and violent nature.

The duke leaped from the coach and pounded upon the entry door with the butt of his heavy stick. I peered at the Lady Genevieve. She did not move at first. Only when the duke shouted that he would have the door down did she finally rise. Her movements were slow and so very graceful. She turned toward the window for a moment, and I saw her beauty and her great sorrow. To my great surprise, there was no fear in her that I could see. Then she disappeared from my view, and a moment later I heard the scraping of the entry door against the sill along with the shouts of the duke. "Where is she?" he screamed. "Where is the young witch?"

In an instant I knew he must mean Mistress Eliza. I don't know why, for I had never thought of her in that way. We all knew witches were evil and cruel and cast horrible spells to torment the righteous. Mistress Eliza was an angel. She was kind and thoughtful, a little headstrong perhaps, and willful in some ways. But she was unfailingly courteous toward all of us who served at the pleasure of our master. There were some oddities about Mistress Eliza, to be sure. She seemed to know things that hadn't yet happened, but I never worried. My old grandmother had a bit of the "seeing eye," as we called it. No one ever thought less of her, or us, for it. She followed the old ways, even in secret. But I knew the duke was accusing Mistress Eliza of being a witch, and I was sorely angered. I wanted to rush into that room and defend her honor. But what could I, a boy, do? The drawing room was filled with rough-looking men. I remember thinking how angry the housekeeper would be at all the mud on the carpets. It was a foolish thought, but it stuck with me—the beautiful room and those ugly, dirty villagers.

The old priest and the duke were shouting at Lady Genevieve. She backed away to the fireplace and stood there, her hands folded in front of her. I couldn't hear her voice at all. The duke's face was flame-red in the light of the lamps, and spittle flew from his mouth. He menaced the lady with his stick, and again I wanted to defend her, but something held me back. Surely he only wanted to frighten her into telling him where her daughter was. He barked out orders to the men to search the house. Several of them left the room and I heard them pounding up the stairs from the front hall to the first floor. Doors slammed and I heard the breaking of porcelain and glass.

A man returned to report failure. The duke demanded he go the stables and see if the master's coach and horses were still there. The man ran out and I almost left then, fearing I should warn my fellow servants. But still I remained rooted to my little patch of earth. The duke continued to berate Lady Genevieve, and still she said little or nothing.

Then I knew. Mistress Eliza was not there. She must have gone in the carriage that had flown so swiftly from the house, and Lady Genevieve had stayed behind. But why? She, too, could have made good her escape. If she'd sent away Mistress Eliza, then she'd had foreknowledge of the duke's arrival.

"Where is she?" he screamed, his face contorted into a horrible mask like the gargoyles I'd seen once in a picture book. Lady Genevieve shook her head and said something.

"Hiding where? I'll search every inch of these grounds."

The great commotion within the drawing room made me bolder, and I crept close enough to reach the knob of the glass door. With my breath caught in my throat, I teased it open a tiny fraction at a time. I felt a blast of warmth, then I could hear the lady speaking.

"Do you not think it absurd that a man of your position is forcing his way into a private home at this hour in search of a tiny child who has done no one any harm? How dare you presume so much!"

"I'll presume anything I wish!" he roared.

"You would not if my husband were still alive."

"If your Sir Francis were still alive, he would certainly assist me in removing this evil from his hearth and home. And perhaps he, himself, tried. Perhaps that is why he is dead." The duke paused. "Or was he as evil as you, and the Lord punished him for it by sending him straight to hell?"

Lady Genevieve's voice rose in anger. "Do not defile the memory of my beloved husband. If you and these good citizens," and even I could hear the scorn in her voice when she said that, "do not wish us to live among you, then we will depart. We will move our household to a more hospitable location."

"Escape is just what you would like," he sneered. "I have it on the authority of God that this child is a devil, a witch, a spawn of a demon. I'll not let her craft her evil to poison our water and turn our children into animals and worship Satan in our midst—not here or anyplace else."

Lady Genevieve's answer was the last thing I would have expected. She laughed. It was a full, rich sound that exploded from her mouth as if the duke was the funniest thing she'd ever seen in her life. Everyone in the room was stunned into silence, and I thought for a moment that it might all end there. That they would all see the awful absurdity of what they were doing and simply leave quietly. But it was not to be.

"You'd laugh at God, you demon of hell!" shouted the duke.

And he struck her. He actually struck the Lady Genevieve with the heavy piece of carved wood he carried. He swung so hard, she was thrown down onto the carpet. I thought surely she had been killed outright. But there was more strength in her than I imagined. I saw her hands reach up to grasp the scrolled arm of the chair by the fireplace, first one hand, then the other. Slowly, she pulled herself to her knees. The men watched in silence as she brought herself completely erect. Blood gushed from the side of her face. She wiped it away with one brush of her hand.

Lady Genevieve looked at the priest and the man who served as the sheriff. "This is what you, a man of God, and you, a man of the law, would allow? That a defenseless woman of gentle birth be attacked in her home?"

They said nothing, the cowards. But I noticed that several of the villagers had gone slinking out of the room, and I heard their footsteps on the loose stones of the drive. Apparently they had no stomach for what was happening. For my part, I wept in frustration that I could not help her.

"I will ask you once more, where is the demon child?"

"Like many old manor houses, this one has secret places. My daughter has been instructed to remain hidden, no matter how many times anyone may call to her."

I was most surprised at her words since I was convinced that Mistress Eliza was nowhere in the house or on the manor grounds. Then I realized she was playing for time, time for her daughter to get farther away. The lady's courage took my breath from me.

"But she would come if you called, would she not?" snarled the duke, raising his stick.

"Perhaps," answered the lady. "But I shall not do so for any reason."

"I think you shall!" He struck her again, this time the stick coming down on her shoulder. I knew full well that a blow such as that would have broken a man's bones, let alone her delicate ones. But she barely staggered this time, supporting herself with one hand on the mantelpiece.

"No," she said in a clear and powerful voice, as if raised to reach every corner of the house. "I shall not let you harm my child."

I can't bear to say how many more blows she withstood before crumpling to the floor in a swoon from which I feared she would never awaken. By then, most of the villagers had fled. In their drunken frenzy, the idea of capturing a witch had seemed a novel adventure. But that their mission might involve physically assaulting a woman of noble birth had never occurred to them. Seeing it was frightening and shameful.

As the odds began to turn in my favor—I, after all, was young and strong, and entirely sober—I began to feverishly work out a plan to get the Lady out of there and to a physician in the next village. I would hide her in the tiny aspen grove and get the pony cart from the stables. I doubted I could manage to hitch up a horse without attracting attention, but I myself could pull the small cart. Perhaps the duke, the sheriff and the priest would begin searching again, and I could carry her from the house whilst they were not on guard. Then my hopes were dashed when the duke ordered the sheriff to bind her hands and put her into the carriage.

"Take her to the prison in Roundhall," he commanded. "Hold her there until I make arrangements for her passage to France. She'll spend her days in a madhouse, I guarantee it."

"But what of the demon child?" muttered the priest. "That is our purpose, here. Not this…" he waved his hand at the still form of Lady Genevieve.

"The mother has told us all we need know," said the duke, his voice almost gleeful with the pride of a man who has won the day. "The Satan spawn is right here in this house in some secret hole or other."

"It may take days to find her if the child is obedient to her mother's will."

"That might be true. But we shall not have to wait that long." He glared at the few remaining villagers. "Take your torches within," he said. "Fire the house. The brat will either scream for help or be destroyed."

They hesitated, looking back and forth between the duke and the priest. The sheriff stayed in the shadows beside the carriage.

"Do it, you fools!" the duke shouted angrily. He picked up a torch from the ground where it had fallen. "Who is there to defy me?"

No one spoke.

He strode into the house, and from my vantage point I saw him touch the flame to the draperies. They were fully afire in moments. Then he grabbed a fireplace tool and raked glowing embers of the fire out onto the carpet. He swept the sheets of music from the pianoforte and poked the torch into the pile. The minutes went by, and I heard his curses from within. But I could not reach the Lady Genevieve. I had visions of seizing the carriage and driving her away to safety, but the coachman had stayed on his box, and the sheriff and the priest had remained outside. The last men from the village had fled down the drive as soon as the flames became visible through the windows and they understood that the duke intended to burn a child alive.

I heard cracking sounds, and the delicate hand-blown glass in the drawing room windows began to shatter as the fire reached the bubbles of air beneath the surface. I moved stealth-ily backward, away from the shards, and waited to see what would happen. I was quite convinced that Mistress Eliza was far away, but fear nagged at me. Should I go inside and search? But what would I find that the men had not? I heard heavy banging sounds coming from the rear of the house, then the duke emerged from the front door, an evil grin of satisfaction on his fat, ruddy face. "That will do," he said. "That will do very nicely. I have barred the rear door so not even a rat will escape." He leaned against the carriage wheel. "Now we shall wait and see."

I saw him peer into the open door of the carriage. "A pity the demon's mother isn't awake to see the sentence of God carried out."

There is no more to say of the duke or what became of Lady Genevieve, because I have no knowledge of that. When the house began to burn in earnest, I crept away from the bushes and ran toward the stables. There, I took Boromir out from his stall, put on his tack, and led him through the copse toward the road. Once out of sight of the house, I mounted and rode faster than I thought possible toward Chillwater, for I knew from the direction of the coach and four I'd seen earlier that they must be headed for the docks. As the great horse thundered down the road, I realized I had made myself a thief, and I had left the manor without permission. But it did not seem to matter a great deal. The master had died, the lady was perhaps already dead, and Mistress Eliza had fled. There was nothing left there for me, and my only thought was to reach my young mistress before she sailed away. Never had I felt so angry and sad and alone in the world.

By God's good fortune, I did find Mistress Eliza and her Uncle Fitzhugh, the master's brother, before they sailed. I went to the ship that lay tied to the dock, and him alone I told of Lady Genevieve's fate as we stood on the deck of the ship, the young mistress safely tucked into her cabin. He asked for every detail and I was loathe to provide them, but I obeyed his wishes and trembled to see the fury in his eyes and the tears that coursed down his cheeks. His enormous hands gripped the railing with enough strength to rip it from the deck plates had he wanted to.

"Do you know if she yet lives?" he asked.

"No, sir. I do not know. I didn't see her move again after she fell the last time. I'm sorry, sir. If only I could have done something." I cast down my eyes to the toes of my muddy boots. Then his hand lifted my chin. He looked me directly in the eyes.

"There is nothing you could have done to save her, Jack. She chose this path of action, even though I feared in my heart that it was a grave mistake. You saw her courage, and you did me a great service by coming here to tell me of it. For that alone, I would take you into my household and under my protection. All I ask is that you keep this from Eliza. She must never know the suffering her mother chose to endure to keep her daughter safe."

"Yes, sir. But, sir?"

"What, Jack?"

"What shall you tell her when her mother does not come?"

"A lie, I suppose, or a half-truth. She's too young to understand now."

"Yes, sir, she is."

And that is how I found myself on a sailing ship bound for a new land, a new world. Weeks later, we came in sight of the colony of Massachusetts.

*

Entry of August 13 in the records of John Burkett,
Warder, St. Agatha Asylum for the Insane.

I received this day a communication from the chief physician at the asylum on the continent to which Lady Genevieve Fitzhugh was consigned shortly after her arrival at my institution. She was transferred there at the insistence of the duke of Crevier, though against my recommendation. M. Cleville informs me that one of the sisters there attended the lying-in of patient Fitzhugh and that a child was delivered. As there is no relative of record, the child was sent to another institution, an asylum for orphans. Patient Fitzhugh did not survive the birth. Although my instructions were to inform the Duke of Crevier of any change in the patient's mental or physical condition that was communicated to me, I have recently learned that his lordship was struck and killed by a runaway horse and drayman's cart in the city of London. The duke died of numerous fractures to the skull and other bones.

As there are no family funds to underwrite the cost of funeral arrangements for Patient Fitzhugh, she will be interred at what I assume is a sort of pauper's field Saturday next. I, myself, will provide a small marker, with an appropriate epitaph, as it has been such sadness to see a noblewoman, however stricken with mental disease, treated in such a manner.

CHAPTER SIX

Bell, book, and candle shall not drive me back,
When gold and silver becks me to come on.
—William Shakespeare, *King John,* act II, scene 3

Malcolm was standing, hands in his coat pockets, in the middle of an empty parking space just outside the Hallowell House restaurant when Connor and Laura pulled up. He waved them into it as he stepped back onto the curb.

Laura angled the rental into the tight space in one flawless reverse move, with a tiny forward adjustment before turning off the car. "And you can parallel park, too," said Connor. "What a woman!"

"Thanks," smiled Laura as she checked oncoming traffic before swinging open her door. There was a line of vehicles passing within inches, so she waited.

Connor, however, jumped out on the passenger side and was immediately folded in her friend's enormous hug.

"Are you okay, hon?" he asked. "I'm so sorry about your mom."

"Thanks, my friend. And I'm doing all right," she mumbled into his lapel before pulling gently out of his grasp. "But can we not talk about my mom right this minute? It's been a long night."

Laura finally gave up trying to wait out the traffic and slid across the center console to exit on the curb side of the car. "Do I need to ask how we got the primo parking spot?" she laughed.

"Only if you want me to admit to public menacing," he replied, "though I think that's only a misdemeanor."

"You actually stood here and wouldn't let anyone park?" said Laura as she joined them, and received her own hug.

"I didn't tell anyone not to," he shrugged. "But no one seemed to want to ask me to move."

Connor surveyed him from head to toe. "I think with the outfit and the sunglasses and the height, no one dared." Malcolm was wearing a dark suit and tie under the black cashmere overcoat Connor had given him for his birthday, and he sported a pair of Oakley wraparound sunglasses. "You know, with that expression on your face, if I didn't know you were an upstanding police officer, I might think you were a dangerous man."

"Little old me?" said Malcolm, placing his palms against his mammoth chest. "Imagine that."

"Oh, stop it," said Laura, giving his arm a gentle punch. "Let's get inside. It's been months since I've had the chance to watch you pack away twenty or thirty pounds of food."

"I think that's highly exaggerated, Ms. Nez," he said with mock indignation. "I don't believe I've ever consumed more than ten pounds of food at one sitting."

Once they'd ordered, Malcolm propped his chin on one hand and looked squarely at Connor. "I know you said not to talk about it, but..." He stopped.

"I meant I didn't want to talk about my mother, or maybe what I mean is about my relationship with her, which wasn't much to speak of."

"Not your fault," he declared.

"I don't think it's about fault," she replied, with a glance at Laura. "I'm starting to get a different perspective on a lot of things. But I need time to sort it out. "

"Then maybe you really shouldn't be involved in this investigation. Maybe it'd be better if you got out of Boston, went back to your place in Santa Fe."

"No!" said Connor sharply. "I'm not running away from this."

Laura laid a hand on Connor's arm. "I don't think that's what Malcolm's saying."

"No, it isn't," he frowned. "But Benjamin—"

"So that's it," she snapped. "You've been talking to Dad, and he thinks I'm too emotional to be involved in the investigation. Well, you'd both better think again. Excuse me!" She tossed her napkin down and scraped her chair back hard.

They watched her walk toward the back of the restaurant.

"What did I say?" asked Malcolm, his face a study in bewilderment. "I was only…"

"I know. She had a rough night."

Malcolm sighed. "The dream travel thing, right?"

"Something like that. But she's starting to see her mother in a different light, and maybe even miss her a little. So don't be surprised if she's kinda cranky."

"I don't care if she's cranky or a bitch on wheels," said Malcolm. "I just hate it when she's hurting like this."

"You and me both. We love her, and there's not a lot we can do."

"Except maybe figure out who did this, and why."

"My sentiments precisely."

By the time Connor returned from a ten-minute absence, Malcolm and Laura were chatting amiably about Ayalla and the FBI's take on the Fore River Bridge incident. Neither said a word about Connor's abrupt exit, or acted in the least bit solicitous of her mental health. Instead, Malcolm quickly drew her into the conversation.

"They don't have final reports from the FBI techies, but a guy at the lab told Ayalla that there were at least half a dozen mechanical devices under the hood and the dash of that limo that aren't original equipment on a Caddy. One of them probably caused the throttle to stick wide open, and another trashed the brake cylinder."

"Sounds as if we're dealing with a toymaker," said Laura, using an old security agency term for a criminal with a flair for electronic devices, especially remote-controlled ones.

"According to Ayalla's source, the perp's very good at what he does. Says the work is top quality—not something your average scumbag could come up with."

"What about the explosion?" asked Connor.

Malcolm waited to answer until the exceptionally bright and friendly waiter (who continued to remind them his name was Gregg with three *g*'s) had placed their salads and refilled their water glasses.

"That's one place the doer might have screwed up," he replied, picking up his fork. "Not all the charges detonated, and they may have even gone off a few seconds late. It was probably supposed to look like a freak accident, and a full gas tank would have caused a massive fireball if it was rigged just right. And if the car had exploded before it hit the water…" He paused, looking uncomfortably at Connor, who waved her hand for him to continue as she took a bite of salad. "Well, if it had, then the wreckage and all the parts would have been scattered all over the Fore River for hundreds of yards, and sunk to the bottom. Because the damage occurred after it was underwater, the blast wave was sort of smothered. So they recovered just about the whole car. That's why they've got those devices to study."

"That can't make the guilty party very happy," said Laura. "They almost always leave some sort of signature when they build a device."

"Nothing identifiable yet, but they're working on it."

"I think Underwood is involved in this," Connor interjected. "So why don't we start there?"

"Underwood?" Malcolm's eyebrows arched questioningly.

"The funeral director. He was Billy Dagle's business partner."

"You think he had something to do with killing Florence Gardner and your mother? But why?"

"I have no idea. But there's no rule that says we have to find a motive first. Sometimes you don't figure that out until later."

"Okay," Malcolm shrugged. "Between means, motive, and opportunity, I'd say we could probably establish the other two, well, at least the opportunity. Do you have any idea if this Underwood character could rig up a car like that?"

"No," said Laura. "But he might have enough money to pay someone else."

"Hand-tailored clothes and a big BMW," added Connor.

"Unless he's all flash and no cash," suggested Malcolm.

"Possibly, but Laura's going to ask my father to get us a little background on Mr. Underwood. Then we'll see how real he is."

"In the meantime, though," said Malcolm slowly, "there is the whole inheritance angle. I hate to say it, and I don't even know her, but there is a chance your friend might be worth looking at for this."

Connor didn't reply as sharply or as indignantly as he'd feared. Instead, she sat silently for almost half a minute, staring at her water glass. "I don't think Grace could be involved, but," she took a deep breath, "I've hardly talked to her for over twenty years. Maybe she isn't the same person I knew."

Laura's cell phone rang. Malcolm and Connor waited in silence as she took the call. "Thanks, Benjamin, I'll let her know."

"Let us know what?" asked Connor impatiently.

"Your dad has uncanny timing," replied Laura. "On the subject of Grace Wainwright's motive…he had a chat with one of the Boston detectives who's already been around to see the Wainwright family lawyer. Seems Grace had quite a lot to gain from her aunt's timely departure."

"Didn't Grace already stand to inherit?"

"Yes and no," said Laura. "Apparently her mother was still unwilling to accept Grace's lifestyle. She wrote her will with some weird provisions, including that unless Grace married *and* bore children, she would only receive a limited trust fund with a $50,000 annuity for life."

"But what about the rest of the money? That estate must be worth several million dollars."

Laura raised her very expressive eyebrow. "More like thirty to forty million, and Florence could control the entire fortune until such time as Grace fulfilled the requirements."

"But that doesn't change just because Florence is dead," protested Connor. "The terms of the will—"

Malcolm shook his head. "Don't tell me you've already forgotten how to think like a lawyer. Do you actually think Grace wouldn't be able to contest those provisions in the will?"

"She could have contested it without killing her aunt."

"Sure, but *now* there's no one to fight her on it. Just think…the aunt could have spent a big chunk of that fortune on lawyers and kept the case in court for years. In the meantime, Grace is out of the money and down quite a few notches in her standard of living."

Laura nodded. "I'm sorry, Connor. But you wanted a motive, and there it is, big as life. Fifty grand a year versus complete control of a huge estate. She gets to go back to the house and live there. Who's going to call her on it? No one. If Florence hadn't died, I imagine the old lady would be sitting up there on Beacon Hill, gloating to beat the band."

Connor sighed and rolled her eyes toward the ceiling. "All right. I'll grant the outside possibility, but that's all."

"Maybe we ought to be looking for a connection between Grace and the funeral director. What did you say his name was?" asked Malcolm.

"Devin Underwood," replied Connor. "And if there is something to your pet theory about Grace—and Underwood's involved—they'd have to have planned it together."

"I don't have pet theories, only questions," Malcolm scowled. "I'm not trying to make a case against your friend. Hell, I don't even know her. But someone had better stay impartial."

"I'm perfectly capable of remaining unbiased during an ongoing investigation," snapped Connor, reverting to the stiff verbal formality that served as a generally reliable barometer of her mood—the more pedantic the language, the more angry or nonplussed she was. "However, I see no reason to impugn a person's character, particularly one who is grieving the death of a parent, without substantive evidence of wrongdoing."

Malcolm and Laura glanced at each other. They recognized the signs. "I don't think Malcolm is saying the police have probable cause to apply for search warrants, honey. We're theorizing, looking at all the possibilities."

Connor's shoulders sagged. "I know. You're right, and you're both going to have to bear with me a little."

"Don't we always?" teased Malcolm, the spark returning to his brown eyes.

"Geez, you make me sound like a genuine burden," replied Connor, but the tilting-up at the corners of her mouth took the edge off the complaint. They both knew she was conceding a point and let it go at that.

Three sizzling steaks arrived a few moments later, and Gregg-with-three-*g*'s deftly positioned each entrée with a stern warning that the metal serving platters were very hot. He officiously rearranged everyone's water and iced-tea glasses, then reached down, retrieved Malcolm's napkin from the floor, and flicked it into his lap with the air of a mother picking up after her children. Malcolm scowled and, ignoring the heads-up about the hot platters, grabbed his with both hands and pulled it closer to him. The waiter, startled into silence, waited for his patron's howl of discomfort, but Malcolm simply shrugged and reached for his knife and fork. Gregg departed, shaking his head.

Laura leaned in. "You burned your fingers, didn't you?"

Malcolm kept his attention on the slab of beef. "Yep."

"And it hurts?"

"Yep." He began sawing at his steak.

"And you know it would probably help to stick them in the ice water, but you're not going to, are you?"

"Nope."

"Why?"

"Well," he said, chewing his first bite, "it's a guy thing."

"Got it," said Laura, scooping up her own knife and fork. "Just wanted to be clear on that."

Connor looked from one to the other—two of the most important people in her life—and laughed out loud. It was a rich, deep, delighted chortle, and it was the most welcome sound that either of her companions had heard in a long time.

*

Devin Underwood was not amused. Arthur Raley was nowhere to be found. He'd not appeared at their appointed meeting place the previous afternoon. Then a phone message on

Devin's cell had instructed him to go to the Arnold Arboretum on The Arborway. He'd wandered around trying to find the visitor center, but discovered it was closed and locked.

When he got back to the funeral home, there was a sealed envelope on the back door. The note inside read, "I'll be seeing you very soon." It was signed 'A.' So Arthur was playing with him. Devin felt a spasm of fear ripple along his spine. He couldn't imagine what sort of rules Arthur played by, but they were hardly likely to be sane, sensible, or fair. Devin had to resist the urge to get back in his car and drive—out of town, out of state—hell, out of the country. But even if he were able to elude Arthur, there was no getting away from Friedrich. The man had tentacles everywhere, and the money to find out anything he wanted to know… well, almost anything. It almost pleased Devin that his fearless leader hadn't yet identified the other player in this bizarre drama. They had Grace Wainwright, yes. But the other half of the plan hung in abeyance until Friedrich's genealogy experts had followed the threads of history to their modern-day conclusion. Something was holding up the works.

For his part, Devin had become more and more convinced that the whole plan was a crock. But on the other hand, he'd read a many of his grandfather's letters, and Hitler *had* almost won, after all. And the Führer had been convinced that the initial source of his mighty army's power lay in the few artifacts he'd managed to ferret out from their secret hiding places around the world—the wood and iron hammer wielded by the last king of the ancient Viking warriors, the sword of St. Michael, the circlet of gold worn by Richard the Lion-hearted, an ivory and gold amulet that had once hung from the neck of Hannibal as he crossed the Alps with his troops and elephants. Even the shield of the warrior woman, Boudicca, had made its way into Hitler's private treasury. Still, the most important pieces had eluded him.

He had offered immense rewards to the man who could bring him the spear that was said to have pierced the side of Jesus Christ as he was crucified, or—and this was something Adolf wanted even more—the fabled Ark of the Covenant.

In the last year or so of the Reich, according to one long-winded letter, the Führer suddenly seemed to abandon faith in all his objects of power. Instead, he had focused on one person, a certain Wilhelm von Adler, and the supposedly magical object he carried, to the exclusion of all other concerns. There had been a sudden surge of activity ordered directly by Heinrich Himmler. Spies had been sent out all over the world looking for something. And it all had to do with what Devin's grandfather had referred to as *le voleur d'âmes*. Since Devin had studiously avoided any chance of being mistaken for a scholar while at school, he'd been forced to consult a French dictionary to translate the phrase, oddly jarring in an otherwise precisely German account of a military officer who'd found himself on the losing side. Literally it means, "thief of souls." But that made absolutely no sense to Devin. Even if he'd believed in the human soul, he didn't see how anyone could steal something so intangible and, to his mind, about as burdensome as a conscience.

But Devin strongly suspected that items like the Ark and the spear, and the stupid French thing had been destroyed or, more likely, had existed in myth alone. To Devin, whose sense of history was sorely lacking, it seemed damned likely that the old Führer was little more than a nutcase who was snatching at straws as the Allies closed in around his armies. His ambitions had outstripped his strategy. But one thing in his grandfather's writings was of intense interest to Devin—vivid descriptions of the avarice of the highest-ranking officers around Hitler. They'd plundered their way through Europe, seizing gold, gems, tapestries, paintings, and sculpture with the appetites of fat, spoiled little boys who couldn't stuff enough chocolate in their mouths or shiny marbles in their pockets. Entire trains of freight cars left cities like Paris, Brussels, Amsterdam, Vienna, and Budapest laden with stolen booty. And despite years of legal wrangling, not all of it had been returned to its rightful owners. Yes, most of the art, so clearly identifiable, had found its way back to museums around the world. *But who needed art?* thought Devin. *What could you do with it except sell it?* And nowadays it was almost impossible to get away with selling a masterpiece unless you had the right connections. The only powerful connection Devin had was Friedrich—not someone likely to endanger his financial empire by trafficking in stolen artwork.

Rich people took so much for granted, Devin had decided. He was embittered at Friedrich for keeping him on a short leash. So much of the substantial sum Friedrich had transferred to him so that he could buy into the funeral home and give the appearance of solid respectability was already gone, much more quickly than planned. But then Devin's idea of solid respectability had been more expensive than the Doktor's. The old fool lived in the past, tottered around his mansion dressed in clothes right out of an old movie. What did he know about life in the big city? You needed the right clothes, the right jewelry, the right address. So Devin had squandered better than a million dollars in less than a year, though in his own defense he kept reminding himself of the big chunk that had been paid over to Dagle & Sons for a substantial interest in the business. *And wasn't that a waste of cold hard cash,* he grumbled to himself.

Once Friedrich had learned that the Wainwright family had used Dagle & Sons as their family's mortuary for years, he had tried to convince Friedrich that he could just a get a job there and then take care of the preparations. But no, the old man had said that part ownership would assure that Devin had his hand in everything. When the time came for Claire Wainwright to have her tragic auto accident, it must be Devin Underwood himself who dealt with the daughter, Grace, and who was granted admittance to the family home to discuss the arrangements. Devin could maintain close contact with Grace without raising anyone's suspicions. And only Devin could be sure that their "contractor" would have access to the funeral limousine the night before the services were to be held.

The overall plan had gone pretty much as laid out by Friedrich, and Devin had pretended to have something to do day after day as he sat behind his big oak desk in the front office, fending off boring inquiries from Billy Dagle—about contracts and funeral trusts and the embalming equipment breaking down.

His amusements were few but expensive—the car, his bespoke tailor, fine dining, and costly but beautiful women from an exclusive agency in Boston. He suspected Friedrich would not be too pleased with the latter activity, but Devin wasn't as worried as he might have been a few months earlier, because now he had a plan of his own. The solution to his penurious condition lay in solving a puzzle, and Devin had no doubt he could succeed.

He'd spent the past few weeks in a veritable orgy of self-abnegation—no women, no bouts of high-stakes gambling at the Foxwoods casino. Devin had, for the first time in his life, been seriously dedicated to something other than hedonistic pursuits. Much of his time had been spent in libraries, archives, and on the Internet, tracing names, dates, and maritime shipping records. He had his grandfather, Karl, to thank for his partial success. The old man, who'd spared no vitriol in denouncing the greed of the senior officers of the Reich, had been a man of precision. His accusations of cowardice against those whose intention was to cut and run when the war turned against them, were documented—surnames, military ranks, methods of escape, and—this was the best part—the ways in which they'd schemed to take personal fortunes along with them.

References to gold and gems appeared frequently in these accounts. One individual in particular had captured Devin's attention. The man disappeared from Berlin well before the bombardment began. His eventual destination had been unusual. While most high-ranking Nazis would eventually flee to South America, Africa, or island nations in the Pacific, this man hinted of a new life in the United States. This had enraged Karl, that Hitler's golden boy would run straight to the heart of the enemy, but there was little he could do as a young, untried officer in the S.S. under the protection of the Doktor—a man he had grown to distrust and fear. But he burned with loyalty to the Reich.

Devin, as he dutifully conducted his research, thought there was a pleasant irony in the fact that Friedrich never knew how much Karl despised him. That's why he'd mailed dozens and dozens of letters to himself over the years in care of a half-brother in France. Later, Devin's father had handed them on to his son. Karl hadn't dared keep a journal that Friedrich would find. But he referred to the Doktor as a psychopath and a vile murderer of good men. He'd had no choice but to accompany Friedrich into the mountains, but terrible memories of the last days of the Third Reich were burned into his heart, and he determined to thwart Friedrich—to be the Judas who sat at his right hand.

It was perhaps fitting then that Devin's grandfather would provide the means for Devin to break free of the Doktor's obsession with revenge and cabalistic plottings to establish a new world order. That scenario was so unlikely as to be laughable. What mattered in the world, he was quite convinced, was the power conferred by wealth. With enough of it, he would cover his tracks and disappear into a life of ease. He had what he thought were some rather clever ideas about how to accomplish this. First and foremost, he must find a way to stage his own death. In the meantime, he carefully pieced together the evidence.

Friedrich, himself, had unwittingly helped. In the initial flush of excitement over finding some musty old diary written by an English servant in the 19th century, the Doktor had been a little loose-tongued during Devin's last visit to the estate. The old man had literally trembled as he babbled out parts of the story to his young protégé, though not all of it was unknown to Devin.

Wilhelm von Adler (the one Karl so resented) had left Germany with the Führer's blessing. With him he took sufficient wealth to keep him and his future family comfortable for several generations if properly invested. But according to Friedrich, the real treasure was the amulet he wore around his neck. Devin seriously doubted that. Magic was for fairy tales. But he was secretly thrilled to have confirmation of his grandfather's stories. This had to be the same von Adler. If so, he'd been planning on going to the United States. What if Devin could find the family first? Perhaps a spot of blackmail would be in order. After all, who would want to admit being related to a Nazi of Hitler's inner circle?

"He took most of the gold," Friedrich had said, and Devin had been shocked out of his pleasant daydreams of being as rich as the old Doktor.

"What?" he said, sitting up straight and paying full attention.

"He took the almost the entire store of gold from the bunker, more than a ton. It was the Führer's direct order. He knew the Reich would survive and rise again, and Wilhelm would be the key."

Devin's heart hammered in his chest. A *ton* of gold. Not possible.

"How could he carry that much gold?" asked Devin, trying to sound curious but not urgent.

"Cleverly concealed in two specially engineered trucks. I saw to that myself. We also sent the Führer's personal collection of jewels and a small fortune in stolen British pounds sterling and French francs. Wilhelm was in the lead vehicle when they left for France."

"He gave all that to one guy, just because of some necklace?" sputtered Devin, realizing immediately he should have kept quiet. He'd gone too far and broken the spell in the room.

Friedrich had stared at him narrowly. "What did you say?"

"Nothing."

"You questioned the Führer's judgment!"

"No, not really. I didn't mean it that way."

"And you said Wilhelm wore a necklace. How would you know that?"

"You just said…"

"I said he had an amulet. That could be any object at all. Why did you assume it to be a necklace."

Devin did his best to look less than bright. "I thought that's what amulet meant…you know, a necklace."

Friedrich had scowled and let it go. But the very next day, Devin was on a plane back to Boston. He hadn't had even the slightest chance to snoop around the Doktor's study, or discover any more details about Wilhelm von Adler. He suspected that Friedrich, with all his resources, must have already tried to trace Wilhelm's heirs. But Devin was fairly sure he would know if the old man had succeeded. He was Friedrich's representative in the United States, and his go-between to the Supreme Aryan Brotherhood—its roots dating from the time of Hitler. Friedrich had found them useful in the past and provided carefully laundered funds to support their genealogical research as well as some of their more clandestine efforts.

It was this very connection that had led Devin to Arthur Raley, who was somehow involved on the fringes of the S.A.B. That association was the primary deciding factor in Friedrich's decision to employ Arthur. Devin hoped it would also keep Arthur from acting too rashly about his unpaid fee until Devin had managed to find the heirs of Wilhelm von Adler and hit them up for some very substantial hush money. He had this feeling, a gripping sensation in his chest, that told him he was close. Maybe then he'd reveal the name to Friedrich, or maybe not. As far as he was concerned, the whole scheme of reuniting bloodlines and finding magical amulets was crap. He wasn't going to spend his life living in some fantasy novel. But he was going to live as wealthy man, current emphasis on "live," which meant he'd better find Arthur Raley very soon. Every time Devin started his car, he held his breath. And that was certainly no way to enjoy life.

CHAPTER SEVEN

That's villainous,
and shows a most pitiful ambition
in the fool who uses it.
—William Shakespeare, *Hamlet,* act III, scene 2

"It will be interesting to see who shows up," Connor whispered as they waited in the same cemetery where they'd chatted with Billy Dagle only a week earlier.

Laura tilted the umbrella back a little more fend off the wind-driven rain. "Wonder why there doesn't seem to be an open grave anywhere. Don't they dig them in advance?"

"I think so." Connor looked around and shrugged. "Somehow I doubt Mr. Underwood will be on hand to make sure everything goes well."

"They did the embalming at Billy's funeral home, though. Which makes me wonder what becomes of his share of the business. Your dad says the only relative is a sister, and no one knows where she lives."

"Maybe she hated the business even more than her brother did."

Laura shook her head. "Maybe so. But if there's someone your father can't find, then I'd have to assume that person is probably no longer with us."

"He didn't find any record of her death."

"You know as well as I do how many people, especially young women, just disappear without ever being heard from again. Think of that serial killer up in Oregon. He murdered dozens of women and buried them in the woods. It was only a fluke they caught him."

"So you're thinking Billy's sister is dead."

"Only speculating," Laura shrugged. "I don't mean to be morbid, but…look, the hearse is arriving."

From their vantage point near the entrance gate to the cemetery, they could just glimpse the long black car as it pulled up and parked. A small four-door sedan slid into a space in front of the hearse.

"That has to be the oldest hearse still running," said Laura. "I'd say late '70s, maybe."

"Something tells me that Mr. Underwood spared as much expense as possible in sending his former business partner to his final reward."

Two bedraggled men in rumpled suits got out of the hearse and opened the rear door. The driver of the sedan, a physically imposing man in his thirties with short-cropped hair as black as the well-cut suit he wore, got out of the sedan and waited as the funeral home staff prepared to slide the casket from the hearse onto a rolling cart.

"That must be Chris, the boyfriend," said Laura. "Nice-looking guy."

"Looks as if he shared Billy's penchant for working out."

"Probably. We should introduce ourselves."

They moved quietly down the path alongside the church to the brick walkway. The single mourner looked a question at them.

"We don't mean to intrude," said Connor smoothly, putting out her hand. "But we met your partner the other day, and we wanted to pay our respects. He seemed like a good person. Are you Chris?"

Tears glinted in the corners of his eyes. "Yes, I am." His voice was thick with emotion. "Billy...um...sorry." He took a deep breath and reached for Connor's hand. "Chris Falcone."

"I'm Connor Hawthorne, and this my partner, Laura Nez."

Chris nodded. "I recognized you, of course." He paused, clearly uncomfortable. "But you're, that is, your mother..."

"Yes, she was in the car."

"Oh God, I hope you're not paying attention to those disgusting stories in the scandal rags about Billy. He would never—"

Connor cut him off with a wave of her hand. "Please, we're not that naïve. Just talking to him for a few minutes, we'd know the idea of him putting that car in the river on purpose was absurd."

"Thank you," he said, with obvious relief. "And I'm very sorry about your mother and Florence Gardner."

"It's kind of tough," Connor sighed. "Though my mother and I didn't exactly get along. For you this must be really hard. To lose your partner..."

"It sucks," he said, his shoulders sagging. "This is so fucking unbelievable! That anyone would want to hurt him."

"I'm not so sure anyone really did," said Laura gently. "He may have been an innocent bystander. The police are still trying to sort out what happened."

"That would be like Billy, always in the wrong place at the wrong time. But you know, he was so excited to have met you, Ms. Hawthorne. He called me from the car right before he...before it happened. He couldn't wait to tell me that he'd talked to one of my favorite authors in person." He paused. "I'm glad that he was so happy that day." He turned away from them and wiped at his face with both hands.

The two attendants thudded the casket in place and began rolling it up the path.

Chris fell in behind, with Connor and Laura on either side. "Would you rather be alone?" asked Connor. "Or perhaps you're expecting some friends. We only wanted to tell Billy goodbye."

"I'm the only one here. Billy had so many friends, and they all came to the wake last night at our house. Before they left, I told them I didn't want them to drive all the way out here in the rain, that I wanted to do this by myself."

The two women immediately stopped. "Then we'll say good-bye here," Laura said softly.

He turned to them suddenly. "But I was wrong. I can't do this alone. I can hardly bear the thought of them putting him in…"

"We'll walk with you then," said Connor, taking his arm. "Maybe it will help a little."

"Thank you."

The three of them followed the creaky-wheeled cart along the crooked path until it stopped in front of an imposing mausoleum. The iron door stood open, the rusty chain that ordinarily secured the door hanging from a weathered ring set into one of the stones.

"Not exactly a New England custom," said Chris, his voice shaky. "Billy always thought it was a big old joke that his family just had to own a mausoleum. Maybe it's something about people in the funeral business."

"So his family's been around here a long time?" asked Laura.

"I guess. Or else they bought this from someone and put their name on it. I don't know if you can even do that. But I'd imagine this thing is a couple of hundred years old."

Connor peered through the rain at the bronze plate above the door—DAGLE. The plate was appeared newer than the mausoleum. "Billy's dad is in there, then?"

"I guess. Other ancestors, too. He always said how he couldn't imagine sleeping where it was so cold in the winter." At that, Chris lost his composure completely. He turned and walked farther into the cemetery until he was twenty or thirty yards away.

Laura turned her attention to the two men who stood beside the casket, displaying almost no interest in the proceedings.

"Did you know Billy?" she asked. Connor looked at her questioningly, but Laura kept her gaze focused on the attendants. "How long did you work for him?"

"We didn't work for *him*," snapped the taller of the two. "Mr. Underwood is our boss."

"But Mr. Dagle was one of the owners."

"Yeah," shrugged the shorter one. "Whatever. Let's get this done."

"Shouldn't you wait until Mr. Falcone comes back?" asked Laura.

They ignored her and began maneuvering the cart through the door of the mausoleum. It was a relatively tight fit, and much shoving and complaining ensued. Laura hoped Chris wouldn't come back in time for their display of ill temper. Finally the passage of the casket was complete, and the shorter attendant came back outside and crooked a finger at the two women. "One of you wanna come in here and see him put in the crypt? If it scratches up the wood, it ain't our fault."

Laura was not fond of burial grounds, or mausoleums, despite having overcome by necessity her Navajo abhorrence for contact with dead bodies. She glanced at Connor, who took the hint. "I'll go. Why don't you see if Chris wants to be here for this?"

Laura gave a tiny sigh of relief that elicited a quick smile from Connor before she followed the man into the mausoleum.

The air was sharply colder inside, and for a moment Connor entertained the fanciful notion of death as a frigid force of nature that dwelled permanently in places like this, and emanated from the closely fitted paving stones in the floor beneath her feet. But then she turned her attention to the two sullen funeral attendants who were struggling to lift and slide the casket into a crypt in the far wall. She noticed there were a number of sealed crypts, but with the metal cart in the way, she wasn't close enough to read the inscriptions on them. She wondered how many of the Dagle family were entombed here, and why anyone would want to be closed up in a box, and then sealed into a stone enclosure. The mere thought gave her shivers. When her time came, cremation was the only option. She'd made it clear in her will, a document she'd changed a year earlier to add Laura as a beneficiary in addition to Connor's daughter, Katy. Laura didn't know about the alteration, and wouldn't have approved. Money meant very little to her. But Connor couldn't imagine not leaving something for Laura when the time came.

"Aw, for Christ's sake," muttered one of the attendants. The casket had jammed halfway into the opening. "Something's blocking it."

"I told you it looked too narrow."

"I think it's just on a bit of an angle," offered Connor. "If you back it out a little and lift up on this side…"

They both glared, but clearly they wanted to get this done and be on their way, so they grudgingly followed her suggestion. Within seconds, the casket slid in with only a slight scraping. The taller attendant looked at Connor as if daring her to say something about having damaged the casket, but she stared back at him impassively.

"Come on, we're outta here," he said to his associate. "The cemetery people are the ones who close it up and cement the front."

Connor had to step back against one wall as they wheeled

the cart past. When they were gone, she took a moment to examine the markers on the walls. To her surprise, there were only a few Dagles memorialized on the walls. The other markers bore different surnames. "Hmm," she muttered to herself. "Different branches of the family? Who knows?"

She stepped outside and found Laura and Chris huddled under an umbrella. He looked up, clearly miserable. "Sorry. I couldn't go in there and…well, I just couldn't. I don't know which is worse, burying him in the ground, or sealing him up in a wall. This crypt—God, it's all so medieval." He struggled to pull himself together, and extended his hand, first to Connor, then Laura.

"Thank you both for coming here. You helped me a lot, and I didn't even know I'd need it." He reached into his pocket. "I hate to ask for another favor, and maybe you won't be able to help. But the police will hardly talk to me, and I *have* to know what really happened. All these stupid rumors and innuendo. It makes me crazy. And now that the cops and the FBI interviewed me, they won't give me the time of day. Won't return my calls. Maybe you have a better connection to them." He cleared his throat. "I know who your father is. Maybe he knows something."

The pleading look on his face would have been enough to melt even the coldest of hearts, and Connor was a well-camouflaged softie of the first order. She took his card willingly. "I'll do everything I can to get at the truth," she said. "And I'll share what I find out," she added with slightly less conviction, though only someone who knew her well would have detected the subtle shift. In reality, Connor would share what was necessary and proper, but she'd been around long enough to know that sometimes the entire truth was more painful than helpful, and sometimes very dangerous.

They left Chris standing in the cemetery, after giving him a scrap of paper with the number of their bed-and-breakfast. He still seemed torn as to whether he'd enter the mausoleum. Once they reached the car, Laura turned over the engine and got the heater and defroster running. They were both shivering from the cold and damp.

"So what was it like in there?" asked Laura.

"The mausoleum? I don't know. Cold, weird, kinda spooky. Chris was right. Sealing people up in walls. It's medieval."

"Reminds me of that Edgar Allan Poe story, *The Cask of Amontillado*," said Laura.

"Oh, God, that one always gave me the creeps," replied Connor. "Of course, the victim was still alive when what's-his-name started bricking up the niche."

"True. But it's even creepy when they're definitely dead. This fascination with preserving bodies. What's the point? They're nothing. Just shells that people used to inhabit. Once they're empty…" Laura shrugged eloquently, and Connor remarked to herself how much her lover could convey with a dip of her shoulder, a raised eyebrow, or a tiny frown.

"I don't understand it myself. For instance, it's one thing to maybe put flowers on someone's grave, you know, just as a sign of love and respect, but some places I've seen families decorate graves at Christmas, for heaven's sake…with trees and lights and fake snowmen. I mean, what's up with that? Here's this person gone off on the next great adventure of cosmic existence, and there's people standing around the place where some moldering body is pushing up daisies."

Laura laughed. "Pushing up daisies? No one says that anymore."

"Well, they should. I think it's a rather colorful and evocative image."

"It might have been almost lyrical except for the 'moldering body' thing."

"Hey, everyone who's buried is going to end up as food for the worms, eventually."

"This just gets better and better. So how do the worms and the daisies tie in?" Laura quipped.

"Oh, stop it," said Connor with a grin. "Isn't the progression obvious? Bodies feed worms, and worms poop, and flowers are fertilized."

Laura looked at Connor incredulously. "I think it's time for a change of subject. Somehow we've gone from human burial customs to worm poop. And even for you, that's one helluva of segue."

Connor sighed. "Yep. And now let's segue from cemetery to hot bath. I'm pooped."

"Connor!"

"Sorry. I didn't mean worm-pooped."

"You're impossible."

"Yeah, but I'm cute."

*

"We finally got something!" Benjamin announced with undisguised satisfaction.

"On…?" asked Malcolm.

"Mr. Devin Underwood."

"Ah, the funeral director. Ayalla didn't seem to think much of him as a suspect."

"Probably because on the surface he seems reasonably respectable, a little sleazy in his personal habits maybe, but not criminal."

Malcolm stretched his legs straight out and settled further into the comfortable easy chair in the living room of Benjamin's suite.

"So what is it we've got?"

Benjamin paged through a sheaf of faxes he'd just received. "This," he said, handing Malcolm a grainy black and white photograph. "I imagine it's only a matter of time before our friends at the Bureau make the connection, too."

"Which one is Underwood?" asked Malcolm.

"The one on the right in the dark suit."

"And who's that with him?"

Benjamin consulted the fax sheet. "Subject: Arthur Raley. Under periodic surveillance for the past six months."

"Who's interested in him?"

"Actually, some NSA boys."

Malcolm raised an eyebrow. "Why them and not the Bureau?"

"According to this, the information has been shared. But the military has concerns about Mr. Raley because he may be someone else entirely. They suspect he has ties to a neo-Nazi group based in Berlin. He may even be a German citizen."

"So why haven't they had a heart-to-heart with him yet?"

"It's all speculation. But he has been seen in the company of members of the Supreme Aryan Brotherhood."

Malcolm's lips tightened into a thin line. "Those sons of bitches with the white sheets with swastikas painted all over them. They marched in Washington two months ago. Not a damn thing anyone could do about it, either."

Benjamin laid a hand on his shoulder. "I'm sorry. Seems our Constitution is a two-edged sword."

"In theory, it's a fine document, Benjamin. In practice..." he sighed deeply, "in practice it means we have to let hate walk the streets." He looked at the photograph again. "So we have this weenie funeral director cozying up to a Nazi. So what? Maybe Mr. Underwood wants to join up."

"True. And that wouldn't exactly make him a murder suspect.

But there's more about Mr. Raley. If he *is* the guy who's wanted in Germany, then he's a very talented demolitions expert and maybe even a genius with electronics."

Malcolm's eyes lit up. "Now I see where you're going with this. Limousine is rigged to blow, all sorts of interesting gizmos to take control of the steering, brakes, and accelerator. Okay…this is getting better. But there are still a lot of holes."

Benjamin nodded. "I know. There doesn't seem to be any motive whatsoever for Underwood to kill a client and his business partner."

"Not forgetting your ex-wife," said Malcolm quietly.

"No, but I'm fairly convinced she was in the wrong place at the wrong time. Connor said Amanda had her own car and driver at the church. She probably just wanted to ride in the limo with Florence Gardner. Things like that were always important to her." His jaw tightened, and he moved over to the window to stare at the view of glittering buildings.

"It's harder than you let on, isn't it?"

Benjamin didn't answer for several moments, and when he did, his voice was ragged with suppressed emotion. "Yeah. It is. There was a time when I loved that woman more than I could ever tell her. I shared a big chunk of my life with her. But…"

"Things change," said Malcolm. "No matter how hard you try to make them stay the same."

"You're right, as always." Benjamin stood up straighter, his shoulders back. "This is a helluva lot harder on Connor. I can't even figure out if it's better or worse that she had such a bad relationship with her mother."

Malcolm thought about that. "I don't think it's really a question of degree. I think it's just a different kind of sadness. My sister once told me that when someone you really love dies, your heart hurts for what you had and you've lost. But when it's someone you wanted to love and couldn't, your heart hurts for what might have been and never was. But both of them hurt just as bad."

Benjamin came to sit down across from Malcolm. "Your sister is a wise woman."

"I'd like to think she learned it from me," he grinned, "but she's older than I am…and she never lets me forget it."

"Someone's got to keep you in line."

Malcolm laughed. "That she does." He reached for the papers that Benjamin still held. "So let me read the rest of the story on this S.A.B. bastard."

"Maybe you ought to give Ayalla a call when you're done. Make sure someone's brought this to her attention."

"Good idea. She can get mighty pissy when people don't share."

"Though as I recall, that street doesn't always run both ways," remarked Benjamin.

"What can I say?" Malcolm shrugged. "Once a Fed, always a Fed. And I'm just little hick cop from D.C."

"Right," replied Benjamin in his driest tone. "And I'm the tooth fairy."

*

Devin got in and closed his car door, but before he could lean forward slightly to put the coded key into the ignition, something very cold and hard pressed against his neck. *Oh, shit,* he thought. *Damn the fucking black tint on the windows.*

"Where's my money?" Raley's voice hissed beside Devin's right ear.

"I talked to my boss, and…"

"That isn't what I asked." The object ground into his neck just below his jawbone. He tried to pull away, but the man's other hand held his head in a vise.

"I know," Devin yelped. "But he's pissed off about the car. The cops have it, and they have the stuff. He's got a guy on the inside who—"

"What stuff?"

"Your electronic…whatever. The remote-control things. Most of the limo was intact except for the interior. My boss, he said now they know it wasn't any kind of accident. And that Billy didn't do it on purpose. He's pissed, I tell you. I've been trying to get the money."

"You'd better try harder. I don't give a fuck what the cops think. They'll never trace that stuff back to me. So tell your boss if I don't get paid I'm gonna start by sending you back to the Fatherland in little pieces, one at time…you know, a finger here, a testicle there."

Devin felt his gonads shrivel. He almost cupped his hands over his crotch. "You don't know him. He's…he's a nutcase, and he's so fucking stubborn you can't tell him anything."

"Then I guess I may as well kill you right here, you stupid little shit."

"No!" Devin screamed. He felt the sweat trickling from his armpits. "Wait! We don't need his money. I know how we can get more…a lot more…than he ever promised you for this job."

"So where is it?"

"I don't have it yet."

"Don't think you can con me, you little jerk-off."

"No! I'm not. I know some things my boss doesn't know. I found out one of Hitler's top guys came here with a fucking fortune in gems and gold—a whole fucking ton of gold—I'm not kidding."

For the first time, Raley's grip relaxed slightly.

"If this is some sort of goddamn fairy tale, you are so fucking dead."

"It isn't. I swear it." Devin's whole body was tied in a knot. His custom-made shirt was completely soaked through, and he felt as if his tie was strangling him. "I've been researching for months. I've looked at all the shipping manifests. And I'm close." He held up one trembling hand. "I'm this fucking close. I swear it. The man I've been looking for…I know he ended up in Massachusetts. He had some sort of family connection here. It was in my grandfather's letters."

"So who was he?"

Devin gulped. "That's the last detail I'm working on."

"That's a *detail,* you moron?" The gun barrel dug in again and Devin squirmed in the seat.

"I mean it's just a question of matching up the guy with whatever name he took on. I've got this hotshot researcher working on the data. He said he's narrowed it down to about five possibles. Once he gives us a name, we can squeeze that family for every dime they've got. My boss says this guy was one scary dude—the Nazi hunters never stopped looking for him."

"Your boss is looking for the *same guy*? And you think a little pissant like you is going to beat him to the prize? What are you? Just stupid or fucking crazy?"

"No! I told you…I have my grandfather Karl's letters—whole bunches of them. There are so many, I've never even read them all, just the ones about this Nazi who took off with the gold. And what my boss *doesn't* know is that my grandfather hated him. My boss always thought he was this, you know, big-brother figure for Karl. My grandfather actually hated him. He never told my boss *anything* he knew about this Nazi who escaped. And he did know some stuff my boss didn't. But he put it down in his letters. He mailed them to himself at this place in France, and then told my father where to find them. Before my father died, he sent them to me. My boss has no idea I know any of this."

"If you had enough, jerk-off, then you'd have already found the family."

"I had to combine it with stuff my boss had learned. I started snooping on him every time I was back in Germany, and a friend of mine is real good with computers. He snagged some E-mails."

The pressure of the gun lessened again. "So there's someone else in on it, too, some other partner of yours."

"His name's Gerhard. He does research. He's like a fucking ferret. Finds anything you want."

"He gets a share?"

Devin thought quickly. "Not if you don't want him to."

"Good answer, 'cause I don't like sharing. And if you're fucking with me, you're dead."

"I know," said Devin shaking with relief as the gun was withdrawn.

"So how long before you know the name we're looking for?"

"Any day now. Gerhard said he'd narrow it down. But I had to sort of put him on something else temporarily."

"What?" Raley snapped.

"My boss—"

"Enough with the 'boss' shit! What's his name?"

"I don't know what his real name was. Nowadays people call him Friedrich. My grandfather sometimes referred to him as the 'Doktor.' "

Devin heard a sharp intake of breath.

"Well, I'll be a son of a bitch!"

"What?!"

"Nothing," muttered Raley from the backseat. "So what is it you have this Gerhard working on?"

"Um…Friedrich is really pissed off about that other woman who got killed—the wife of some politician or something."

"Amanda Hawthorne."

"Yeah. Her husband's got big-time connections, and Friedrich wants to know how big. Plus the daughter and her lezzie girlfriend showed up at the funeral home, trying to make arrangements. Maybe it was for real, maybe not."

"So your boss isn't too happy about the Hawthorne woman getting toasted?"

"He said it meant too much attention."

"No shit! I wouldn't like to lay odds on whether the Feds are sniffing up my ass…or yours either."

"Mine?" squeaked Devin.

"Yeah, yours, pretty boy. So I suggest you stay home and take care of business. And don't try to contact me. I'll find you."

Devin heard the back door open, and if it hadn't been for his beloved leather upholstery, he might have just peed his pants out of sheer relief that he wasn't yet dead.

CHAPTER EIGHT

La foi consiste à croire ce que la raison ne croit pas.
(Faith consists in believing when it is beyond the power of reason
to believe.)
—Voltaire, *Questions sur l'Encyclopédie*

Grace smiled as she opened the door. "Thanks for coming on such short notice."

Connor stood back and let Laura precede her through the wide oak entry door and into the generously proportioned foyer floored in black-and-white Italian marble. Against the wall to their left, a wide staircase covered in an Oriental runner led to a landing on the second floor. Grace asked them to go through the first hall door on the right into an expansive space that would once have been called a drawing room. Laura had no idea what a modern-day resident would call it. Perhaps a living room, though it certainly gave no sign of being *lived* in. Every reflective surface in the room sparkled; the deep warm tones of the mahogany and cherry furniture shone with years of careful polishing. Several vases of flowers, fresh cut and aromatic, were arranged with precision. The upholstered sofas, love seats, and armchairs situated near the fireplace showed not even the trace of a previous occupant's derriere. It was all eerily perfect, as if the room had been flash-frozen and then thawed out just in time for their visit. Not even the merry little blaze on the hearth could lend any emotional warmth to the space. Laura wondered if the rest of the house looked like this.

"Please, let's sit over here by the fire," said Grace, lowering herself into a deep armchair and still managing to look uncomfortable.

Laura and Connor sat together on a small sofa at right angles to Grace. "When you called, you said you thought you were in trouble. What's going on?"

"It's the police and the F.B.I."

"What about them?" asked Connor cautiously.

"They won't let up. They keep questioning me about my mother's finances and her will and why I didn't ride in the car with my aunt that day."

Laura nodded. "It sounds trite, Grace, but they really are just doing their jobs. Most people don't like being questioned."

Grace scowled. "Once, maybe. Or even a second time to follow up on something. But the Boston police have been here three times. And that…that *black* woman from the FBI, well, she's been insufferable and rude."

Laura glanced at Connor, whose expression barely changed. No doubt Connor had also thought of Ayalla Franklin as insufferable and rude. But Laura knew that prejudice was anathema to Connor. She wouldn't let the racial reference go unchallenged, and Laura didn't have long to wait.

"I'm sorry, Grace," said Connor, her voice tight. "Are you annoyed that the FBI agent is rude and insufferable, or that she's black?"

Grace looked mildly startled. "Oh…well, I didn't mean anything by that. But you know, when some people get into positions of authority, they tend to get a little, well, arrogant."

"No, I guess I don't *know* that."

Grace sat back, as if Connor's sarcasm had struck her physically. Laura, though liking Grace Wainwright less and less, thought it time to intervene or let the encounter deteriorate into a full-scale argument.

"So why do you think the authorities continue to question you, Grace?" said Laura mildly.

"Because they think I had something to do with my aunt's death," snapped Grace. "And, apparently by association, something with my mother's accident as well. They seem to forget that I was the one who demanded an investigation into that car crash. I know it wasn't accidental. I just know it."

"It's hard to accept certain things," replied Laura, "We'd rather think there was someone out there we can blame."

"There is someone out there!" Grace's volume went up several notches. "There is!"

"You mean—"

"I mean, there is someone out *there*." Grace leaped from her chair and strode to the tall sash window at the front of the house. Someone's been watching me, following me. I can feel his presence even if I can't see him."

"Him?" asked Laura, who was perfectly willing to accept that people could sense when they were being watched or followed, but less doubted that intuition could positively establish gender.

"Yes, I'm quite sure."

"Why?"

"A glimpse. It was definitely a man."

"Height? Hair color? Race?"

Connor piped up, unwilling to let go of the racial issue. "Surely you would have noticed if the man was white…or black."

Laura ignored her. "If you have any description at all, you should pass it on to the police or the local FBI field office."

Grace threw her hands up in despair, but to Laura's practiced eye, the gesture seemed calculated for visual effect rather than an expression of genuine emotion. Something was wrong here. She'd gotten that "vibe" from Grace before, as if the outer woman and the inner woman were out of resonance with each other. But which was the "real" Grace?

"You just said the police think you may have had some involvement in what happened to your mother and aunt. But why?"

Grace hesitated. Laura waited, her face impassive. She and Connor knew about the unusual terms of Mrs. Wainwright's will, but did Grace know they knew? Or would she dissemble, hoping to appear lacking in motive to commit not one but two murders?

Laura watched the inner struggle that played itself out on Grace's finely sculpted features. The silence grew into an oppressive presence all its own. Laura still said nothing, and Connor seemed to be taking her cue from Laura.

"You already know my mother didn't approve of my lifestyle," Grace said softly. "And my aunt was even worse. She harped on it constantly. I think, in the end, my mother would have been much more accepting of me, but Aunt Florence wouldn't let it go. Eventually, she talked Mom into changing her will."

"How exactly did she change it?" asked Connor. "Did she discuss the new terms with you?"

Now you're back on your game, love, thought Laura, who had feared that Connor's bias toward Grace would prevent her from asking the hard questions.

"Yes, she did discuss the terms. Right after it was signed. It was only a week or two before her death, which made it even more bizarre." Grace returned to her seat near the fireplace, and wrapped her arms around herself. "She said if I didn't get married and have kids, I couldn't inherit. I mean, how stupid is that?! And my dear aunt, that ill-tempered old maid, would have control of the entire estate. It wasn't fair. But what could I do? Aunt Florence was going around grinning like a Cheshire cat, as if she knew damn well I'd never fulfill the terms of the will."

"Would you have tried?" asked Connor, her eyes fixed on Grace's face.

"No…I mean, I don't think so. I couldn't. But…"

"There *was* all that money," Laura interjected.

Grace sighed. "A whole lot of money. And this house." She swept her arm in a semicircle. "I grew up here. Granted, I haven't lived here since I was out of grad school, but still."

"Why do you think it was so important to your mother that you have children?" asked Connor. "Just to prove that you had consummated a marriage?"

"Oh, that," Grace shook her head. "No. My mother could be so incredibly weird sometimes. She had this fixation about my having a daughter. Talked about it since I was little. It was so bizarre. I hate even talking about it. All her friends thought she was such a level-headed society matron. Who would have guessed she was into all that woo-woo New Age nonsense."

Almost as if on cue, both Connor and Laura sat forward on the love seat. "What?" asked Connor. "She was into consulting psychics or something?"

"Even worse," said Grace, pursing her lips. "At least that way she would just have wasted some money on a few charlatans. No, she actually believed she was a descendant of some witch cult or magical priestess family, or something like that. And she actually tried to convince me that I was, too. Just because I was her daughter." Grace laughed humorlessly. "Can you believe it? She even saddled me with that ridiculous middle name because of it."

"Miranda," said Connor quietly. Laura wasn't surprised—Connor had a remarkable memory for detail. Still, though, a slightly childish part of her wished Connor hadn't been so quick to recall that bit of information.

"Yes, and I'd assumed it was because that was her middle name. But she told me all the eldest daughters before me had that middle name. And she babbled on and on about some gift or other."

"Some kind of object?" asked Laura.

"What? No, nothing like that. God, I'm almost embarrassed to say it. Some sort of special 'power.'" Grace crooked her fingers to convey the quotation marks. "Although, now that I think about it, there was something about a necklace…was that it?" She rubbed her temples as if willing herself to remember. "I started tuning her out completely when I was ten or eleven. The topic was just so silly. And she'd ask me the most bizarre questions."

"Such as?" asked Connor.

"Oh, like did I ever know things before they happened, or sense what people were thinking, or whether they were telling the truth. It was all so strange, and she seemed so desperate about it."

Laura leaned forward. "Was your mother able to do those things?"

"I don't think so. It's not as if she ever predicted disasters or read minds or anything. Thank God, or she would have caught on to me a lot sooner than she did."

"Caught on to you?" Laura frowned.

"You know, about being gay and all. She didn't even suspect until I was in college."

"Parents are often the last to know," said Connor.

"I only know that she acted as if there was some sort of inherited ESP thing, and I should have it. And she insisted it went back generations." Grace shrugged. "I still don't know what she was really talking about."

"You said something about a necklace?" Laura reminded her.

"Oh, yeah. I must still have it somewhere. I remember thinking it was an incredibly ugly little thing, sort of line abstract art gone really bad."

"I'd love to see it," said Laura.

Grace looked puzzled. "Why? I'm sure it's a piece of junk, some sort of family legend my mother took too seriously."

"I'm interested in esoteric subjects. Made sort of a study of unusual occult items that have surfaced over the centuries." To Laura's ears, her claim sounded only barely plausible, but Grace seemed to take it at face value.

"If you want to wait a minute, I can go look for it. I can't really remember if my mother took it back when I showed no interest in it. But it would be in her wall safe if it's anywhere."

She rose and left the room. After several seconds, Laura moved swiftly across the room and peeked out into the entrance hall.

"What are you doing?" asked Connor.

"Just making sure she went upstairs."

"You really don't trust her, do you?"

"It isn't a matter of trust. To me, she's an unknown quantity. What are you thinking right now?"

"That she isn't the same person I used to know. That crack she made about black people, for instance. She just wasn't like that in college. We were both outspoken when it came to equal rights and equal protection. I just don't get it."

"She's under a lot of stress right now," Laura said quietly, still in a position to keep an eye on the hall and the staircase. "You're not catching her at a very good time."

"Now you're defending her?"

"I'm keeping an open mind."

"All right. Now tell me why you're so anxious to see some old necklace of Mrs. Wainwright's."

"Doesn't it seem odd that an upstanding Boston Brahmin would harbor an obsession about some sort of psychic ability she was supposed to have passed on to her daughter?"

Connor thought about that for a few moments. "Having met her a few times, I'd have to say it was very odd. But then you never know what goes on in people's heads. Obviously, Grace doesn't put any stock in it."

"Maybe she should," said Laura, and when Connor raised one eyebrow. "Yes, I do have a hunch about this. There is something to the woman's story, whether or not Grace has any gift at all. Besides, why are you being such a skeptic? You're the one with the Celtic priestess for a grandmother."

"Yes, I know. But I'm not psychic or anything."

"Oh, really?" said Laura.

"Well, it's not as if I run around predicting the Dow Jones, or bending spoons with my incredible mental powers."

"You know, you're lucky your grandmother Gwendolyn isn't here right now. I have a feeling she would have some choice words for you."

"No doubt. And if you keep talking about her, she's going to show up."

Laura chuckled. "Not planning on going to sleep tonight, huh?"

"Not if I can help it. Now, what's your hunch?"

"It's a little tingle I got as soon as Grace mentioned a necklace, almost like familiarity."

"You've never met any of her family, have you?"

"Not as far as I know, at least not in the everyday way."

Connor sighed heavily. "I keep forgetting you never limit yourself to good old-fashioned reality."

"Why should I when there's so much to discover out there?"

"And you think you may have some knowledge of this inherited psychic gift, or the necklace Grace's mother tried to give her?"

"I do. Shh. I think I hear her." Laura darted back to her place on the love seat, put one hand gently on Connor's arm, and looked as if she hadn't budged since Grace left the room.

"I found it," announced Grace, as she came through the door with a small wooden box in her hand. "Hard to believe, but there it was on one of the shelves in the safe." She glanced at Laura's hand on Connor's arm, and Laura saw the flicker of emotion in Grace's eyes. *Long time to still be jealous,* thought Laura. *So what's really going on?*

Grace made a point of handing the box to Connor, who took it and immediately passed it to Laura, who again saw the brief flash of resentment. But she decided to puzzle over that later. Right now all she wanted was to look in the box. The tingle had grown into a sensation like an electric current running down her arm and into her chest. She tried not to seem too anxious as she flipped open the lid, but what she saw there almost took her breath away. Nestled in a cocoon of black velvet lay a pendant of gold. To Laura it literally glowed. It was, she knew, an abstract sculpture of a goddess figure. She'd seen only one picture of a similar figure in her lifetime. That photo had depicted a stone carving dating from the ninth century found near the stone circle of Avebury in England. But this one had a significant difference—it seemed somehow incomplete.

Connor, who was looking over her shoulder, merely shrugged. "Interesting."

Laura, on the other hand, was trying desperately to find her voice. She reached into the box and carefully plucked the pendant from its cradle. She held it up to the light, examining it carefully. But as it revolved slowly on its chain, the room began to spin around her, and she quickly dropped it back onto the velvet.

Grace's voice seemed to be coming from some distant location, and then the volume ramped up like a radio signal growing stronger. "…so do you see anything special about it?" Her tone was curious, no more than that, and her eyes were on Connor rather than Laura. Grace seemed disappointed at Connor's indifference, and unaware of Laura's spiritual vertigo.

"I'm not sure," said Laura cautiously, not wanting to convey in any way the potential importance of the piece. She felt sure Grace would immediately snatch it away, and though Laura didn't know why, she didn't think she could stand for that to happen. "I'd be happy to have a friend of mine here in Boston take a look at it, just to confirm its age maybe and give you an appraisal in case it's worth anything." With a supreme effort, she closed the box and handed it back to Connor, willing her to understand its importance.

"I can't imagine it's worth much," shrugged Grace. "I mean, just look at the ugly little thing. It hardly compares with anything in my mother's jewelry collection."

"I daresay," said Connor, slowly turning the box over in her hands. "But we'd like to research it a little. You *know* I was always fascinated by history." She gave Grace a conspiratorial smile. "If you wouldn't mind lending it to me, of course."

Grace positively preened under Connor's gaze, and Laura allowed herself a tiny sigh of relief. Connor had understood Laura's silent message, and was even turning on a little flirtatious charm to get Grace to relinquish the pendant. Or at least she hoped that was a ploy. *Oh, stop,* she said to herself. *Keep this up and you'll start sounding as jealous as Grace Wainwright.*

"Well, if you're that interested, I suppose it would be all right. I suppose it's mine to do with as I like." Grace gazed over their heads as if summing up the totality of all that was hers now.

In that instant, Laura saw something around Grace—like the ghost image in a double-exposed photographic negative. It was as if the woman were somehow larger than her physical self. It was an aura of sorts, but not of the type Laura was used to seeing. This wasn't simply an extension of her soul energy, but instead appeared to Laura's finely honed senses as a projected self, an intentional aura. As Laura watched, the image dissipated. But what had prompted its manifestation? Was Grace aware of it? Or was it spontaneous and related to her genetic makeup? She glanced at Connor, but couldn't tell if she'd seen it, too.

"I'll return it within a couple of days," said Connor, casually placing the box on the end table beside her. "So, to get back to the reason you asked us here. I'm not sure what you think we can do about an ongoing investigation."

"You have influence," said Grace, with a hint of petulance. "Your father, he's important. He's a power in Washington."

"*Was*," corrected Connor, a maneuver Laura silently cheered. Benjamin hadn't necessarily retired from a practical standpoint, but it was imperative that it appear he had. "My dad isn't a senator anymore, and he doesn't do any work for the White House either."

"But still—" Grace started to argue.

"I'll ask him to inquire," Connor cut her off. "But he won't interfere."

"But your mother is the reason the FBI is involved at all."

"What?!" said Connor, her lips a tight line.

"If this were just a local incident, no way the FBI would be involved. It's such a big deal because of Amanda Hawthorne."

Connor took a deep breath. "There may be some truth in what you say. But, on the other hand, given what's been going on in the world, the FBI tends to look into more incidents than it used to, including local crimes. And remember, there were explosives involved. I imagine they want to find out where those materials came from. Otherwise, they'll leave it to the local cops."

"Well, if not your father, then *you* could have a talk with them."

Laura could feel a coil of anger building inside Connor, and she bent her entire conscious will on heading that off. If Grace reacted badly to what she perceived as a lack of friendly cooperation, she might, out of pure spite, take back the box with that incredible amulet. And Laura believed without doubt that they must have it for a while, to find out what it truly was. *Calmly, my darling, calmly. Don't let her see your anger now. Stay in the light. Stay with me.*

Instantly she felt Connor relax. *Gee, I must be getting better at that,* thought Laura.

"You're right, Grace. Let me see what I can do, what I can find out. They're probably just hurting for suspects, and you're one of the only leads they have."

Grace smiled broadly, as if she'd won. Laura had to wonder just what it was Grace really wanted from Connor. She didn't particularly like any of the possibilities.

Connor stood and scooped up the wooden box. "Sure you don't mind?" she said, with yet another smile.

"Of course not. I'd trust you with anything."

Grace's remark transparently excluded Laura, but Connor simply ignored the intent. "We are remarkably trustworthy," she replied. "We're just a couple of Girl Scouts." Before Grace could respond, Connor was halfway to the door, with Laura close behind.

"I'll let you know as soon as I talk to the police," Connor said, "In the meantime, if you see the person who's watching you, call 911 right away, and try to give them a good description." Grace started toward them. "No, that's all right. We can see ourselves out."

They were on the sidewalk seconds later.

"Whew," said Laura. "That was the fastest exit I've ever seen you make."

"Keep walking and don't turn around. She was about to change her mind and ask for the necklace back."

"So you got my message then?"

Connor glanced at her and picked up the pace even more. "What message?"

"That I didn't want you to get pissed off at Grace's stupidity, and say something that would make her take back the pendant."

Connor didn't answer for three blocks. Laura silently kept pace beside her.

"Let's go in here." Connor pointed to a coffee shop. They went in and ordered—Connor a latte, Laura an espresso. Once they were seated with their drinks, Laura looked at Connor steadily, wanting to know what was going on, but the question died on her lips. Her lover was far away, at least in thought. Laura sipped her coffee and watched the other patrons come and go.

"It wasn't a message from *you*," said Connor very softly.

"What?"

"You said I must have gotten your message. But it wasn't you. I know what you in my mind feels like. God, that sounds so ridiculous, but you know what I mean, right?"

"Of course I do, sweetheart."

"It wasn't you. And yet it was familiar. So when I finally sat here and thought about it, then I knew perfectly well it was my grandmother."

"Gwendolyn was with you?" said Laura incredulously. "But you haven't heard from her in a long while."

"No. And I think I was a little sad about that…and maybe relieved, too." Connor glance around. "I wonder if she heard that."

"Wouldn't matter if she did," said Laura with a smile. "Once you get out of this human existence, I think your priorities are a lot different."

"Is that something *your* grandmother taught you?"

"One of many things."

"And how would she know? She's still hanging out with us humans, isn't she?" asked Connor.

"Yep. Still alive and kicking, though I have a feeling she's about a hundred years old."

"So she's an expert on dead people?"

"I think that's kind of a broad category, and you know better than to generalize. Some people just die and are confused, and wander around. They're kind of like children. Some go off to other planes of existence. Some actually think they're in heaven or hell for a while. Some travel the Dreamtime. A lot of them act in the capacity of guardian angels. There are as many possible faces to death as there are to life."

"Gwendolyn always told me that nothing is ever simple. I'm beginning to see her point."

"So you heard from her while we were in there?"

"I felt this very strong presence for a few moments. And it was loving, and calming, and then I saw words, as if they were written on a chalkboard in my head."

"What did they say?"

Connor chuckled. "I guess I should have known right way who it was, just from the tone. The words were: *Mind your manners. Kindness works much better than judgment. Placate the child. Do not fail to take the amulet when you leave.*

Laura nodded. "No wonder you knew it wasn't me. I was only asking you to be nice, not ordering you about."

"But it didn't feel like orders. It just seemed to make damn good sense at the time. Once I went over it again in my mind, I could almost hear those perfect English vowels of hers."

"So she thinks the necklace is important, too."

"Yes, although I have to tell you it still makes me nuts to talk about her in the present tense."

"That's enlightenment for you," said Laura, grinning. "Nothing's the way you always thought it was."

"No kidding." Connor took a sip of her latte. "So you were trying to get me to mollify Grace, too? And you were just as anxious to get this necklace. What's so special about it?"

Laura explained the sensations she'd had just holding it, and that it was strongly reminiscent of the ancient goddess figurine discovered more than a century earlier. "It has to be one of the power objects."

"Power objects?" Connor's expressive eyebrows arced into a skeptical curve. "Not like..." Her sentence trailed off.

"Sort of," replied Laura softly. "The...um...item your grandmother's circle fought to protect, the one you saved up on the Tor."

"I'd just as soon not have a repeat performance of that night," sighed Connor.

"I agree, but that's only one example of an object that has inherent force or magic to it."

"You're saying there are significant numbers of these things in the world?"

"I have no idea how many there are. But they've been around for centuries, or more like millennia. Periodically, one turns up. Generally they attract the power-hungry." She paused. "Hitler's a prime example. He had his followers searching all over the world for various objects like the Ark of the Covenant and the Holy Grail and some sword or other that belonged to one of the Knights Templar, I think."

"And they really exist?"

Laura puffed out her cheeks as she exhaled. "Who can say for sure? I tend to believe some of them are secretly handed down through families or closely guarded by religious orders."

"This necklace was apparently handed down through Grace's family."

"Yes, and that alone tells me it may be important. But it's also hard to read. What I felt when I held it was both powerful and, at the same time, I don't know…maybe ambivalent is the word."

"You mean it's neither light nor dark?"

"Maybe. Or incomplete? I felt it. All right, this will sound weird, but I felt it vibrating steadily as if it were *waiting* for something."

"For someone to use it? For Grace to figure out what it does?"

"I'm not sure. You can't always put intuition into words."

Connor shrugged. "So where do we go from here? Other than looking up that sculpture you talked about, what else is there?"

"We could trace the family's genealogy," suggested Laura. "That might give us a clue."

"I suppose. But does any of this have to do with the limousine crash? And Grace's mother's death, for that matter?"

"Perhaps nothing. But I'd lay money on there being a link."

"I thought you were leaning toward Grace as the murderer with pure greed as the motive."

Laura thought for a moment. "I'm not saying that theory is out the window. But the picture just got bigger. There are elements to all this that I don't think Grace is even aware of, at least not consciously."

Connor finished her coffee and tossed the cup into the trash receptacle behind her. "I've got another idea. If this goddess figurine was found near Avebury, then it may have some connection with the ancient faith of my ancestors. Who would know better about it than—"

"The Carlisles," Laura finished for her. "Of course. Let's get on to them right away."

Connor checked her watch. "It's already after 11 in England. I think it can wait until tomorrow. And let's run it by my dad. We're supposed to meet him at the hotel in less than an hour."

"Agreed."

They left the coffee shop arm in arm and circled the block, walking up a parallel street to retrieve their car, parked a block from Grace's house. In the gloom of twilight on an overcast evening, neither of them noticed a shape that emerged from the shadows on the side street and kept pace with them. Once, Laura felt a twinge of alarm and she spun around. But nothing on the quiet street appeared the least bit menacing. Across from them, an elderly woman admonished her bichon frise to hurry up and go.

"What's wrong, honey?" asked Connor once she realized Laura had stopped abruptly.

"Oh, nothing. Just a case of the willies, I guess."

"That's not like you," said Connor, frowning. "You're not the paranoid type."

"Hey, don't knock the state of overcautiousness," said Laura. "It's saved both our butts."

"True," replied Connor mildly.

"And besides, sometimes even paranoid people are right."

"Uh-huh," said Connor as they reached the car. "Are you driving?"

"Sure," said Laura. "Toss me the keys."

Connor flicked the key ring over the hood toward Laura. In the darkness, however, her usually quick hands failed to snatch it out of the air. The plastic tab clipped the side-view mirror and she heard a clink as the keys hit the ground. She bent to get them and in that moment felt something pass close to her left ear. It took her only a fraction of a second to identify the spit of a silenced gun, and the sound of glass breaking somewhere behind her. "Get down!" she shouted at Connor, who hit the sidewalk without asking questions.

Laura thought fast, trying to estimate the direction from which the shot had come. Quick calculations—and a glance over her shoulder at a broken shop window on the other side of the street—told her the shooter was probably not that far away, and closer to Connor's side of the car.

"Stay down, but get around the back of the car," Laura hissed urgently, trying to make herself heard above the sounds of cars passing on the cross street.

Again, Connor complied. She'd learned the hard way not to question Laura's tactics in life-or-death situations. She wriggled backward and felt her way around the car until she came up behind her partner's back.

"What the hell is going on?" whispered Connor.

"Someone just took a shot at us."

"I didn't hear anything."

"Silencer. No one was supposed to hear anything. If I hadn't bent over to pick up the keys."

Connor's arms tightened around her shoulders. "Son of a bitch! If I find the bastard …"

"You and me both. But right now we need to figure out a plan."

"Other than crouching here in the street."

"It's already getting old."

"So what do we do?"

"I'm thinking we drive away."

"Are you nuts? We'd be sitting ducks."

"I'm pretty sure whoever it was is gone. He failed and retreated."

"Is this an intuition thing?"

"Partly, but also logic. He can't wait around here indefinitely.

Everybody and their brother carries a cell phone these days. We could already have called the cops. For all he knows the cavalry is on the way. And since he can't actually see us, how does he know we didn't already crawl along behind these cars and get away. No, he's gone."

"I take it we're not going to call the cops?"

"Not unless you want to stand around here all night. Once they find out who you are, they'll make a federal case out of it, probably literally."

"Okay. But you're sure it was just one shot? A stray bullet might have found its way into one of the houses, and not just that shop window over there."

"Only heard one hit," said Laura quietly.

"All right. We'll keep this to ourselves for the time being."

"Good. It's time to go. I'm getting pretty damn cold kneeling on the ground."

"You're not just going to stand up, are you?" said Connor holding firm to Laura's arm.

"No. First, I'm going to unlock the car, like so"—she pressed the button on the remote—"and swing the car door open."

The interior light came on, and they stayed put, waiting.

"You see? Nothing to it. You open the back door and slip in."

Connor did as she was told, still keeping below the level of the seat back, and closed the door behind her. She heard Laura do the same. They stayed low since the interior lights would stay on until Laura slipped the key into the ignition and turned it one notch. Once the interior was dark, Connor peered over the backseat. "What do you think?"

"I think it's time to go to dinner."

"Go for it."

Laura held her breath, and in one smooth motion she started the car, slapped the gearshift into drive, spun the wheel hard to the left, and hit the gas. They peeled out of the parking spot, barely missing the beige Lexus sedan in front, and shot down the street. Connor leaned over the seat and squeezed Laura's arm. "I love how you handle a car."

"Thanks, hon."

"Of course, if we'd hit that Lexus, we'd have to go back and leave a note."

Laura laughed. "That's one of the things I love about you. Unwavering integrity even in the face of danger."

"Oh, stop it. I didn't mean we'd go back this very minute. Which reminds me—"

"You want to pay for the shop window, don't you?"

"Yeah, I do. We'll get the name and address tomorrow and I'll send them a money order."

"Anonymously, I presume."

"Yep."

"Hungry?"

"Starving."

"I think adrenaline does that to you." Laura paused. "Are we going to tell Benjamin about this?"

"My first impulse is not to tell anyone else until we get a better idea of who shot at us, but maybe I'm just rationalizing. I'd love to avoid the fallout from this. My father will be worried to death and want to hire round-the-clock bodyguards. And Malcolm will be hot to find the shooter and tear him limb from limb."

"Goes with the territory," Laura said.

"How's that?"

"They love us. They want to keep us out of harm's way. And their natural protectiveness is testosterone—amplified by about a factor of ten."

Connor laughed. "Are you claiming women aren't protective?"

"Hell, no! Back us into a corner and threaten our loved ones, we're a bad guy's worst nightmare. But we generally don't circle the wagons and pull out the big guns unless we're sure there's an actual threat."

"I think saying that men are the overreacting gender goes against centuries of propaganda."

"Probably."

"Could you pull over for a second?"

"Sure, how come?"

"I want to ride in the front seat with you."

Laura smiled and found a space along the curb. Connor hopped out and slid into the front seat.

"Feels like déjà vu," said Laura.

"What? Oh, yeah. I did the same thing in New Mexico, not wanting you to chauffeur me around."

"Even when you thought that's what I was—a chauffeur."

"As opposed to a machine gun–toting pint-size Stephen Seagal."

"Either way, I'm glad you wanted to ride in the front. Made me realize you weren't some elitist rich girl."

"Why thank you, ma'am. Just think, I could have taken after my mother." Connor started to laugh, then fell silent. "I guess that isn't very funny anymore."

Laura laid her hand on Connor's knee. "Death doesn't change what is or what has been. So don't beat yourself up. Now you know a lot more about Amanda, but that didn't make her any more pleasant to be around when she was alive. I tend to think she's probably amused by some of her antics as a human being."

"Maybe so," said Connor. "Maybe so."

*

"Goddamn it!" Devin screamed as he pounded his fists on the steering wheel, grateful for the excellent soundproofing of the BMW. "I can't fucking believe I missed!"

In reality, it wasn't all that surprising that Devin's first and only shot at the two women had gone wild. His experience with the sniper rifle was minimal, and he couldn't even remember how to adjust the scope for distance. For that matter, he didn't even like guns. The rifle was simply part of the equipment with which Friedrich had outfitted him. He carried it in a sleeve that was sewn into the side of his golf bag. No one knew he didn't play golf, so the ruse had worked perfectly.

Friedrich had ordered him to keep an eye on Grace Wainwright, an assignment that purely annoyed Devin, but he didn't dare disobey, at least not yet, not until he figured out the rest of the equation that had Ms. Wainwright on one side and an unknown on the other. So he'd hung around the neighborhood, changing jackets occasionally, trying to be inconspicuous. It wasn't easy. The Wainwright home was only one opulent house on a street of rich people. Interestingly, officers in patrol cars "happened by" rather more often than they did in poorer neighborhoods. And they were less tolerant of loitering. Fortunately his car and clothes fit the neighborhood, and the tiny yet powerful binoculars folded flat into the pocket of his jacket without much of a bulge to ruin the drape.

He'd been unpleasantly surprised to see the Hawthorne woman and her girlfriend arrive. He'd checked with the funeral director of a rival mortuary and learned that Amanda Hawthorne's body had been released from the medical examiner's office and prepared for shipment to Washington that night. Devin had assumed the family would go with the body. So what the hell were they doing at the Wainwright home? Anything that even hinted of interference in Friedrich's plans for Grace was enough to give Devin palpitations. And the report he'd received from Gerhard indicated that Connor Hawthorne was a first-class meddler. Worse, her girlfriend was some sort of government employee, but no civil service data was available anywhere. Gerhard told him that meant she was probably someone with a high-level security clearance. When you factored in ex-National Security Adviser and ex-Senator Benjamin Hawthorne, it could spell disaster.

He didn't decide to kill them just because of who they were, however. Devin was not the sort to act on a hunch. But he'd gotten as close as possible to the front windows of the big living room where they three women were sitting. The heavy overcast made it possible to see clearly into the room. He'd watched Grace leave, and puzzled over what she was doing … maybe going to the bathroom or something. When she returned, she had something in her hand, something she passed to the Hawthorne woman. A moment later, the Indian woman held it up. He quickly dialed in the zoom, and the object came into focus. His heart thumped wildly in his chest. The necklace! Surely it was the one Friedrich talked about, the one Devin had seen in old pictures, photos that dated from World War II. He thought Friedrich said it was silver, but this seemed to be gold. Still, in this light, who could tell for sure? And he didn't always listen carefully to Friedrich's obsessed monologues.

The pendant dropped from sight, and he strained to see what she was doing with it. Then Connor Hawthorne had laid a box on the table. That must be it. Was Grace going to take it back to wherever she kept it? He crept closer so that he had a good angle of view. The conversation went on another minute or so, and the two visitors stood up. The Hawthorne woman picked up the box. *No!* he thought. *Don't let them leave with it.* But clearly they were going to. The box went into Connor Hawthorne's shoulder bag, and within seconds they were out the front door and starting down the sidewalk at a brisk pace. He pushed his way through the shrubbery, tearing his jacket, and for once not minding the damage to a custom garment. He had to keep them in sight. He followed for blocks until they turned in to a coffee shop. He couldn't possibly go in. They'd recognize him instantly.

Once they ordered and sat down, he figured they'd be there for at least fifteen or twenty minutes, maybe longer. But what to do? Outlandish ideas crossed his mind, such as finding a street bum or some juvenile delinquent to snatch the woman's handbag. But those two would probably just beat the crap out of anyone who tried, and besides, bums and thugs were extremely rare in this part of town. He could try mugging them himself after they came out, but again, Gerhard's warning that the Indian woman was connected with one of the intelligence services made him think twice about taking them on personally. Besides, he'd need a gun. And that's when it came to him. He had one, not a handgun of course, but a state of the art sniper rifle that had only been out of its hiding place once when Friedrich insisted he take it to a practice range owned by the Supreme Aryan Brotherhood. After firing off several dozen rounds, Devin had decided he was accurate enough.

Now the solution to his problem was clear. The rifle was equipped with a suppressor that reduced not only its noise but the muzzle flash as well. He would wait until they were off the busy, well-lighted street. Surely they'd parked their car near Grace Wainwright's house. He'd shoot them from a distance, retrieve the pendant, and be gone before anyone even knew what had happened. By the time some dog-walking old geezerhead stumbled across the bodies, he'd be safe at home.

Devin turned and trotted quickly back they way they'd come. The closer he got to the Wainwright house, the more carefully he scrutinized the cars, looking for a rental license plate or company sticker. He was starting to sweat. Possible flaws in his plan suddenly occurred to him. What if they didn't drive here at all?

What if they'd taken a taxi? But no, he would have seen it drop them off. Still, they might decide to leave their car and come back for it tomorrow. Maybe they needed to be somewhere. Devin was riddled with doubt by the time he stumbled across a four-door sedan that was unmistakably a rental. He looked around him, then pulled a tiny penlight from his shirt pocket and shone it within. In the front he saw nothing besides a couple of maps. But in the back, he hit pay dirt. A dark brown leather portfolio lay on the seat. Near the handle was a monogram of just one letter—a calligraphy "H." He took a deep breath, praying this wasn't the rental car of someone named Henderson or Hartman, but surely the odds were in his favor.

Time was getting away, though. The two women might show up any minute, considering how fast they'd walked to the coffee shop. He ran around the corner to his car and opened the trunk. Devin looked around before he turned the golf bag over and carefully peeled back the panel that seemed to be (but was not) sewn on. He briefly acknowledged the inventor of Velcro before sliding the rifle out and quickly swung the shoulder stock into position and slid the scope onto its mounting brackets. Next he screwed the custom-made suppressor onto the barrel. Then he opened the back door of the car and grabbed his long coat, the excellent black cashmere number that had set him back a couple of thousand dollars. He carried it to the rear of the car and before he thrust his arms into the sleeves, he looped the short strap attached to the stock of the rifle over his shoulder before putting on the coat. The rifle dangled next to him, completely hidden.

He closed the trunk and the car door and set the alarm with his remote. He had just turned the corner when he saw two figures at the other end of the long block. *Shit! They'll be here in a less than a minute.* He jumped over a hedge, and the rifle prodded his ribs painfully. But he ignored it and ran across a small lawn and a brick walk and shoved his way through more shrubbery until he was almost parallel with the car he'd identified. But his angle was poor. He kept moving until he was sure he was ahead of the car. Then he heard voices—their voices. The women passed by and he risked peeking out from his new vantage point. He swore through gritted teeth. He'd come too far. The shot was maybe fifty yards now, and the light sucked. He fiddled with the scope, aware that he had only seconds.

The Indian woman stood on the driver's side, Connor Hawthorne on the curb next to the passenger door. He would go after Laura Nez first. That was the harder shot. And no doubt the other one would come around the car to see what happened, and he'd have an easy target. He put the crosshairs on her forehead and began to slowly squeeze the trigger. In that instant, something flew through the air, something shiny and white. Laura Nez's hand went up. He hesitated a split second before he fired. Even as he did, though, he saw to his deep dismay, that her head was no longer visible. He heard the distant tinkle of breaking glass.

She'd ducked. But why? She couldn't possibly have heard him.

He swung the rifle left. Connor Hawthorne wasn't there either. What the hell was going on? He panicked. If the Indian woman knew she'd been shot at, she'd call for help. The cops would be here fast. He ran, aware that he didn't dare leave his car parked. The cops would probably run every license plate for two or three blocks in each direction. With those two goddamn women involved, his name was bound to attract someone's attention. He plunged back across the low hedge and out onto the sidewalk, snagging the hem of his coat on something. He heard it tear when he yanked it loose. *Fuck! Can this get any worse?*

Devin was almost afraid to use his remote. That little beep

when you unlocked the doors—the noise he'd thought sounded so cool—suddenly seemed like a homing signal anyone could follow. But he had little choice. He had to get in the damn car and drive…now! He was afraid to leave the rifle on the seat of the car, so he quickly popped the trunk, threw it in, and ran around to the driver's side. He forced himself to start the engine and pull away slowly, carefully, as if he hadn't a care in the world. He U-turned to avoid the possibility of being seen by the two women as he passed the end of the street where they were. A block later he turned right, then left. He zigzagged his way for several blocks until he came to the expressway and the road that would take him back to the funeral home in Hingham.

It wasn't until he joined the flow of the traffic on the express-way that he let himself relax. Still, he didn't dare open it up on the straightaways. Much as he loved giving the big BMW its head, and feeling the G-forces press him into the leather seat, he didn't think he could stand the emotional strain of getting pulled over on this particular night. One flashing light in the mirror would put him right over the edge. So he maintained a sedate sixty-three m.p.h. until he exited, signaled every turn, and finally pulled his car into the driveway of the funeral home. He'd have to get the gun out of the trunk, clean it, and hide it again. Then he'd head back into the city to his apartment and pour himself a very large drink. Eventually, he'd have to call Friedrich. That part he dreaded most.

*

"You didn't get even a glimpse of him?" demanded Malcolm, his fury barely under control.

"No," said Connor. "And I wish you'd settle down."

"You're saying I shouldn't be upset?"

"No, I'm saying you need to take a deep breath. You know we actually considered not telling either of you about this."

"You're kidding!"

"No. I'm not. You're both so predictable. Look at Dad." Outside the window that separated the hotel restaurant dining room from the sidewalk, Benjamin was speaking into his cell phone in a decidedly animated fashion. "He's obviously mobilizing something or someone."

"You notice the vein in his right temple?" Laura asked, her attention fixed on her former boss.

"Yeah. The one that pulsates when he's angry."

"He gets kind of freaked sometimes."

Malcolm stared at them in disbelief. "Ex*cuse* me! Someone tried to kill you tonight. Do you mind if we take this seriously?"

"No," said Connor, sipping at her Chivas on the rocks. "But it doesn't seem logical for you to be more indignant than we are. So let's try to keep it in perspective."

"Besides," Laura chimed in as Benjamin snapped his phone shut and headed back inside. "The more I think about it, the more amateurish this shooting looks. The guy picked a bad location, a bad time of day for visibility, and I'm thinking he might have missed even if I hadn't ducked."

"Not a professional hit man, then."

Laura snorted slightly. "We'd be dead...and we're not. Ergo, an amateur."

Benjamin pulled out his chair and sat down. "You're probably right," he agreed, reaching for his drink. "But that doesn't mean we won't be taking precautions."

"Oh, Dad. Not bodyguards. Please."

He sighed. "I knew you wouldn't agree to that. But you will have shadows for the next few days. I'll arrange for you to meet them in person at the hotel in the morning, so you'll know them by sight. But if they do their jobs right, you shouldn't notice them at all."

Connor sighed. "You're not going to give up on this one, are you?"

"Nope," said Benjamin, and Malcolm smiled.

"Wipe the smug satisfaction off your face, my friend," Connor told him as she picked up her menu. "It's hardly becoming."

"Becoming what?"

"Oh, hush up and order something."

"I will, and then we'll tell you what we've found out about Devin Underwood."

"This ought to be good," said Connor, nodding emphatically.

"He's got some nasty friends," said Benjamin. "But if you don't mind, Malcolm, let's hold the briefing until we get back up to the suite. Just in case." He let his eyes roam over the people seated near them in the dining room, and they all got the message. Too many ears in the vicinity.

Malcolm shrugged. "Sure thing. Now...how big are the steaks?"

"If they're not big enough," replied Benjamin with a smile, "order two."

CHAPTER NINE

There is some soul of goodness in things evil,
Would men observingly distil it out.
—William Shakespeare, *King Henry V,* act IV, scene 1

"The problem is, we can't find any connection between Grace Wainwright and Devin Underwood." Ayalla scowled and slammed the folder shut. Other than the photographs Benjamin's sources had uncovered (and Malcolm had promptly delivered to Ayalla), Devin Underwood was almost an informational void. And other than Grace's one visit to Dagle & Sons Funeral Home, and Devin's return visit to the Wainwright residence, when both Grace and her aunt were present, they hadn't uncovered a single meeting or phone call or fax passing between them. If there had been a conspiracy to get rid of Grace's mother and then Florence Gardner, the FBI hadn't any evidence that the funeral director was part of it.

"You've checked out everyone else at Dagle & Sons?" asked Malcolm.

"Of course."

"And?"

Ayalla scowled. "And *nothing.* One of the morticians, or whatever they're called, might be into a bookmaker for five or six thousand bucks, but that's a rumor. And the rest are basically average employees with nothing more sinister in their files than parking tickets. Not a one of them has gotten suddenly wealthier, including the one who gambles."

"What do you think of this neo-Nazi connection?"

"Revolted."

"Me, too."

"Seriously, though…" she sighed and closed her eyes for a moment. "you're saying Underwood is playing militia with those bastards—"

"And he might have access to explosive ordnance."

"All right. But all you have is a string of suppositions: *if* he actually knows who the S.A.B. guy was, *if* he's actively involved, *if* he had access to explosives, and *if* he had any idea how to use them."

"Back up a minute," said Malcolm. "Who says Underwood had to actually carry out any of this? What about this Arthur Raley creep? Benjamin told me that the NSA is interested in him because he might be a German terrorist type, one who knows about gadgets and bombs."

Ayalla frowned. "There you go again. *Might be* a German terrorist. I can't run an investigation and assign resources based on total guesswork. This doesn't add up to one solid lead, and you know it."

Malcolm leaned forward in his chair. "What I know is that someone took a shot at Laura and Connor last night, probably with a sniper rifle."

"What?" Ayalla came out of her chair. "Why didn't you call me immediately? What did the cops find when they responded?"

"No cops," said Malcolm.

"That's just fucking great!" Ayalla exploded. "Why is it those two always seem to think they're above the law?

Someone discharges a weapon on a city street, and your pals don't think it's necessary to let at least one law enforcement agency know about it? Now any sort of forensic evidence is completely compromised."

Malcolm bristled, but he tried to keep his temper in check. His first compromise was not jumping to his feet so he could be the tallest person in the argument. And he let Ayalla vent all her frustration before responding.

"At least *you* should have known better. What if this wasn't a one-shot deal? What if the killer tries again? If we're not actively working on the case, we don't have a chance of preventing a murder! One of them, hell, *both* of them, could end up dead, and on *my* watch."

"So that's the point of all this?" he snapped. "You're worried something will happen to the senator's daughter and you'll be to blame?"

She paused and stared at him hard. "No. That *isn't* the point. Is that really what you think of me? That all I care about is my job security?"

"No," said Malcolm slowly. "But it might seem that way to someone who doesn't know you as well as I do."

She locked eyes with him, but he kept his expression completely neutral. Finally, she said, "If Connor or Laura get hurt, I'd feel responsible, the same way you would." She sat down heavily. "No one else here is going to give a shit about anything *except* the political ramifications. Even my boss. He isn't stupid. He knows Benjamin Hawthorne could hurt him, professionally and every other way. And he figures Grace Wainwright knows some important people. Money talks. But that doesn't keep him and his cronies from their little jokes about what two women do in the bedroom."

Malcolm swallowed hard. He was used to prejudice; it had

followed him all his life. But it was worse, somehow, when people he cared about were the targets. "Sounds like your boss needs a little sensitivity training."

Ayalla looked at him and flashed a tiny smile in his direction. "Were you thinking of tutoring him personally?"

"What do you mean?"

"You're clenching and unclenching your fists."

"Oh," he looked down at his hands. "Sorry."

"It's all right. I feel the same way about his bullshit attitude."

Malcolm cocked his head to one side. "Toward Connor and Laura...and Grace Wainwright?"

She sighed. "I don't really know Grace Wainwright, though I don't think I trust her. Now Connor and Laura...all right, I'll admit it. I do like them. They're good people, and they've both got guts. Okay? I've said it. Now, don't make me say it again."

Malcolm grinned. "I promise I won't. But it might be nice if you said that to them someday."

"Maybe I will when the opportunity presents itself." She paused a beat. "Or not."

"All right," he smiled. "So we'll get back to the subject at hand. We have nothing that ties Grace to a conspiracy to commit murder, but she does appear to be the one who will benefit from all this."

"Exactly! We're talking millions of dollars. Money, sex, retribution," she ticked them off on her fingers. "As far as I'm concerned, those are the all-time leaders in the murder motive list. And money is definitely number one."

"Agreed. But motive without means and opportunity will get you nowhere."

"We're bound to find it—the connection, I mean. She can't have done it alone. Let's face it, prissy white girls with Ivy

League educations and designer clothes don't know shit about rigging up bombs."

"Is that prejudice rearing its ugly head?"

"Just common sense."

"So you're saying maybe a prissy black girl with an Ivy League education and designer clothes *would* know how to make a bomb?"

"Oh, shut up! You know what I mean."

"Just keeping you honest."

"Like I need a spare conscience. I've already got one, thank you."

"Yes, ma'am. It's just that…"

"What?"

"You're so focused on Grace Wainwright as the instigator, with some hired hit man to do the dirty work, that I wonder if you've considered a little twist on that scenario."

"Such as?"

"Well," he paused, wondering if the source of the idea would put her off before she gave it a fair listen. But then he figured, what the hell. "Connor brought it up last night. She agreed that millions of dollars made a good motive, but what if it's someone else's motive?"

Ayalla stared at him, frowning. "She's the only heir, the only one named in the will besides her aunt…except for small bequests to servants and a few substantial ones to some charities."

"Have you checked them out?"

"The servants, or the charities?"

"Either, or both."

"Yes. And it was a waste of time. The people who benefited from Mrs. Wainwright's death had nothing to gain from Florence Gardner taking an unscheduled drive into the river."

"All right, so that brings us back to Grace. But," he sat forward in his chair, "what if someone who wants all that money decided it would be easier to get it from Grace herself than from the mother or the aunt?"

Ayalla started to open her mouth, then stopped. "Hmm."

"What if the murderer is just paving the way for Grace without her knowledge?"

"Making sure she gets control of the entire Wainwright fortune." Ayalla appeared at least a little intrigued. "But then what? Are you postulating some sort of gigolo type who's waiting in the wings to start a romance? That doesn't seem likely under the circumstances, now does it?"

"I can't say whether or not there are lesbian gigolos," he said, "or whatever they would be called—maybe gigol*as*. But it's not outside the realm of possibility. And besides, let's not forget the weird terms of the will—that she's supposed to get married and have a child. She may be able to beat that in court, but what if she can't. Maybe there's a Mr. Wonderful just waiting to be needed, or waiting to show her how to get around the prospect of living a heterosexual charade."

"How is it you know the exact terms of the will?" asked Ayalla, frowning yet again.

Malcolm shrugged sheepishly. "News gets around?"

"Is there anything your senator buddy can't find out?" she sighed, shaking her head.

"Not as rule," he said. "Sorry."

"Don't be sorry. It's just annoying how I struggle to pry information out of other government departments, other law enforcement agencies, potential witnesses, and Benjamin Hawthorne snaps his fingers."

"You're not going to start in on him again, are you?" asked Malcolm.

"Hell, no. I've decided to like him, too."

"Wow. All in one day. Listen, since he does have good access, why don't you use him?"

"Use him?"

"He'd share anything he has with you. Just like I brought those photos of Underwood and Arthur Raley. All you have to do is ask."

"Hate asking," she replied curtly.

"I know. Too proud."

"Too independent," muttered Ayalla.

"There is that."

"Don't give me a hard time."

"Hardly ever," he said with a smile.

"So get out of my office and go chase…him." She picked up the photo of Devin Underwood and Arthur Raley.

"Which one?"

"Either. But I still think it's a dead end. Can you even see Grace Wainwright falling for Mr. Armani funeral director?"

"Not really. But there's something else you ought to know."

"Yes?" Her tone as vaguely menacing.

"Connor and Laura have this pendant on a chain that Grace said they could borrow. Laura gets a sort of weird…vibe…off it."

"Vibe?"

"Okay, I don't know what the right word is, but you get the idea. This thing has been in Grace's family for years, and it seemed really important to Grace's mother."

"So?"

"When Connor and Laura left the house with it, well, a little while after they left the house, that's when someone shot at them. It just occurred to us that maybe the pendant was really valuable."

"And is it?"

"We can't find out anything much about it, but Connor's getting in touch with some experts in England."

"Whatever," said Ayalla, clearly not interested in "vibes" off inanimate objects. "I'm getting in touch with experts right here. I've got a meeting in five minutes. Sorry."

"That's okay. Will I see you tonight?"

"Call me at six, and I'll let you know."

He ached with the desire to rub the tension out of her neck and shoulders, and kiss the top of her head. But he didn't dare. Not here. She'd kill him.

He leaned over and whispered, "You're beautiful," and dashed out of the room before she could tell him he was being completely unprofessional.

*

"No, the connection is fine," said Connor, taking a seat at the desk in Benjamin's hotel suite. "I'm just amazed to hear from you so soon. We only sent the images of the pendant a couple of hours ago."

"I showed them to Ellen as soon as she came in." Lord William Carlisle's deep English-accented baritone echoed across the trans-Atlantic connection. "She's been dragging out all the old books from the library. I'd wager you haven't any idea what you've got hold of."

"No," frowned Connor, signaling Laura to pick up an extension. "Laura's getting on the line now."

"Good, good. Glad you're there, Laura. Connor's E-mail said you felt some energy from it."

"Yes, Lord Carlisle, although it was a different sort than I've experienced before. Then when I realized how it resembled the goddess of—"

"Best not be too specific, my dear. And enough with the Lord Carlisle bit. Good heavens, you'll make me feel a right old geezer. It's William to you. Ah, here's Ellen. She's made some copies of materials you ought to read. If you'll stand by your facsimile, she'll send them now. You'll see what you can see."

"Can we talk more about this?" asked Connor, surprised at his haste to close the conversation.

"Of course, my dear, of course. We'll see you later. Cheers."

The connection was severed. Connor stood there holding the phone. "That was incredibly uninformative. And what did he mean by 'we'll see you later'?"

"He obviously didn't want to discuss it over the phone." Laura pursed her lips thoughtfully. "He doesn't seem to me like someone who goes in for drama, so…" she paused.

"The pendant is important." Connor suggested.

"Could be. And there's the fax." They crossed the room to where Benjamin had set up his laptop, fax, scanner, printer, and a few other electronic gadgets that would never be found in any computer store.

One by one, sheets emerged from the machine, as they began reading the cover letter from Lady Ellen Carlisle. Neither had the patience to wait, so they held the page between them so both could read.

My Dear Connor,

Now what have you gotten yourself into? I'd have thought you'd had quite enough of magic since our encounter with those nasty buggers on the Tor. If this piece is authentic (and I tend to believe it is because of what you wrote about its provenance), you have stumbled onto something for which many individuals, some more nefarious than others, have been searching these many decades. You already know from experience that there are indeed some powerful objects knocking around the world. Be warned that this one can easily be turned to evil use in the wrong hands. Of course, you've only got half—and my eldest mentor tells me that it is not sufficiently powerful to do great harm unless it is reunited with its twin. The joining of the two halves creates a third force more powerful than either could possibly summon alone.

I am including copies of drawings from our archives. They may be of help to you.

I know nothing of this Grace Wainwright, but I am putting my best efforts into discovering her ancestry. We have extensive files on all those who have been associated with the Circles of Light over the centuries.

For now, keep it…and yourselves…safe. My love to your precious Laura, and warmest regards to your father and the wonderful young policeman. Has he gotten over his experience in Glastonbury yet?"

E.C.

"Whoa!" said Connor. "I guess you were right. There is something about that necklace."

Laura was pulling several sheets from the fax. She stared at the first one so long that Connor said, "I wanna see!"

Almost absentmindedly, Laura handed her the other sheets, but kept the top one.

Connor began flipping through the faxed pages. Surprisingly, they hardly seemed like images of the same item. But they had obviously been drawn by artists of various talent, or perhaps different perceptions, and certainly in a different media—one a minimalist sketch, another a carefully detailed pen-and-ink, a third rendered in charcoals. "So that's what Ellen meant about us only having half. Look! The entire pendant is supposed to look like this. But we only have the darker piece—the other segment must be made of silver, or some very light metal. It's amazing the way they fit together. But you clearly see the shape of our half. What is it supposed to depict anyway?" She looked up and Laura was still studying the image. "Earth to Laura!"

"What? Oh. I'm sorry. I got a little carried away looking at this. It's beautiful, isn't it?"

Connor reexamined the other pictures she held, and shook her head. "I suppose," she shrugged. "I wish the captions were more legible."

Laura peered at hers more closely. "Kind of blurry, but I think it says, 'Goddess of Avebury pendant, c. 1663.' Do you suppose that's the date of the drawing, or the date they think it was made?"

"We'll have to ask Ellen. You know, I think this sketch is of the figurine that was found at the archaeology dig, rather than the pendant. Wait, there's one more sheet in the fax."

Laura, who was closest, picked up the page, glanced at it, then started to hand it over. But she suddenly snatched it back.

"What?"

"This is a photograph instead of a drawing."

"From when?"

Laura held it under a table lamp. "From the archives of the Schutzstaffel (SS), Berlin, 1943." She frowned. "But that doesn't make any sense. Grace got this from her mother, and you said the family's been in Boston for generations. How would her pendant end up with the Nazis during World War II?"

Connor reached for the photo, then held it at arm's length. What was it about this picture? Then it came to her, and she couldn't believe she hadn't seen it at once. She quickly rummaged in her bag, pulled out the little wooden box, and snapped it open. She held it up to be sure. "*This* pendant didn't end up in Germany...the one in the picture is the *other* half."

Before Laura could respond, Connor's cell phone rang. She pressed a key. "Oh, hi, Tracy. Yes. I'm sorry we didn't call, but it was getting so late, I didn't want to wake you. We stayed in Boston last night… What? When did it happen? Is anything missing?… Oh, I'm sorry. How would you be able to tell? No, we'll drive over there right away. Are you two all right?… No, no, stop worrying about it. This isn't your fault at all… No, I mean it. We certainly wouldn't blame you. Sometimes things just happen." Connor disconnected.

"What's up?"

"Tracy and Laura went in to straighten up our room at the B&B this morning, and the place was trashed, like someone searched it, went through everything. She's just about in tears thinking they must have gone out last night and left the door unlocked."

"Just *our* room?"

"Yes," replied Connor grimly. "So I guess we can probably draw some conclusions."

Laura glanced at the pendant still dangling from Connor's hand. "Starting with that, I imagine."

"Maybe someone wants it back."

"But Grace would simply ask for it. So it has to be someone else. You know," said Laura, "we were just talking about Nazis last night, and whether Devin Underwood has anything to do with the Supreme Aryan Brotherhood. You don't suppose—"

"That some Nazi wannabe *has* this half," Connor held up the photograph. "And is determined to find this one." She raised the pendant in her other hand.

"Maybe. If we're on the right track, then this is beginning to make sense in a weird sort of way."

"Or we could be grasping at straws."

"True. I can't even imagine that Devin Underwood would be deeply dedicated to any particular cause, except perhaps his own. I doubt he has the slightest interest in anything but money."

"I agree. He doesn't fit the profile of a fanatic."

"But let's not forget his pal, Arthur Raley. We know nothing about *him.*"

Connor sighed. "We need more. Remember what Malcolm said last night. He was fairly certain Ayalla wouldn't take well to guesswork."

"So we'll keep digging."

"Agreed. And maybe I'll put this in the hotel safe, just in case." She paused. "Maybe I should find a way to lock up my dad's computer and this other communications gear."

Laura shook her head. "No place in a hotel room is secure. But don't worry. The stuff is useless without the passwords and key codes, believe me. Anyone who messes with any of it will fry every internal circuit."

"Good. Then let's get going." She paused on the way to the door. "You know, now that I think about it, Tracy didn't say anything about having called the police. I wonder if they did."

"I have a feeling they're trying to figure out if they should. They have a real obsession with privacy for themselves and their guests."

"I'd be perfectly happy if they didn't call the cops. Just makes it more complicated."

"True." Laura scooped up the fax. "I think we'll take these with us."

They started down the thickly carpeted corridor, their steps barely a whisper. Laura scanned over Ellen Carlisle's note once more. "This part about 'my eldest mentor.' You don't suppose she means…"

"Oh, yes, I do suppose. That has Gwendolyn Broadhurst written all over it."

"Sounds as if we're going to have reinforcements."

"Yeah, but are we talking living and breathing reinforcements, or the dead and hovering?"

"We'll have to wait and see," said Laura, pressing the elevator button. "But either way this is going to be very interesting."

*

"You saw the pendant!"

"Yes, sir."

"And you let them take it away?"

"I tried to…um…"

"Tried to what!?"

Devin cleared his throat. He wished he'd never mentioned the pendant to Friedrich. He was fairly sure he should keep the failed murder attempt to himself. "I intended to steal it, but I couldn't get the opportunity. Then I found out where they were staying, went there, and searched the room thoroughly. It wasn't anywhere to be found."

"How did you discover where they were lodging?"

"I called a friend of theirs and explained that I wanted to get in touch about funeral arrangements."

"You used your own name?"

"Of course not. I said I was from the place where they prepped the Hawthorne woman."

"Were you careful not to leave any trace of your search?"

Devin winced. He hadn't been careful at all. He was in too much of a hurry thinking someone would be home any minute. "Um, yes, pretty much."

"Does that mean 'yes' or 'no' in your vernacular?"

"It means yes."

"Good. Then we may have a window of opportunity to retrieve the pendant. I would not have believed that foolish young woman would part with it. I wonder why she did."

"It might be—" Devin hesitated.

"Might be what?"

"I got research back on Connor Hawthorne. Seems her last two books have been a little out of character for her—more about the occult than the law. Some of the reviewers were critical of what they called the 'spooky stuff' in the newest book. But she's acquiring a whole fan base because of it."

"So she has an interest in the unknown. Perhaps that's why Grace felt compelled to mention the family heirloom."

Devin suddenly blurted out, "So are you ever going to tell me what's so important about this thing?"

Friedrich was deadly silent, and Devin truly wished he'd kept his mouth shut. He already knew a few odds and ends about the pendant, but he wanted more, and he was sick of being out of the loop. Still, if even half the stories were true, it was incredibly stupid to openly challenge Herr Doktor.

"You'll know more when it is necessary. For the time being, you are to do nothing about retrieving it. I will see to that part of it. Do you understand me completely?"

"Yes, sir," Devin replied, grateful to have escaped the old man's wrath. Of course, if Friedrich should find out that it was Grace Wainwright whom he'd called to find out where the women were staying or about Devin's sloppy search of the room at the bed-and-breakfast…no, he didn't want to think about that. Besides, he'd disguised his voice quite well. Grace didn't seem the least suspicious.

"Send me this information you've obtained on the two women. I'm curious."

"I'll fax it to you immediately."

"Good. And Devin?"

"Yes, sir?"

"Don't disappoint me.""

"No, I won't."

Friedrich hung up, and Devin dropped his cordless phone on the table beside him. He didn't feel anywhere near as confident as he had the day before. He didn't doubt that Arthur Raley was lurking nearby, waiting for him to come through on his promise of a small fortune in blackmail proceeds. And he was no closer to identifying the American descendants of Wilhelm von Adler. Well, at least he knew more than Friedrich, but that was no longer of much comfort to him.

He took a deep breath. The tightness in his chest was the pressure of fear bordering on sheer panic. Arthur Raley, the Supreme Aryan Brotherhood, Friedrich, the cops and the FBI, and now the Hawthornes. He was surrounded, and the walls of his chic apartment felt as if they were closing in on him. He needed to go for a drive.

*

The Doktor was not pleased with his young protégé. He was not cool under pressure, he didn't think creatively, and he was more greedy than ambitious. Friedrich wouldn't have minded ambition; he appreciated its stabilizing influence. Once the mind was sufficiently focused on a prize worth having, then all distractions and minor considerations were burned away in the fire of achieving that prize. Power was worth struggle, deprivation, pain, and blood. Power was a magnet for those who wanted to stand in its reflected light and were willing to die for it. He would gladly have given his life for his Führer and the principles on which the Third Reich was built—the merging of warrior and proud farmer, the purity of the Aryan people, the expansion of their empire, the conquest of the weak, and the eradication of bloodlines that would sully the great rebirth.

Were there truly any today who understood that depth of

loyalty? He secretly despised most of the so-called neo-Nazi organizations. Many were manned by nothing but undisciplined ragtag louts. Their visions of glory were the stuff of adolescent wet dreams—guns to shoot, weaker men to bully, women to use and abuse. It reminded him of some of Röhm's brown shirts— the S.A. thugs who supported Hitler in the early years—whose brutality brought down the wrath of the Weimar Republic just as the fledgling Nazi party was beginning to gain strength. It was only by the clever maneuvering of Friedrich's boss, Heinrich Himmler, that Röhm and his would-be army were brought to heel.

Himmler had never ceased carrying out one strategy after another in building the tiny regiment of bodyguards known in 1925 as the *Schutzstaffel* into the mighty and dreaded SS. Eventually, every security service was under his direction— including the Gestapo, the German State Police, the Prussian Secret State Police, the SD, and all local police forces. To Friedrich, though, the crown jewel in Himmler's acquisition of power was the creation of the *Einsatzgruppen*—the extermination units. Friedrich's first posting had been to a one of the camps that had originally begun as a prison for dissenters during the early years of Hitler's rise to power. Manned by troops of the Totenkopf regiment, it had been transformed into a killing machine where hundreds died every week and eventually every day. He had been sensitive once to the cries of the condemned, but his zeal for the goals of the Reich had soon hardened his heart against the pleas for mercy or at least a quick death. Friedrich was bent on discovering something his Führer needed to know—the seat of psychic power in the human brain, and the observable genetic qualities of talented psychics. Others had scoffed at his work, but he had carried on.

Each day at the camp, he chose a new batch of subjects to

test. The ones who showed a glimmer of ability were segregated for further study. The ones who could not guess a single hidden image or one of the words concealed on a chalkboard turned to the wall were sent out to be shot. The remaining subjects might have wished for that fate. Friedrich's experiments were carried out with no regard at all for the agony of the patient. Brain surgery without anesthetic was common. But, Friedrich reasoned, how else was he to know what parts of the brain controlled the man?

As time passed, and he had nothing to show for his efforts, Friedrich grew desperate. Then came a reprieve from the Führer whose moods had grown more and more mercurial with the horrible reversals of fortune on the Russian front. The Doktor was ordered to Berlin, to join the staff. He was technically being posted to the Leibstandarte Adolf Hitler, the Führer's personal regiment, but in practice he was to undertake new experiments—on unsuspecting young German soldiers. The Führer had concluded that the tests in the death camps had failed simply because the subjects were racially impure. Friedrich must now work with Aryan subjects of good background. Naturally, he was less cruel in his work. He gave them drugs to ease the discomfort, and not all of them were particularly courageous in giving their all for the Fatherland. In the end, they all died.

Friedrich always wondered if that was why Wilhelm had left in secret. Did he actually think the Führer would allow him to be sacrificed to the cause? Not that Friedrich had never considered it, at least in theory, because here was a subject worth understanding. His powers were formidable, his vision sometimes frighteningly clear. What it would have meant to see inside that remarkable brain! Yet Hitler would never have put his pet psychic at risk, and Friedrich was not sure he could even bring himself to cut into the young man. But rumors were rampant in those final months. Or perhaps Wilhelm had actually seen something in the future of Berlin that he interpreted as mortal danger. In any event, with the Führer's blessing, he had disappeared.

Much of this had been set down in Hitler's own hand. Yet why, in the name of all that was sacred to them, did he not include the most important details of the long-range plan for von Adler's future? The only facts Friedrich had gleaned from Hitler's cryptic notes about von Adler indicated that the young man returned to France where he would have once again assumed his French surname. That was easy enough to trace, and once Friedrich had emerged from his mountain exile and moved cautiously back into the flow of the world, he had sent Karl to make exhaustive inquiries in France. Yet every time Karl returned, he had nothing of value to report.

Some few remembered the tall, athletic, and *très gentil* son of M. de L'Aigle. He had returned home after escaping from a German prisoner-of-war camp. But to Friedrich's profound frustration, no one remembered where the young man had gone. There were rumors, all unfounded and contradictory: He'd gone to join the French Foreign Legion; he'd married and moved his household to Paris; he'd volunteered to join the British Expeditionary Forces in North Africa; he'd enlisted in the United States Army to fight in the Pacific theater of operations. Each was more absurd than the last. Not a shred of documentation could be found. It was as if the man had vanished, along with the silver pendant, *le voleur d'âmes.*

The only thing with which Friedrich could content himself was tracing the history of the other half of the pendant. Fortunately, Hitler's researchers had been precise and thorough in their endeavors. Sketches of the complete pendant, its two mirror images united, had been recovered from a French museum after Paris fell to the Germans. Every legend and story and rumor about it had been recorded and analyzed. Most telling, however, was the discovery of Wilhelm's true ancestry—an Englishwoman named Genevieve Miranda Fitzhugh committed to an asylum for the insane early in the 19th century. Her child had been taken from her and adopted by the de L'Aigle family in Alsace-Lorraine. She had been a widow, and the old hospital records indicated she spoke of a daughter. But the trail ended there.

Years upon years passed, and Karl died. Friedrich mourned his comrade, but his ambitions were not dimmed. He placed monthly advertisements in every trade magazine and paper in Europe and the Americas that catered to book and memorabilia collectors, offering a large reward for any correspondence, journal, or public record including the names of Genevieve or Eliza Fitzhugh. He continued to send graduate students to libraries, archives, and private collections of old documents all over the world. They found a brief mention of the burning of the Fitzhugh manor house near Chillwater, and the disappearance of Lady Fitzhugh and her daughter, Eliza. Friedrich reasoned that the woman might have had the whole pendant in her possession and perhaps given the other half to the child, but there were nights when he was equally convinced that it was lost forever. Then a miracle had occurred, one that convinced him beyond any doubt that his cause was just and his mission blessed by the gods of his Aryan ancestors. A book dealer in the United States had sent him a letter, timidly inquiring if the gentleman was still offering a reward for such materials. At first, Friedrich had been curt. This was no doubt another disappointment among hundreds. He told the man to fax him copies of the first few pages, but ignored the papers for over an hour after they arrived. When he did finally take them up, his heart began to pound. Instinct told him he had struck gold!

Friedrich took no chances. He called the man and asked for a bank account to which he could wire the funds. Then he sent a courier to collect the old diary. From that moment, discovering the descendants of Genevieve Fitzhugh had been child's play. The last female in the line was Grace Wainwright. And she had the golden half of the pendant. Or at least she'd *had* it, he thought. Until the fool lent it to Connor Hawthorne. But that would remedied easily enough. She didn't know what it was, and certainly not enough time had transpired for her to find out. He doubted there were more than a handful of people in the world who would recognize *le voleur d'âmes,* certainly not anyone of the American woman's acquaintance. By the time she got around to satisfying her childish curiosity, it would be too late.

*

Arthur Raley was paranoid. But he had a right to be. The security services of more than a dozen countries considered his capture a high priority. And most of them had no interest whatsoever in bringing him to trial. He was a "shoot on sight" target. He was a enough of a threat to warrant a death sentence, but of insufficient political importance that anyone would need special permission to put a bullet in his head. He'd spent more than twenty-five years making bitter enemies, and there was no one in the world whom he considered a friend. There were clients and objectives, and there were occasionally useful allies to help execute his strategies. But no one knew him personally, certainly no one understood him, and he didn't particularly care one way or the other. It amused him to contemplate what sort of profile the FBI and the CIA had created for him. It would be so like the Americans, with their penchant for psychology, to paint a picture of him as a garden-variety sociopath with a history of cruelty to small animals and playmates, or perhaps a neglected and abused child crying out for attention. In truth, his childhood had been comfortable. His parents, though undemonstrative by nature, had demonstrated the proper concern for his safety and upbringing, had sent him to private schools and a fine university. Hans (his real name) had been a moderate student who played team sports and was generally liked among his companions. He was neither a leader nor a loner. He got good grades with very little effort, but he had no desire to earn top marks if it meant exerting himself. Hans simply fit in, played the academic game, and coasted through life, waiting for something more exciting to come along.

His chance came during his last year at university. He and a few friends were swilling cold brew at a beer garden near the campus. They grew rowdy, and one of his soccer teammates, Fritz Mannheim, began to hold forth on the glories of German history and spout fulsome praise of the now-banned Nazi Party. Hans pretty much ignored the idiot until a pudgy but well-dressed man suddenly appeared at the table, dragged Fritz to a corner, and apparently gave him a good dressing-down. It was the 1970s, and Hans, who couldn't hear them over the din, figured it must be one of those bleeding hearts who were always worried about political correctness and West Germany's image in the world.

A minute later, Fritz rejoined the table, sinking onto the bench next to Hans. "Whew," he'd said. "I had no idea old Kesselmeyer could be such a tiger."

"You know him?" asked Hans, his curiosity only slightly aroused.

"Of course. Everyone knows Kesselmeyer." Fritz leaned in. "He's head of the party faction here."

"What party?"

"You know," said Fritz, trying unsuccessfully to wink.

Hans thought about it for a moment. "You mean he's in the Nazi Party?"

"Shh! Someone will hear you."

Hans laughed. "Oh, be serious, will you? Everyone knows about modern-day fascists, whatever they call themselves. Banned or not, the fanatics come out of the woodwork periodically."

Fritz stiffened as if highly offended, and Hans shrugged. "Look, everyone should believe whatever they want. I personally don't think there's the slightest difference between one party and the next, or one politician and the next."

"That's where you're wrong," said Fritz firmly.

"So if he's on your side, why was he giving you such a hard time over there?"

"He said I was being unnecessarily indiscreet in voicing my views. He insists we need to keep a low profile."

"Can't get much lower than impotent and out of favor," said Hans.

Fritz scowled at him. "You have no idea what you're talking about."

"Maybe I'm wrong, but then again, I don't really care."

"You should."

"Why?" asked Hans, raising his stein for a last long gulp.

"Because you could be a part of a better future for our country, a better future for the Aryan people."

"Aryan people? I think I've read this before somewhere…like in a history book. This is old news, Fritz."

"No, it isn't old at all. If you're the least bit interested in learning your true destiny, then come with me tonight."

"Where?"

"A meeting."

"Will the fat guy be there?"

Fritz's face flushed furiously. "Don't insult him. You should never insult him. I'm only trying to do a favor for you, my friend, to make you a part of a glorious future."

Hans sighed. "All right, all right. I'll go to your meeting if it will make you stop nagging me about it. Perhaps it will be educational and entertaining. I need a good laugh."

Hans had been at least partly right. The meeting was indeed educational, but he didn't laugh, not even once. He discovered that Herr Kesselmeyer was not the least bit amusing, nor did he find any aspect of life amusing. Everything he said was in deadly earnest, and had it not been for the frisson of fear that ran through Hans when he looked in the old fellow's eyes, he would probably have been tempted to poke fun at Kesselmeyer's fanaticism. Somehow he didn't dare. A couple of hours into the meeting, he had no desire to ridicule anyone. Hans had finally discovered something he could care passionately about—the Nazi Party—and it promised to care about him, reward his loyalty, and give him a reason to get up in the morning. The more Kesselmeyer talked, about the glories of the past, about the bright future of a united, expanded Germany controlled by pure Germans, the more Hans felt his chest swell with pride. He was an empty vessel, waiting to be filled with purpose. This was his land, these were his people.

By the time they left the meeting, Hans was completely enthralled and Fritz was elated with his friend's reaction. "You see, I told you! Couldn't you feel the power in that room? And Kesselmeyer is the source of it. He raises the energy just by his presence, even before he begins to speak."

Truth be told, Hans had felt something. He was skeptical of

feelings, but he couldn't deny that his attitude toward life had changed. From that day, he was the staunchest of Kesselmeyer's supporters, even after the man was arrested and jailed for his illegal activities. Hans rapidly rose to leadership rank in the semi-secret, paramilitary organization, though his parents were appalled and his former university friends deeply puzzled. Hans severed all contact with his family, content to live frugally in one of the modest "safe house" apartments owned by the organization and shared with his friend, Fritz. The men roamed the streets at night, vandalizing the businesses of Jews, blacks, and others they judged undesirable. They always escaped just ahead of the police, whom Hans began to believe must also be secret supporters of the New Reich. When the Nazi troopers reached their headquarters after these forays, they sang and drank and enjoyed the company of women. This, he thought, was the life of a true warrior.

Did he become too arrogant? In later years, he sometimes wondered. Whatever the reason, this ideological idyll soon came to an end. Less than a year into his tenure as a commander, Hans decided a bold stroke would rally new support to the cause. Thus, against the explicit instructions of Kesselmeyer, who had finally been released from jail, he planned an assault on an armored car. Giddy with a sense of his own role in what would become the glorious history of the Fourth Reich, he put together what he deemed a perfect tactical plan. That he had almost no military training, and only moderate experience with high-powered weapons, bothered him not at all. Zeal had supplanted good sense. He had moved into the dangerous mind-set of a man who believes fate is inevitably on his side.

Still, despite his puerile attempts at mounting a military operation, they might actually have succeeded, if only by virtue of sheer surprise. Major crime was exceedingly rare and guards were liable to be lax. Hans and his men could have made off with a fortune in cash. But even Hans, in considering a worst-case scenario, hadn't come close to what awaited them that morning shortly before dawn. The plan had seemed to be working. They shunted the armored vehicle into the alley as the driver tried to avoid impact with a car that pulled out in front of him. Quickly, Hans moved his troopers into position and banged on the back door with his rifle butt, demanding they open up.

He waited; all was silence. He raised the rifle again, but before he could strike the metal door, one shot rang out. He turned angrily to see who had disobeyed his orders. There was to be no shooting that would attract attention. But his men stood mute, their eyes fixed upward on the rooftops of the buildings. Hans looked up, too, as an amplified voice echoed through the alley. *"Polizei!"*

His heart almost stopped. The police! It wasn't possible. Yet there they were, black-clad figures ranged along the roofline, their rifles trained on the would-be robbers. Hans and his men were like ducks in a shooting gallery. Instinctively, Hans wanted to fight. He raised his gun barrel, and again the voice barked out, *"Lassen Sie Ihre Waffen fallen!"*

All round him, the weapons of his comrades rattled as they hit the ground. So much for the warrior blood. *Cowards!* his mind screamed. *To give up without a fight.* He tried to aim at the nearest policeman and shots were fired; it was not a warning, but a takedown. And had it not been for his body armor vest, Hans might have died. As it was, he suffered a fractured femur, three broken ribs, and would have bled to death in the alley if the medical team had not acted promptly. But the police wanted a trial, not a martyr. He recovered enough to stand trial, and on the day of his appearance before the judge, Hans received a blow worse than the gunshots of the police, one that would stay with him far longer. The chief witness against him was none other than Kesselmeyer. Hans stared in mute disbelief as the man admitted to having tipped off the police about the planned crime, and smugly distanced himself from the rabble of criminal hangers-on who had infiltrated his perfectly legitimate political organization, one which, by the way, had adjusted its views to be more in keeping with the laws of modern Germany.

Given the least opportunity, Hans would have leaped at the man and strangled him to death. But he was shackled, and the traitor was out of reach. The finding of the court was inevitable—prison. From that day until his release four and a half years later, Hans spoke no more than absolutely necessary. Other prisoners learned quickly to leave him alone, for his temper flared instantly to violence, and he fought with an intense enmity that made even the most obtuse criminal back away.

In his cell, Hans brooded for hours on end. He was no longer the idealist because there were no longer any ideals worth having. He had been profoundly betrayed, and he would not be that foolish again, to put his trust in venal, corruptible, spineless men. The only cause for which he would fight now would be his own. His goals were fairly simple, and he learned much in the prison that would assist him.

On the day he was released, Hans went to his father, who, though heartbroken, was too kind to disown his son. Hans, in a well-rehearsed plea, said that he wished to leave Germany, leave the disgrace of his imprisonment behind. He had his university degree in electrical engineering, and he knew he could find a job elsewhere. But who would hire Hans in this country?

As he anticipated, his father was deeply impressed by his son's obvious rehabilitation and anxious to help him make a new life. After two hours of discussion, and a long, boring dinner with his parents, he left their house with a substantial bank draft, enough to set him up in France, or Belgium, or even England. Two days later, with a set of excellent false identification, he made plane reservations from Stuttgart to Montreal. He carefully sewed the cash securely into the lining of a fine but battered leather suitcase. His suit was well-cut, his overcoat excellent quality, and the handmade black leather driving gloves fit like his own skin. He looked every bit the moderately successful businessman.

In the taxi on the way to the train that would carry him to Stuttgart, he asked the driver to stop near a cable office. "I might be a few minutes," he explained. "I have several messages to send. Please wait." He handed over a generous tip and left his suitcase in the car to reassure the driver of his return. He didn't worry about the money. He'd noted the driver's name, and should the man leave, Hans would find him.

Hans, briefcase in hand, walked briskly into the cable office, through the lobby, and out a side door he'd identified the previous day. It was less than two minutes' walk to his destination. He bounded up the back steps of the old, but still elegant stone residence, pulled a small crowbar from his case, and had the door open in seconds. The wood splintered, but subtlety wasn't important. He ran up the stairs to the second room on the right of the landing, and flung open the door so that it banged against something behind it.

The action in the room froze. A nurse dressed in white had been about to administer an injection. The patient stared, his mouth an O of puzzlement. A man in a dark suit and tie, seated on a chair in the far corner, had been leafing through a magazine that dangled in his hand.

Then time ticked forward again, and the nurse screamed,

the patient tried to sit up and the bodyguard reached toward his belt. Hans swung his silenced automatic toward the man in the chair and two red dots appeared on the man's forehead. The nurse scrambled backward, but not fast enough. Two more red dots.

Finally, Hans stood beside the bed and savored the terror in Kesselmeyer's eyes. He would have liked to prolong the sweetness of his revenge, but there wasn't time. He leaned over and put the gun against the old man's ear. "You betrayed me, you stupid swine. And now you die." He fired twice and watched the life go out of the red-rimmed eyes before finishing up his plan. He quickly and thoroughly went through every cupboard and drawer, tossing things onto the floor. He preferred that this initially appear to be a burglary turned to murder. He took all the jewelry he could find, ran downstairs with several sheets and pillow covers and filled them up. He dumped them all in the rear hall, left the door standing open, and slipped out.

The driver was waiting patiently as Hans came out of the cable office with a sheaf of flimsies, copies of the messages he'd sent. All appeared just as he wanted it to. The driver reached over the seat and popped the door open. Hans made small talk about the slow clerk in the office. They laughed about stupid people.

A block from the train station, he asked the driver to turn onto a side street. Hans had reconnoitered the area and discovered a block of warehouses where drivers often stopped for a quick nap. Hans asked to be let out, insisting that the walk would do him good. He handed the man a large denomination. As the driver focused on making change, Hans shot him behind the right ear and caught him by the shoulder before he fell against the steering wheel. He closed the man's eyes and leaned the head against the window. No blood showed. At a casual glance, he was sleeping.

He reached over and shut off the ignition. Then he took all the money, the man's wallet and gold wedding ring, and stuffed them in his briefcase. With a quick survey of the area to ensure that no one was nearby, he grabbed his belongings and hopped out of the car, moving at a normal pace. At the next corner, a street beggar accosted him. For an instant Hans thought of shooting him, but he had a better idea. He reached into his briefcase and took out the wad of cash from the taxi driver and handed it to the man. It would have only the driver's prints and now the beggar's.

He was in good time for his train, and he settled in to his first-class seat with a sigh of contentment. He smiled when he imagined the beggar flashing that money around and then trying to explain to the police that a well-dressed businessman had simply given it to him. It was all too perfect for words. Hans closed his eyes and wondered why people made such a fuss about killing. He'd committed four murders in less than an hour, one of them a rendering of justice, the others acts of practical necessity. But he experienced not a twinge of guilt. In fact, he felt liberated, free of moral rectitude and free of the need to belong. He had acquired a skill—killing—and for the next twenty-five years, he honed his talent and sold it to the highest bidder.

CHAPTER TEN

To die, to sleep;
To sleep: perchance to dream: ay, there's the rub;
For in that sleep of death what dreams may come
When we have shuffled off this mortal coil...
—William Shakespeare, *Hamlet,* act III, scene 1

The plane hit the runway a little too hard, but Connor barely noticed. Landings at Reagan Airport in Washington were often less than elegant, especially in bad weather.

"Geez, it's pouring," said Laura, peering out the window. "Ducks could drown in this."

"Forecast says more rain tomorrow."

"I'm sorry, hon. That's going to make it harder, I know."

Connor shrugged and tucked the paperback she'd been reading into her shoulder bag. As soon as the seat belt light went off, she stood up and opened the overhead. She and Laura had only brought small carry-ons. They only planned to be in Washington for forty-eight hours or so, just long enough to attend the wake and funeral of Amanda Hawthorne.

Within an hour, they were on the George Washington Parkway headed into the city. Connor's cell phone rang. For the next minute and a half, she was uncharacteristically terse, answering the caller in monosyllables. "All right then, 2 o'clock." She stabbed the end button and said, "The lawyer."

"Your mom's lawyer?"

"Yeah. I've been dodging her calls all week. Seems Dad gave her my cell phone number."

"He must have thought it was important."

"He also knows I have no desire whatsoever to hear anything about Mom's will."

"I know that. But the woman is just trying to do her job. Isn't she legally bound to do certain things to get the will probated?"

"Yes, and she also has to inform the heirs of the terms of the will."

"So what's happening at two o'clock?"

"We're going to her office. It's on Old Georgetown Road in Bethesda."

Laura glanced at her watch. "We've got a couple of hours to kill. How about one of those cheese steaks you used to rave about?"

"You must have a strong mothering streak," Connor smiled. "Whenever I'm stressed, you prescribe food."

"Yes, but would a *good* mother prescribe a cheese steak sub, greasy chips and a large Dr. Pepper?"

"Probably not."

"Good. Then once again I've proven I'm not perfect."

"Perfect enough for me." Connor took the exit ramp for the Capital Beltway toward Maryland. "Next stop, Philadelphia Mike's."

An hour and a half later they left the rental car in the parking lot beside a dignified two-story red-brick office building and climbed the stairs to the second floor. Elaine Medford's outer office was a textbook rendering of understated elegance.

Everything from the subdued flame-stitch fabrics of the sofa to the pleated lampshades matched, but not obviously so. The dark Thomasville mahogany chairs and coffee table conveyed prosperity without overindulgence. It was a lawyer's office that didn't try too hard. Connor approved.

The receptionist's desk was unoccupied, the computer off, and the surface bare of any work. Connor was about to knock on the inner door when it swung open and the lawyer herself invited them in. She was about five foot six, and wiry rather than slender. Her hair was pure white and cut into a sort of pageboy style that Connor hadn't seen in years. She wore a pair of pearl-gray corduroy slacks, a mauve silk blouse, and a short white wool jacket. Reading glasses hung from a beaded chain around her neck, and earrings shaped like little books dangled from her earlobes. This, thought Connor, was an eccentric lawyer.

"Sorry about the empty office. My paralegal, Eric, is off this afternoon. His partner was having surgery today. I figured he wouldn't get much done while he was worrying about Calvin. So, let's get down to business. I know you probably still have some arrangements to make."

"Actually, that's all taken care of."

"Good." She slid a stack of files closer and opened the top one. Placing the glasses halfway down her nose, she scanned the first page. "Oh, hell," she said, closing it again. "I don't know why I'm stalling. I know perfectly well what it says. I drafted it myself. Didn't like it, but I did it."

"What is it, then, I mean, that you didn't like?"

"I don't like it when people use a last will and testament to beat someone over the head. It's almost as if they've just got to have the last word, even from beyond the grave."

Connor stared at her for a moment. "I take it I'm the person she wants to beat over the head."

"Yes, and I'm not happy about it." She took a deep breath and leaned back in her chair. "I believe a person has a right to do as she wishes with her property. But I also happen to know that your mother's estate consists almost entirely of the money and real estate she received from your father in the divorce settlement. And he gave her all of it free and clear without a single argument. At the time, I thought he was nuts, but it was the easiest fee I ever earned. Then, a few months later, she wanted me to redraft her will. Obviously she had no intention of letting anything go back to Benjamin, which seemed a little vindictive, but what can you do? So, I did what she wanted, and I tried to alter her thinking, but—"

"Elaine, if you're this upset over the will, what on earth did she do?"

"She disinherited you completely!"

Connor burst out laughing. It took her a moment to regain her composure before saying, "That's what's got you in an uproar, that my mother didn't leave me a dime?"

"Yes, it is," said Elaine, clearly baffled at Connor's reaction. "And I don't see the humor in it."

Laura laid a hand on Connor's arm. "Honey, perhaps you'd better explain."

Connor wiped her eyes. "I'm sorry, Elaine. Here you are, terribly concerned on my behalf, and I'm acting like a crazy person. But the fact is, I didn't want any of my mother's money or property. I have a nice home, I earn extremely good money, and I never could stand to be given something with strings attached. So this is perfect. The irony is that my mother thought she could punish me even after she was gone. But now that she's dead, I'd wager she really regrets having been so mean-spirited."

"Excuse me," said Elaine, frowning over her glasses. "Now that she's dead...?"

Laura intervened. "It's kind of a long story. Depends on whether you believe in the afterlife."

The lawyer shook her head. "I don't believe in anything I can't see, touch, hear, smell… I'm a show-me kinda gal."

"Missouri?" asked Connor with a smile.

"Actually, Montana."

"Good. So…did Mom split everything up between charities, or commission a building at her old prep school?"

"There were a few charitable bequests," replied Elaine. "But the house in Potomac and the bulk of the cash as well as non-liquid assets go to your daughter, Katy."

It was Connor's turn to be dumbstruck. "She did that? She left her estate to my daughter?"

"Almost everything."

Connor shook her head. "I'll be damned. I never thought she really cared about Katy, at least not since Alex and I were divorced."

"Apparently, she did. But I don't suppose she ever told you."

"No, but then we didn't have much in the way of quality time."

"I gathered that."

"So why am I here, then?" asked Connor.

"Two reasons. One, you *are* an heir. Your mother left you the sum of one dollar."

"Good legal strategy," Connor nodded. "That way I can't claim that a bequest to me was simply overlooked in the drafting of the will."

"Exactly. And two, you are named as your daughter's trustee. She doesn't get control of the full estate until she's twenty-five unless—"

"Unless what?"

"You waive the waiting period. It's up to you to decide if Katy is mature enough to handle the responsibility. It's a lot for a young person, and you may want to—"

Connor held up a hand. "You can stop right there. I know you only want to give me good advice, but this is just one more foolishness my mother dreamed up. Maybe she thought I would somehow turn into her, but that's not going to happen. And maybe she thought it would be some sort of nasty little joke to put me in charge of money that was supposed to be mine. But you know what? Katy is over twenty-one, and she's a levelheaded, smart young woman. As far as I'm concerned, she can have her inheritance right now."

Elaine shook her head. "You're sure?"

"Yes, I assume you have the waiver documents in that file."

The lawyer smiled a little sheepishly. "Actually, I do. But that's only because Eric is the best paralegal in the business and he's prepared for everything." She flipped through the manila folder until she found a particular sheaf of paper, then slid them across the desk. Connor took a pen from its brass holder and quickly scrawled her name and/or initials in all the places where little yellow stick-on arrows had been neatly affixed on each page.

"There," she said, replacing the pen in the stand. "Is that it?"

"Indeed it is," replied Elaine. "I have to say I didn't expect this to go quite so…um…smoothly."

"You may have gotten a slightly biased impression of me from my mother."

"Seems I did." The lawyer stood up. "If there's anything else I can help you with, let me know. I have a limited power of attorney and signatory rights to her bank accounts for the purposes of paying expenses, and I've already made payments to Ryerson's for the wake, the funeral, and the interment. If you find anything unsatisfactory, let me know. I'll be at the funeral tomorrow."

"Thanks, Elaine," said Connor, reaching to shake the woman's hand. "You appear to be one of my mother's better choices."

The lawyer blushed slightly. "All goes with the job. Nice to have met you, and you, too, Ms. Nez."

Outside, Laura slid her arm through Connor's as they walked to the car. "Nice lady. Not as sharkish as some lawyers I've known."

"We're not *all* ambulance chasers."

"I sometimes find it hard to think of you as an attorney."

"Former attorney is more like it."

"I thought it was a more or less permanent affliction," said Laura with a grin.

"Well, they don't exactly tattoo the word *esquire* on us when we pass the bar."

"True. I would know if they'd done that, now wouldn't I?"

Connor laughed. "Indeed you would."

*

The opulent, high-ceilinged reposing room at Ryerson's Funeral Home was already beginning to fill with visitors when Laura and Connor entered. They'd spent half an hour with Rick Ryerson, the senior funeral director, assuring him that everything looked just fine. He was so determined to please that Connor had a feeling Amanda's estate was paying top dollar for these arrangements. Rick had assured them that many flowers had been delivered during the day, but for the sake of appearances, his floral staff had still filled in with some large arrangements, including a magnificent casket spray of roses, lilies, orchids, freesia, and ivy. By the time all was put in place, the air was so heavy with floral scent, Connor asked one of the assistants to open a window. As she turned back toward the casket, she saw a lone guest standing behind it, between the casket and the wall.

That's odd, she thought. *Why would anyone squeeze back there?*

Connor moved along the wall, until she was parallel with the elderly woman. There was something familiar about her, but for Connor, whose distance vision was not what it had been in her younger days, the features of the woman's face were blurry. She moved closer, and then it hit her—the dark tweedy jacket, the longish skirt, the pale ascot—Connor's breath caught in her throat. "Grandmother?" she whispered as she stepped closer, her heart hammering. Still, the face and form did not come fully into focus, and yet…the eyes, those keen-sighted eyes—so familiar, so welcoming—were riveted on Connor. "Grandmother?" she said once more.

Yes, my child. I thought it best that you see me here. Of course, no one else can. She smiled. *Except perhaps your lovely companion. Not much escapes her notice.* Connor felt Laura beside her. *Greetings to you as well, Ms. Nez. I've come to help Amanda with her transition, though she's doing much better than I'd hoped. I was there with the two of you in the Dreamtime. Well done, child! And, Ms. Nez, stay alert.*

The late Gwendolyn Broadhurst quickly faded from sight.

Laura exhaled loudly. "Wow! That woman sure knows how to make an exit. I wonder what she meant by 'stay alert.'" She turned to Connor, whose cheeks were damp. Laura gently brushed away her tears. "You still miss Gwendolyn."

"Always," said Connor softly, still staring at the spot behind the casket. "She made my life bearable when I was young. Those long summers with her in England, those were the best times. And when I was older, she was still there, standing in the door of the cottage when I arrived, the tea service laid out, and somehow I thought she'd *always* be there. Sounds stupid. People always die eventually."

Laura put her hands on Connor's cheeks. "But she still *is* here, and you're one of the lucky few who understand that life never truly ends."

"Maybe, I mean, you're right. But...she can't hug me any-more."

*

For the next hour, Laura stuck close to Connor, who remained near the entrance door to welcome guests as they signed the guest book. She studiously avoided getting near the open casket, even though Rick had assured them the restoration was "perfection itself." Laura did likewise. She found the practice of viewing dead bodies as one of the least comprehensible of Anglo funeral rituals. But many visitors clearly did not share her reluctance. The line of people waiting to pass in front of the casket had grown to more than a dozen. Laura suspected a number of them were there out of ghoulish curiosity rather than grief over Amanda's untimely death. She yanked her attention from the queue of bejeweled matrons and their dark-suited husbands when she heard a familiar voice.

"You didn't think I'd miss being here, did you?" Malcolm was saying to Connor.

"But you just went to Boston. I figured you'd be too busy to come back."

"Never too busy for you. And Benjamin and I are taking the shuttle back tonight. We won't be here for the actual funeral."

"That's all right. My dad's probably uncomfortable enough being here tonight."

"I don't think it's all that unusual anymore—divorced spous-es attending a thing like this."

"Nice to know I'm part of a trend," said Connor's father as he joined them. He hugged his daughter, and then Laura. "I'm not sure Amanda would agree, though. This is probably annoying her, wherever she is."

"I wouldn't be so sure of that, Dad," replied Connor. "As a matter of fact, we need to chat about Mom when we have some time together."

Benjamin looked at her quizzically. "Okay. Sounds as if you know something I don't."

"Maybe. But in the meantime, don't worry about the past. It's a lot less important than we think."

"Senator!" boomed a voice from the line of people coming through the door.

Benjamin closed his eyes in a perfect imitation of martyrdom. "Please tell me that isn't Mariah Fulton."

"Sorry, Dad. I believe it is."

Malcolm whispered, "Who's Mariah Fulton?"

"Only the most unrelenting lobbyist in Washington. And rumor has it she sells stories to the newspapers to supplement her income."

Benjamin turned away from the little group. "I'll intercept her before she traps us all." He slid quickly through a gap in the crowd.

"What a guy," smiled Connor. "Sacrificing himself for our safety."

Malcolm could see over much of the milling crowd thanks to his significant height advantage. "That woman with the big hair and horsy face?"

Connor peered between heads and shoulders. "Yep. Though I doubt she'd appreciate the description."

"She won't be bothering you and Laura," Malcolm declared firmly.

"You're not going to arrest her, are you?" said Laura. "I'm not sure bad hair is grounds for slapping on the cuffs."

"Humph!" was Malcolm's response.

Connor smiled. "He's big enough that we can just hide right behind him. She'll never see us."

"Let's go find some refreshments," suggested Laura.

They edged away from the incoming traffic with Malcolm providing a rearguard presence and were circumnavigating the room when Connor suddenly stopped. "Oh, shit!" she hissed.

Laura, squeezed between her lover and Malcolm, who hadn't been warned of the abrupt halt and thus bumped into them both, and tried to see what had so alarmed Connor. "What?"

"Alex's mother."

Laura had to think for a second to make the connection. "Ah, your former mother-in-law."

"Yes. If there's a Connor Hawthorne rabid anti-fan club out there, she would be its president."

Laura looked past Connor's shoulder toward the buffet table. "Which one?"

"Black suit with the pearls."

Laura frowned. "That describes half the women in here."

"Plate in one hand, highball glass in the other, really red lipstick… She's just to the left of the guy with his arm in a sling."

"Yes, I see her. I don't know if I've ever seen anyone stand up quite that straight."

"No choice. She's old school—super-hold girdle, long-line bra with stays, the whole shebang."

"Ouch."

"Tell me about it. My mother tried to make me wear all that so I'd fit into a size smaller wedding dress."

"And did you?"

"I flatly refused. I called it the armor of the virgin. I remember saying who in their right mind would want to work their way through all that rubber and nylon."

"Look out, I think she's seen you."

"Yep," said Connor, firmly arranging her face in what she hoped was a pleasant expression. "Now we'll find out if a funeral setting will require her to be marginally civil to me."

Cecily Vandervere was coming right at them, her ruthlessly lifted and separated bosom parting the crowds like the figurehead on an ancient Greek warship. The man with whom she'd been speaking, the one with his right arm in a cloth sling, followed uncertainly in her wake.

Malcolm, who'd finally gotten the relayed message from Laura about the woman approaching, moved around so that his bulk deftly prevented Mrs. Vandervere from getting too close to Connor.

"Lydia," she said, her nose wrinkling as if offended by an unpleasant odor.

"Cecily," replied Connor tonelessly.

"My condolences. Your mother was a fine woman."

"Indeed she was."

Mrs. Vandervere frowned. Clearly she thought protocol required that Connor thank people for expressing condolences and make suitably appropriate comments, thereby leaving a conversational opening. Laura could see that Connor was refusing to play the game and silently applauded her restraint. Just as Laura was about to say something suitably innocuous, the man who'd been standing behind Cecily Vandervere pressed slightly forward, as if buffeted by the growing crowd of guests tempted by the free Nova Scotia salmon and imported pâté de foie gras. The back of Laura's neck tingled with electricity and she stared at the man. His gaze was fixed on Connor, and the man's expression startled Laura badly. She didn't know who he was, but she instantly knew *what* he was. The man was a hunter.

In an instant, her practiced eye took in the slightly askew toupee, the moustache that didn't quite match the hair, and the eyeglasses that were too broad for his face. Finally, something triggered his awareness and he swiveled his head toward Laura. His dilated pupils were fathomless black discs floating in a web of tiny bloodshot veins. She shivered slightly and quickly pushed forward, determined to put herself between Connor and the stranger.

Malcolm, too, had given the fellow with the sling a second glance, an old habit from days working special security details. He didn't necessarily see what Laura had, but his own little inner voice seemed to be clearing its throat to say something. The man looked vaguely familiar. And yet... Then Laura moved, and Malcolm was obliged to shift his bulk to the side. His left arm came in contact with the man's sling for a few seconds, and that's when his internal alarms went off. Where there should have been a man's arm, he'd felt something hard and unyielding, something metallic. His instincts screamed, *Gun!* He swiveled around abruptly, with Laura right beside him. The man slipped sideways behind Cecily Vandervere, his eyes shifting back and forth between the two people now totally focused on him.

Malcolm stepped sideways, his body an effective shield, and reached out with his left hand to grasp whatever lay concealed in the sling. Laura said, "Excuse me, Mrs. Vandervere," and none too gently pushed the woman toward Connor. Instantly she had a clear view of the man's other arm, and his closed left fist in which something silvery and metallic shone in the soft light. That fist was headed straight for Malcolm's hand as it closed around the man's right arm. She saw the shank of a needle and reacted instantly. Laura grabbed the man's wrist and twisted his arm, pushing back hard against him. She heard Malcolm beside her: "Shit! What was that?" Laura looked down and saw a thin line of blood well up on the back of Malcolm's hand. The stranger jerked his wrist from Laura's grip in that brief moment she was distracted by Malcolm's injury. He backed up quickly, ignoring the indignant protests of the guests behind him.

Drinks sloshed, plates of hors d'oeuvres were overturned.

Thirty feet away, Benjamin felt a surge of anxiety flow through him. Ignoring the guest extending his hand in greeting, he turned toward where he'd last seen his daughter. He couldn't find her, but he instantly picked out Malcolm, and the back of Laura's hair. Where was Connor? Then he heard the raised voices and saw Malcolm moving toward the other door into the corridor. But then the big man stopped and even from a distance, Benjamin could see something was very wrong.

Laura, torn between the desire to stay near Connor in case the man with the fake sling had other allies in the room, and her instinctive response—catch the guy—chose the latter. The voice in her head said, *Go!* She fell in right behind Malcolm, whose bulk was clearing the way, and checked side to side for additional threats. Thus it was that she ran right into Malcolm's back when he stopped. His shoulders sagged and he swayed backward toward her. She had the absurd thought that she might be able to catch him if he fell. "Malcolm, what's wrong?" she asked, trying to turn him around.

"Laura, what happened?" Benjamin was at her right elbow. He and Laura finally managed to move around in front of Malcolm as the other guests stared at them with frank curiosity.

"I don't know. We were going after that man in the gray suit with one arm in a sling." She looked at Malcolm's hand. It was still bleeding. "The guy scratched him with something, a needle maybe."

"What's wrong with me?" Malcolm's words were slurred and heavy. "We gotta…we gotta get…" His eyes closed and he swayed even more on his feet.

Benjamin quickly lifted one of Malcolm's eyelids. The pupils were enormous. "We have to get him out of here."

Connor burst through the ring of onlookers. "What the hell is…"

she began, then stared at her friend. "Good God, is he sick? What is it?"

"We'll figure it out later," said Benjamin. "You two grab his other arm." Benjamin slid his left arm through Malcolm's right and stood close to steady him. At the same time, he snatched the cell phone out of his coat pocket and hit a speed-dial number.

"Emergency pick-up," he barked, giving the address and orders to come to the rear entrance. He then rattled of a complex series of letters and numbers that Connor and Laura both recognized as a code giving both clearance and specific instructions, before snapping the phone shut. "We've got to get him out of here and, I think, keep him as upright as possible."

"Why didn't you just call the Rescue Squad, Dad?"

"A hunch. Don't ask me where it came from, but it was clear as a bell. There's a transport coming from Bethesda Naval. It's less than two miles from here, and they have a crew on instant response standby twenty-four hours a day. They were scrambling the ambulance before I hung up."

"You think you know what's wrong with him, don't you?" said Connor as they struggled to walk the big guy down the hall to the rear door. Malcolm was mumbling incoherently and stumbling over his feet.

"Maybe, though I'm not sure. But his eyes, and his lips, they're turning blue. And look at his nail beds. Reminds me of the reaction to some toxins I saw in the Far East."

"Like venom?" asked Laura. "Seems I heard you use the code calling for antivenin to be on hand."

"I did, just in case."

"Is there a problem?" Rick Ryerson appeared beside them, clearly alarmed. "Does your friend need to lie down? There's a couch in my office."

"We've called for an ambulance," said Benjamin. "Just show us the quickest way to your back entrance."

"An ambulance! But...well, I suppose, if it's in the back. It's just that I hate to make a scene. We try to—"

"The door, sir!" Benjamin snapped.

"Of course, of course. Right this way."

By the time they got outside and propped Malcolm against a wall, they could already hear a siren in the distance.

Rick Ryerson clearly didn't know quite what to do. He paced back and forth, opened his mouth twice to say something, then changed his mind. Finally, Connor put a hand on his arm. "Rick, it would be a great service to us if you would let the guests know that our friend became ill, possibly a heart problem, and they are welcome to stay as long as they wish. If you would act as host, I'd appreciate it."

The funeral director sighed with relief. "Naturally. Yes, of course. I'll make sure everything runs smoothly until the last person leaves." He disappeared into the building.

Connor put her hands on Malcolm's barrel chest, and swallowed hard. "You keep breathing, you big idiot! Don't you dare die on me!"

They heard the squeal of tires, and a wholly innocuous white panel van sped around the rear corner of the building. Its only distinguishing feature was a light bar of revolving red lamps on top. On the doors, in small letters, were the words MEDICAL RESPONSE TEAM. They slid to a halt, and two paramedics jumped down from the back as a third came out of the passenger seat. Within seconds they were half carrying Malcolm toward the rear of the van.

The driver called to Benjamin. "Got here as fast as we could, sir."

"Thank you," he replied. "Now let's get going. Connor, you want to ride in the back?"

"Yep," she said, trotting around the van.

Benjamin and Laura climbed into the front, and the driver pulled down a jump seat in the center for Laura. As soon as he heard the back door slam, he stepped on the gas.

"Sir, about your code for the problem…" He eyed the two women cautiously.

Benjamin said, "Speak up, lieutenant. Ms. Nez has clearance about ten levels above you."

"You didn't say what sort of antivenin was needed."

"I'm not even sure it is needed, but it's a strong possibility."

"They're administering temporary measures. We'll be at the intake in under five minutes… What the hell!" The driver was reaching for the siren switch as he swung out of the driveway, and almost collided with an ambulance on its way in. "Did you call someone else just in case?"

"No, I didn't," said Benjamin, his brow creased with a frown.

"Well, maybe someone else called 911 on their own."

"Maybe."

"Or maybe not," said Laura, reading her former boss's mind.

The lieutenant jammed down the accelerator. "Funny about that ambulance, though. This area's covered by the Bethesda-Chevy Chase Rescue Squad, and that sure wasn't one of their units."

"No," said Benjamin, thoughtfully. "It certainly wasn't." He turned to Laura. "I've got a team fanning out to look for our man with the sling, but what are the odds?"

Laura shrugged. "Slim to none. The guy's no amateur."

Chapter Eleven

*Ein einziger dankbarer Gedanke gen Himmel
ist das vollkommenste Gebet.
(One single grateful thought raised to heaven is a perfect prayer.)*
—Gotthold Ephraim Lessing, *Minna von Barnhelm*

Arthur Raley tried to control his fury as the white van flew by the ambulance in which he was riding. Within a minute and a half of leaving the funeral home, he'd abandoned his disguise and donned a paramedic uniform. The hired attendants and stolen ambulance were waiting less than a mile away. But they were late arriving to pick him up around the corner from the funeral home. Still, he thought they'd have time. People usually panicked in medical emergencies, running around trying to decide what to do. That had clearly not been the case. The white van leaving the driveway screamed "government" to Raley, which meant the whole plan, now a complete shambles, had been flawed from the very beginning because it had not taken into account the long reach of Benjamin Hawthorne. Arthur Raley silently cursed Friedrich. Unbeknownst to Devin Underwood, Arthur was now dealing directly with Devin's boss. Arthur rather liked the idea of playing both ends against the middle, especially when there was the glimmer of a true prize at the end of it all. The intrigue was a welcome respite from the tiresome routine of his career—take a contract, kill the target, collect the fee.

Thus he'd accepted the risks of the plan outlined by Friedrich, even though it seemed unnecessarily public. But as the old man had pointed out, Connor Hawthorne was almost never alone. She had the pendant. Friedrich wanted it. She must be separated from her friends and family so that the artifact could be recovered. Carrying out an abduction under the guise of a medical emergency would reduce the chance of anyone intervening. Arthur had gone to the funeral home armed with a syringe and his favorite light .22 hidden in a sling. In it he'd placed a preparation of snake venom and tranquilizer designed to make the human body mimic the signs of a heart attack. Even in the relatively likely event there were a doctor present at the wake, deliberate poisoning would not be anyone's first thought.

According to plan, he'd get close enough to the Hawthorne woman to inject a modest amount of the poison, just enough to make her collapse. The rest he would hold in reserve in case anyone interfered. Then he would shout that he'd called an ambulance. When the unit arrived, the men inside, discreetly armed with stun guns, had strict orders that no one was allowed to accompany the patient. Within seconds, they'd be gone, and then a deal would be struck. Connor Hawthorne's return in exchange for the pendant. Friedrich was certain that the father and the girlfriend would acquiesce instantly.

The strategy had failed miserably. Even though he'd managed to get almost close enough by following that odious woman around the room and pretending to be with her as they approached the target, he'd been unable to slip by Mrs. Vandervere. So intent had he been on finding an opening, he'd noticed too late that the Indian woman was staring at him, and not in a friendly way. She'd moved toward him purposefully, drawing the attention of the big black guy next to her. Arthur had known from the moment the cop brushed against the sling that the gun was no longer a secret. He saw it in the cop's eyes, and Arthur needed a diversion. He slipped the syringe from its mini-holster in the left coat pocket and raised it just as Laura Nez grabbed his wrist. He fought her off, backing away, as the cop reached for him. Arthur stabbed at the man's hand, the only good target he could find. But his angle was bad. Even though he pushed the plunger all the way down, the needle was skipping across the cop's hand. Arthur knew it hadn't really sunk beneath the epidermis. Still, it should have been enough to drop the son of a bitch in his tracks. It hadn't, and Arthur did the only thing he could do—he ran.

Even in his flight, however, he kept his wits about him. He had the sling off and his radio out before he'd reached the rear fire door, its alarm disconnected earlier. At the very least, he could still get rid of the evidence of the toxin. His phony paramedics could pick up the cop and dump him somewhere, maybe even cremate the body just in case. Arthur prided himself on his ability to keep one step ahead of failure. This time, however, he'd been one step behind.

The speed with which the Hawthornes and the Indian woman had dealt with the crisis was breathtaking. If he weren't so angry, he could almost admire their tactical sense. But as he watched his quarry speeding away in the white van, he silently cursed them, and Friedrich, too, for seriously underestimating the depth of the resources on which Benjamin Hawthorne could call. The subtle markings on the van hadn't fooled Arthur. He knew who they were, and only an individual with pervasive influence and high security clearance could have ordered up a team in so short a time. Now, even if the black cop died, they'd know how it had been done. That was the inherent weakness in using an unusual method— the more esoteric the weapon, the more obvious a trail it could leave. And disguised or not, he knew Laura Nez had seen him up close. That would have to remedied at the earliest possible moment. For now, he needed to cover his tracks here in Washington. He had no intention of spending any more time in the Hawthorne's home territory. In Washington, D.C., they clearly had the advantage.

Arthur directed his hired help to drive the ambulance into Rock Creek Park where he said he'd hidden their transfer vehicle. Even with the aid of streetlamps, the area was almost pitch black in the shadows. The driver parked, switched off the lights. Before he could open the door, however, Arthur put a bullet into the back of his head. The man in the passenger seat barely had time to register his partner's slumping over the steering wheel before he received the same treatment. The third man, riding in the back with Arthur, had already been dead for a full minute.

He got out of the ambulance, quietly closed the door, and slipped into the trees. The unit would be found soon, he supposed, but there was nothing to connect him to it. The D.C. cops would puzzle over three dead men in a stolen emergency vehicle, probably find out they were low-level scumbags, and file it away. Arthur took very seriously the perhaps apocryphal pirate maxim: Dead men tell no tales. Which is why he was rather hoping Malcolm Jefferson was among them.

*

Miles away, in a secured area of Bethesda Naval, Malcolm Jefferson was on complete life support and fighting for his life.

Doctors had as yet not identified the precise composition of the poison that had been injected into his hand. A Navy commander, however, had confirmed Benjamin's suspicion that some type of venom had been administered. He'd prescribed a protocol of antivenin treatments, but the patient was not responding as expected. The commander had sent blood samples for a tox screen. They'd know more within a half hour.

In the meantime, Laura, Connor, and Benjamin paced the waiting area.

"Should we call his sister, Eve?" asked Connor.

Benjamin shook his head. "I've sent a car for her, and they'll drop off someone to watch the kids. I hate to worry her, but it wouldn't be fair if anything…" His voiced trailed off.

"What about Ayalla?" Laura suggested.

"She's too far away to do anything but worry. Let's wait until we know something more definite."

Connor went and got three cups of tepid coffee, and they tried to distract themselves with an informal debriefing. Connor, of course, had not realized what was happening, as her view was almost entirely obstructed by the armored bulk of Cecily Vandervere. She'd only vaguely noticed the man behind her.

Laura had gotten a good look as well as a strong sense of familiarity. She sat quietly on a chair and let the images play, while mentally stripping away the hairpiece and moustache. It was a skill few could master, as facial hair was the one characteristic that most often confused eyewitnesses. A man looked strikingly different with a beard or moustache. But she built a composite in her head of the man's face clean-shaven, and within a few minutes she was fairly sure. "Benjamin, you wouldn't happen to have those surveillance photos of Devin Underwood you got from the NSA guys?"

"No, they're in a file I put in the safe at my apartment.

Thought it would be more secure. I can call and see if Jeannine's still there, though at this hour I doubt it."

"That's all right. We'll look at it later. But I think the man who attacked Malcolm is the same one in the photograph with Devin Underwood.

Benjamin thought hard. "Raley. His name was Arthur Raley."

Laura nodded. "Yes. I'm almost sure of it. Something about the shape of his nose and the set of his eyes."

"Those pictures were taken with telephoto lenses, hon. Not very sharp."

Laura shrugged. "I know. But still…"

"If you say so, I tend to agree," said Benjamin. "I've rarely known you to be wrong about an identification."

"Actually, I kind of wish I were wrong."

"Why?" asked Connor. "This gives us a lead."

"In that sense, it's a good thing," agreed Laura, "but on the other hand, it also means that our suspicions about the death of Grace's mother and the limousine being sabotaged aren't just suspicions anymore." She waved toward the door of the emergency bay where Malcolm was being treated. "All of this is connected—Underwood, Arthur Raley, someone searching our room at the B&B, getting shot at in Boston." She paused. "And that pendant. Ever since we got the information from the Carlisles, I've been thinking about it, and someone wants it."

"But why?" asked Connor, frowning. "It's just an old amulet with a colorful history behind it—not to mention Grace has only half of it."

"Correction, sweetheart. *We* have only half of it. And since we've had it, there have been at least two attempts to kill one of us, probably you."

Connor took a deep breath. "Gee, thanks."

"Sorry. But think about it. Grace gave *you* the pendant.

Someone knows that. Granted, that shot in the dark the other night could have easily been for either of us, but today that man was looking right at you, not me, not Malcolm, and certainly not Benjamin. His attention was completely focused. I have a feeling that either the gun or the needle was for you. I tend to think it was the needle."

"Why?"

Benjamin spoke up. "The other ambulance."

"What other ambulance?" asked Connor.

"When we left the funeral home," Benjamin explained. "we almost ran into a paramedic unit coming into the parking lot."

"So? Maybe one of the staff called."

"But they would have called the rescue squad. This unit had the wrong markings completely. It might even have been from a private company. So why was it responding, unless it was stand-ing by for a *prearranged* emergency? If our van hadn't arrived so fast, I'd be willing to bet they were going to snatch the victim and be out of there before anyone was the wiser."

Laura nodded. "And the victim was supposed to be you."

Connor looked baffled. "But why? Why make up such an elaborate scheme? They could go steal the damn thing out of the hotel safe more easily than commit a kidnapping or a murder in front of a roomful of witnesses."

Laura pondered that for a moment. "But they don't know where we put the pendant. I don't think the goal was killing you, at least not right away."

"Boy, you're really a breath of sunshine today, aren't you?

Laura shrugged again and extended her hands, palms up. "What can I say, sweetie? You'd hate it if I just made stuff up Pollyanna-style."

"I suppose."

"So your theory is kidnapping?"

"They may have decided it would be more expeditious to simply offer to trade you back for the pendant."

"But I still don't get it! That stupid necklace. Its importance is based on a legend, for crying out loud. A legend, I might add, we don't even know much about."

Benjamin put his hand on Connor's shoulder. "Well, someone knows about it, besides the Carlisles and people in their circle. And that someone is relatively obsessed with the idea of having it to risk an abduction like this. But we're going to catch up on information very shortly. The Carlisles left a message at my office. They were delayed leaving England, but they'll be here in time for the funeral tomorrow."

"They're coming here?" asked Connor. "Because of the pendant?"

Benjamin frowned slightly. "No. They're coming for Amanda's funeral. It just happens that they'll also be able to tell us some things we need to know."

Connor shook her head. "Sorry. It's just that I didn't think they knew Mom very well."

"They didn't. But they loved Gwendolyn. And Gwendolyn loved her daughter, despite everything that happened between them. William and Ellen have never felt anything but compassion for your mother's difficulties. They're paying their respects and honoring the lineage that you and Amanda and Gwendolyn are part of."

"Funny, it's still hard to think of her that way."

Laura cocked her head to one side. "What way?"

"As being related to me and my grandmother. Mom hated everything that she thought made Gwendolyn seem strange. She didn't want to believe in anything mysterious or magical."

"Your mom just didn't know who she really was," said Laura. "That she had a beautiful soul."

"I'm starting to see that, especially since the dream I had the other night. All my life, I felt so separate from her. There were times I couldn't even believe we were related."

"But you know," Laura smiled, "you look like your mom and your grandmother."

"True." She stood up. "I need some more coffee. How about you guys?"

Benjamin and Laura demurred, and Connor walked down the corridor.

"I'm anxious to get back to Boston," said Benjamin. "Maybe day after tomorrow. We *all* need to put our heads together."

Laura looked toward the treatment room door again. "You sound pretty confident there, Benjamin. You think we'll all be going back."

"Yes," said Benjamin firmly. "This team isn't losing any members. That's the only thing I'm allowing myself to believe."

"I'm with you, Dad," added Connor, appearing around the corner of the waiting area.

"Me, too," Laura agreed. "Now, did you tell your Dad who we saw at the wake?"

*

"You can be as angry as you wish," the elderly physician sighed. "But if you won't agree to the treatments, there's nothing more I can do for you."

Friedrich gripped his old leather swagger stick so hard his knuckles were white. He wanted to leap across the desk and throttle the stupid old quack with his bare hands. But it had been many decades since Friedrich could have actually done so. He had to content himself with imagining the satisfaction of cartilage crushing under his once-iron grip.

"You know perfectly well the radiation and chemotherapy would leave me completely immobilized. I have…I have a business to run."

"The tumors are inoperable. Three years ago, perhaps…" The doctor shrugged. "As it is, the surgery on the lymph nodes has only the slightest chance of success, and the brain, well, the infiltration is too profound. Removing it would leave you a vegetable, *mein Herr*. Four other specialists agree with me."

Friedrich closed his eyes for a brief moment. A shudder of despair ran through him. "Then how long?" he barked. "Tell me how long."

The physician shook his head. "These are only estimates."

"I said, how *long*?!"

"Three months," the man said softly. "Perhaps only a few weeks until your motor skills are affected, your ability to think and reason seriously compromised. The brain will go before the rest of the body. It has already begun."

Friedrich stood, with some little effort. "Get out! Get out of my house!"

The physician shook his head, and picked up his black case, seemingly unfazed by Friedrich's fury. "I'll be back if you need me."

"Never come here again!"

"As you wish."

As the door closed, a soft beep signaled a call on the secure line. Friedrich breathed deeply and picked it up. No doubt his plans were proceeding. He'd had to accelerate the timetable, and act more aggressively than prudence dictated. But all alone in his sanctuary he had to admit that he was running out of time. If he were to survive to see at least the beginning of the new order, no one could be allowed to bar his way. The phone beeped again. Raley would be reporting his successful acquisition of their bargaining chip. That realization alone made him stand a little taller, despite the pain in his limbs. "Your report," he snapped as he recognized the voice on the other end. He stood there mute, the sibilance of the caller's voice through the receiver the only sound in the darkened room. The voice stopped. Friedrich said nothing. But his anger could not be contained. He slammed the phone onto the surface of the antique desk so hard that plastic pieces flew. Again and again, until there was nothing left but one bit of circuitry at the end of the cord.

✳

"He's stable and the prognosis is good," the Navy commander announced, as he banged through the swinging door.

"What does that mean, exactly?" demanded Connor.

The officer scrubbed the hours-old stubble on his face. "That the treatment protocol is working. His vital signs are much stronger, and we'll probably be taking him off the ventilator in a few hours. He even had a spike of consciousness, started to fight the trachea tube. Strong guy."

"Yeah, he is," said Connor, tears of relief glistening in the corners of her eyes.

"The tests came back showing the venom was laced with an animal tranquilizer."

"Good God," said Benjamin. "That could have killed him."

"A full syringe could have," the doctor nodded. "But scans of the injection site showed the needle didn't go very deep. Mostly skittered across the skin, like the guy aimed and missed while he was pressing the plunger. Anyway, I'll ask the orderly to keep you updated."

Connor turned to Laura. "He's gonna *make* it," she shouted.

They hugged each other hard, then reached out to include Benjamin in the group embrace. "Looks like you and Malcolm are finally even, sweetheart," said Connor.

Laura looked puzzled. "Even?"

"Don't be modest. From what the doctor said, if it hadn't been for you grabbing the guy's arm, Malcolm would be dead."

"I think that's leaping to conclusions," replied Laura. "I didn't really do much of anything. I shouldn't have let go of his wrist at all. Then he might not have gotten the syringe even close to Malcolm."

"Well, when you're done critiquing your performance, I'll remind you that ever since Malcolm showed up in the New Mexico desert and carried you out on a stretcher, you've been itching to return the favor. Now you have. Be glad!"

"All I'm glad about is that he's alive. Next time I save his life, I'm going to do it in a much more definitive way, so that he doesn't end up in the hospital on life support."

"You're impossible," grinned Connor. "Dad, can we contact the driver who's bringing Eve in? I want her to stop worrying at the first possible moment."

"Already on it," he said, and they turned to see him with the phone to his ear.

"Let's go downstairs and meet her," suggested Connor. "And then food. I'm starving."

"How is it you can go from queasy with worry to flat-out ravenous in under five minutes?"

"Just little old mercurial me," Connor replied.

"Hmm," said Laura. "Is that anything like moody?"

"Nope. Mundane people are moody. Interesting people are mercurial."

Laura chuckled. "Good. I'd hate to think I've fallen in love with a mundane person."

*

Ayalla Franklin grabbed her handbag and briefcase and slammed her office door behind her. A couple of the other agents turned to stare, but she kept walking toward the elevator. Not until she reached the nearly empty parking garage and slid into the driver's seat of her agency vehicle did she allow herself to really breathe. When she did, the tears came—tears so unexpected, and to her mind unwarranted, that she wiped them from her cheeks and stared at her damp fingers in dismay. Why? Malcolm Jefferson would be all right, or so Benjamin had told her. She had a strong sense that he'd downplayed the gravity of the original situation, but she knew he wouldn't lie to her about Malcolm's survival, and of that, he assured her, there was no doubt.

Oddly, she was sort of angry. It seemed every time Malcolm got involved with Connor and Laura, he took stupid chances and risked his life. She resented it, or maybe simply wished she herself was someone for whom he'd risk his life. Yet knowing him as well as she did, she thought he probably would be just as protective toward her.

She took a tissue from her bag and daubed at her eyes. Maybe she was crying out of sheer relief that he was all right. But even that bothered her. Emotional ties were the last thing she needed right now. For that reason alone, she'd kept Malcolm at arm's length. She cared about him, but she was terrified to realize there might be more to it than that. Ayalla had the absurdly impractical urge to drive straight to the airport and take the next shuttle to D.C. It was more than an urge, really. She *needed* to see with her own eyes that he was all right. She wanted so much to hold his hand, hear his voice.

Get a grip, girl. This isn't a damn soap opera. Ayalla shook her head as if to banish the rampant sentimentality that threatened her ordered mental world. There was work to do here. Benjamin had shared their theory that Arthur Raley had been the one who had attacked Malcolm. The only lead she had to him was Devin Underwood. It was time for a chat with the funeral director.

*

From the Personal Journal of Jack Fortis

It was only by accident I learned the importance of the pendant that Mistress Eliza wore until the day she passed it along to her eldest daughter. I knew it had been her mother's, for I'd seen it around her ladyship's neck on one occasion, and thought it merely a keepsake. The one I'd seen the mistress wear didn't look quite the same, but supposed it was only a poor memory on my part.

Then one day whilst I was working in the kitchen, I overheard Mistress Eliza and Master Fitzhugh in the pantry. I might say they were arguing a bit. And I didn't understand it all. But the master kept insisting that the pendant was "harmless"—that's what he said all right, "harmless"—without the other half. But the mistress said she'd been having dreams about it, and something bad was going to happen with the other half. That's when I realized why the pendant didn't look right. The one her ladyship had worn was different, fuller somehow. And it had been of silver and gold. The mistress's piece was only of gold.

They stopped talking all of a sudden–like, and I crept away, not wanting to be thought to spy on them. But my mind kept going back to what she said, and I wondered if her ladyship had kept the other half and what had become of it.

Mistress Eliza, even then, had not been told of her mother's treatment at the hands of the duke, and I, for one, hoped she would never know.

*

"You think we should have stayed at the hospital?" asked Connor as they filed wearily into Benjamin's apartment at his private club, leaving their dripping raincoats in the foyer.

"Eve was there," said Laura. "And I think it was a family sort of time."

"We're family!" protested Connor.

"In a manner of speaking, hon. But still, she's his sister, and I think she wanted to sit by his bed and do some praying."

"She is the prayingest lady I've ever known," said Connor.

"Works for her," Laura said. "Personally, I do a fair amount of praying, just not the same way."

Benjamin, who'd stepped into the bedroom to shed his jacket and tie, returned with a the case file he'd begun compiling. "Gwendolyn told me you can live your life as one ongoing prayer."

Connor's brow creased slightly. "You believe that?"

"Probably, though I can't say I've ever mastered the path."

"Path? What, you think it's some kind of Zen or something? Or maybe living in a convent."

"Your grandmother hardly struck me as a Buddhist," Benjamin smiled. "And she certainly wasn't nun material."

"Too opinionated, you think?" smiled Connor.

"At the very least."

"I understand what she meant," volunteered Laura. "It's not much different from what my own grandmother taught me. The Navajo desires to live in harmony with the natural world, with his fellow beings… It's all part of the whole. I think Gwendolyn was talking about living your life in resonance or maybe alignment with the Creator."

Connor sighed. "Why does theology have to be so complicated? And ambiguous!"

Laura shook her head. "Honey, I don't think we're talking theology. It's just *being*. And there's nothing ambiguous about that."

"Being how?"

"Loving, I think. Kind, nonjudgmental, stuff like that."

"That last one...not my strongest suit."

Benjamin laughed. "It's very hard, daughter of mine. You a lawyer, me a politician and a spook. Not exactly ashram material, are we?"

Laura put her hands on her hips. "You're both impossible, and Benjamin, you're full of it. You're one of the most spiritual men I've ever known."

The ex-senator looked at her with some surprise. "Seriously?"

"Very," said Laura. "And Connor knows full well who she is and what she can do."

"Do not!" said Connor, her emphatic denial belied by the upturned corners of her mouth.

"All right. That's it. Topic closed. Let's look at the photos again." Laura flopped down on the comfortable sofa. Benjamin began spreading out the papers and photos. Connor read the reports while Laura leafed through the photos. "I'm certain," she said, finally. "This the man who injected Malcolm." Her finger tapped the glossy print. "Arthur Raley is now at the very top of my personal shit list."

*

Unaware that he, himself, was the topic of discussion, Arthur Raley stood in a steady downpour a half-block from the club where Benjamin Hawthorne had lived since his divorce. Had Raley known he was being discussed by name (at least his most common alias), he would have been somewhat alarmed. As it was, he knew his face was imprinted on at least one person's memory. And if the black guy survived, that would be at least two. He still hadn't been able to confirm whether Jefferson had died. He guessed where the man must have been taken, but the security unit at Bethesda Naval was not your average hospital. You didn't just call up, pretending to be a relative.

A quick reconnaissance of Benjamin Hawthorne's building had revealed first-rate security and vigilant staff. No one entered through the front or rear without authorization. He wouldn't be able to get at them while they were in there. But he couldn't trust to fate that they wouldn't leave in the middle of the night. So he'd dressed in a private security guard uniform and posted himself as close as possible to the entrance. And still it rained. Every inch of his clothing was soaked and he stood there cursing the day he'd ever heard from Devin Underwood. And he was now reconsidering having contacted Devin's deranged boss, Friedrich.

At first, learning of Friedrich's existence had pleased him because he'd suspected for some time that there was a single mind controlling the actions and direction of the Supreme Aryan Brotherhood. But he'd never been admitted to their inner circle, and they were obsessed with maintaining a cloak of secrecy even Arthur could not breach. But he had certainly heard of the "Doktor," an almost mythical figure in Nazi lore. That the man was alive and kicking added an entirely new dimension to the drama. Since Arthur always preferred dealing with the top man, he'd been in touch with Friedrich only hours after he'd gotten the information out of Devin Underwood. He was greeted first with terse denial, but a brief résumé of Arthur's career allayed the old man's suspicions. Arthur was impressed. The one-time Reich officer was quite a strategist and knew when he'd acquired a potentially valuable asset. He'd quickly sketched out the plan to get hold of Connor Hawthorne. Arthur had agreed to carry it out, without revealing that it was Devin who'd given Friedrich's identity away. He fully intended to play both ends of this game, to see who got to the prize first.

Unfortunately, Friedrich's bold *Blitzkrieg* strategy had backfired badly, and Arthur had called to relay the results. Now, *that* had been a weird conversation. One minute he was talking to the guy, and the next, all he heard was loud banging, as if the receiver had been dropped at the other end, and then silence. Something about that silence worried Arthur, but he there wasn't much he could do about it. Reluctantly, he'd dialed the call again, only to be greeted with an answering machine. He hung up.

For the time being, he needed to focus on three things—eliminating as many of the opposition as possible, cashing in on this huge payoff that both Devin Underwood and Friedrich were promising, and not getting caught by either the authorities or the rabid inner circle of the S.A.B. This would constitute a full-time job. Arthur was beginning to think about retirement, and as he stood in the cold rain, he decided to move up the timetable. A warm beach, a cold beer, and a succession of women. He simply needed this one last addition to his already sizable accounts in the Caymans and in Zurich. But he'd always believed you could never have too much security for the future. And part of that security lay in killing everyone associated with this travesty of an operation.

CHAPTER TWELVE

When vain desire at last and vain regret
Go hand in hand to death.
—Dante Gabriel Rosetti, *The House of Life: The One Hope*

Well after midnight, Devin Underwood was finally slipping into a Nembutol-induced sleep when his doorbell rang. His first thought was that the sound was part of this weird dream he'd been having, the kind of dream that floats into the human mind when it balances on the border between waking and sleeping. In his dream, people were running back and forth in an enormous graveyard, and they kept stopping to ask Devin where their relatives were buried. He had a map in his hand, but the print was so small he couldn't read the numbers. Then someone said it was closing time, and he heard a warning bell…but his mind finally registered that it was his own doorbell ringing repeatedly. He shook himself awake, groaned, and stumbled out into the hallway. "Who the fuck is it?" he snarled, but didn't wait for an answer before flinging open the door. He instantly wished he'd looked through the peephole first.

Under other circumstances, Special Agent Ayalla Franklin would have been amused. Devin Underwood was a well-endowed young man who apparently slept in the nude. His shock at seeing an FBI agent at his door, followed by the sudden realization that he wasn't dressed, made him blush to the very roots of his hair, and Ayalla decided that phrase applied to *all* his hair. Underwood stepped back, tried to cover himself and look indignant at the same time. It didn't work.

"Perhaps you'd like to get a robe, or something," said Ayalla, walking past him into the living room. He started to follow her, obviously to protest her presence, but his lack of clothing precluded an extended argument. By the time he returned in a T-shirt and boxer shorts, Ayalla was firmly ensconced in the chair by the gas fireplace—his chair, of course. She knew every technique for getting the upper hand in an interrogation, and she didn't think this one would require her entire bag of tricks. Without his expensive clothes and perfectly styled hair, Devin Underwood looked young—and more than a little scared. She also noted the dilated pupils and slightly slack-jawed expression. Some sort of drug, she supposed, and whether it was legally obtained might prove an interesting sideline to her inquiries.

"Look," he protested, "you can't just come barging in here in the middle of the night."

"I don't think I barged, Mr. Underwood. I rang the doorbell; you opened it. I walked in, and I don't recall you asking me not to sit down."

"Well, I couldn't very well do that, now could I? Not with…" he squirmed. "Well, not under the circumstances."

"I do apologize for the late hour, but you see, some new developments have come up in this investigation. I thought it would be prudent to consult you immediately." Her tone was almost a purr.

Underwood's eyes narrowed slightly, but she'd caught his interest. He relaxed ever so slightly, enough to take a seat on the couch that faced the fireplace. "About what, exactly?"

"Because it was your firm's limousine that was involved," she continued, "I thought it wise to let you know that we have a lead on the person who may have set the charges that blew up the car, and, of course, the three victims."

"Three?"

Ayalla frowned. "Ms. Gardner, Mrs. Hawthorne, and your business partner, Mr. Dagle."

"Oh, yeah, Billy. Sorry, I took a sleeping pill a little while ago. Been having a tough time get any shut-eye. Everything's been so stressful, what with poor Billy and those two unfortunate women. I just feel so bad about it."

Ayalla suspected Underwood was doing his best to sound sincere, but he was in no danger of winning an Oscar for his performance. His act was well below the standards of some of the felons she'd interrogated in her career.

"I'm sure you do, Mr. Underwood. That's why I know you'd do everything possible to help us."

"But I don't see how I can."

"Well, as I said, we've got a line on someone who might have been the perpetrator."

"Really?" he said, clearing his throat.

She watched his eyes. They were not the eyes of an innocent, puzzled individual. She could read the fear in him. His legs twitched slightly, and he drummed his fingers on the arm of the chair. He was showing the signs that his natural fight-or-flight responses were vying for attention.

"Yes, although we're really digging for a motive. There doesn't seem to be a logical connection."

"Connection?"

She smiled at the stalling ploy. "Well, you know the public always thinks there *has* to be an identifiable motive behind a particular crime, and that prosecutors have to prove why someone committed a crime. But that's not strictly the case. Most of the time, we rely on hard evidence, forensic science, and expert testimony. The motive is more of the icing on the cake, something to sway the jury. In this case, the physical evidence could prove to be a little…" She held her hand up palm down and parallel to the floor and waggled it, "…iffy."

"Oh," he replied, and she watched him relax a little more. He clearly liked the twinge of uncertainty in her voice.

"So a motive for the crime becomes a little more important. It's useful in knowing on whom we should focus our investigation. For example, if we look at a crime like arson, it's easier to start with who had reason to burn something down. In this case, of course, we have a lot of variables to deal with. Who was the intended victim? That's really the foundation. After that, it's easier to identify suspects."

"I still don't see how I can help," he muttered. "I barely knew the two women, and I didn't spend much time with Billy Dagle. So how could I help?"

"That's the interesting part," Ayalla said, smiling as she opened her briefcase. "In one of those amazing coincidences that really do happen from time to time, the man we suspect is someone you may know." She watched his perfectly tanned countenance go pale.

"B-b-but I don't see how that's, I mean, that's not possible. I don't know anyone—I mean, anyone like that."

"Criminals rarely *appear* any different than the rest of us, Mr. Underwood. As a matter of fact, they can look like anyone. So I'm sure it was some sort of bizarre quirk of fate that brought you into contact with our suspect. But I thought I'd better come and see you about it. I'd really hate to see the Bureau jump to any premature conclusions about all this." She pulled out a single photograph from her case and slid it onto the coffee table. Underwood had to stretch himself to see. Ayalla watched him intently. She expected a reaction, and she wasn't disappointed. She saw his Adam's apple rise and plunge as he swallowed hard. His complexion paled. Underwood's struggle to remain nonchalant was almost ludicrously obvious, as he kept his face turned slightly away from her until he thought he was sufficiently composed.

"That *is* you, isn't it, Mr. Underwood?"

"Um…I guess, maybe it is. Not a very good picture. But I don't understand why…" His eyes kept flicking back to the photo.

"Why what?"

"Why you'd have a picture of me. I mean, why would someone be taking a picture like that?"

"As I said, it's probably just a bizarre coincidence that you're sitting at this particular table with him, but we at the Bureau don't really like coincidence. You see, this man," she tapped her pen on the face of Arthur Raley, "is the one we suspect as being involved in the homicides."

"But why…um…why would he…?"

"That's just it, we don't know why. But criminals always leave a trace of some sort, Mr. Underwood—a signature if you will." She leaned closer to him, lowering her voice to an almost conspiratorial level. "I feel that I'm able to share certain information with you. And we haven't let it be known that we recovered parts of devices in the limousine that carry that 'signature' I mentioned. Seems this man," she tapped the photo again, drawing Underwood's attention to it, "uses explosives as tool of the trade, so to speak."

"The trade?"

Ayalla nodded. "He's a killer, Mr. Underwood, that much we're sure of. And he has a penchant for using bombs as well as other more exotic weapons." Ayalla kept her voice steady. She was pretty much writing the script as she went. In truth, they knew hardly anything about Arthur Raley. Everything gathered to date, except the attack on Malcolm, was sheer conjecture. But she was determined to present a different picture to Underwood—one he would no doubt pass on to his coconspirator. Her superiors would not have approved of her strategy one bit, and even the act of showing the surveillance photo to Underwood could get her reprimanded, even suspended. But she was acting on instincts that told her time was a critical factor.

"Now, despite appearances"—once more her pen went *tap-tap-tap* on the photo—"I, for one, am convinced that you've been some sort of innocent pawn in all this."

Underwood nodded emphatically. "Of course. I don't even *know* who this man is."

Ayalla smiled indulgently. "You know, it's understandable to want to avoid admitting we might have done something foolish. I mean, who likes making mistakes? And criminals can be so convincing sometimes, just like first-rate con men who talk people into doing things they'd never even *think* of doing otherwise. So my feeling is that our suspect may have contacted you at some point, perhaps given a perfectly innocent explanation of why he needed to know certain information, or have access to certain areas of the funeral home—you know, something like that. Naturally, you wouldn't have any idea that his intentions were violent or illegal." Ayalla looked at Underwood as if he were the original choirboy.

For his part, the young man was sweating, even in the chill of the room. Every time Ayalla's pen drew his gaze back to the photo, his heart skipped a beat. *There it is. They have proof. They know.* He tried to breathe and find his energy center, just the way his Tae Kwon Do instructor had taught him. But he felt as if he had a 500-pound weight on his chest that kept his lungs from expanding. And if he had any *chi* left in his whole body, he couldn't feel it.

"So," Ayalla was speaking again, and his eyes skittered back to her. "As the senior agent assigned to this case, I am determined to cut you as much slack as possible, Mr. Underwood, because I simply don't believe for a moment that a successful and outgoing businessman such as yourself is deeply involved in this mess. And I'm willing to really go to bat for you with my superiors if you'll be as honest as possible about this." The pen resumed its rhythmic tapping. Ayalla waited. She'd gone as far as possible. If he were going to cave in, this was the moment. She sensed that Underwood was right out there on the edge. He took a deep breath.

Here it comes, she thought. *Here it comes.*

The phone rang, startling them both. Underwood lurched forward in his seat, almost ran around the couch to grab the cordless phone lying on a table near the entry. Ayalla cursed silently. She knew without a doubt the moment had passed.

"Hello," he spoke into the receiver. "No, nothing. I was…uh…just surprised by the phone so late." He kept his back to Ayalla. Although she couldn't see his facial expression, she clearly saw his shoulders hunch with tension. Whoever was on the other end was making him nervous. She glanced at her watch and took note of the precise time. One way or the other, she'd find out where the call had originated.

Underwood wasn't contributing much to the conversation other than the occasional "uh-uh," "yes," or "no." Ayalla wondered why he didn't just leave the room. Perhaps he was sufficiently rattled by her presence that he didn't want to appear to be acting suspiciously. At least she could take some solace in having gotten under his skin. If there was some sort of conspiracy between Underwood, Arthur Raley, and the Supreme Aryan Brotherhood, then Underwood was mostly likely the weakest link. Nothing in his background check identified him as an experienced criminal or political extremist. Other than multiple trips to Europe, which somewhat exceeded the frequency of simple tourism, his life to date appeared unremarkable. It occurred to Ayalla that, much as she might dislike the notion, she might have to call on Benjamin's Hawthorne's many-faceted resources to dig a little deeper.

"No, later!" Devin stabbed the disconnect button on the handset. The phone rang again. He held it rigidly by his side but didn't answer.

"Aren't you going to get that?" Ayalla asked. "I don't mind waiting."

"It's a nuisance call," he snapped. "And if you'd please leave, I'd like to get some sleep." Obviously, he'd regained enough composure to start reasserting control over his personal space.

Ayalla feigned surprise. "But you still haven't explained this photograph."

"I don't know that person. And the picture is fuzzy. That might not even be me."

Yeah, right, thought Ayalla. Though taken with a long lens, and enlarged, the image on the print was acceptably sharp.

"The identity doesn't seem doubtful to me," said Ayalla. "And you are facing each other, at the same table, with—"

"I don't care!" Underwood's voice rose. "That's your opinion. Now unless you have a warrant or something, I want you to leave my house."

He's been watching too many crime shows, thought Ayalla. *Or whoever he just talked to scares him a lot more than the FBI.* She picked up the photo and put it back in her briefcase. "You're tired right now. But we'll have this talk again later, and perhaps it would be best if we conducted the interview at our office. I'll be calling you tomorrow to set up a time."

"I'm busy tomorrow."

"Everyone's busy, Mr. Underwood. The entire staff of the Boston field office is busy investigating three deaths. So we expect cooperation from private citizens. Surely you'd like to know who used your company's resources to commit murder." Underwood stared at her, his breath coming quick and shallow. She watched the rise and fall of his chest beneath the thin T-shirt. "And surely you can explain your meeting with a primary suspect."

Underwood swallowed and his eyes blinked rapidly. "I told you. It's some sort of mistake. And I don't know anything about it." He turned around, walked down the hall, and opened his front door. Ayalla had no choice but to leave. She certainly couldn't arrest him, and she couldn't have made a case for a search warrant.

"You'll be hearing from us, Mr. Underwood."

"Whatever," he snapped, and slammed the door behind her.

A couple of minutes later, she started her car and pulled away from the curb. She'd observed that Underwood's apartment windows overlooked the street. On the off chance he was watching, she drove out of sight, circled the block, and held her position for three minutes. Then she snapped off the headlights and slid into a space a little farther away, but with a clear view of both the front of the building and Underwood's car—the black BMW M5 she'd seen outside the funeral home. Through a pair of binoculars she double-checked the license plate: 2FST2C. *That must get him some police attention,* she thought, and found herself wondering how someone as flamboyant and materialistic as Devin Underwood could be involved in a murky and deadly serious conspiracy such as this. But then, she corrected herself, we don't know this is anything more than an elaborate plot to steal a multimillion-dollar estate. And Underwood wouldn't be averse to a share in a large payoff. Maybe money was the lure for him, as well as Arthur Raley, but those white-sheeted neo-Nazis had a different agenda. She yawned. Her day was twenty hours old and not likely to end soon.

Ayalla kept herself completely upright in the seat. Too much relaxation and she might fall asleep. At least once every minute, her eyes made a circuit of the rearview and side mirrors, the front of the building, the street ahead of her, and the black BMW. More than once, her thoughts were on Malcolm. She was almost tempted to pray, a practice she had abandoned when her father was framed by a political enemy and then forced to resign in utter disgrace from the D.C. police force. He'd been a man of prayer and integrity, a man who never failed to choose what was right rather than what was expedient or career-enhancing. And he'd paid the price for his personal morality. Only a few years after his retirement, he'd been felled by two heart attacks within weeks of each other, the second one massive. She'd seen the despair in his eyes on her visits home, the shame he'd felt at donning a rent-a-cop uniform every day and patrolling shopping malls. That's what had killed him—the shame. At his funeral, she didn't make even the least pretense of bowing her head when the minister prayed, nor did she utter an "amen." She stood there, eyes wide open and blazing with anger, jaw clenched, hating God. Her mother was shocked, but Ayalla was adamant. Her father had been duped into believing that a pure heart would ensure justice. But she knew better. Justice could be bought, sold, or bartered, and it was hardly color-blind. Trying to work in a predominantly white male world, she knew the score.

An old aphorism ran through her mind, "A woman has to do her job twice as well as a man to be thought half as good." *Try being a black woman,* she mused. Ayalla straightened her spine and stretched her arms as much as possible in the confined space. Not for the first time, she let herself wonder if there was any future with Malcolm. She was almost afraid to think too much about it. She had what she herself admitted was a childish superstition—if you wanted something too much, it would be taken away. Maybe it didn't make sense, but it fit her personal cosmology—one formed by years of bitter experience.

Before she could follow this train of thought to its next depressing step, she saw a brief glow of light. The front door of the apartment building had opened for a moment. She kept her eyes trained on the sidewalk and, sure enough, Devin Underwood, now dressed in dark slacks and a leather jacket, made a beeline for his car. Ayalla slid down in the seat, but her quarry never even glanced at his surroundings. She saw the lights flash as he deactivated the security system, and then heard the motor roar to life within seconds. The car shot away from the curb with a slight squeal of tires. So…Mr. Underwood was in a hurry. Ayalla eased her car into the street, so intent on keeping an eye on the target, she failed to see a subcompact sedan pull out and fall in some distance behind her.

Ayalla kept a loose tail on Underwood. The streets of the city were relatively deserted at this time of night, and she could identify his taillights at a fair distance. He drove as if the devil's minions were breathing down his moon roof, and she was beginning to worry that a Boston cop would pull him over, and ruin her chances of following him to a meeting with Raley. For that was her first thought—Arthur Raley had called and demanded a get-together. This could be her best chance to catch the conspirators together. Raley was already a wanted man. She would be justified in arresting him. Underwood would be icing on the cake.

She checked her rearview again. A set of headlights, far back, but they'd stayed with her for the last several minutes. Perhaps it was coincidence, perhaps not.

Ahead of her, the funeral director braked hard and took a sharp left turn. She sped up to get to the corner. Amazingly, he was already a block away. He must have had the accelerator to the floor. Could he have spotted the tail? She swung the Bureau car into the turn and stepped on the gas. Ahead, a stoplight turned red. She slowed slightly. The view was clear, no oncoming traffic at all. She kept going, but clearly Underwood was still pulling away. She slapped the dashboard. *Damn this piece of junk.* In the distance, she saw Underwood's brake lights. Maybe he'd have to slow for something. She just needed a few extra seconds to close the gap a little.

The siren startled the hell out of her. She looked in the mirror and a colorful string of epithets rolled off her tongue. A Boston P.D. cruiser was right behind her. Then the light bar came on, the headlights flashed. Ayalla ignored them. Then the police car pulled right beside her. With her left hand, she took out her badge case, flipped it open, and pressed against the side window. She pointed ahead of her, clearly indicating she was in a pursuit situation. Still, the cop driving once again blasted a burst on the siren.

For a moment, she started to accelerate again, but common sense prevailed. Inciting a police chase through the streets of Boston was not a good idea. Still, she fumed. They could see the government plates on the car. This was harassment, nothing more, nothing less. It was a game they played, and now she was "it."

She screeched to a halt, noting with some satisfaction that the cop driving had to slam on the brakes hard to avoid rear-ending her vehicle. *That would have been a nice touch,* she thought. Ayalla was out of the car, her badge held high, before the cops could even get their seat belts off. Out of the corner of her eye, she saw a car turn the corner she'd just passed—a black or dark-blue subcompact sedan. But for now she had other things on her mind. She walked right up to the driver's window and slapped her I.D. against the glass. The other cop jumped out, his hand on his service weapon.

"F.B.I.," she snarled. "Just what seems to be the problem?" The cop inside the car obviously wanted to get out, but he couldn't do that without shoving her out of the way. He was basically trapped unless he wanted to crawl over to the passenger door.

The other cop walked around the car. "Hey, you're the one who ran that red light back there."

Ayalla stood her ground. "And you probably didn't notice the black Beemer that went flying through that intersection about ten seconds before I passed."

"Um," the cop looked a little sheepish, and he'd taken his hand away from grip of his pistol. "No, we only saw you. We had just turned the corner on Bakewell."

"So, having nothing else to do tonight, you thought pulling over an official U.S. government vehicle would be a nice little diversion?"

The officer in the driver's seat finally decided to roll his window all the way down. "We pull over drivers who break the law," he announced pompously. "We didn't know you were a lady Feeb." He grinned at his own stupid joke.

She turned to him, "Not only that, officer, but I'm also the 'Feeb' in charge of the investigation into the Fore River Bridge murders." She leaned closer. "I take it you've heard of that."

His smile faded. "Yeah."

"And you may recall having heard the chief of police talking about all this cooperation between law enforcement agencies, you know, in the interests of solving three homicides."

"So?"

"So this doesn't look much like cooperation, Officer…" she glanced at his name plate, "Giordino. I want to be sure I get the spelling right." She swung around to examine the other cop's nameplate. "And Smith…ah, now there's an original name. I'll need your first name and middle initial, too." She reached into her raincoat pocket and took out a small spiral-bound notebook, and a pen. "For my report."

"Report?" said Smith.

"Of course. My boss is gonna ask why I screwed up, let a suspect lose me. And I'm not gonna take the heat for it. Life's bad enough without a lecture about fucking up a simple surveillance. So I can explain that two of Boston's finest—Giordino and Smith—decided to stop a government agency car in the middle of the night, after an agent demonstrated she was acting in the line of duty."

"Hey, you coulda been flashing a fake ID," Smith protested.

"Of course," answered Ayalla, continuing to write in her notebook. "And this could be a fake government-issue sedan, with fake U.S. government license plates. I'm sure your commanding officer will commend you for your exceptional fucking diligence." She stalked back to her car, got in, and drove away, fighting the acid fury that rose up in her gorge and threatened to choke her. In her heart, she knew they'd stopped her not for the red light, but because she was a black woman driving alone. She had no doubt whatsoever, that under the same circumstances, had a white male agent flipped his badge into their view, they would have saluted and let him go. The tragedy of their ignorance and prejudice made her want to scream with grief, but she swallowed it down and kept the tears inside, burning in her chest and her belly, where they could hurt only her and no one else.

As she expected, there was no sign of Underwood or his

BMW. Since the file contained no known address for Raley, she had nothing to go on. The restaurant where they'd been photographed was miles away in a commercial section of the city, and undoubtedly had been closed for hours. She had two choices: go back to her apartment, or drive to the funeral home in Hingham and see if Underwood was there. She was too full of adrenaline to do anything but lie in bed and stare at the ceiling, so she opted for what would probably be a pointless trip to the suburbs. With a sigh, she headed for the expressway.

*

Friedrich sat back in his chair. Some decisions were more difficult than others. Only his wise foresight in having Devin Underwood's home and office watched by officers of the S.A.B. had prevented a potential disaster. One phone call had alerted him that an FBI agent was calling on Devin late at night. Friedrich had no illusions about Devin's strength of character. He was weak, just as Karl had been weak. Friedrich believed without doubt that Karl could have found a trace of Wilhelm von Adler, if only he had been willing to 'persuade' people to talk. But Friedrich's idea of persuasion was profoundly different than Karl's. And the old man didn't trust anyone else to pursue the elusive psychic warrior and his descendants.

He'd hoped that he might be able to protect Devin from his own shortcomings if only because he was Karl's grandson. Now he found himself faced with a distasteful choice. Devin had been his "man on the ground" so to speak, his frontline warrior. Sadly, the boy wasn't much a of a warrior but more of a wastrel. Friedrich couldn't afford to lose any more ground in this particular conflict, and now that he had Arthur Raley's skills at his direct command, Devin had shifted into the liability column.

Perhaps it was time to once more test the dedication of the S.A.B. contingent. He knew that most of their recruits were only play-acting at being soldiers—motivated by discontent and a thirst for bullying, but the core group of officers had some semblance of discipline. They had proved useful as a front, and, as Friedrich planned, would prove even more useful as scapegoats.

*

Devin was more frightened than he'd ever been in his life. He knew as soon as the phone rang that it could only be Friedrich—no respecter of time zones when he wanted to issue orders. Devin had been in a panic of indecision at that moment, with the FBI agent tapping her damn pen on the photograph of him and Arthur Raley when the phone rang. Should he answer? Would it seem suspicious if he didn't? But if he did, what would he say? He was as scared of the old man finding out the FBI was breathing down his neck, as he was of the FBI finding out about his connection to Friedrich. As it was, he'd come off sounding like an idiot, but fortunately, he wasn't expected to converse, only listen. Friedrich's tone had sounded colder and crueler than ever. He'd insulted Devin, said he was incompetent, stupid, and a lot of other things. And with the FBI agent a mere fifteen feet away, all Devin could do was listen and try to quell the rage in his chest. He wanted to throw the phone across the room and then stomp it to bits, but instead he took the abuse, and agreed to the orders—go to the funeral home, meet one of Friedrich's emis-saries, and give the man the keys to a hearse.

But after the agent left, Devin was almost paralyzed with indecision. He didn't actually *have* to obey Friedrich. The old bastard was thousands of miles away. What could he really do? *Sic those goddamn Nazi boys on you,* his mind answered.

Wouldn't they just love to surround your apartment and play commando?

Devin couldn't think straight. The sleeping pills had dulled his thought process and his reaction time. He realized he was still standing in the entry hall. What was he going to do? He went back to the bedroom and mechanically began picking up clothes from the floor and putting them on. He had the fleeting thought that he never wore wrinkled clothes, but it passed. He picked up his keys from the dresser and slipped them into the pocket of his leather jacket. He had to go, but go where? To the funeral home? To a hotel? Or just away? Anywhere but here. He was so tired, the decision seemed to be made for him. Almost as if the BMW were on autopilot, it made the series of turns that would take him to the funeral home. Finally, he glanced in his mirror. Headlights. They stayed with him. His heart began to beat faster. Who would be following him? Then the absurdity of the question hit him, since there were so many possibilities: FBI, police, Arthur Raley, the S.A.B. wackos, or someone he hadn't even thought of yet. After he negotiated the next turn, he stomped the accelerator and felt himself pushed back into the seat by G-forces. He loved that feeling. If he weren't so frightened, he might even be enjoying this. He'd gone from zero to sixty in about five seconds. When the headlights finally turned the corner behind him, he was blocks away. Devin almost laughed—one tiny victory in a situation that, to his mind, totally sucked.

He slowed down on Route 3. No sense in getting nailed for a ticket. At this time of night, he was an easy target for a bored cop with a radar gun. Once in Hingham, he slowed to the exact speed limit of the surface streets, then groaned in frustration as his fuel light blinked on.

"Shit!" he muttered. He reversed course to an all-night

service station where he filled up his tank while leaning against the side of the car, still in a fog of confusion and incipient fear that threatened to overwhelm him if he thought about the situation for more than a couple of minutes at a stretch. But as the pump handle clicked off, he made a decision. He wanted to live. The big score was no longer very attractive. He wanted to go far away, maybe even the West Coast. At the funeral home, he had about $15,000 stashed in a huge wall safe that had been installed courtesy of Billy's old man, who'd had a thing for security.

Then there was the car. He hated to think about selling his pride and joy, but even used, it was worth over eighty grand. He might need that money to lie low. He got back in the car and glanced at the Rolex glinting on his wrist. There was another nest egg if he needed it. Devin began to feel a little better. As he drove, he even convinced himself that Friedrich would be too busy chasing his pipe dream of the Fourth Reich to really worry about what had become of him.

He pulled into the driveway of the funeral home and was relieved to see there were no other cars around back. A plan began to form itself in his mind. If the S.A.B. goon showed up right away, he'd give him the keys to the hearse. Then he'd grab the cash from the safe, along with his grandfather's letters, and start driving. He wouldn't be able to use his credit cards—too easy to track. So it would be cash all the way. He'd take the Mass Pike west and get as far as possible before morning, then turn off and start using secondary highways.

Devin got out, left the engine running, and went in through the back door of the funeral home. He'd almost reached his office, turning on lights as he went, when he heard a creak behind him. Devin whirled around as a man stepped out of one of the viewing rooms.

"What the fuck!" he gasped.

"I'm here for the hearse," said the man in a rumbling, harsh voice

"How did you get in here?" Devin stammered.

"Not hard. So get the keys."

"Sure, they're on the board in the back office." Devin had to go past the man, and as he did, stepped into a malodorous cloud of cheap aftershave, pungent body odor, and fetid breath that almost gagged him. He resisted the urge to suggest the man bathe once in a while. No sense in appearing uncooperative.

Devin stepped into the bookkeeping office and turned on the overhead light. "Over here," he said, opening a small metal key cabinet. He lifted a set of keys off the third hook. Might as well give the creep their newest funeral car. Devin wouldn't be worrying about it anymore.

"Let's go," his visitor muttered, gesturing with his chin for Devin to precede him.

"What? You need me to show you which car. It's in bay three, just what it says on the key tag."

"You're driving."

Devin felt his bowels churn. "What? Why? Friedrich didn't say anything about that. He told me to give you the keys. That's it."

"Plan's changed. You're driving."

"But I need to—"

"Hey," the guy snarled. "I've got my orders." He opened his much stained raincoat and drew a pistol from the leather holster attached to his belt.

Devin's mouth went dry, and everything became horribly, painfully clear. This wasn't about helping out the S.A.B. with a funeral home hearse. This disgusting man was going to drive him somewhere and probably kill him. He felt as if his brain were filled with white noise. The only thought that surfaced was absurd beyond belief: How would he be able to stand the man's stench in a closed car?

"Come on," the man snapped, waving the pistol. "We don't got all night."

Devin's legs trembled as he sidled past and through the doorway. "Outside, hurry up!"

They started across the parking area toward the garage. The rain that had teased the city with intermittent drops all day had begun to fall in earnest. *And I just washed my car? Oh, shit. What am I thinking?* Devin tried desperately to get a deep breath. *Oh shit, oh shit, oh shit.* He swallowed hard. *Run! I've gotta run. But he'll shoot me. Or would he? The gun doesn't have a silencer on it. Or does it?* Devin reached the garage door of the third bay. *If I get in the car, I'm dead.* His muscles tensed, adrenaline coursing through him. *Now! Go now!*

Simultaneously, three things happened. A pair of bright headlights swept across the front of the garage building and stopped, lighting up the two men as if they were on a stage. In a heartbeat, Devin ran. He wasn't aware of making a conscious decision. It was as if his legs had a will of their own. He lurched toward the lights. And the man behind him fired.

Devin stumbled as if he'd been shoved him from behind. He stopped, looked down in silent wonder at the stain blossoming on his white shirt. In the bright wash of lights, it looked almost black. He put his hand to his stomach. Another heartbeat, and the nerves reacted in concert to the insult his body had been dealt. *Oh, God!*—pain like nothing he'd ever imagined. Another explosion behind him, and he pitched forward, dropping to his knees. This time there was no delay in feeling the hideous impact of the bullet between his shoulder blades. And he noticed fat drops of rain hitting the pavement. There was a voice behind the light.

"FBI! Drop your weapon!"

Another shot…did it come *from* the light, or from behind? He couldn't tell. He didn't really care about it anyway. Devin had a fleeting moment to wonder why nothing hurt anymore. And why he could see the rain was coming down hard, but it didn't feel wet, didn't feel cold; actually it didn't seem to touch him at all. A silhouette took shape in front of the headlights. A hand reached out just as he saw the black, wet, hard pavement coming toward his face. He heard the roar of a motor, tires spinning on wet pavement. The engine sound, it was very familiar. His car. Wasn't that his car? He felt himself yanked hard to one side and something large passed near his face. There was a rending scraping of metal, then silence.

It really isn't that bad, he thought, opening his eyes to find the FBI woman looking back at him. *I didn't really wanna die, though.* It suddenly occurred to him that someone should know, about Friedrich, about the S.A.B., about Arthur Raley. But he didn't have time to explain it. The woman was talking to him. He could barely hear her voice. Devin swallowed with much effort. He started to speak. His voice sounded so strange to him. The FBI woman bent closer. She held his face in both her hands.

"Hang on, damn it! There's an ambulance coming."

He saw her hands move to his chest. Seemed she was trying to press on him, but he didn't feel it. Only the cold, icy rain on his face. That was the only thing that bothered him. Except that it felt as if he couldn't get enough air. He didn't like that very much. He tried to speak, and once again the woman's face was near his.

"Get them," he whispered as loudly as he could.

She leaned even closer. "Get who?"

Devin focused his mind, fighting the blackness. "Nazis. The…Reich…it's…Friedrich."

"Who's Friedrich? Devin, who is Friedrich? Is he the one who shot you?"

Devin almost smiled. "The devil." His eyes started to roll back in his head. "The Doktor."

＊

When the first local police cars pulled up, they found Special Agent Franklin sitting in the middle of the funeral home driveway, cradling Devin Underwood's head in her lap. Her car was still running, the high beams blazing a path through the rain and darkness, lighting up the white garage building twenty yards away. Moments later, the paramedics showed up, and Ayalla told them the victim had been dead for several minutes. She was covered with the blood. The medics wanted to examine her for injuries. "It's not *my* blood," she snapped.

Ayalla showed her identification and began to bark orders. "Get out an APB. The suspect is about 5 foot eight to five foot ten and on the fat side, maybe 200-220. Beige raincoat, balding, and he's driving a black BMW M5 with beige paint transfer on the left front fender where he struck my vehicle. He may also be seeking medical attention. I hit him at least once, so notify clinics and hospitals. Now get it out on the radio." She paused, remembering. "Wait a second. Get some people out searching the streets for a couple of blocks around—black or dark-blue small sedan—you know, like a Sentra or a Passat."

"You gotta be kidding," said the cop. "There's a ton of cars like that."

Ayalla started to argue, then realized he was absolutely right. "Yeah. Never mind. But the shooter left his car somewhere near here."

The patrol officer went back to his car and Ayalla watched

them put a yellow plastic sheet over Devin's body to protect it for the crime scene investigators. Part of her was frozen with shock at having been shot at just as she stepped from her car; another part ached for this beautiful young man, his life drained away on a patch of asphalt. She rarely pitied criminals, and she was pretty sure that Devin had been involved in the murders of Florence Gardner, Amanda Hawthorne, and Billy Dagle. Yet he'd seemed more scared than sinister. And those last few words. He'd wanted very badly to tell her something, yet he seemed somehow amused. But about what? *Nazis. Friedrich. The devil. The doctor*—sounded like so much nonsense.

Another car pulled up and inwardly she groaned. Her boss had arrived, and Ayalla had a lot of explaining to do. One of their prime suspects was now dead.

CHAPTER THIRTEEN

The Light of Lights
Looks always on the motive, not the deed,
The Shadow of Shadows on the deed alone.
—William Butler Yeats, *The Countess Cathleen,* act IV

As might have been expected, the turnout for the Amanda Hawthorne funeral was substantial, despite a capricious rain that alternated between deluge and drizzle. A storm system had blanketed the entire Northeast corridor, and meteorologists were predicting an ice storm beginning late that night. At 10 A.M., though, the temperature was still above forty degrees. The angry, gray sky loomed far too close for comfort, as Connor, Laura, Benjamin, and the Carlisles stood huddled together under umbrellas. The church service at St. Sebastien's Episcopal Church had been tasteful, neither too brief nor too long. The priest had delivered a pleasant homily, laced with platitudes, designed to soothe rather than incite additional waves of grief. The only event of note was the one they were now discussing.

"It glowed," admitted Connor, a little reluctantly. "But I still think it could have been the lighting effect."

Ellen Carlisle smiled. "Logic and intelligence are among your most wonderful gifts, Connor dear, but they don't always work for everything."

"And the side chapel had no lights of its own," added Laura. "The statue of the Lady just lit up from within—it glowed."

Before the service began, the Carlisles had expressed a desire to visit the church's Lady Chapel. It was their habit to pay homage to all representations of the Divine Mother they encountered in the world. She was the central figure of their spiritual lives, and their circle was firmly dedicated to invoking Her presence in a world that had run amok under the guidance of a self-limiting patriarchy. Connor's grandmother had been the priestess of this circle before her passage into other realms of existence.

As a courtesy, Laura and the Hawthornes accompanied the Carlisles. When they stepped into the small chapel, Ellen Carlisle drew a sharp breath. "Oh, my," she said softly. The figure of the Mother was particularly beautiful, and she was depicted with her arms stretched out in welcome and blessing. Her skin was dark, reminiscent of the black Madonnas scattered throughout the world. And her face was naturally in shadow. Yet, as they watched, her countenance began to glow, and the warm light spread from the top of her head down to the hem of her robes.

Lord and Lady Carlisle immediately knelt on the small padded kneeler in front of the statue. Connor saw their lips move in silent prayer. Their faces, too, shone with joy as well as reverence. Slowly, but without hesitation, Laura moved to the side and knelt. Benjamin followed, leaving only Connor standing. She stared at the statute, then at her friends and family. Her heart was gripped with indecision, fear, and an odd sensation she could identify only as a longing for something. Finally, she took up a spot beside Laura. She didn't know how much time passed, but they heard the opening hymn, and the spell, whatever it was, dissolved. They walked briskly to their seats at the front of the church.

Connor sat through the service with only half her attention on the proceedings. Her insides churned. The luminous simulacrum of the Mother remained fixed in her mind. Even her grief at seeing Amanda's draped casket before the altar was somehow softened by a presence that had insinuated itself into her heart. Connor was almost dizzy from feeling both profoundly sad and inexplicably joyful. She felt Laura take her hand, and the sense of vertigo abated slightly. Connor focused on sensations—the cold marble beneath her feet, the unyielding wood of the seat beneath her, the warmth of Laura's hand. She opened her eyes once more, and breathed deeply. To her surprise, the priest was concluding the service. The organ swelled again, filling the neo-Gothic church with the strains of melancholy. The guests waited politely in their pews for the passage of the casket and the family, then filed out with a smattering of whispers and nudges.

Benjamin and Connor stood side by side at the top of the church steps to accept the condolences of the guests. There would be no graveside service where such an exchange would ordinarily take place. Amanda had left a handwritten note with her attorney that she did not want, under any circumstances, to be buried next to Benjamin Hawthorne in the plots they had purchased years earlier. But she had made no other arrangements, no doubt because she never suspected her life would end so abruptly and so soon.

Laura stayed off to one side with the Carlisles. "Connor's making arrangements for Amanda to be sent to England," she explained. "That's one reason her daughter and great aunt aren't here. She talked Katy and Jessica into waiting until the service in St. Giles."

"We stopped in London to visit Katy very briefly," Ellen said. "She was still concerned that she should have flown over, but she also just took a new post with a firm in the City. I think she was relieved at the way the plans turned out."

"It'll take at least a week, maybe two, before the paperwork is done and the casket is shipped," Laura nodded.

"That will give us some time to look into the matter before us," said William, his expression grave. "There is some quite malevolent mind at work in all this, and we'd best prepare an effective defense against it."

Laura looked at him quizzically. "A malevolent mind?"

"We've been doing some ceremonial work since you and Connor inquired about *le voleur d'âmes*." He didn't elaborate, yet Laura understood. The powerful Celtic circle, now guided by Lady Ellen Carlisle, had convened to conduct a very different sort of inquiry...in dimensions unfamiliar to most people.

"We might have learned even more had Connor been present," said Ellen quietly.

Laura sighed. "She still isn't comfortable with the idea. I can't say exactly what she's afraid of, but—"

"She'll come to it one day," Ellen replied. "It's her place, you know. I'm only filling it temporarily. She's Gwendolyn's heir. But it makes our circle one short of the thirteen. We and our predecessors have stood against evil, time and again, but only at full strength. The circle was complete when Adolf Hitler's occult magicians came against us, and they failed."

"Is that why you are so familiar with this pendant? You sent us old photographs from the Nazi archives."

"Yes, we do know about the connection, and that is why we are deeply concerned. We might not have prevailed back then if his occultist had possessed *both* halves. But we will talk more of this later," William cautioned as press people began drifting toward them. "I think it also might be wise if we avoid photographs." He deftly evaded the approach of a photographer and shepherded the two women back into the church where photos were not allowed for any reason.

"She did glow, didn't she?" asked Laura.

"Yes, my dear," replied Ellen. "Of course. Her divine energy is once more manifesting on this planet. I'm sure you've felt it yourself."

"I've seen some interesting images in the Dreamtime, but I still haven't been sure what to make of them. Oh, and speaking of images, Mrs. Broadhurst paid us a visit at the wake."

William and Ellen both smiled. "We rather thought she'd done so," said William. "She's a wily old girl and likes to have her way. Appearances aren't strictly forbidden, of course, but they aren't exactly encouraged, either. Still, Gwendolyn was always a trifle stubborn."

"There was something else, too. Connor had a dream about her mother."

"Ah, so Amanda must have shaken off the illusion of her life here much more quickly than we expected."

"Illusion?" asked Laura, though she was at least partly clear on what they meant.

"Just that we thought she might wander for a very long time, wrapped up in a little world of her own, before looking into the mirror of the Mother," said William.

"That's simply a way of explaining the process of awakening," added Ellen. "Most do not come to it until after they die, and some not even then."

"It meant a lot to Connor to see her mother in such a different light," Laura said. "Then she could grieve for the real Amanda, not the unhappy, hateful person she became."

"Good," said William. "Very good. I know Gwendolyn is

pleased, and I suspect she may have had a hand in that as well. There are those who have to be given a shove into the light of awareness, and Gwendolyn was never patient."

Laura nodded. "I knew her so briefly, only a matter of hours when she arrived in New Mexico. And yet…"

"You felt as if you'd known her much longer," Ellen smiled gently. "That's because she so embodied the Divine Mother's energy—gentle yet fiery, calm yet implacable—it's familiar to all of us whether we recognize it or not."

Laura nodded. "She was all that and more."

"Who was?" said Connor, coming up behind them.

"Gwendolyn," replied Ellen.

"Ah, yes. Don't suppose she's around here anywhere?" Connor eyed her surroundings with an air of caution that made them all smile.

"You never know, my dear," Ellen said. "She's rather unpredictable."

"You're telling me. I suppose you heard she put in an appearance at the wake."

"Indeed," nodded William. "And I imagine we'll be seeing more of her."

Laura took Connor's hand. "You okay?"

"Yeah. Dad's talking to the last few. I couldn't take much more insincerity from our guests. I don't think there were a dozen people in this church who genuinely cared about my mother." Connor's voice trembled slightly. "I don't even know why the rest of them came."

"Curiosity and puzzlement and maybe a little fear," answered Laura.

"Fear?"

"Dying scares most people. When it's someone they know, a funeral gives them a chance to feel grateful they're not dead."

"Well, as long as it serves a purpose," said Connor with more than a touch of sarcasm. "Now let's get out of here."

The five of them rode in the limousine to Bethesda Naval, where Malcolm, though still weak, was demanding to be released. His doctors were at a loss to explain his rapid recovery and tried to insist on another day of tests. He'd refused. Thus, at midday, Connor was trundling the somewhat surly cop out of a rear entrance in a wheelchair, with Laura and Benjamin bringing up the rear.

"This is so stupid," he grumbled. "I could have walked."

"Humor me," said Connor. "How often do I get to push you around?"

"Literally or figuratively?"

"Hey, watch it," she said, tapping the back of his head.

"You watch it. I've been at death's door."

"Well, you didn't make it through, pal. So no mollycoddling."

Laura, walking beside Benjamin several paces behind Connor, smiled and whispered, "Sometimes they're like a couple of kids."

"Kids who adore each other but absolutely won't say it out loud."

"Yep!"

The door to the limousine swung open, and the Carlisles got out. Malcolm immediately ordered Connor to stop the wheelchair and let him out. He swayed on his feet for a moment and she grabbed his arm. He didn't resist, but gently pulled away to shake William Carlisle's hand and then Ellen's.

William clapped him on the shoulder. "Damn glad to see you up and about, old man. Your friends tell me you had a run-in with a nasty bugger."

"Next time he'll be the one in the hospital," Malcolm declared, and by his tone no one doubted it for a moment.

"Let's hope there is a next time," said Benjamin, shepherding everyone into the car. "Arthur Raley isn't anywhere to be found around here, or in Boston. I had a call from Ayalla this morning. They've been diligently searching for him." He paused, and rolled up the privacy screen. "And there've been some other developments. I was waiting to tell you when we were all together again."

"What is it, Dad?"

"Devin Underwood is dead."

Laura, Malcolm, and Connor were clearly shocked. The Carlisles, unfamiliar with the funeral director's part in the drama, quietly waited for clarification. Benjamin provided it, giving a brief but thorough résumé of the events to date.

"Ayalla was following Underwood when he left his apartment late last night. But thanks to a couple of blue suits in a radio car who pulled her over, she lost him. On a hunch, she went to the funeral home. Just as she pulled into the driveway, she saw Underwood with another man who took a shot at her."

Malcolm sat forward instantly. "She's all right?"

"She's fine," Benjamin assured him. "You would have been the first to know if there were anything wrong. There are some holes in the windshield of her car, but more importantly, holes in Devin Underwood's back. The man shot him very deliberately before running away."

"You think someone was sent to kill him?" asked Laura.

"Seems likely. Maybe Devin was becoming a liability."

"Ayalla also said she'd gotten Underwood pretty spooked with that photo of him and Arthur Raley together. Then he got a phone call, though it was really late in the evening, and minutes after she left, he was out the door in a hurry."

Benjamin ran down the rest of the past week's events and concluded, "So what we have are a lot of pieces that may or may not fit. We know Arthur Raley was acquainted with Devin Underwood. We're fairly sure that Devin was involved in the sabotage of the limousine that killed Amanda, Florence Gardner, and Billy Dagle. We also know that Grace Wainwright has the gold half of the pendant which you folks," he nodded toward the Carlisles, "know a lot more about than we do. We also know that someone tried to search the girls' room at the bed-and-breakfast right after Grace loaned Connor the pendant. That may or may not be the same individual who took a shot at them on the street near Grace Wainwright's house. Finally, we have what I believe was an abortive attempt to abduct Connor and ended up almost killing Malcolm. We have Laura's identification of Arthur Raley as the man wielding the syringe."

"Let's not forget the Supreme Aryan Brotherhood," growled Malcolm.

"Indeed not," William Carlisle spoke for the first time. "I believe they are very much involved in all this."

"But what *is* this?" Connor blurted out. "So far, nothing makes particular sense. And how is it you know about some fascist militia group here in the States?"

"Perhaps when we've had a chance to show you the documents we've brought and bring you up to speed on the results of our most recent, er, inquiry," said William. "But I'm afraid we'll need some time and privacy."

Benjamin nodded. "Then it will have to wait until we get back to Boston. I've reserved a larger suite with a conference table and arranged for rooms on the same corridor for all of us. We're going to stick together." He eyed Malcolm, whose skin still looked gray. "Insofar as possible, I don't want anyone out on the street alone."

William leaned forward. "The item…it *is* secure?"

Benjamin nodded firmly. "It's still in the hotel safe."

"Will we be able to examine it? To confirm its authenticity?" asked Ellen.

"Absolutely. And I suggest we all be even more cautious than usual, aware of our surroundings. Ayalla told me that some members of the Brotherhood are on the move. There's even a chance the man who shot Underwood was one of them."

*

Friedrich's rage was all-consuming. Karl's grandson was dead, and the American agents were hot on the trail of Devin's killer. Worst of all, Arthur Raley had done nothing to rectify his failure in Washington. The Hawthornes, the Nez woman, even the cop whom Raley had injured—all were alive and well and possibly getting closer to stumbling upon a secret Friedrich had pursued for most of his life. He hadn't wanted the boy killed, just taken somewhere out of the way until the plans for the restoration of the Reich were fully realized. He didn't want Devin talking to people. Then he learned that the man sent to do a simple job had panicked under fire and killed Devin—and almost killed an FBI agent.

All his thoughtful, meticulous plans were being systematically decimated by sheer stupidity. But he'd had no choice but to leave the groundwork to others. That, however, would change as of now. He'd already alerted his valet to pack his luggage. He had reservations on a Lufthansa flight at 10 P.M. to New York City. From there he would travel by car to Boston. It was time, or more likely past time, for a true leader, an oath-sworn Nazi officer of the greatest brotherhood of all time to take command.

The glass case in his study stood empty now. He had ordered his valet to pack his uniform, along with the boots, the cap, the decorations. The secret compartment was also minus its contents—the journals and other papers. Friedrich had no intention of returning to this house. For him, it represented a despised past—the decades of hiding, of pretending to be someone he wasn't. That was over. He would live out whatever time he had left in the heart of the old enemy's territory and destroy them from within. He would cast off the distasteful role of Jew and industrialist. He would be once again Hitler's trusted aide, Himmler's eager collaborator, and the brilliant Herr Doktor. The Fates had called to him once more, and this time their message was clear.

*

Six o'clock in the evening and the sun hadn't made an appearance in person the entire day. Its presence was nothing but a rumor passed on by thick, huddled clouds presiding over a bleak, wet city. Ayalla's shoulders ached, her head hurt, and her legs were remarkably difficult to motivate as she made her last circuit through the funeral home. Teams had been searching half the day, once the inevitable jurisdictional squabbles had been settled. The local police in Hingham had been righteously indignant at federal interference. This was a homicide on their turf. But as it was immediately tied in with the Fore River Bridge murders and the current FBI case, the locals eventually had to give in. They left, but not before they'd barged through doing a half-assed search, more designed to assuage their damaged pride than aid the investigation.

As a result, Ayalla's team was hampered by having to determine the original condition of the interior of the funeral home. In the long run, it hadn't mattered. Nothing of genuine significance had been discovered. Files had been boxed up for later analysis, and phone records would be pulled. But there was definitely no smoking gun. After interviewing the handful of staff members (most of whom seemed more concerned for their future employment than the death of their employer), the team had moved on to Devin Underwood's apartment, but Ayalla didn't hold out much hope for any major revelations from examining his hair gel collection and trendy wardrobe.

After more than thirty-six hours, she was tired beyond belief and wondered why she hadn't had the good sense to go home and sleep. Malcolm would be back tonight, and she hardly dared admit to herself how much she wanted to see him alive and well. Ayalla walked into Devin Underwood's office and sat down in the ostentatious leather desk chair. It was comfortable, maybe a little too comfortable, she thought, closing her eyes. Sleep would be so easy. Ayalla shook herself and methodically went through all the desk drawers again. Nothing new. She was fully aware she was clutching at thin air. Some part of her, though, needed to understand the man's link to these murders. She needed to know why someone so clearly inept at criminal conspiracy had been involved in the first place. Ayalla strongly suspected that her presence at Underwood's apartment the previous evening had a lot to do with his execution. For that was what it had been—an execution. He did not simply stray into the line of fire. He'd been running toward her, running for help. "Shit!" she said out loud.

Ayalla leaned forward and picked up a lovely antique snow-globe on the desk. It seemed rather whimsical for someone like Devin Underwood. Perhaps it had come with the office. She shook it and watched the swirling flakes descending over a miniature copy of Michelangelo's *Pietà*. She shook it again, this time turning it upside down to achieve more snow action. When she turned it back, she heard a metallic clunk, and two objects fell onto the desk blotter—one, a brass circle that appeared to be part of the base of the globe. The other was a key. She picked it up and held it under the banker's lamp on the desk. This was no run-of-the-mill key. It was heavy and thick, the top rounded, and the wards a series of rectangular indentations rather than grooves and scallops. It was vaguely similar to a safety deposit box key, yet too large and heavy for that purpose.

She hefted it in her hand wondering if Devin Underwood had even known of its existence. Perhaps it had been hidden in the globe for a long time. Yet it wasn't the least bit rusty. And it seemed high-tech in its way. *What about a lockbox or a safe?* she wondered. Yet the official search had been thorough and by the book. Her team was good. Still…

Ayalla leaned back in the chair and surveyed the room. Energy she hadn't thought she could muster was pumping through her again. The odds were good that the key was to something in this room. Well, maybe not good, but one had to start somewhere. After an hour of checking every inch of wall space, and removing every painting in the large room, she began to wilt. The surge of adrenaline was gone more quickly than it had arrived. She needed sleep, and then she'd come back and try again tomorrow.

Pocketing the key, Ayalla left the office, closing the door behind her. As she stood at the end of the carpeted hallway, she noticed again the amazing precision with which all the paintings in the hallway were hung. Each was a copy, albeit a good copy, of historic paintings depicting the American Revolution. She had a feeling they'd been chosen by a decorator with an eye to their size and potential placement rather than any particular devotion to patriotism. They were all horizontal images, identically framed. Even without a measuring tape, Ayalla estimated that their separation from each other, or from the occasional intervening doorway was precisely the same. At the end of the hall, however, in a small niche, hung the painting she'd noted earlier in passing, its brass plate identifying the subject as the founder of Dagle & Sons—W. V. Dagle, III, Billy's grandfather. It was a traditional portrait from the 1950s: formal, stiff, dignified. She'd seen the portrait's twin in Billy's office, that one done some twenty years later of Billy's father, Dagle the fourth. She had yet to see a portrait of Billy, though she had several snapshots in his file. No doubt he'd been too young to consider the idea anything but foolish. Still, he had strongly resembled both his father and grandfather.

Ayalla tugged at the corner of the painting halfheartedly. It didn't budge. She didn't expect it to. The searchers had already checked every one of them, looking for a safe or a stash of contraband. It was an obvious place, but some people still did it. She sighed. Maybe she'd find what the key fit, but probably not. As she let go of the edge of the portrait, the band around the sleeve of her trench coat caught on one of the single candle sconces attached to the wall on either side of the portrait. She yanked at her sleeve and instead of slipping free, the metal buckle on the strap lodged firmly over a protrusion on the sconce. She reached up to untangle herself and as she yanked at the buckle, the entire sconce turned sideways. If it hadn't been so completely quiet in the building, she might not even have heard the tiny click of metal on metal. Her first thought—that she'd broken the damn thing and would have to fix it—gave way to an entirely new one. A bubble of excitement formed in her chest. *Hold on. Don't get carried away, girl. This isn't some Nancy Drew book.* But still she reached for the edge of the painting nearest the sconce, and tugged. Her heart fell. It didn't move.

That's what you get for watching The Avengers *in rerun,* she reminded herself sternly, as she finally dislodged the sleeve buckle of her coat and started to walk away. She stopped. "Oh, what the hell," she muttered. "No one here to see me acting like an idiot."

She reached for the wall sconce on the left side and realized she was holding her breath. She exhaled and turned the brass arm. It swiveled easily clockwise, and she was rewarded with the same metallic noise. "Okay, this time, if nothing happens, I'm outta here." She pulled on the painting's edge. Nothing. "Figures," she shrugged. Then she pushed, just to be sure. The spring catch on the inside of the frame released instantly and the painting swung away from the wall. Behind it was the door of an old but sturdy wall safe. "We're gonna have to start x-raying walls," she muttered and withdrew the key from her pocket. The lock looked just as odd as the key itself. There was no doubt in her mind they were made for each other. It slipped in and turned effortlessly. Slowly, wondering about potential booby traps, Ayalla opened the safe door.

"Whoa!" she said, immediately spying stacks of U.S. currency. "Little mad money, Mr. Underwood?" She still wore her latex gloves, so she gingerly extracted the bundles of cash to see what was behind it. The safe at first appeared empty, a rather shallow model, she thought, if this small amount of money was all it held. But using her penlight, she became aware that in the back of the safe was a black cardboard box, almost the size of a standard banker's file box. She reached in and pulled it out. The safe was actually pretty big, though not big enough for a body, she was relieved to confirm. She was already sufficiently creeped out from spending the day in a funeral home with dead bodies "reposing" in various rooms. She reminded herself they'd have to make arrangements to get all the stiffs sent to other facilities. There wouldn't be any more wakes and visitations at Dagle & Sons for a long time, if ever.

Removing the lid, she saw tight, neat bundles of envelopes, all somewhat yellowed. Ayalla gently removed one bundle and noted the address was in France, though she couldn't read the date on the postmark cancellation stamp. She could, however, see that the word *Deutschland* appeared in the return address on the back of the letter. *Germany: It had to mean something—* Ayalla sighed with fatigue—*or nothing.* But something was gnawing at her stomach. Granted it might be hunger, but maybe not. Of course, if these letters were all in German, she wouldn't be able to read them. French, maybe, depending on the handwriting and the dialect of the writer. But German, no.

She replaced the letters and started to put the box back in the safe, but something stopped her. Why would someone put dozens and dozens of old letters in the safe? Presumably they had to be at least as important as the money, maybe more so. And no guard would be posted here tonight. She had planned to set the alarm and make sure all the outer doors were locked. She stood there, her hands through the handles of the cardboard box. *This is stupid, leave it.* She lifted the box, but again, she couldn't fight off an inexplicable reluctance to let it go back into the wall safe. *Oh, what the hell!*

Ayalla put the box on the carpet, stacked the cash in the safe, closed the steel door, pocketed the key, and then swung the painting back into place. She then turned the sconces to their upright positions. *Like something out of a dime novel.* Grabbing the file box, Ayalla headed for the back door. Her car, complete with bullet holes, had been taken away as evidence, and a new (well, *different*) vehicle had been left for her to use. It was only a few feet from the rear entrance. She tucked the box under her arm and stepped outside, still protected from the rain by the portico. Carefully locking the door, Ayalla dashed to the sedan, opened the trunk, put the box inside, then hurried to the driver's door.

She was suddenly and inexplicably anxious to leave. She started the car with a roar—it needed some muffler work, but she was going to be punished for weeks in subtle ways, and this was just one of them—a crappy car. Breaking with her usual habit, Ayalla didn't even fasten her seat belt before throwing the gearshift into reverse. She backed up quickly, twitched the gearshift into drive, and stepped on the gas. Thanks to her haste, the rain, and the fogged-up windows, she didn't see the watcher who had emerged from the shadows beside the back porch and was only a few feet away from her government sedan. Whatever his intentions may have been, Ayalla's abrupt exit left him with no choice but to leap out of the way as her car shot backward and then forward again.

The man picked himself up off the wet pavement and scowled. What had she taken away in that black box? Bert knew his superiors would ask specific questions and were not warmly receptive to excuses—something his comrade in arms, Lieutenant Gunther, had already learned to his extreme detriment. Even now, old Rudy was locked in a makeshift cell at the S.A.B. headquarters fifteen miles outside Boston. He was, for all intents and purposes, a dead man. He had demonstrated neither grace nor valor under fire. Now the only question was whether his indifferently treated gunshot wounds or the legendary Herr Doktor would kill him first.

Bert shivered as a gust of wind blasted down the collar of his wet wool overcoat, and he started thinking about his brother's fishing boat in the Florida Keys. How long would it take to get there if he started out right now? Eighteen hours? More like twenty-four probably. And his vacation wouldn't last long. According to his commanding officer, membership in the Brotherhood was for life. Bert had found this comforting the first time he heard it. Then, a couple of years later, he'd been summoned to an emergency muster of the entire local chapter of the Brotherhood. He'd stood at attention with the other soldiers as the officers read out the charges against one of their own. The man's "crime" was simple. He had tried to quit the Brotherhood. For that, the sentence was death. He was taken to a basement room and shot.

No, he wouldn't be doing any fishing in Florida anytime soon. Everyone was in a lather because this big-time S.S. Nazi was coming. Bert would just as soon have skipped the whole thing, and now he was probably in trouble because he didn't stop that woman FBI agent from taking something out of the funeral home. But what could he have done? Even Rudy hadn't stood a chance with her, and he was an *officer*, for crying out loud. He wished he knew what was in the damn box. If it turned out to be something that Devin Underwood was keeping for the Doktor, and the Doktor asked for it, there'd be hell to pay. And Bert was the only one who knew what had been taken. He would just keep his mouth shut. But still, his job was to watch the place. He'd even gone so far as to creep inside when only the woman had stayed behind. Bert had stood inside the door of one of the viewing rooms and discovered he could observe the entire hallway in a large decorative mirror that hung at one end. Thus he had seen Ayalla discover the safe and open it. He almost salivated over the stacks of cash she took out and was rather surprised that she didn't pocket any of it. He would have. But instead she put the money back and took the black cardboard carton that appeared to have bundles of papers in it. Maybe they were important.

He wracked his brain—not a complex process in Bert's case—for a workable solution, something that would prevent any fault from attaching to him personally. When the idea finally came to him, he was nearly frozen to the pavement, but he no longer cared as much about the cold. Bert made a quick trip to his car, parked a block over, and returned with the supplies he would need, supplies he'd learned to use during his Marine tour of duty in the Gulf War. While no great thinker, Bert was adept with explosive ordnance, and demolitions had become his hobby when he was discharged. Of course it was an illegal and dangerous hobby, but the Brotherhood was glad to have him and his skills.

After stopping off in the garage where he'd noticed several fuel cans, Bert broke into the funeral home through one of the back doors. Being careful not to show his flashlight, he moved quickly to the end of the corridor. After fiddling with the wall sconces, he freed the painting that camouflaged the safe and inspected it closely. *Not enough light in the hall,* he thought. In the nearest office, he found a tall floor lamp. Its extension cord reached out into the hall. Satisfied with the illumination, he deftly shaped small but effective charges of C-4 around the hinges, and inserted a pair of detonator wires and attached them to an electronic circuit capable of receiving a signal from his remote. Next, he went through the first floor systematically pouring gasoline in a pattern most effective in spreading fire quickly. He dumped file drawers and spread papers to increase the amount of fuel. He closed the door of each room and left the long hallway untouched. It wouldn't do to have gasoline fumes filling the corridor when he set off the charges.

When he was ready, Bert stepped into the office farthest away, the one that had a reflected view of the wall safe, and switched on his transmitter. One press of the button, and a muffled boom shook the other paintings. From his vantage point, he saw the door of the safe swing open. Bert ran to the safe, opening the doors along the hall as he went. He billowed out a plastic trash bag he'd brought from the kitchen, and tried to elbow the twisted metal door out of the way. Unfortunately, its weight could not be supported by the lock alone, and it fell. The door was dense and amazingly heavy for its size. Bert, wearing only thin rubber galoshes over street shoes, yowled in pain when the door, with gravity as its primary motivation, plummeted to the floor and broke several bones in his foot. In his anguish, he began hopping around on the other foot, not heeding the placement of his equipment bag directly behind him. Arms flailing wildly, he sailed backward, at which point Bert experienced one of those cruel cosmic jokes that are only humorous from a very broad perspective. It was a chain of tiny events that required the utmost coincidence to achieve such an unexpected result.

First, he'd been in a hurry to find the right detonator wires, and had carelessly left his favorite long screwdriver sticking up out of the bag at a rakish angle. Then, of course, there was the safe door difficulty—and the pain and the hopping and the falling down, none of which would have been life-threatening in itself. But taken together, the result was most unfortunate. The tip of the screwdriver slipped neatly between Bert's ribs, plunged through soft tissue, and drove directly into the heart. He felt the pressure as he was impaled, yet oddly, there was no pain. He looked longingly at the stacks of the cash in the safe, and only then did he notice the lazy movement of the floor lamp, swaying, teetering. He stared up at the hot light bulb, its filament like a tiny blaze under glass, smelled the gasoline fumes all around him, and saw the outcome with horrible clarity. Desperately, he tried to snatch at the lamp. As he did, the screwdriver tip moved, too, and tore through his aorta. Blood flooded into his chest cavity. The lamp's bulb exploded on contact with the floor and ignited the gasoline with an enormous *fwoomp* of searing heat. Providentially, Bert was already dead.

It was almost twenty minutes before anyone noticed the flames dancing in the windows of the funeral home, and another twelve minutes before firefighters began arriving.

Before they could start pouring water through the windows, the enormous old structure was fully involved. Fifteen minutes later, the roof collapsed and the walls began to fall inward. The firefighters turned their entire attention to protecting neighboring buildings and the garage in the rear. The realization that there might have been deceased persons in residence raised no immediate alarm, but did give rise to a number of cremation jokes, some of them clever.

It was two hours before the fire was knocked down and another two before Bert's body was discovered. The FBI wasn't alerted until the next morning, a little payback for the jurisdictional squabble it had won the day before.

Chapter Fourteen

They are all gone into the world of light,
And I alone sit lingering here;
Their very memory is fair and bright
And my sad thoughts doth clear.
—Henry Vaughan, "They Are All Gone"

The six of them gathered around the conference table, though the hour was late and the entire company tired. As the Carlisles had traveled from several time zones ahead of the States, Benjamin suggested they might want to put off the meeting until the morning. But the Carlisles spent only an hour in their rooms in meditation before joining the others.

"I don't think we have the luxury of time," William began, as he passed out a set of file folders from his voluminous briefcase. "It will take a little time to explain, and there are some gaps. Let me begin by describing what we encountered when our circle met night before last." He looked at each of them in turn, as if gathering their full attention. "I warrant this will sound a bit strange, but bear with us." He smiled at Ellen. "We cast the circle with a particular intention. Ordinarily, we meet on a regular basis simply to check in with the state of the world, if you will. We sometimes encounter areas in the fabric of this dimension or others that are strained or damaged: the sort of problem that might arise from an irresponsible or, on occasion, a malevolent use of magic."

Though he wasn't looking directly at Connor, his finely tuned senses intercepted the spasm of disbelief that passed through her. "You don't like that word, do you?" he said, raising his eyes to meet hers.

"Not really. It makes me think of guys pulling rabbits out of hats."

William chuckled. "The word *magic* is open to misinterpretation because performers and sometimes charlatans pretend to employ it. But that isn't the kind I'm talking about. I use the word only because it's convenient. In our sense, it means the manipulation of power, of soul energy. That kind of energy forms a grid that connects all of creation, and, if properly understood and respected, it can be used to alter reality, or delve into the mysteries of other dimensions of being. You've seen it happen, Connor," he added softly.

She stared at him for a moment, then nodded. "Yes. In Glastonbury. I can't explain it any other way."

"Good, then we can proceed with moderate faith in the truth of what I'm saying." He opened a file. "The first few pages summarize with extreme brevity the workings of our circle between 1937 until 1945. Naturally, neither Ellen nor I were part of it. I was a tiny child, and Ellen just born. But your grandmother was there." He paused. "Would you like to read it to yourselves, or shall I simply relay the salient points?"

Benjamin nodded. "We can read it in detail later."

"All right then. During World War II, Britain eventually stood alone as the last European country not conquered or occupied by Hitler's armies. There are those to this day who cannot understand why he was unable to overrun our tiny island. He had massive land, sea, and air forces at his command,

and he had a detailed plan in place to land troops on British shores. At the time, only the Royal Air Force stood between our nation and Hitler's soldiers. Even their gallantry and tenacity, however, could not keep us safe. You may recall stories of the air raids, the many nights that thousands of Londoners spent in the underground Tube stations to escape the destruction. More and more of the RAF planes were shot down, and fewer and fewer pilots were available to fly the aircraft that remained. The Americans were coming to our aid, but they, too, had been forced to gear up for a war that took so many people by surprise." He paused to take a sip of water.

"The people of your circle weren't surprised, were they?" said Laura suddenly.

William looked at her and smiled. "You're quite right. They knew of Adolf Hitler as a threat long before anyone else took notice. To so many people, he was just a funny-looking little man, shouting his ridiculous speeches to a handful of fanatics. But our circle saw something else. And they weren't the only ones. We are by no means the only group of adepts in England. At the time, a number of groups following various paths and spiritual traditions were getting quite anxious. Back then, however, there was a certain tradition of separatism. Wiccans didn't work with Druids, who didn't work with Goddess circles, and so forth. So not enough information was shared. But each group, in its own way, had picked up the danger signs years before."

William took another sip of water, and turned to Ellen. "Would you carry on, love? I'm afraid I'm a little hoarse from so many days of talking."

"Certainly, darling. What the adepts of each tradition saw long before Hitler came to so much power was that his ambitions were not based solely on raising an enormous army. Yes, h did that, and he formed organizations like the S.S. in order to perfect his plans. But he also was relying heavily on the use of occult power. The skilled light workers knew he existed even before they knew his name. They saw the drawing in of the darkness, the formation of a vortex in its earliest stages. If he were able to acquire sufficiently powerful adepts of his own, Hitler was going to be very dangerous."

"And he was," said Benjamin.

"Indeed. But at the time, there weren't many in our government who would have even listened politely to such warnings. Yes, there were a few, praise be, but not enough. The light workers, the adepts, the priests and priestesses of the traditions simply had to do the best they could."

"So why didn't they all get together and give him a big psychic blast or something?" asked Malcolm.

"But that's exactly what they couldn't do," answered Ellen, "though I'm sure it was very tempting for our predecessors. But," she hesitated for a moment to gather her thoughts, "the use of true magic carries with it grave responsibility. And, quite frankly, there are rules. We all acknowledge that darkness has its place in the fabric of creation, as does every opposite, just like matter and antimatter. Each of us has ventured into the dark places. Darkness exists as surely as light. It is a teacher."

"What does that mean?" asked Connor. "What can we learn evil?"

t evil, Connor. Darkness. And yes, before you accuse me semantics, there *is* a difference. Darkness is the opposite. It is the stuff of which fear is made. And fear courage and faith and hope. From darkness comes a s of envy or lack. But it can also teach us gratitude.
e   he other hand—that is darkness turned in upon

itself, molded and formed into a power that is angry, aggressive, and abusive. Evil seeks power over others, and it feeds on rage and despair. At the heart of evil is the intent to destroy."

"So you're saying it wouldn't be right to destroy Hitler?" asked Malcolm in disbelief.

"No. The man *had* to be defeated, but if the circles of power in Britain had chosen to actually assault him and his occult workers on that plane, the only outcome would have been the triumph of darkness. I know," she said, reaching out to lay a hand on Malcolm's arm. "It may not make total sense, but believe me, there was really only one answer.

"Once the Germans had overrun France, we knew we were all in great jeopardy. For the first time, the leaders of many different traditions managed to overcome their mistrust of each other or their skepticism about other paths and work in concert. It was agreed that the alliance must first encircle the island with all their collective power. Then, and only then, they would send out a single message, specifically to Adolf Hitler—over and over they told his consciousness that the time was not right to invade England, that to do so before late summer of 1944 would prove disastrous. The alliance did not assault him psychically or other-wise. To have done so would have been suicidal because the power of a violent intent would, by nature of universal law, come back on them."

"That's in the Wiccan tradition, isn't it?" asked Laura. "That anything you send out comes back threefold."

"Yes," Ellen agreed. "And there's a connection there with the holy trinity, but we haven't time now for a detailed lesson."

"You said my grandmother was part of this," Connor said.

"It was in the year of the worst crisis that she came to the role of priestess of the circle of Light, the circle of the Lady."

"Wouldn't she have been awfully young?"

"She was barely into her thirties. Gwendolyn had not expected to assume the mantle for many years, as was the tradition. But her predecessor, only about sixty at the time, fell ill and died, an event we believe may have been caused in some way by Hitler's chief occultist—a man named Wilhelm von Adler."

"Von Adler?" Connor repeated the name. "That sounds familiar."

"It was in the few pieces of documentation we sent you earlier."

"The file photos from the Nazi archives," said Laura. "Yes!"

"So Gwendolyn stepped in," said Connor.

"She did indeed, and the accounts we've read indicate she was nothing short of magnificent." Ellen glowed as she talked about their former leader. "The power and presence of the Lady ran so strongly in her that even those who had refused to join the alliance were inspired to cooperate. Those skeptical of her abilities because of her youth were converted in a single meeting with her. And with all this power at her disposal, and the threat of evil at our very shores, still she would not breach the tenets of our faith."

"Must have taken a lot of self-control," said Connor.

"I believe it did. Those who were there at the time say that Gwendolyn grieved for the soldiers and pilots we lost every day. She wept openly for the children whose bodies were dug out from the rubble of London. And the circle actually felt the horror of the human beings sent to the death camps. But no matter how many times she may have wished to gather up this power and hurl a veritable bolt of thunder at the heart of Germany, she did not break faith and become like the dark ones. We believe that to draw magic from the grid of Soul energy and use it to kill is evil. And to use evil against evil is pointless. The victim becomes the perpetrator. And the light is extinguished. Our circles would likely have been destroyed, or turned to evil purpose."

"So she chose to defend and delay," Benjamin commented.

"Exactly. The Americans were pouring in to assist, although they had their hands full in the Pacific Theater. D-Day was less than a year off."

"They knew about D-Day?" asked Malcolm.

William smiled at him. "Our circle can see the patterns developing out in the future. The members didn't know the precise dates, but they saw it as a distinct possibility if Hitler could be distracted long enough. Earlier on, we'd spent a great deal of time encouraging him to continue his campaign on the Russian front. We may have even given him the impression it would be extraordinarily successful."

Benjamin smiled. "He apparently believed you to the bitter end. He sent tens of thousands of troops to be chewed up by the Red Army."

Laura leaned forward. "I hope I'm not jumping ahead here. I mean, I want to know all this, but you said time was pressing. Back at the church this morning you said that if the Nazis had had both halves of this pendant, they might have prevailed."

William frowned. "I think that is true. As it was, the circles and covens barely held together under the onslaught from Hitler's cadre of occultists. Most of them were extremely powerful and profoundly committed to the use of darkness as a weapon. But one of the saving graces, at least for our part, was that evil is by its own nature remarkably uncooperative in sharing power and influence. Whereas we could overcome our differences and work together, each of Hitler's black magicians truly wanted power for himself. Thus the Reich's fortunes ebbed and flowed. At first it seemed there was nothing that could stop them. When our people were not yet working together, Hitler's armies and the S.S. overran country after country. So well did the occultists do their work that in some cases there was hardly any resistance at all. They put around Hitler and his inner circle something like what old-time witches would call a 'glamour.' It made thousands of people see them as heroes and glorious conquerors."

"So what changed?"

"Other human beings weren't fooled," said Ellen. "And they got to work on the problem."

"So his plans started going awry," said Benjamin. "His armies got almost to Moscow and then started losing ground until they were in full retreat."

"Everywhere, an underground resistance had sprung up, and we sent them our light and love. They could do things on the human plane that we could not, in respect of the Lady, the Holy Mother, do in the ethereal planes."

"You mean armed resistance?" asked Malcolm.

Ellen nodded. "Precisely. What we are about is essentially prayer. That is how we draw power from the Source, from God, if you will. The resistance movements acted in self-defense, not in aggression. Yes, they used force, and that was their right and choice. We sent them hope and faith."

"But you said the alliance could have been defeated."

"Sorry, we got a bit off track there," said Ellen. "Yes, that is true, because at one point, something happened that began to swing the balance toward the black magicians. They began acting in complete concert." Her expression was troubled. "Gwendolyn, who had become the nominal leader of the alliance, was nearly overwhelmed while in the other plane, and she came face-to-face, so to speak, with a symbol as large as life. She recognized it at once because it had been associated with her tradition for hundreds of years."

"The Goddess of Avebury," Laura blurted out, then blushed a little. "Sorry, didn't mean to interrupt."

"That's quite all right, my dear, and you are correct. What Gwendolyn saw was part of the pendant that had been made in honor of that goddess's power. But the key to the pendant and its enormous potential power lies in a paradox, and it's one we've touched on tonight." She turned to Connor, who was staring into space as if in a trance. "You already understand, don't you?"

Connor swallowed hard. "I do. I'm not sure how, but it just came to me. Unlike the object we discovered in Glastonbury, the pendant is neither light nor dark. It's both." She took a deep breath, and when she spoke again her voice carried a faintly different inflection. "It is both faces of the Mother, both terrible and wonderful. She is the dark earth and the womb from which all is born. She is water and she is fire." Connor fell silent, and Malcolm made as if to reach for her, his face creased with concern. William put a restraining hand on his arm and whispered, "Let her be."

They waited and within a minute or so, Connor sat back in her chair and looked around the table. "Well, that was weird."

"What happened, sweetheart?" Benjamin asked.

"Kind of waking dream, I guess. But my grandmother was there, telling me about the pendant. I think I was repeating some of that to you."

"Yes, and since you could see her so easily, Connor, you will be more open to understanding the rest of this story."

Laura put her hand on Connor's knee in a gesture of support, and all eyes were once more on Ellen.

"The figure Gwendolyn encountered was indeed half of the pendant, the silver half. Somehow the Nazis had acquired not only the pendant, but—and this was the shock—someone associated *by blood* with the line of keepers of the pendant."

"You mean one of the original light workers had turned against you—that is, the alliance?"

"No, the pendant had been lost for more than half a century. Gwendolyn's circle of adepts had searched for its energy signature quite diligently on many occasions. Of course, they'd been seeking the balanced vibration of the complete pendant. I don't know that anyone had considered it might have been separated, or that it could be separated. Only those entrusted as its guardians would know all of its secrets."

"So Gwendolyn was surprised?" said Malcolm.

"More than that, she was shocked almost into losing her connection to the circles that protected her journeying out onto the astral planes. My mother later told me they almost lost her completely. The conflict between Gwendolyn and the one we came to know as Wilhelm von Adler sent huge waves across the grid they'd established. When Gwendolyn finally returned to her earthly form, she was unconscious for two days."

"But why?"

"The worst aspect of the pendant's power is why it came to be called *le voleur d'âmes,* the thief of souls."

"I don't get it," said Malcolm, his face screwed into a skeptical frown. "Stealing souls sounds like something out of a Dracula movie."

William smiled broadly. "Oh, my dear fellow, don't let's get started on the story of vampires, or we'll be here all night. But yes, I understand it sounds bizarre. It isn't possible to literally steal a soul, of course. Each one is quite attached to its host body and personal realities quite firmly. And a soul isn't a commodity to be possessed. But this is more of a figurative theft, and only becomes a problem when the pendant is separated and thus, unbalanced in its power."

"So what does it do?" asked Laura.

Ellen took over the narrative once more. "Somehow the pendant imbues its wearer with the ability to see beyond the veil of ordinary mortal reality, to see right into the darkest corners of the individual soul. This isn't necessarily a negative power. The priestesses of the particular circle in that era would no doubt use the pendant to help their followers survive what are often called dark nights of the soul. The priestess would have enormous insight into the causes of both spiritual and emotional pain and be able to serve as guide. The other half of the pendant, made from gold that symbolizes the heart center, ensures that this work is carried out with great love, compassion, and delicacy."

"And without the golden half," said Connor, "there is only the raw power, untempered and unchecked, and susceptible to misuse."

Ellen nodded in obvious approval. "Exactly. But only if it is wielded by a person of the pendant guardian's bloodline. Since Wilhelm von Adler was able to use it, the alliance had to assume that he was of that line."

William flipped several pages in the folder. "We've included a research report that's been compiled after many years' work. And we did find the answer to Wilhelm. But first let us finish the story of World War II.

"Please do. What happened after Gwendolyn's encounter?" asked Laura, on the edge of her seat.

"The word went out among them to find the other half, and in the meantime, the power base of the alliance was reinforced tenfold. They went into round-the-clock meditation, prayer, and ritual. And still it was touch-and-go for several weeks. Finally, a very elderly gentleman, the chief celebrant of a sect of Gnostic Christians, came to Gwendolyn with a story about the pendant. His grandfather had been a village priest some miles inland from the coastal town of Chillwater. This was around the turn of the century, 1800 or perhaps a little later. One night, his grandfather accompanied the Duke of Crevier to a manor house where the duke accused a child of being a witch. The little girl was the daughter of Genevieve Miranda Fitzhugh, and we suspect she probably had already displayed some of the psychic powers that ran in that family."

"But surely they'd gotten over the witch scare by the beginning of the nineteenth century," said Connor.

"Generally, yes. But this particular nobleman was obsessed with the idea that his family's honor depended on stamping out so-called evil. Anyway, the vicar was drawn into this by virtue of his being the only local cleric, and was apparently horrified when the duke assaulted Lady Fitzhugh, who had been recently widowed. Then, when he failed to find the child, he set fire to the manor house, because the mother had insisted the child was well hidden and would never show herself."

"Dear Lord," said Malcolm. "He burned a child alive."

"Well, perhaps, and perhaps not. The vicar insisted that the child could not have been there, for they remained until the structure was fully in flames, and there was no sound of any person in distress. He became convinced that Lady Fitzhugh had been warned and had sent the child away. Apparently a stable boy also went missing that night," William consulted his report. "Jack Fortis."

"What became of Lady Fitzhugh?" Laura asked.

"According to this man's story, the duke had her confined to a prison and then sent to an asylum for the insane in France. Before her death a few months later, she gave birth to a child, a son, who was adopted by a wealthy family because of his noble lineage. We believe Wilhelm von Adler was a direct descendant of that child, and that somehow the pendant, or rather, half of the pendant stayed with him, and was passed down in the family."

"But how did he get involved with the Nazis?"

"They recruited heavily, especially during the latter years of the war. There were far more Nazi sympathizers than most people realize. Our theory is that Wilhelm was one of those recruits and one of the black magicians somehow recognized him on a psychic level, or perhaps saw the pendant. Much of this is conjecture, but we think these are viable theories."

"So, how does all of this connect to Gwendolyn and Wilhelm?" Laura asked.

Ellen went on. "The old man's story held the key to Wilhelm's defeat, or more accurately, the defeat of the black magicians. Once she understood who the young man really was, it occurred to Gwendolyn that he wasn't nearly experienced enough to command Hitler's occult circle. For that is what was happening. Someone was commanding it. The power of the pendant had literally taken over the soul volition of the occultists and was being channeled into one extraordinarily potent weapon. Gwendolyn surmised that there was a powerful and undeniably evil intelligence at work, controlling Wilhelm."

"Hitler himself?" asked Benjamin.

"No, he wasn't really at all talented in that way, though he longed to wield that sort of power. Instead, he had to rely on others. Chief among them was Himmler, of course, but there was also a more shadowy figure, only referred to as Herr Doktor. We don't know his surname, but his Christian name began with an *f*, according to a few letters that were found after the fall of Berlin."

"But the investigation was incredibly thorough," Connor interjected. "They amassed thousands of documents for the

Nuremberg trials. I don't see how they could have failed to identify any of the men on Hitler's staff."

"Nor do I," said William, who had served with British intelligence before his retirement. "There had to be something else at
work. We think this Herr Doktor had planned far in advance to
conceal his identity. And we think he may have been able to exercise some form of power over the minds of others to literally
erase his existence from their conscious memories."

"Like some sort of Svengali," Benjamin commented.

"Very much so, but not with uniform success. Two months
before D-Day, Gwendolyn broke through Wilhelm's astral projection and literally flew like an arrow of light to the very center
of the black magicians' power. As she later told the story, she
finally encountered the man she dubbed the puppeteer of the
whole show."

"But how did that help?" asked Connor.

William explained. "You see, she now *knew* him. On the
astral planes. She could set her field of energy to directly offset
his. As long as the alliance could not find him in that sense,
they could not stop him from exercising the combined power
of the occultists. But Gwendolyn had torn away his mask.
Wilhelm himself was far too inexperienced to be a threat to the
alliance, and the Doktor couldn't muster enough power by
himself to defeat all of the power being wielded in the defense
of England. Basically, he gave up."

"You mean my grandmother ran him out of town on a rail."

"Spoken like a true John Wayne fan," smiled Laura.

Connor blushed. "I'm into bigger-than-life heroes."

Ellen nodded. "Your grandmother was extremely courageous.
She went back to the field of conflict, even after the incident that
nearly killed her."

"She was also stubborn as hell," Connor added.

"No argument there," said Ellen with a broad smile. "Thank Spirit for that."

Malcolm was starting to fidget. "I don't mean to be rude, and I'm trying hard not to be impatient, but how does any of this help us now? And Connor and Laura have a gold pendant, not a silver one."

Ellen sat up straighter. "The pendant tucked away in your safe is the gold half. It wasn't really very difficult to trace Grace Wainwright's ancestry once we had a starting point, or rather, an ending point. Up to now, none of us has known what became of the golden half, or whether Lady Fitzhugh's daughter even lived.

"Grace's middle name, by the way, is also Miranda. All the guardians of the pendant have had that as their first or second name as part of the tradition. We found an unbroken connection leading back in time from your friend Grace to one Eliza Miranda Fitzhugh, the daughter of Lady Genevieve. The pendant is always passed to the eldest daughter, thus the surnames change over the generations, but 'Miranda' as a first or middle name makes it easier to follow the thread."

"So she's theoretically the current guardian?" asked Laura.

"Yes, although we seriously doubt she has any knowledge of this."

"I doubt it, too. She wouldn't have been so willing to turn over the pendant to us if she'd had any inkling of its significance. And maybe her mother didn't truly know either."

"What can this half of the Goddess of Avebury pendant do by itself?" asked Benjamin with his usual pragmatism.

"Nothing really, unless it is wielded by a guardian," William hesitated, "or by one who has been initiated into its secrets."

"Well, that lets all of us out," sighed Connor with visible relief.

"Not precisely," replied William, and everyone in the room except Ellen waited for the other shoe to drop. "Gwendolyn would have been able to use it to counteract the negative force that the *le voleur d'âmes* embodies. She was intimately familiar with its strengths and weaknesses."

"But Gwendolyn's not here," Connor reminded them a bit sharply. "At least not in the walking-around wielding-magical-objects sense."

"Yes," said Ellen. "But *you're* here."

Connor stared at her for several seconds. "You can't be serious!"

"But I am," Ellen replied calmly, meeting her gaze. "For all that you pretend to disbelieve, you've felt the magic coursing through you, just as you did in Glastonbury."

"That was different. I had no choice but to help, because of my Dad."

"Perhaps at the time, because you thought his life was in the balance, you persuaded yourself to move past fear, but the strength to do so has always been within you. Of that, Gwendolyn had no doubt."

"But why do we have to do anything with the pendant?! Why can't you simply take it back to England and keep it safe?"

William shrugged. "We can do that, and eventually we will. But not until it is reunited with its sister and those who would use that other half for ill have been disarmed."

"But you just said it has no power without a guardian to use it. I'd have to assume this Wilhelm character's been dead for a very long time."

"And his descendants?" asked Ellen.

Connor shook her head. "You don't know for sure if there are any."

William leaned forward in his chair. "We do know. You see, where the possibilities of discovering truth in the physical realm may be limited by intellectual knowledge and the absence of written records, there is much one can discover in the nonphysical. This is one of the reasons we're so concerned. Not only did Wilhelm have descendants, but as of the last meeting of our circle, shortly before we got the news about Amanda, one of those heirs is in possession of the silver half of the pendant."

"But how do you know that," asked Malcolm. "What evidence did you discover?"

William turned to him. "Asked like a true copper," he said quite seriously. "But I doubt you'd find the answer very satisfactory. Would you be willing to take our word for it?"

Malcolm paused, mulling over the idea. "Pretty much, but at least tell us what it is you've discovered with your… um…investigation."

"We've told you about the grid of energies that crisscross the planet," he began, but Connor interrupted.

"Wait a second. We didn't discuss the pendant with you until after my mother was killed. We didn't even know about it. Now you're saying that you were focused on it before then."

"We hadn't focused on it yet. But we'd become aware of a connection between a power object that had once drawn Gwendolyn's energies to it, and someone at this very time who wishes so desperately to control it that his own innate powers have become visible to us on the astral planes. One of the reasons for this is because of the locale from which we felt this obsession emanating—the heart of Germany."

"Someone in Germany has the silver half of the pendant?" asked Laura.

"No, fortunately. The person who wants it is not the person who has it."

"So let me get this straight," said Benjamin. "The person who seeks its power would then have to control the rightful heir in order to exercise the inherent power of *le voleur d'âmes.*"

"Indeed."

"But what assurance could he…I'm sorry, is this person male or female?"

"The energy signature is of a male incarnation," said Ellen.

"How could he be sure of controlling the guardian?"

"If the legends are reasonably accurate, and we believe they are, the pendant isn't passive. In other words, in the hands of an unskilled and untrained person, the pendant would tend to direct the actions of the guardian rather than the other way 'round. There is a powerful centuries-old link between the object and its keepers. And the link is about balance. But the living guardians—Ms. Wainwright and the descendant of Wilhelm von Adler—are neither skilled nor trained nor even consciously aware of their own souls."

"Who is Wilhelm von Adler's descendant?" asked Laura

Ellen shook her head. "That's the limitation on our method. We can follow an energy or a vibration to its approximate source geographically speaking, but we can't then peer through the ethers and see a nameplate on someone's desk." She chuckled. "This isn't science fiction, after all."

The others laughed aloud, and Ellen, who'd sensed a need for comic relief to ease the tension, was glad of it.

"If this isn't science fiction, I don't know what is," said Connor, as her mirth subsided.

"I know it may seem that way," Ellen nodded. "But, again, take it on faith if you can. Someone in Germany has been actively and ruthlessly pursuing the pendant."

"Which half?" asked Connor.

William shrugged. "Either, although given the possibility of the Nazi Germany connection, I suspect it's the silver half and the guardian related to Wilhelm. Still, since someone has made a clear effort to steal the gold half from you and Laura, it seems logical to assume that the Wainwright women have been identified as the descendants of Lady Fitzhugh. Thus, this malignancy we've felt in Germany is now focused on both halves."

"But they didn't try to steal it when Grace had it," argued Connor.

"Why should they? It's of little or no use without Grace, or her mother. If someone wants the pendant for what it can do, they probably know they would need someone of the bloodline to at least activate its energy."

They were all silent, until Laura spoke. "So maybe Catherine Wainwright's car accident was no accident."

"Someone thought Grace would be easier to control without her mother around," suggested Connor.

"And what about the aunt?" asked Benjamin. "You suppose they were afraid she was also an obstacle."

"Very likely," said Ellen. "I believe you told me there was a question of dispute over the will Grace's mother left. And all this tragedy is bound to keep Grace off balance, and susceptible to some very unwholesome influence. The persons behind this may also be interested in Grace's wealth."

"She has been acting strange," said Connor.

"Strange how?"

"Not like herself, at least not entirely the person I once knew." Connor paused for a beat, looking mildly uncomfortable. Laura, next to her, squeezed Connor's hand. "She always was a little temperamental and even jealous. But now she's so—how shall I put this?—changeable. One minute she's acting selfish and difficult, and the next, she's completely different, almost apologetic."

Ellen and William nodded simultaneously.

"You think she's being influenced?"

"Again, it's quite possible," replied Ellen, "but we mustn't leap to conclusions. Her behavior could simply be due to emotional strain, or some sort of psychological imbalance. I think tomorrow we'll contact our other members and attempt to form a cohesive circle in the astral plane."

"Why do you say 'attempt'?" asked Laura, her expression curious.

"Because, since Gwendolyn's departure, we've never successfully held the circle for more than a few minutes unless we're together in the same physical space that has been psychically sealed for everyone's protection. I'm only a stand-in for Gwendolyn. I've never been able to access the level of power that she could."

Again the attention shifted to Connor, but Laura intervened. "But you said you have been able to detect something happening on the astral plane."

Ellen sighed ever so slightly. "Yes, of course. We're able to actually see the grid of energies when our circle is operative in the astral planes. Imbalance, danger, conflict—all these are evident to us because of their colors and vibrations." She paused, noting Malcolm's attempts to keep his natural skepticism from showing. "I know it all sounds unlikely, my friend. But that's how it is."

"Sorry, please just keep going and ignore me."

"You're not a man I'd ever choose to ignore, Captain. But, as I was saying, we can detect certain conditions, if you will, that exist. There's a dark, highly powerful concentration of malevolent intent centered in Germany. From that core we sensed an old connection, the one to Gwendolyn. The energy pattern of that thread was old; it corresponded to the one our circle felt during World War II. Keep in mind that our circle's experiential memory is collective, stretching from the long-distant past. Any work the circle has ever done in the astral realms is part of our current knowledge." She paused for a sip of water.

"In addition, the energy signature of the concentrated intent is also familiar."

"The occultists working for Hitler," Connor blurted out.

Ellen nodded vigorously. "Yes. Not necessarily the same individuals, but the same sort of power they raised fifty years ago." She shuddered slightly. "It isn't pleasant to encounter, even with the protection of one's colleagues."

"So now explain about the silver half being here."

"Once we began to sense what to look for, we made a thorough examination. We focused each astral journey on combing the grids of energy. It took a long time because the von Adler pendant is no longer in use and no longer vibrates at its active energy. We found residual traces through time and followed the clues to America."

"Where?" said Benjamin, Laura, and Malcolm almost simultaneously.

But before she could answer, Connor said one word, "Massachusetts."

After a moment's silence, William looked hard at Connor. "Why, yes," he said. "But is that a guess or a knowing?"

Connor squirmed slightly in her seat, and then sighed. "I guess...I know, even if I don't know how. But my grandmother always said there's no such thing as coincidence. Events are always part of one divine pattern, even if it's too enormous to see clearly."

William smiled broadly. "I imagine Gwendolyn is quite pleased to know you were listening to her teaching."

"I listened," Connor protested. "I just didn't always agree."

"Spoken like a true priestess," said Ellen. "It's occurred to you that all the threads of this long story appear to be converging here."

"Yes. The deaths in Grace's family, my mother, Devin Underwood. The link between him and Arthur Raley and the Supreme Aryan Brotherhood. And now whatever this is you're sensing in Germany. Something's happening, and it isn't good."

"Try not to attach a value judgment to the events themselves, Connor," Ellen chided gently. "We have no idea if what is happening will turn out positively for us, or for the world at large. All we can do is set our intentions and stand in the light."

"You really think I need to be involved in this...I mean, in the circle? You think I can do something about the pendant?"

"It's a possibility, Connor," said William. "We only want you to be aware that the need might arise. In the meantime, just keep on pursuing the truth the way you always have. Dogged information-gathering and analysis might be more prosaic, but it, too, has great value."

Ellen yawned. "There is still much to discuss, but I have to admit I'm knackered. How about we reconvene early in the morning?"

No one objected, and they retired to their respective rooms. In the hallway Laura took Connor's arm. "You're really bugged about all this, aren't you?"

"Yeah, I suppose I am. The thing is, I don't mind taking on a challenge, but everything associated with my so-called heritage seems more like a burden, like the job is choosing me instead of me choosing it."

Laura squeezed her upper arm. "That's because it is, honey. Now let's get some sleep."

★

She stood in the midst of a circle of women, a part of her remembering dimly that at some time, in some place, she was a person named Connor Hawthorne. Yet here she was something quite different, something much more. Their mouths did not move, these silver-robed figures, yet she heard their thoughts as clearly as if they spoke aloud. Her mind did not perceive a jumble of words or images projected all at once, but rather an harmonious blend of visual and auditory input that stretched from past to present to future in an unbroken stream. This, she knew, was the sacred sisterhood of which Gwendolyn was a part.

Gradually, her grandmother's voice grew distinct, and the other voices gently receded as if providing a musical accompaniment to the main melody.

"Still afraid, my child?"

"Yes."

"Of what?"

"What I don't understand—what I can't see and touch and take hold of with my hands."

"It sounds as if we're losing ground, dear, instead of making progress in your education."

"You know I already have a very good education, thanks to my parents."

"Don't be impudent, child."

"Sorry. But being here scares me."

"Then why did you come?"

"I don't know that I meant to. It just happened."

"Fortunately, your Soul knows its path," said Gwendolyn. "Even if your human ego is a bit bruised in the process."

Connor felt the circle contract around her. The women moved closer until she could see starlight in their eyes. Their bodies were indistinct in their robes. She had the sensation she could almost see right through them.

"You can see through them," Gwendolyn said.

"What?"

"You can see through them because they aren't really there, not in the sense you're thinking. Their souls are gathered, but I doubt you'd be able to detect them without some manifestation of form in the Dreamtime."

"You mean they've taken form so I can see them?"

"In a sense."

"What am I supposed to do, Grandmother?"

"About what?"

"This pendant for one thing, and the circle for another. I don't know how to be what they want me to be."

"Of course you do, but you're not ready. William and Ellen and the others will wait patiently until it is time."

"But what about right now?"

"For now, be your true Self. Live every minute with great love for your fellow human beings, even the ones it is difficult to love. Which reminds me, the one you call Ayalla needs your friendship. Do not withhold it from her."

"But she hates who I am."

"No, she fears what she does not understand. There is a great difference."

"I'll do my best."

"That is all anyone can ask of you, my dear granddaughter. Your work with Ellen and William is paramount. The amulet you call the Goddess of Avebury pendant must be reunited and safely tucked away where it cannot be used for harmful purposes."

"But I still don't see what the harm is exactly. William and Ellen said it had been used to focus dark magic."

"That isn't what it was intended to do. They will explain it, my dear. Keep your questions for the light of day. We are here, you and I and my sisters in Spirit, simply to be with each other, to share our joy in being present in the Presence of the Creator of all things."

The music of golden voices rose again, this time spiraling higher and deeper, into the earth plane, into the dimensions of time, wrapping all manifestation into a single, eternal note. Connor slipped into the mists, wrapped in unspeakable joy, and she slept.

CHAPTER FIFTEEN

Time's glory is to calm contending Kings,
To unmask falsehood, and bring truth to light.
—William Shakespeare, *The Rape of Lucrece,* preface

By the time Ayalla reached the new crime scene—the burned-out shell that had been Dagle & Sons Funeral Home—she was ready to face the music. Her first inkling of fresh disaster was a furious summons from her boss. He hadn't bothered to brief her on many details. All she knew was that a fire had consumed the place and at least one "mystery" body had been found. The others had been deceased and embalmed before the fire started. This one had been fresh and had not died of natural causes.

When she arrived, her hair pulled back in a tight, still-wet ponytail, a lone fire engine remained, its personnel raking through the rubble. Police and crime scene investigators were poking about. She identified herself and joined the small huddle of FBI agents standing in the rear parking lot, wondering how she would broach the subject of the wall safe and the box of letters that had apparently belonged to Devin Underwood's grandfather. When she walked up, Ken Morgenstern, the SAC in charge of the Boston field office, glared at her. The other agents, the team she was currently supervising, kept their gazes fixed on each other's neckties.

"So what the hell happened here?" Morgenstern growled. "You secured this scene last night, didn't you?"

"Yes," she said firmly, her voice steady.

"Then how is it we've got a fresh crispy critter in the corridor?"

"I assume he broke in, sir."

"You assume? And how is it we find a whole lot of charred money in a wall safe? I was under the impression that you and your crack team had done a thorough search."

Ayalla's mind raced. If she admitted having found the safe but hadn't reported it immediately, there would be hell to pay. Morgenstern would use it against her. Of that she was sure. Then there was the matter of the box of letters. She'd taken them into her apartment the night before, too tired to even think of reading any of them. After so many hours without sleep, she'd simply peeled off her clothes and landed face down on the mattress. But having potential evidence in her possession for that many hours was a serious breach of the rules. Her stomach churned with acid, and before she'd made a conscious decision one way or the other, Morgenstern tipped the scales with his warm, sunny personality.

"The rest of you take a hike," he snapped at the other agents. "I want to talk to *her*."

Ayalla gritted her teeth. Not even the courtesy of using her rank or title. The guy was a real son of a bitch.

Morgenstern leaned in close, and she almost gagged on the mixture of cheap cologne and even cheaper cigars. "You fuck this up any more than you already have, and you're goin' back to Washington with your tail between your legs. Some affirmative action schmuck thought he could shove you down my throat, but I don't have to like it, and I don't have to give you diddly-squat to do. But Skinner wanted you on this one because you know that big shot Hawthorne and his queer daughter." He paused, a malicious little smile on his lips. "Been wonderin' just how well you know her."

Ayalla stepped back. "What the hell are you implying?"

"Like you don't know. But I don't give a flying fuck about your lezzie friend and her daddy. I've got two years to retirement, and you're not going screw it up for me. So you get this investigation closed in seventy-two hours, or I'm turning it over to someone I can trust." He started to walk away, then turned back. "And don't even think about filing a complaint on me. You're not the only one with pals in the Bureau."

He strode to his car and drove away with a characteristic screeching of rubber. Ayalla tried to find the impetus to move. She knew the other agents were staring at her. She couldn't lose it here, not in front of them. She closed her eyes for a moment, took two deep breaths. Her intermittent yoga practice was coming in handy these days.

"All right," she told them, finding her voice. "Let's get to work. We need an ID on the body in the corridor. Let the locals handle notification of the families of the deceased who were awaiting funeral services. Morgenstern said there was cash in a wall safe…" She hesitated only a fraction of a second. "Let's recover every scrap we can and try to lift serial numbers. Dietrich, you get with the arson people and see what they have. Not that it will come as a surprise. I can smell the gasoline from here. Just remember, people, we need to move fast. You already know one of our chief suspects was shot last night. We need to find out who was in the house after we left."

Three of the agents moved away briskly to carry out her orders, but one guy, a thirty-something agent by the name of Bob McLuskey, stayed behind.

"What, Bob?" she asked.

"I, that is, I wanted you to know that most of us think you've gotten a raw deal from Morgenstern. The way he's treated you…"

Ayalla was surprised how only a few kind words made the tears prickle at the back of her eyes. Thank God for her sunglasses.

"Anyway, even though some of the agents are like Morgenstern, most of 'em aren't. Just thought you should know that." He walked away.

Ayalla sighed. "Well, I'll be damned." Just when she thought she had this bunch figured out. She watched the crime scene people at work, and her mind wandered to that box, now locked once more in her trunk. She had to find out what was inside, because maybe, just maybe, that's what someone had been after last night.

A medical examiner's team was carrying a body bag toward their van—the victim from the hallway. Who was it? Arthur Raley, the only other conspirator they suspected, or someone else entirely?

Her cell phone rang. She flipped it open and punched the send key.

"Hey, girl. I've been tryin' to reach you since last night." Malcolm's silky baritone was a balm to her spirit.

"Sorry, we've had some problems. Are you okay? I tried to call, but your cell phone didn't answer."

"Don't worry about it, and yes, I'm fine. But how about you? Benjamin told us what happened."

"I'm in a lot better shape than Devin Underwood."

"Any idea who shot him?"

"No. And now there's the fire."

"What?"

"Someone torched the funeral home last night. We've got a suspect, but he's toast. And my boss is just itching to make me look bad, like I screwed up."

"Shit."

"Yeah."

"So I think maybe we can help."

"Who's we?"

"You know, the gang's all here, kind of."

"Yes, I figured. But I've got a lot to do, Malcolm."

"Believe me, you need to take some time. If you're gonna have a prayer of solving this, you need to know what we've found out."

"I thought you were at death's door. And you've been running around investigating?" Ayalla realized she sounded more annoyed than she really was and took another deep, hopefully cleansing breath.

"Believe me, I haven't been running anywhere, thanks to Arthur Raley."

"I'm sorry."

"Don't worry about it. When can you break away?"

Ayalla looked at her watch and back to the other agents carrying out their assignments. "Oh, what the hell. I can be there in an hour."

"Good."

"Wait a second. Where *is* 'there'?"

Malcolm gave her the name of the hotel and the suite number where they'd be meeting.

"This better be good," she warned him.

"It'll be interesting," he said, and she could just about hear his smile.

"What does that mean?" Ayalla asked, but he'd already hung up.

"Damn!" She snapped the phone closed, and walked over to where Bob McLuskey was talking to a local cop. "Bob," she said, "a minute?" When he stepped toward her, she said, "I'm going to follow up a lead. It's probably nothing, but I have my cell if you need me. Keep me up-to-date, please."

He smiled at her in his slow, easy way. "Yes, ma'am."

*

Friedrich was exhausted but alert. He refused to succumb to the temptation to sleep in the back of the limousine. It would be a sign of weakness, and, moreover, he never let anyone near him when he slept if only because old habits die hard, especially paranoia. He'd never been to America, and as one who watched only news programs and business reports on television, he was thoroughly unfamiliar with the culture and even the geography. He hated the Americans on principle. It was they who had tipped the balance against the Führer, with all their war planes and fleets of battleships, and their jingoistic foreign policy. Americans believed bigger was better and everyone who arrived on their shores would be subsumed in the "melting pot." Well, one day they would dance to a different tune, even if he could not live to see it.

If Adolf Hitler had taught Friedrich anything, it was that the "public" was a remarkably easy group to manipulate. If discontented, any appeal to their emotions, their greed or their fear would whip them into a frenzy and prime them to do almost anything. By the same token, if content, the body politic would lie as quietly as an old hunting dog that has lost its will to so much as roll over. That is how Friedrich saw most of the world's democracies—fat, rich, and lazy. The people didn't care what their leaders did, as long as the cable TV worked and the grocery store shelves were well stocked. They could be lulled into such complacency that the world could change drastically without a peep out of them. Friedrich understood this, and also understood that the new Reich did not need to directly control millions of people, only those who made the decisions—some politicians, but mostly business executives and military commanders. People would follow like the sheep they were.

At the very least, he needed the Wainwright woman and the golden half of the pendant. He had little hope anymore of finding Wilhelm's family, or his half of the pendant. But he could not wait any longer. He was too close, and he had to believe the omens were in his favor, despite the loss of Devin and the Brotherhood's failure to obtain the pendant. Now that he was here, it would be all right. Friedrich sensed an unfamiliar strength flowing through him, as if his tired arteries and veins had expanded, his body tuned up. He almost thought he could do everything he'd once been able to do as a younger man—and then some.

"Sir, we are at the gate."

Friedrich hadn't been paying attention to the scenery, so he was surprised that the road was hemmed in on both sides with thick stands of trees, many of them without their leaves. Ahead, a barred metal gate sat between heavy steel posts. To the right and left of the gate, an eight-foot fence topped with razor wire stretched as far as he could see. Friedrich approved. The occult work he had been doing alone for years had helped protect this installation from prying eyes. No one who passed saw anything but a benign wooden fence leading to what must surely be a farm. The wards and charms he'd created and sent to the Brotherhood's commanding officer kept out the curiosity seekers, for no one ever became curious about it. Once they had passed by, the location's very existence passed from their conscious awareness.

The limousine was properly checked by two sentries, and Friedrich noted with satisfaction that they wore the correct field dress of the Waffen-SS, the purely military arm of the Schutzstaffel. The car moved on, and another minute and a half brought them to the compound. The driver was quick to open the rear door, and Friedrich stepped out, again marveling at the strength of his legs that had felt so feeble when he boarded the plane in Germany.

Georg Gruber strode from the door of the commandant's office. "*Heil* Hitler!" he shouted, his arm extended smartly.

"*Heil* Hitler," Friedrich responded, returning the salute, and almost smiled at the sight of the handsome, muscular blond man, a mere thirty-four years of age, yet superbly trained and highly dedicated. This, he thought, was the New Reich: men like this one.

"Sir, we have long awaited your arrival. May I show you to your quarters?"

"No, Kommandant, have my luggage sent there. We shall talk now."

"As you wish, sir." Gruber led the way into the office. "Shall I summon the other officers?"

"Not yet. There are things we must discuss first, sensitive matters."

Gruber started to say something, but Friedrich raised his hand to command silence. "I realize your officers are carefully selected and well trained. But you will learn that it is imperative to keep vital facts to yourself. Never share information unless you must. Need I point out that if your Lieutenant Gunther had been caught, he might have proved a serious security risk."

"My men have not been given the details of what we are seeking, or why. They do know of your arrival."

"I suppose that was inevitable, but be extremely careful from this moment on. The future depends upon it."

"Yes, Reichsmarschall."

Friedrich regarded him for several moments, and said a silent prayer to the gods of war that he had chosen the right man for the job. Georg didn't know it yet, but he was destined to command much more than a handful of men hidden away in a tiny enclave.

"Sit down, Gruber, and listen carefully."

*

Ayalla knocked on the door of the suite, the cardboard box tucked under her arm. After much inner debate, she'd decided to enlist their aid in analyzing the contents. She couldn't do it alone. She didn't have enough time. And even though she wasn't terribly fond of Senator Hawthorne's cowboy-style method of getting things done, she knew he was smart and experienced.

Benjamin answered the door, greeting her with a broad smile. "You made it! Good. Come in and sit down. Take off your coat. Can I get you some coffee or a soda? There are sweet rolls and muffins and toast on the table."

"Coffee would be good," she replied, putting down her box just as Malcolm came out of another room. The minute he caught sight of her, he grinned and moved swiftly across the room. He had incredible grace for such a big man, she thought, then immediately chided herself for mixing business with personal matters. *Don't hug me, don't hug me, don't hug me,* went her mental chant. He hugged her, then held her at arm's length.

"You look like death warmed over."

"Well, thank you, and may I say you don't look so good yourself."

He released her and Ayalla, suddenly dizzy, swayed on her feet. He caught her arm. "What is it?" he asked, his face creased with concern.

"Nothing," she snapped, trying to wrench her arm from his grasp. "I'm probably just hungry." When she thought about it, she realized it had been at least twenty-four hours since her last meal, maybe more. "Yes, I'm sure I'm hungry."

"Then eat!" He escorted her to a chair at the conference table and began filling a plate with baked goods.

"Gee, you think that's enough?" she said, when he plunked it down in front of her.

"You want more, you have to clean your plate first."

Ayalla started to argue, then realized her mouth was watering. She picked up a bear claw and took a very large and possibly unladylike bite. Then a sip of scalding hot coffee. Then another bite. At this rate, she'd feel human in no time. Benjamin had discreetly adjourned to the living room of the suite, still within sight, but apart from them as they sat side by side.

"You really okay?" she asked.

"Yeah. I'm tough to get rid of."

"Tell me about it."

"Okay."

Quickly Malcolm outlined every detail of the attempted abduction and the price of his intervention.

"You're sure it was Raley?"

"I've already told you—"

"I know, sorry. I'm having a bad day."

"On the news this morning, we heard about a fire at a funeral home. It was the same one?"

"Yep," said Ayalla, mumbling through a mouthful of cheese danish. "And they found a body."

"That's not exactly a surprise," he said with a tiny smirk.

"Oh, please. Enough with the dead jokes. This body was not a client. We don't know who it was, but he was probably in the process of cleaning out a safe when he died. I haven't gotten cause of death from the medical examiner yet, but the tech found a screwdriver impaled in his back.

"Sounds as if he wasn't doing the safe alone."

"Maybe. But he had to have already known it was there. Four agents missed it completely, and I only found it by accident."

"You found it? But then how—"

"Don't ask, just like you're not going to ask how I came by that box of papers over there, which is one reason I'm here, by the way. I need help figuring out if they've got anything to do with this case."

The bell rang again. Benjamin went to the door, looked through the peephole and then swung back the safety latch. Ayalla didn't know the tallish older couple who entered, and she started to panic a little. This meeting was supposed to be private, very private. Who were these people?"

Benjamin made the introductions. "Lord Carlisle, Lady Carlisle, this is Special Agent Ayalla Franklin. Ayalla, William and Ellen Carlisle."

"How do you do?" said William. "We've heard a great deal about you from Captain Jefferson. All of it good, I might add."

Ayalla stood as she swallowed the bite of muffin quickly. "Well, thank you."

They were all frozen in an awkward silence until Benjamin came to the rescue. "I think we can sit down. Laura and Connor should be here any moment." He looked at Ayalla and immediately responded to the skepticism she so eloquently displayed as she regarded the Carlisles. Her very body language told the story. She was not happy at having outsiders here, people she didn't know. But she'd have to *get* to know them.

"Ellen and William were instrumental in helping us with a situation in England," said Benjamin. "This situation may have more unusual overtones than the FBI thought."

Ayalla's eyes widened in alarm. "How unusual?"

"Very, I'm afraid."

"Look, Senator—"

"Ayalla, please," he said with a hint of chagrin in his voice.

"Sorry, just habit. I mean, Benjamin. When Malcolm asked me to come over, I thought it was to discuss new evidence that could shed some light on the murder investigation."

"That's exactly what we intend to do. I imagine you won't be happy to hear it, but all I ask is that you give it a fair hearing. Ah," he said, as the bell sounded again, "that must be the girls."

"The 'girls'?" Ayalla whispered to Malcolm, who had resumed his seat next to her.

"Shh. He's a father. That's how fathers talk."

Ayalla's heart contracted. He was right. She could hear her Dad's voice—*How's my baby girl?*—even when she was a grown woman. God, how she missed him.

"We're ready to get started," she heard Benjamin say, and she looked up to find Connor and Laura sitting down directly opposite her. Laura gave her a friendly smile, and even Connor's expression was open and welcoming—something of a surprise. The potential for anything other than an uncomfortable truce with Connor took Ayalla off guard. She didn't know what to do with it, so she simply nodded.

"If it's all right with everyone, I'll summarize for Ayalla everything we've discussed so far." He focused on her. "Remember, even if all this sounds bizarre, hear it out, okay?"

"Okay."

"I sent for a whiteboard this morning," he said, pulling it out from under the conference table, and propping it on the arms of one of the chairs. "Thought it might help us make some additional connections."

With his usual precision and logic, Benjamin began to unfold the story of the Goddess of Avebury pendant from its separation into two halves at the beginning of the 19th century up until the present. Using information the Carlisles had provided, he showed, in quick sketches, the path they had theorized for the von Adler half-pendant (beginning with Lady Genevieve Fitzhugh's son, born in France), and then the history of the Eliza Fitzhugh half-pendant on down to the present day Wainwrights.

Ayalla, who had been fighting to keep her expression neutral in the face of all this bizarre talk of magical power objects, at last found something for her analytical mind to latch onto. "You're saying the motivation for the murders had something to do with this…this pendant?"

"Yes, we are," replied Benjamin. "It has everything to do with what's happening now."

"All right. I can see a possibility for the Wainwright connection. But this still doesn't explain Devin Underwood or Arthur Raley or the Supreme Aryan Brotherhood."

"Actually, it does," said Malcolm. "But you have to hear the rest." He laid a hand gently on her arm, and in her frustration it was all she could do not to slap it away.

Benjamin continued. "I won't go into all the details, but let me give you a short version of what happened during World War II that concerns the pendant." He glanced at the Carlisles. "If I go wrong anywhere, stop me," he said.

"Carry on, old boy," said William. "You're doing fine."

If Ayalla had been skeptical before, Benjamin's story of Gwendolyn's circle, and the alliance of spiritual traditions to ward off Hitler's invasion, left her speechless with disbelief. When Benjamin had concluded that portion of the tale, he looked at her for a long moment. "You don't particularly buy any of this, do you?"

"No," she said, then instantly regretted her lack of tact. This man was, after all, a former U.S. senator and an adviser to presidents. She should try to overlook the obvious fact that he'd lost his marbles. "I mean, I don't see how it's possible."

"Of course you don't," said Malcolm. "Neither did I, once upon a time. But just because you don't understand something doesn't mean it isn't so."

"This isn't about understanding; it's about reality!" Ayalla's voice rose higher than she intended. "I've got four people dead—no, make that five with the body found this morning—and nowhere to go, no real leads at all. And you're all sitting around here talking about fairy tales and magical necklaces! Well, I've got better things to do." She stood up so abruptly her chair would have fallen over backward, had Malcolm not reached out to catch it. She strode around the table, grabbed her raincoat, and slammed out the door. Malcolm got up quickly to go after her, but Connor was already on her feet. "No, I'll go," she said firmly.

Laura looked at her quizzically. "You?"

"Yes, me."

Connor turned the corner and saw Ayalla leaning against the wall next to the elevators, her shoulders sagging. As she drew closer, she saw that the FBI agent hadn't yet pushed the down button.

Connor knew the thick carpet had muffled her footsteps, so she said "Ayalla," softly so as not to startle her. "wait a minute."

"No," she replied, not even turning around.

"Please, it's important."

After several seconds, she finally shifted to face Connor. "For you to come after me, it must be important to you. I thought it would be Malcolm."

"He wanted to, but I beat him to the door. And yes, this is important, to all of us." She paused. "I haven't been much of a friend to you, and I'm sorry for that. But—"

"How can you stomach all this? You're a lawyer, for God's sake. And you were a prosecutor."

"Ayalla, please. Think back. Don't you remember what happened to us in the garden at that mission in California? You heard and saw the same things I did."

"I don't know *what* that was. Some kind of hallucination. Probably from something growing in the garden."

"So that's what you've decided? To file it away as a drug-induced vision?"

"That's the only way I can cope."

Connor wondered if Ayalla was as miserably confused as she looked. "I know what that feels like. It happened to me a few years ago when suddenly nothing made sense: Nothing was the way it was supposed to be. And I fought it with every ounce of intellect I could muster."

"So what happened to make you change your mind? Your girlfriend?"

Connor took a deep breath, choosing not to take the question as a demonstration of Ayalla's apparent homophobia.

"Laura was part of it, but most of all, my grandmother changed my mind."

"Your grandmother's…deceased, isn't she?"

"Physically, yes. At least I assume so."

"Assume?"

"That's another long story I'd be happy to share with you when we have time. But the thing is, the weird stuff kept happening, and finally, my mind couldn't deny what my heart knew. My grandmother has stayed with me, not always near, but within call, so to speak."

"What?"

"Okay, that's story number two that we'll tackle later. Right now we have a crisis. I wish I could lay it out for you in black and white—photos, fingerprints, DNA—the whole works. Yes, it's manifesting in our reality as murder and mayhem, but we can't stop it until we really understand why it's happening. And the 'why' is the Goddess of Avebury pendant. At least for now, even if you don't believe in its inherent power, then accept that there are other people so convinced of it, they'd kill for it. Would that work for you? We can each tackle this problem on different levels. You and Malcolm prefer the hands-on digging, and so does my Dad. Laura and I can team up with Ellen and William to go at it from, well, let's just say, a different direction."

"You mean the psychic stuff?"

Connor smiled. "You're actually a lot kinder in your terminology than I used to be."

"As long as you don't expect me to buy into it."

"I don't. But can you just bear with us a little longer?"

Ayalla sighed and straightened her shoulders. "I don't have other options. That's why I came over here in the first place. I'm at a dead end, and my job's on the line, and I don't have much in the way of support."

"Then maybe you can make do with us for a while," said Connor, laying a hand on the FBI agent's shoulder, then quickly withdrawing it.

Ayalla looked at her for a moment. "I'm not afraid of you, Connor. And I'm really not a raving homophobe either. It took me a while to understand it, that's all. I grew up with certain ideas, certain beliefs. But I've done some thinking. And I respect you and Laura because of the kind of human beings you are. Let's leave it at that. Okay?"

"Sound's all right to me. So, are you ready to go back and face the weird and unknown?"

"I suppose. And to be totally honest, I need your help. That box I brought, it has a bunch of letters I found in a safe at the funeral home. I never got a chance to report it to my boss, and now it's too late to say anything. But the letters might give us a lead."

"Have you read any of them?"

"I just glanced at a handful before I took the box away. Problem is, the ones I saw were in German."

"Not a problem," beamed Connor. "Just so happens that William and Ellen have another interesting hobby—foreign languages." They started back down the corridor. "Just between you and me, William's French pronunciation is atrocious, but they're both fluent in about eight languages. And my Dad can get by in a few as well."

Ayalla brightened visibly. "Then maybe it is a good thing I came here after all."

"Nothing like good old coincidence," said Connor with a tiny smile.

"You're teasing me, aren't you?"

"Yep."

"That's okay. I can take it."

"Thought you could."

They reached the door of the suite, still standing slightly ajar.

"You ready?" asked Connor.

"No, but let's do this anyway."

They walked in together and Malcolm stood up. "Everything all right?" he asked cautiously.

"Yes," said Connor firmly. "Let's get to work. Ayalla has a translation job for us, and maybe an explanation as to why Devin Underwood is involved in all this."

Ayalla picked up the carton and placed it on the table. Removing the lid, she dug out bundles of yellowing letters. "These were in the safe at the funeral home. I think all or some of them are in German. Connor tells me you folks," she nodded at the Carlisles, "are familiar with the language." She handed a bundle to Ellen, whose face lit up when she looked for the date on the topmost letter.

"Good heavens," she said, "this was mailed from Germany to France in 1944." She riffled through another stack Ayalla laid on the table. "And these—1949, 1948—well, they're out of order. Quickly then, let's sort them by date, and William and I will begin reading. First, though, let's find a way to indicate this one stack that was right on top. They may have special significance."

Benjamin found a pad of small stick-on notes they attached to half a dozen letters not wrapped in rubber bands. Then each of them plunged into the box for a handful and began sorting stacks. Connor grabbed a notepad and tore off several sheets. In large letters, she printed years—1944, 1945, and so on. She placed these down the center of the table so they could save time by sorting all the letters into common piles. After about thirty minutes, most were categorized by year, though not by month. Some sorting was made easier because a few bundles at the bottom of the carton appeared not to have been opened since the time they'd been gathered up and tied with string. They were already in consecutive chronological order.

Finally, there were some left over that were no longer in envelopes and bore nothing but a month and day. Ellen said that once they had read all the letters, they could probably identify the chronology of the leftovers by their content.

"It's going to take a while to scan these," she sighed. "But we'll proceed as fast as possible. Benjamin, would you be comfortable doing some of it? The writing is pretty legible. Looks like an educated hand."

He frowned. "My German is extremely rusty. But I'll give it a whirl. If I think I'm missing too much content, I'll stop."

"Good, I'd suggest looking for references to the occultists working in Germany and, of course, Wilhelm von Adler."

*

Miles away, at Devin Underwood's empty, cold apartment, his answering machine clicked on in response to an incoming call.

"Hi. This is Chris Falcone, Billy's partner. I tried to leave a message at the funeral home, but there was no answer. I was wondering if you have a better address for Billy's sister in your records. I was going through stuff a few days ago to give away, and I found a piece of jewelry with a note that said "For my sister." I don't know where she is, so if she ever calls, have her get in touch with me. In the meantime I decided to leave it with Billy. It's kind of a funky-looking thing, and I never saw him with it on. But then he never wore silver anyway. Uh, my number here at the office is 555-7117."

The machine clicked off, and the red light began to blink in the dim, gray light.

Chapter Sixteen

*It is a miserable state of mind to have few things to desire
and many things to fear.*
—Francis Bacon, *Of Empire*

Commandant Gruber stood at perfect attention beside his small officer cadre. Friedrich, now resplendent in the full black uniform of an S.S. Reichsmarschall of the Leibstandarte Adolf Hitler, reviewed the troops with extreme gravity. His boots shone in the light of the torches set at regular intervals around the parade ground, and the tip of his swagger stick slapped regularly against the top of his right boot.

To be sure, there were only thirty of these men, but it was a beginning. And Friedrich had no illusions that an army of any size could carry out the master plan. It wasn't about force; it was about cunning. The Norwegian commandos who'd destroyed the Reich's only heavy-water plant and crippled their nuclear bomb program knew about cunning. The members of the resistance in every country the Nazis had conquered knew about cunning. Friedrich was taking a page from their book. His victory would be subtle, yet absolute.

Behind him, he heard a small commotion. He turned, annoyed. The two soldiers, with Rudy Gunther between them, were making slow progress across the yard, mostly because the prisoner was highly uncooperative. Friedrich was displeased. A soldier walked upright to his death, eyes open, emotions in check. He motioned for them to take Gunther to the wall, in front of which were stacked hay bales. To his utter disgust, the man dropped to his knees and begged for mercy.

In a fit of pique, Friedrich took out his pistol, walked briskly to the prisoner, and stood behind him. "*Feigling!*" he hissed, though the poor terrified man probably did not know he'd been called a coward. Friedrich shot him in the back of the head. Trash like this Rudy Gunther did not deserve the honor of dying by a firing squad, face-to-face with his executioners. That was a death for warriors.

"Gruber, dismiss the men, and summon the car. I will change my clothes. We have business elsewhere."

*

More than two hours had passed since the box of old correspondence had been opened. William and Ellen were still scanning the texts swiftly, having grown accustomed to the handwriting as well as the idiomatic turns of phrase used by the author. They had early on confirmed that every one of the missives was signed "Karl" or simply "K." They had yet to find a surname. But they had turned up a wealth of information to support their suppositions about Wilhelm von Adler's role in the occult machinations of Hitler's inner council.

Karl, whoever he was, had clearly been a dedicated soldier, not a fan of "magic and devilment," as he called it. So far, they had followed his story during the last year of the war to when he escaped the Allies closing in on Berlin. The man was writing to a brother in occupied France.

"Listen to this," said Ellen. "He talks about his fellow soldiers being shot down by one of their own officers. Let's see, here it is. *'I watched in horror as the Doktor killed them all after making them carry his enormous antique desk to a truck. I don't know why he didn't kill me, too. He seems to think I'm loyal to him, or too young and stupid to do anything but follow him blindly. Now that we're hidden away, I don't have much choice but to do his bidding. But I tell you, the man is evil, as if there is something dead inside Friedrich that refuses to pass to the other side.'* Nice image," said Ellen.

"What did you say?" Ayalla had been making a chart on which they could record dates and events that might be relevant.

"I said, 'nice image.'"

"No, before that. About Friedrich and a doctor."

Ellen looked back over the text. I don't think it's a doctor, but more like *the* Doktor, you know, as if it's someone's *name*. But apparently he's also called Friedrich."

"Oh, dear God," said Ayalla, leaning on the conference table.

"What?" asked Malcolm.

"Before Devin Underwood died, he said something about Nazis and the Reich. I thought he was babbling, but then he said"—she rubbed her temples—"let me get this right: He said, 'It's Friedrich.' And I asked who that was, if Friedrich was the one who'd shot him. And then he said something that made no sense at all. 'The devil…the Doktor.'"

They all stared at her. Finally, Malcolm spoke. "That's the connection to the funeral home, then. Somehow Underwood got mixed up with these neo-Nazis who are trying to use the pendant to get back into power. But why would he have these letters? Maybe he was blackmailing this character named Friedrich?"

"I think I have the answer to that one question," said Ellen, holding up another letter. "I skipped ahead thirty years. This one contains a brief holographic will, and it's signed 'Karl Unterholz.'"

Benjamin and William immediately got the point, but the others didn't. Ellen explained. "'Unterholz' literally translated means 'Underwood.' I suspect Devin was Karl's grandson."

They all started speaking at once until Benjamin raised his voice over the hubbub. "Wait a second, wait a second. Let's take this one step at a time. If Ellen's right, then we can see Devin Underwood's motivation to be a part of this conspiracy. We need to quickly sort through the rest of this to see if we can find out who Friedrich is and if he's really still alive. I'd very much like to know his last name. Then I can run a database search."

"But he wouldn't be using his real name, Dad."

"No, but we can find out what he did during the war, and why he was called the 'Doktor' back then."

"I have a feeling the answer isn't pleasant," said Connor.

"You're probably right," Benjamin said, his face grim. "But we have to keep after it anyway."

Ayalla spoke up. "There isn't much I can do about the translation. I want to go take another look at Devin Underwood's apartment. We overlooked the safe at the funeral home the first time through. Maybe we missed something at his home."

"If you don't mind, I'll go with you," said Malcolm. "German is pretty much Greek to me."

Connor chuckled. "That's well below the standard of acceptable humor in this room."

"What can I say, I'm just a lowbrow kinda guy."

"Yeah, right. So go investigate already."

"We're on our way," he said, grabbing Ayalla's coat and handing it to her before shrugging into his own topcoat. "We'll be in touch if we turn up anything."

*

"This was the funeral home we owned?" said Friedrich in disbelief, and with some lack of accuracy. Through Devin, he had only acquired a partial ownership in the business, because all they required was that Devin establish a legitimate relationship with the Wainwright family. Friedrich, with his macabre sense of destiny, had chosen death as the uniting factor—first Grace's mother, then her aunt.

"Yes, this is—I mean, this *was* the place," said Gruber. He, along with Friedrich, was now dressed in a simple, well-cut black suit. They were parked across the street from the smoldering shell of the enormous colonial house that had been Dagle & Sons, driving Devin's BMW. The plates had been replaced, of course, and the fender repainted. It was a fast, sleek, and sexy car that Gruber hadn't been able to bring himself to get rid of, after Rudy had brought it back to the compound. Gruber also hadn't thought it necessary to mention the provenance of the car to Friedrich, whose only comment about it was that it was too costly for Gruber, and he should take better care of it by getting the scrape on the fender repaired more expertly.

It was growing dark, but they could still see the outlines of some of the rafters.

"What happened? You said nothing of this."

"I didn't know, sir. It must have only just happened."

"There is no fire-fighting apparatus here. This blaze occurred hours ago."

"Yes, sir."

Friedrich sat there fuming. He had no faith in Devin's ability to maintain strict secrecy. What if there were papers, notes, recordings? Friedrich needed to clean house, literally. But someone else had done it for him. The question was, who?

"You had a man watching?"

"Of course, sir. A good man, one of our demolition experts."

Friedrich's head swiveled toward Gruber. "Do you suppose he had anything to do with this?" He waved his hand toward the blackened hulk. "Where is he?"

"Bert hasn't reported in yet, but he'd have no reason to set a fire."

"Well, *someone* had a reason. I want to know everything about this fire, everything the police have."

"Yes, sir. We have good sources in the police department, certain sympathizers."

"Good. A network of informants can be very useful as long as you don't trust them too far. Now take me to Devin's apartment."

*

"Someone's messed with this," said Ayalla, examining the bands of yellow police tape across Devin Underwood's apartment door. Instinctively, her right hand swept back the cloth of her raincoat and came to rest on the butt of her service weapon. Out of sheer habit, Malcolm nearly mimicked the gesture, until he remembered that he carried no gun. He was out of his jurisdiction and had no legal authority in the Commonwealth of Massachusetts. Ayalla caught the flicker of movement and almost smiled. "There are times when being a Feeb has its advantages."

"You're never going to let me live down that comment, are you?" he said, referring to their first prickly meeting in his office more than a year earlier.

"No. And I take some satisfaction from being the one with the gun…again."

"Don't suppose you still carry that spare?"

"Not tonight," said Ayalla. "You'll just have to stay behind me."

His silence was an eloquent commentary on what he thought of that suggestion as he pulled the tape loose. She reached into her left pocket and extracted the envelope containing the keys to the apartment. Handing them to Malcolm, she drew her weapon and nestled it into a two-handed grip, barrel pointing upward, her finger, for the moment, outside the trigger guard. Malcolm quietly turned the key in the lock and eased the door open and stepped back. She could feel the tension radiating from him.

They moved into the foyer and stopped, listening, their senses attuned to any sound, any indication of another human presence. The air in the apartment, with the heat turned off, was cold and still. Ayalla detected a faint aroma of ripe garbage. Mr. Underwood had not taken the trash out in a few days. If the heat had been on, the place would have really stunk.

They continued through the short entry hall and Ayalla peered into the living room, where she'd sat with Devin Underwood, trying to pressure him into a confession. Everything looked just as she remembered, but then it would. He'd left shortly after she did, and he'd never come back. She forced herself not to dwell on the memory of the rain pouring down on his pale, frightened face as he died. He was a murderer, she reminded herself, or at least an accomplice to murder. To her, it meant the same thing.

Slowly they moved through the kitchen, then the bedroom. They inspected the large walk-in closet and the fairly lavish bathroom. Malcolm even pulled the shower curtain back. After ten minutes, they relaxed and Ayalla holstered her weapon. There was no one there. But she remained convinced there had been. Returning to the living room, she flipped a wall switch. Three lamps came on.

"Nice place. I'd still like to know where Mr. Underwood got his money. Benjamin's working on that angle."

"So is the FBI, by the way," she said with an edge of sarcasm.

"I know, I know. This is a team effort, remember."

Ayalla shook her head and began searching the small desk that stood in one corner of the room. It was then she noticed the blinking light on the answering machine. "We thought it was odd he didn't have voice mail," she commented. "But the tape in the machine was blank. We decided we'd leave the machine just in case someone called and left a number we could track down. Still a strange choice of device for this guy."

"Some people don't like remote voice mail, don't think it's secure. I guess it doesn't seem very private when you call somewhere else to get your messages."

"But this guy was a techie," she said, rifling through the drawers. "The team found a laptop, a PDA, a little dictation recorder, a portable fax, an extra cell phone. There's even a security minicam in each room, really well hidden. There's one in the corner there, right at the ceiling. Unfortunately, we haven't figured out where the signal was going."

"That's weird," said Malcolm, peering upward, "looks like it's still operating. See that tiny red light?"

Ayalla wasn't paying attention. She was examining the answering machine to find the right button. The tape rewound.

"Hi. This is Chris Falcone, Billy's partner. I tried to leave a message at the funeral home, but there was no answer. I was wondering if you have a better address for Billy's sister in your records. I was going through stuff a few days ago to give away, and I found a piece of jewelry with a note that said "For my sister." I don't know where she is, so if she ever calls, have her get in touch with me. In the meantime I decided to leave it with Billy. It's kind of a funky-looking thing, and I never saw him with it on. But then he never wore silver anyway. Uh, my number here at the office is 555-7117."

Malcolm and Ayalla stared at each other. "You don't think…" he began just as she said, "What if that's the…" Together they said, "Oh, shit!"

Ayalla grabbed the tape out of the machine. "We've got to find Chris Falcone, right now."

They raced out of the apartment, stopping only to lock the door and haphazardly replace the tape barrier. Then they ran down the hall, taking the stairs rather than waiting for the elevator. Once in the car, Ayalla fired the engine and maneuvered out of a tight parking spot. "Why don't you call Benjamin, tell him what we suspect."

"This could be a serious wild-goose chase," he reminded her, quickly fastening his seat belt. He'd ridden with her before when she was in a hurry.

"I know. I can't think of any reason why Billy Dagle would have this damn pendant, but I also don't believe in coincidence."

*

Inside Devin Underwood's apartment, Friedrich and Gruber stepped out of a small, cleverly camouflaged compartment accessed through the walk-in closet. This was one of the many precautionary alterations Friedrich (paranoid man that he was) had instructed Devin to undertake when he moved into the building. He had sent two trusted craftsmen from Germany to do the work. The space barely accommodated the two them standing shoulder to shoulder, but it was well ventilated, and they were able to monitor the movements of the visitors through the apartment. Friedrich silently congratulated himself on his foresight. Otherwise, there would have been nowhere to hide. They had only been inside the door for a minute or two when they heard the voices—a man and a woman. Though both he and Gruber carried pistols, instinct told Friedrich this was not the time for a showdown with the authorities. He'd quickly shoved Gruber toward the closet and fought down a few seconds of panic when he couldn't find the series of switches that unlocked the door. But then he'd only seen the plans, not the finished work. They were fortunate in that the agent and the cop didn't come in right away. There was a minute or so delay and that was all the time they needed to close up the door and turn on the monitoring equipment.

When the woman came into view, Gruber whispered, "That's the FBI agent who came here two nights ago."

"And the man must be the one that..." Friedrich caught himself. Gruber didn't know about his side arrangement with Arthur Raley. Best keep it that way. "Turn up the audio," he said, still whispering though the compartment had been thoroughly soundproofed.

Gruber looked at the small control panel in puzzlement, and Friedrich reached past him to turn the up the gain on the microphones.

They were able to follow the conversation easily as the FBI agent and the cop went back to the living room. The woman's body blocked what she was doing at the desk, but they were talking about an answering machine, and she said something about a "techie." Friedrich's English was textbook perfect, but his grasp of idiom was weak. He would ask Gruber later what that meant. Then they heard a third voice in the room, slightly hollow as it played back on the machine.

The voice of Chris Falcone came through clearly. When he got to the part about the necklace, Friedrich thought his heart would stop. Surely not. Not Billy Dagle. What would he be doing with the pendant? Billy Dagle. And then it came to him in such a rush of clarity, it took his breath away. How could he have been so horribly blind? The truth had been there all along. Right under his nose. Right under Devin's nose.

Wilhelm von Adler had been Guillaume de L'Aigle. On his return to France, he'd reassumed his family name—de L'Aigle: Dagle. It had to be. But how? Friedrich gagged on the acid that rose up in his gorge. All this time he'd been focused on the Fitzhugh line, on their half of the pendant. He'd almost given up on the von Adler half. And all the time…. Something came to him then, a vague recollection of a passage he'd read in a scholarly journal article about the Goddess of Avebury pendant. The academician who'd written the article was clearly skeptical of its purported powers, yet he had faithfully recounted some of its legends. "*It is even said that if the halves of the pendant are ever separated, they themselves will manipulate human events in slow and subtle ways so as to be reunited.*"

Friedrich himself had only half-believed it, yet now he saw that it must be true. How else to explain that despite a separation of two hundred years and thousands of miles, the two halves of this wondrous object had ended up not only the same city, but in the possession of people who actually knew each other.

He watched with growing anxiety as the FBI agent and the cop snatched the tape and dashed for the door. There was recognition there, he thought. *They know what the necklace is.* That thought horrified him even more. His most closely guarded secret, and at least two outsiders knew about it. That could only mean that the Hawthornes knew as well. But what had Chris Falcone meant when he said he'd leave the necklace with Billy? The man was dead.

"Quickly! We must go." He didn't bother turning off the equipment but did slam the compartment door as they exited. Adrenaline pumped through him as he strode toward the front door, Gruber in his wake. Again, he marveled at how his body moved, more easily with each passing hour, as if the years were melting away. He flung open the door. They didn't bother to lock it, or replace the tape. Within moments they were in the car. Friedrich punched numbers into his cell phone, and drummed his fingers impatiently. "Find an address for Chris Falcone! Call his office at 555-7117 and see if he is there. On some pretext, discover where Dagle was buried. Report back to me at once… Yes, that is the one. It seems that Billy Dagle had the…item I'm seeking." Friedrich stabbed the end key.

"Pull over to the curb somewhere and wait."

"Sir, we are supposed to meet the team at—"

"I'm sure they have everything under control. I laid the groundwork very carefully."

Gruber assumed that Friedrich was referring to one of the sacred occult rituals of their ancient military order, but he also knew better than to ask about it. That aspect of the Brotherhood he found distinctly uncomfortable, but then he had yet to be initiated into the highest ranks, where the deepest of secrets were held closely. Perhaps one day he would clearly comprehend the terrible forces that Friedrich accessed. He glanced at his commander out of the corner of his eye. Something was different about him. If Gruber didn't know better, he'd swear the old man looked younger.

*

Arthur Raley was inordinately pleased when he finished his conversation with Friedrich. Just as he'd been about to write off this whole operation as a senseless waste of his valuable time, fortune had smiled. He already knew exactly where Billy Dagle had lived and where he'd been buried. He'd made it his business to know everything about Devin Underwood's business associates—a simple precaution against future complications

The hours he'd spent watching the hotel where the Hawthornes were staying had yielded very little. Alone, he had no way of observing all the entrances, so he'd hovered near a corner where he could see the front door and the exit from the parking garage beneath the hotel. As a result, he'd missed the departure of Ayalla and Malcolm, who used the a door on the opposite side of the building to reach her car, parked on the street.

Friedrich would no doubt wait for a return call so as not to waste time heading in the wrong direction. He'd be hampered for lack of information, and Arthur resolved to let him stay hampered. He was a little ahead of the impending rush hour. Another thirty minutes of delay, and Friedrich would be considerably slowed in his attempts to leave Boston. Arthur would get to the pendant that Friedrich so wanted. He had no doubt where Chris Falcone would put it.

*

"Son of a *bitch!*" Ayalla shouted suddenly, and slammed on the brakes, badly startling her passenger who was still trying to get through to Benjamin Hawthorne's room.

"What the hell!" said Malcolm.

"That fucking car! The black BMW Devin Underwood drove. It was there! At his apartment! I pulled around it when we left, and something wasn't quite right about the left front fender."

"But I thought you said the guy who shot him drove away in it."

"He did! And he grazed my car on the way out. Which means whoever shot Devin Underwood went to that apartment. He must have been somewhere in the building while were inside."

"Maybe it was a different car."

"Hey, this isn't L.A. You don't see $90,000 BMWs on every corner. Nope, that was it, and I missed it!" She swung her vehicle in a tight, tire-screeching U-turn. He grabbed the handstrap.

"Didn't you just tell me about a run-in with the Boston P.D. Keep it up and you're going to have another one."

Ayalla hit the switch for the dashboard flasher. "Not this time," she said, stomping on the accelerator.

Malcolm braced himself and kept trying to reach Benjamin. The line was busy again.

*

Only a few minutes after Ayalla and Malcolm left to search Devin Underwood's apartment again, a call came through to Benjamin's suite. He answered, asked the caller to wait a moment, and turned the phone over to Connor. "It's Grace Wainwright," he said softly. "She sounds upset."

The rest of them watched as Connor took the call.

"Hi, Grace. Are you all right?"

For almost a minute, Connor tried to get a word in, but Grace was apparently on a roll.

"All right, please. Just calm down. If that's what you want, I'll be there in half an hour." She hung up, clearly frustrated.

"What's the matter?" asked Laura.

"I don't know. Sounds like plain old-fashioned hysteria, probably a delayed reaction to her mother's death and then the incident on the bridge. She says she's been looking at old pictures and saw ones of her mother years ago wearing the gold pendant. She wants it back."

"Now?"

"Right now, or sooner."

"I don't think that's wise," said William.

"Nor do I," Ellen agreed. "It's a great risk to let it out of our safekeeping."

Connor sighed. "I don't particularly want to. But when I tired to argue, that's when she got so upset. She even went so far as to say she'd call the police and tell them I stole it while I was visiting her."

Laura's face suffused angrily. "Your best friend from college would accuse you of being a thief? When she knows that's a complete lie?!"

"As I said, she isn't thinking clearly. She's crying, and I can tell she's been drinking."

"All the more reason you shouldn't deal with her right now," Benjamin said.

"If I don't, I think she'll actually call the cops. And they'll listen because of who she is. Then none of what we're trying to figure out here will be the least bit secret."

"Perhaps you should go and not take the pendant," suggested Ellen.

"If I know Grace, that will be the first thing she'll ask for when I come through the door. What I'm hoping is that I can get her calmed down—or sobered up—enough to reason with her. I don't plan to leave the pendant with her if there's any way to avoid it."

"What's with the 'I' business?" Laura said, rising from the table. "Where you go, I go."

"She seemed to want—oh, what the hell. Of course you're coming with me."

Benjamin stood also. "Maybe I should come along, too."

"Dad, you can do a lot more good here working through these letters than watching us try to avoid another of Grace's tantrums. Besides, weepy, maudlin women make you crazy."

He sighed and contemplated the piles of letters they had yet to review. "Maybe you're right. I'll go downstairs with you and get the pendant out of the safe."

Fifteen minutes later, he watched them drive out of the parking garage. Trying to quell a growing sense of uneasiness, he reflected that being a parent never got one damn bit easier.

*

Ellen leaned back in her chair and met William's eyes. Two minds with the same idea.

"I'll call Jonathan and Portia," she said. "We're going to need them all to gather at the meeting place."

"It's all coming together, but too fast," said William.

"Yes, it is. And you see how already circumstances have conspired to split up our group here on these shores—Malcolm and Agent Franklin off in one direction, Connor and Laura in another. This is a potent enemy we face."

"I wish we had more time to prepare."

"Don't forget, love. Even time is relative where we're going." She picked up the receiver of the nearest extension and began making calls overseas.

*

"Damn it! Still busy," said Malcolm, slapping the phone shut.

"Don't break your phone," Ayalla warned, "my battery's just about dead and the spare is on my desk back at the office."

"I doubt that car is still going to be there, especially if it's Devin Underwood's. Whoever is driving it must have seen us."

"Then why didn't they leave while we were inside?"

Malcolm considered that. "Maybe they were inside, too."

"You mean in the apartment?"

"Or at least the building. Remember when we were listening to Chris Falcone's message? I was saying that it was weird that the red light on the mini-cam was blinking. I don't know much about that kind of equipment, but it could mean someone was watching us, maybe from another apartment in the building."

"Shit! And if there's an audio feed…" She slapped the steering wheel.

"Then they could hear what we heard."

"But would it mean anything to them, about Billy Dagle and the necklace?" she asked, although from her tone, she already assume the worst.

"Seems like a safe bet."

"But what did Falcone mean, that he was going to leave it with Billy? The guy's dead."

"Yes," said Malcolm slowly, staring ahead at the traffic. "Connor and Laura went to the, uh, whaddayacallit, the interment."

"Where?!"

"I don't know."

Ayalla stopped herself just short of blaming him for not knowing. "Well then, find out! Call the number Chris Falcone gave. Five-five-five, seven-something."

"Seven what?"

"You don't remember? Oh, for crying out loud."

"Well, neither do you, babe."

"Don't 'babe' me."

"Sorry, how about we play the tape."

"How about you notice I'm not walking around with a microcassette recorder in my pocket."

Malcolm shut up. They were back in front of the apartment building, and the black BMW was gone. He also knew that an "I told you so" would not go over well at all. Instead, he had an inspiration. "We could go inside and play the tape on the machine in the apartment."

She glared at him, and he was sure she was about to

explode. But all she said was, "Good idea," before flinging open her door.

*

Connor rang the bell and waited. She and Laura had made excellent time, and it had only been about forty minutes since she'd spoken with Grace. She was about to ring again when the door swung open. Her old friend stood there trembling, her face red and swollen.

"Grace, what's the matter?" asked Connor, stepping across the threshold with Laura right behind her. But the frightened woman backed away from them. "Did you bring it?"

"Yes, and I know you're upset, but everything's going to be all right."

"No," said Grace. "It isn't."

Laura felt rather than saw someone behind her. But before she could turn, strong hands gripped her shoulders. At the same time, Connor was pulled away to the side. Laura caught the glint of a gun barrel out of the corner of her eye. For an instant, she started to fight back. Every instinct in her wanted to drop into the mental zone where she could fight in ways that few people in the world knew how to defend. Her training was impeccable, but then so was her judgment in a crisis. She had to think of Connor and possibly Grace Wainwright. Alone, Laura would have responded instantly with deadly force. But Connor wasn't prepared for that sort of fight. And Laura had no idea of the enemy's strength in numbers, or whether they would just as soon kill their captives as not. So instead she stood rigidly, waiting to see what would happen. Then she felt the cold steel of handcuffs around her wrists and saw her options diminish dramatically.

Before she could catch more than glimpse in the darkened

foyer, a hood was slipped over her head. Laura didn't struggle, but so attuned was she to Connor's energy, that she felt her lover's stab of panic. No doubt she'd been given the same treatment, and for Connor, whose claustrophobia was severe, the hood would be unbearable. Laura quickly focused her thoughts, sending wave after wave of loving strength. She only hoped Connor was not too panicked to feel it.

Moments later, she felt a shove. "Walk!" a male voice growled. Laura tried to remember the layout of the house. The hallway was long, running all the way to the rear. She stumbled, and a hand gripped her arm in a cruel vise, dragging her along. She prayed Connor was near. A door opened, and Laura could hear traffic. Surely they wouldn't risk dragging the women out when there was still enough daylight that someone in a neighboring house might see. But apparently they weren't afraid.

Then Laura felt it—an aura around them all like a sort of damping field. She didn't fully understand how it was caused, but she did know she couldn't hear properly—that is, she couldn't hear the gentle undercurrent of life, a pulse that beat with the rhythm of the universal heart. She'd known that sensation since she was a child, felt in it her connection with all of creation, and never had she been cut off from it, until now. Some ferociously powerful energy enveloped them. Perhaps, she thought, no one passing by or looking from a window could actually perceive what was happening. The idea frightened her. If her suspicions were correct, the situation bespoke a force more powerful than she had encountered, more than her wise old grandmother had ever mentioned, possibly even more malevolent than William and Ellen imagined, or could neutralize. That would be an exceedingly scary situation.

Laura was picked up and half tossed. She rolled over and her elbow struck something hard. Other hands dragged her upright until she was sitting, her back against cold metal. More thuds, and she allowed herself a small sigh of relief when she felt a warm body next to her shoulder and recognized the distinctive aroma of Opium, the perfume Connor wore. At least they were together. Laura took a deep breath and kept firm contact with Connor's arm. A motor started, and Laura felt the sway as they began to move. They were probably in some sort of van. She couldn't tell if Grace was still with them.

She calmed her thoughts, focusing her mind and her spirit as she had been taught.

Sweet Mother, be with us now. We need your help in this, the hour of our peril. I call on our allies among the beings of Light— the council of the Sisterhood, the Priests and Priestesses of Avalon, the Old Ones of my People—to bring us aid.

Over and over she repeated the prayer and call, with more conviction each time, sending out a pulse of vibrant psychic communication like a flashing beacon. If there were a damping field cast around them, she need to pierce through it—and quickly.

*

Benjamin sat alone at the conference table. The Carlisles had just gone into the sitting room to attempt an exceptionally "long-distance" invocation of their circle. Ellen had called them all directly, despite the late hour in England. Within a short time each had responded to the emergency, and all but William and Ellen were assembled at the sacred grove.

He tried to read more of the letters, but he felt himself growing increasingly agitated. Connor and Laura had been gone over an hour, and still no word from them. The phone rang and he grabbed the receiver. Before he could say 'hello,' Malcolm's voice blasted him. "We've been trying to get hold of you for almost two hours!"

Benjamin frowned. "Sorry, but Ellen's been on the phone to England. Why didn't you call my cell phone?"

"I did. It's not answering either."

Benjamin reached into his pocket and was dismayed to see that he had somehow turned it off. "You're right, it isn't."

"Listen, we know where the silver half of the pendant is."

"What?"

"There was a message on Devin Underwood's answering machine from Billy Dagle's boyfriend. He said Billy left behind a necklace—he called it a funky silver necklace—with a note that said it was for Billy's sister. But no one knows where she is. So he was asking Underwood to tell the sister if she ever called. And that in the meantime he was going to leave it with Billy."

"Billy's dead."

"Yeah, I know. We've already been through that. He must mean he's taken it to wherever the guy's buried. So ask Connor and Laura where—"

"They're not here!"

"What? Where are they?"

"Grace Wainwright called. She was on the verge of hysteria. Said she wanted her necklace back, or she was going to call the cops and say Connor stole it. I know, it's bizarre, but Connor figured she could get her to calm down. She's convinced Grace has no idea what the pendant is."

"Fuck!" said Malcolm.

"What's wrong?" Benjamin's heart started to pound.

"Two things—first, we figured out that someone may have been eavesdropping on us when we listened to that message on the answering machine, and second, we have no idea where

Billy Dagle is buried. Only Connor and Laura went there for his burial. You've got to call them right now."

"Stay on the line," said Benjamin, turning on his cell phone and punching in the speed dial for Connor's cell. It rang only once before her voice mail kicked in. "She's not answering. I'll try Laura." He redialed…nothing, not even voice mail. "Something's wrong," he said to Malcolm, trying to keep the fear out of his voice. "Laura told me she'd keep her phone on at all times. It isn't even working."

The door to the sitting room opened. Ellen came out, her face ashen. She locked eyes with him and Benjamin felt his chest compress until he thought he couldn't breathe. "What is it, Ellen?" he finally managed.

"It's here…he's here. Whoever is behind this, the focus for all this old, evil energy, he's not in Germany anymore. He's in this country. And very near. He's actively drawing on the residual darkness that still remains from those days when the occultists opposed our Circle. It's feeding him, and he's feeding it. Already there are veils materializing to block our senses, our reach. We need Connor."

Benjamin could hear Malcolm's voice, but he was frozen to the spot. Ellen moved closer. "Breathe, my friend, breathe." He shook himself slightly and put the phone to his ear. "Go to Grace Wainwright's house right now. Ayalla knows where it is. And Malcolm, hurry!"

William appeared in the doorway. "Have you told him?"

"Yes," said Ellen, "but I think we have a more immediate problem, and I think I know why we couldn't connect with Connor."

Benjamin was dialing furiously. "Thank God they've got digital phones with GPS chips. They don't need to be in use for us to find them." The party he was calling answered, and he gave a series of letters and numbers, then barked "I need a tracking team! Now—and I mean right now! Find the GPS locator chip in each of these cell phones." He rattled off the two numbers. "No, don't converge. Just tell me where they are." He hung up.

Ellen stepped close enough to put her arms around him. "You do what you can with your special resources, Benjamin, and we're going to search in our own way. Even when you track them down on the physical plane, Connor and Laura are going to need us in a very different way."

"Do you know what's going on—I mean, really?" pleaded Benjamin. "Have you seen something? Is my daughter…is she…" He couldn't bring himself to finish the thought.

"She's alive, Benjamin. She is the true legacy of a long, long line of very powerful priestesses of the Light, and Servants of the Mother. She could not cease to exist in this world without us knowing of her transition. We will find a way to make contact with her and with Laura. But *you* must find their physical bodies."

*

Success was, as a rule, elusive, yet once in a while the prize was so easy to grasp one kept looking for the hidden pitfall. That's what Arthur Raley was thinking as he pried off the old padlock that secured the metal door of the Dagle mausoleum in the old cemetery in Hingham. Either the stupid thing was here, or it wasn't. Falcone might not have brought it here yet, in which case he'd pay Mr. Falcone a visit. But Arthur had a hunch.

He switched on his flashlight. Even in broad daylight, little illumination would have penetrated far into the gloom of the musty old stone building. He played the light around the walls, looking for a newly sealed crypt. There, at the other end, a reflection caught the beam as it went by. Slowly he backtracked until he found it again. There it was, dangling from a chain hooked over the corner of the crypt plate that bore the name WILLIAM DAGLE III. Naturally, Arthur was suspicious, but he couldn't identify any obvious risk. He moved to the rear wall and took down the pendant. *Really a very plain and ugly thing*, he thought. But obviously Friedrich wanted it very badly. Thus, he would pay handsomely. *And in the end, I don't think I'll let him have it.*

*

When his cell phone finally rang, Friedrich was in such a rage the veins bulged out in his neck. Arthur Raley sounded maddeningly nonchalant. "Hello, Friedrich. I'm in the town of Hingham. And I'm holding in my hand the item in which you are so interested. I happen to know that this item has a mate somewhere nearby.

"How do you know of that?" Friedrich asked, his mind spinning.

"Old Devin wasn't all that secretive, you know? He was frankly more interested in finding the von Adler family and milking them for some of that Nazi loot. But he did mention the item…and that you had a real hard-on for it. So I figure you'd like to see the two halves reunited."

"You don't understand anything about this!"

"Maybe not. But I do understand what you want, and getting it will be expensive for you… Oh, and *Heil* Hitler," he said, and hung up, but not before Friedrich heard him laughing.

"Drive toward Hingham," he told Gruber. "Get going."

Gruber frowned. "But we're supposed to return to the compound. The team will be arriving there shortly."

"Drive!" Friedrich savagely stabbed at the numbers on the cell phone. "The plan is altered," he said to the man who answered. "Go to the town of Hingham. I'll call you with further instructions."

*

Laura heard the low murmur, felt the van stop, pause longer than the span of a traffic light. More whispers, then the van turned hard, backed up, and turned again. They'd reversed course, but why? She'd lost track of how far they'd traveled, and she didn't know the city nearly well enough to make any sort of guess as to where they were now. All she could do was keep sending her message and believe in her heart that some-one was listening.

*

Malcolm and Ayalla ran up the front steps of Grace Wain-wright's house. He rang the doorbell aggressively. Nothing happened. "Their car is still here," said Ayalla, noting the rental sedan parked at the curb. Malcolm rang again. Still no answer.

"To hell with it," he said, taking his coat off and wrapping it in a bundle.

"That might be a little drastic, if they're inside chatting and just ignoring the doorbell."

"Something isn't right here," said Malcolm determinedly. "And you can arrest me, but not before I break into this house."

Ayalla met his eyes, saw the defiant look on his face. Deep down she agreed with him anyway. "Go for it, but keep it quiet. We don't need the neighbors calling the cops."

He placed his folded coat against one of the leaded glass panes in the graceful door. Then he punched it, right in the middle. The broken glass fell inward, and he reached through to the latch. Within ten seconds, they were in the front hall. It took less than that for Ayalla to notice the leather shoulder bag on the floor. She picked it up, opened it, and fumbled around for a wallet. She withdrew a dark brown billfold and flipped it open, swallowing hard when she saw the government I.D. card with Laura's picture.

Malcolm grabbed it out of her hand, and she didn't chide him. He had to feel it to believe it was real. His voice was completely without nuance or expression when he spoke, and she recognized the tactic. Malcolm was fighting to contain his rage. "Someone was waiting for them, took them right here by the door. We have to call Benjamin, find out what we should do."

"What we should do is call my office," she said with a frown. "I need to scramble the team, get set up for a ransom call, do it by the numbers." She already had her cell phone in her hand but Malcolm snatched it.

"Don't you get it?" he growled. "This isn't a kidnapping for ransom. If they *wanted* the fucking pendant and we still had it, then maybe. But Connor took it with her. And do you honestly think your buddies down at the field office are going to do anything but laugh at this whole situation—magical pendants, evil Nazis, occult spells, a little replay of World War II. Come on, they won't help us, and you'll just get your ass canned in the process. The only way we can handle this is our way. And the best person to get us whatever we need is Benjamin. The woo-woo stuff…well, that's up to the Carlisles. You and me, girl, we're the foot soldiers, so get used to it. That's what we do best, and we've proven before that we're a helluva team." He paused to evaluate whether he was convincing her. He wasn't sure. "Please," he said. "All I can do is ask you to play this my way."

She grabbed her cell phone back and dialed, and Malcolm let it go, sure he'd lost the argument. And now it was going to be one big mess. But she surprised him when she spoke into the phone. "Benjamin, I'm afraid it's bad news. Connor and Laura aren't here, but we found Laura's handbag... Yes, I think it's clear they've been taken somewhere... Good, we're going to have a quick look around. Call us as soon as they get a tri-angulation, but—hold on a minute." She rummaged in the Laura's bag. "Don't bother with Laura's phone. It's still here." She ended the call. "Okay," she said to the big man beside her. "Let's do it your way."

CHAPTER SEVENTEEN

If this be magic; let it be an art
Lawful as eating.
—William Shakespeare, *The Winter's Tale*, act V, scene 3

The members of the Circle were in deep meditation, ten of them sitting quietly in the center of a sacred grove in the southwest of England, not far from the village of Glastonbury, two of them in a hotel in the heart of Boston. The separation was not entirely unique in their experience. They had, on occasion and out of necessity, invoked their powers as a group without being physically present in the same location. But the need had never been so great for their combined strength as it was now. Ellen, before she began her journey into the center of Self, was deeply concerned. They were, after all, only human. For all the profound wisdom and power of their astral-plane selves, each member of the Circle was anchored firmly to a human body, complete with its emotional and physical limitations that could, at times, interfere with their ability to act fearlessly and in total Love.

Connor's grandmother, however, before her transition, had possessed a remarkable ability to bind them all together in the astral, and keep them working as One. The gift of her forebears—the ability to weave together the souls of the Circle for a common purpose—had emerged fully realized in Gwendolyn, and Ellen suspected it would someday in Connor if she allowed it. For now, they were compelled to cast a Circle that was one short of the Divine number—thirteen. Without the true high priestess, they were seriously at risk in a confrontation with the sort of ageless, bottomless evil the occult warriors of Hitler had tried to harness and deploy to their Führer's service. That dark vortex had not yet been fully roused, but in a short time, a matter of days, it had shifted from nearly moribund to thriving. Ellen and William suspected that the individual who had traveled from Germany to Boston was the focus of that evil energy. This man and the dark energy that had never quite been extinguished had moved into a frightening synergy. With the pendant in play, the success of the Circle teetered on a razor's edge.

Her meditation complete, Ellen shifted into an altered state of consciousness. The hotel room melted away, and she floated in a silvery mist, awaiting the others. She called to them with the voice of her heart until, one by one, they began to manifest in their astral forms, not quite solid, yet not quite vaporous either. She felt William's presence across the Circle from her. He would anchor, too. This was one of their keystones—the balancing of the masculine and feminine, the transcendent and the immanent. The makeup of the Circle, five men and seven women, was weighted toward the Divine Mother because the times called for it. Throughout their history, the composition had shifted back and forth according to the spiritual needs of the world.

In her awareness, Ellen perceived the links forming. On the astral, the process manifested as filaments of light connecting soul to soul, heart to heart, in an unbroken chain. She began to build on those filaments, layer upon layer, until they stood as human links comprising the equator of a gridded globe of iridescence that was both their tool and their shield. Slowly, the globe began to revolve.

Using the combined energies of the Circle, Ellen felt her way out into the shadow plane, the one that existed a tiny slice of infinity away from the "real" world. For every level of cosmic awareness that one journeyed away from physical form, the shapes of third-dimensional reality such as most humans perceived became less and less clear, reduced from their "solid" vibration to increasingly transparent shadows. It was akin to seeing a once-sharp image fade. From this place, Ellen could see and not be seen. But in order to affect the balance of cosmic energies, the awareness of the Circle would have to be extended much farther indeed. First, though, she must find a focus point.

Ellen waited patiently, leaving behind, along with her physical self, the complex set of human emotions—such as fear, anxiety, and impatience—that could undermine their work. She floated in a state of timelessness and calm anticipation. Then it happened.

A streak of light, almost like a shooting star, flared its way across the gray-silver horizon. The Circle, seeing through Ellen's awareness, drew in a collective breath. Was this their destination? She moved closer. A heartbeat…then two…and the light shimmered in a brief burst, nearer now. The heart of the Circle expanded, drawn to the pulsating energy. The field of their power seeped toward the source of the beacon, drawing itself around the astral manifestation of a call for help.

On the physical plane, in the quiet darkness of the hotel suite, Ellen's lips moved ever so slightly. *Laura, we're here.*

*

"We've got a signal on Connor's cell phone," said Benjamin. "It's moving toward the South Shore area. I'm heading that way."

"What about the Carlisles?" asked Ayalla, not sure if she wanted to know the answer.

"They're working on the problem right now," said Benjamin. "In their own way."

She was right. She didn't want to know. "Malcolm and I haven't found anything here at Grace's house. We're going to get on the expressway and head in the same general direction your people are tracking the cell. Call us when you have more."

*

Connor was more angry than afraid, at least where she, herself, was concerned. Perhaps it was odd, but since her grandmother's rather unusual departure from the everyday world, Connor hadn't been particularly afraid of death. True, she could hardly bear the thought of being separated from Laura, but something of her grandmother's wisdom comforted her with the understanding that she and Laura would only be separated for the briefest of moments in the cosmic scheme of things. Still, her fear for her lover's safety was gut-wrenchingly real. She was inordinately thankful that she could feel Laura next to her, sense the rhythm of her heartbeat. Now she had to decide what to do. Whereas some would feel helpless, Connor felt frustrated. She'd had a moment of panic when they slipped the hood over her head, but she closed her eyes and reminded herself that she'd never been afraid of the dark. There was plenty of air to breathe, even through the rough, musty fabric of the hood. The handcuffs were seriously uncomfortable, but hadn't cut off the circulation to her hands. And around her neck, she wore the pendant. Connor wasn't sure what had prompted her to put it on, rather than slip it into her pocket or purse. Just one of those promptings that seemed to come from nowhere but she knew should be heeded.

When her thoughts turned to the pendant, a subtle change came over her body. Warmth spread into her cramped limbs. Even the chill metal cuffs heated up. She sensed a glow in her chest, right about where the pendant lay against her skin. Interesting. But what could she do with this?

"Listen, child!"

The voice was so loud that for an instant Connor fully believed someone in the van had spoken. But the voice was unmistakably Gwendolyn Broadhurst. Connor pushed all other thoughts from her mind except one—*"I'm here."*

"You're needed elsewhere. The Circle must be completed."

"I don't know how, Grandmother."

"You most certainly do know."

"But why not you? You already have the skill and the power."

"I, my dear, am no longer connected to the physical world. You are. There is always a reason for the way things work in this universe. Now is not the time to question universal laws. Laura has already drawn the focus of the Circle toward you."

Connor sighed and allowed herself one small human thought: *God, I hate it when she's right.*

Carefully, almost tentatively, she let the warmth in her chest flow upward into her head, and downward into her belly. The sound of the engine, the smell of damp wool, the shifting and creaking of the van—it all receded into the background until she was barely aware of it. Gradually, she felt less connected to her physical body. Something tugged at the space around her heart.

"How am I doing?"

"It's a beginning, my dear one. Now follow me…and try to keep up."

*

Arthur Raley had done some of his best work in record time. Pretending to be someone else, he'd called the S.A.B. compound for an update. As he knew all the appropriate passwords, he'd been informed that the team deployed to collect the "packages" had been diverted to Hingham, and that Friedrich and Gruber were also en route.

After wiring a few well-placed charges of plastic explosive around the entrance to the mausoleum as a sort of insurance on his personal safety, he'd quickly set up his laptop computer on top of the one sarcophagus that stood in the center of the floor. He checked that there was ample battery life, and connected his cell phone to the modem port before turning the unit off again. He'd boot it up when bargaining time rolled around.

Arthur waited another fifteen minutes before redialing Friedrich, who answered instantly. "I imagine you're quite close now. I suggest you rendezvous with your toy soldiers at the town square in Hingham. Bring the Hawthorne woman with you. Leave Gruber behind. Then I will let you know where to meet me. It's less than forty-five minutes away. Remember, this is my game." He quickly hung up before Friedrich could formulate even a word of protest.

*

"Drive on the shoulder!" Malcolm barked.

"That's where I'm going," Ayalla said through clenched teeth as she swung the wheel hard and lurched into the breakdown lane. "You may not have noticed, but there were other drivers with the same idea."

"Go around them!"

"It's been raining for days. We'll end up stuck in all that mud beyond the pavement. I don't think I'd like that." She laid on her horn to draw the attention of the lane-blockers to the flashing light on the dashboard. Reluctantly, the other drivers tried to move left, back into the traffic lanes.

"This is taking too long," he snapped, alternating between second-guessing her tactics and shredding the edges of the map book he held in his lap.

Ayalla wanted to scream at Malcolm. But the words died on her lips when she glanced at him and saw the sheer misery on his face. He felt helpless; they both did. Anger wasn't going to help. She reached out and squeezed his hand. "We'll get there, and we'll take care of business."

"Yeah," he said softly, staring straight ahead. "We will."

*

With the evening exodus from Boston filling the streets to capacity, Hingham might as well have been in another state as far as Benjamin was concerned. He was in the backseat of the lead sedan in a three-car convoy. Beside him, a technician continued to monitor the progress of Connor's cell phone toward the South Shore. Benjamin prayed that the phone was still with her.

"Looks like they're on surface streets now," said the tech, his fingers moving smoothly over the keys of his computer. "Let me blow up this map." He tapped the mouse pad. "Yep, there's the signal."

"But where are they headed?"

"They still have a choice," said the technician. "But it's toward the ocean. My guess is Hingham, but they cross into other towns on the way—Rockland, Norwell—after the get off Route 3."

"Is there a cemetery in Hingham?" Benjamin asked.

"Hang on, let me switch computers." He slid out a tray underneath the work surface built onto the rear floorboard, where a second laptop, with a continuous cellular connection, sat humming softly. Within seconds, he accessed the necessary data. "There's one not far from Hingham Harbor."

"That's it," said Benjamin, with a conviction that puzzled him. He raised his voice so the driver could hear him clearly. "Best possible speed to the cemetery near Hingham Harbor, lieutenant."

"Yes, sir," came the crisp reply. "But we may have to sprout wings."

Benjamin sighed. "Whatever it takes."

*

Laura felt the van stop and heard the soft squeal of a brake pad in need of replacement. Their captors' cell phone had rung again, but she couldn't make out the conversation except for one word—Hingham. But was that their destination?

She detected a mood of discontent among the occupants of the van, but no one apparently dared question orders. The men sat in utter silence. Her one consolation was that she'd heard Ellen's voice, only for a few moments, yet it had been loud and clear. And Laura thought she'd been able to communicate the fact that she and Connor were together. A pity she hadn't also known their location. That would have been useful information to share. Laura, though summoned to the astral by the Circle, hadn't dared stay. Her skills were not sufficient to maintain bi-location for any length of time. Wandering around in the Dreamtime meant leaving her awareness of physical reality—and of Connor.

A low, guttural engine drew up near them. For Laura, whose love affair with cars had occupied much of her youth, thought she recognized the sound, if only because she'd heard it fairly recently. Then it came to her—Devin Underwood's BMW. Maybe. But who was driving it?

The sound of the van door opening, then a welcome blast of

chilly air that dispelled the sour warmth of human bodies sweating in a small space.

She heard a voice speaking in German. *"Bringt die Frau fort— und ihre Handtasche!"*

Laura understood the simple phrases: "Bring the woman— and her handbag."

"Welche Frau?" said another man—"which woman?"

Laura almost prayed, *Me. Take me,* until she realized she had no idea which was the more dangerous alternative for Connor— staying in the van, or being taken somewhere else. Either way, her heart dropped into her stomach at the thought of being separated from Connor, having no way to protect her.

"Frau Hawthorne—stellt sie ins Auto."

Laura felt herself being unceremoniously shoved to one side. They were going to take Connor somewhere else in a car. She strained to hear more, any clue that she might pass on to Ellen. But all she heard was the sound of fabric against carpet, no doubt Connor being dragged out of the van. Laura was puzzled by her silence. Not a word of defiance or even farewell. What was wrong? Was she conscious? Had she been drugged? From sheer reflex, Laura began to struggle to sit upright. A hard fist slammed into the side of her head. Pain knifed through her skull, and she crumpled to the floor.

*

Friedrich got into the driver's seat of the BMW. Connor was in the passenger seat, her hands still cuffed behind her. He ripped the bag off her head, taking enough hairs with it to have made anyone flinch. But she made no sign whatsoever. Her eyes were unfocused.

"Wo ist es?" he hissed. *"Wo ist der Hängeschalter—der Seelendieb?"*

She didn't answer, and he cursed his own stupidity. The ignorant woman didn't speak German. He repeated himself, this time in careful, though heavily accented English. "Where is it? Where is the pendant—the Thief of Souls?"

Something flickered in Connor's eyes, but she didn't reply, or even appear to be concerned with his question. *What on earth is wrong with the woman?* he wondered. He grabbed her chin, turning her face toward him. From his pocket he removed the old Luger he still cherished. "I will kill you," he snarled. Friedrich grabbed the leather bag from the floorboard next to Connor's feet and dumped it out in her lap. "Here? Is it in here? I know you have it—I can *feel* it."

The words were barely out of his mouth when he knew: She had to be wearing it. The thought had never occurred to him. Why would she? Only he understood its significance. Friedrich grabbed the collar of her button-down shirt and ripped it open. The top two buttons popped off. There it lay, one half of one of the most powerful magical objects still extant in the world: the thief of souls. Friedrich's heart soared with sheer joy. He laughed out loud. He reached for it, to tear it from her neck—and nearly screamed as a bolt of pure energy seared through his brain, from one temple to the other. The pain almost made him faint, and the surges of energy he'd had these past two days seemed to drain away for a few moments, leaving him tired and old once more. The dynamic field of energy he'd been building around himself and his men to protect them from prying eyes and tampering magicians was weakened to the point of collapse.

Still Connor said nothing. Through half-closed eyes, Friedrich saw the pendant differently. It appeared to expand, then contract. At first he was sure it was simply the movement of the woman's chest as she filled her lungs. But no, the pendant itself was breathing!

He shrank against the driver's door. This woman could not possibly wield *le voleur d'âmes*. Grace Wainwright perhaps. She was a descendant of the old line. Her powers were of great potential. Thus he had ordered she be taken back to the compound in a separate car. He would kill the other two once he had the pendant, and he didn't want her nearby, sensing anything that would make her even more difficult to control. The files told him she had been a friend of the Hawthorne woman. He had planned to use that friendship to coerce Grace Wainwright into doing his bidding, while holding out Connor Hawthorne's life as an incentive.

But now what? From all he'd learned over the decades, what was happening was impossible. This Hawthorne was nothing! She had no power, no knowledge. And yet the proof was right there before his eyes. Connor Hawthorne was completely enfolded in the field of energy generated by the golden figure that lay just below the hollow of her throat.

His cell phone rang.

"Well, Friedrich, my obsessed countryman, are you ready to pay for your desires?"

"Where are you?!"

"Close enough. Look around you. Not far away you'll see the steeple of a church. Behind the church is what you've been looking for. And, Friedrich, leave your thugs behind, or you'll never see your little objet d'art, at least not in this lifetime."

The connection went dead. Friedrich stared at the gold pendant. He wanted to touch it so badly...an overwhelming lust for it coursed through him until he could hardly draw breath. But how?

Then the solution came to him in one sudden blinding inspiration. An image of the silver pendant appeared full blown in his mind. Flashes of memory, the pendant dangling around the throat of Wilhelm von Adler. That was what he needed. With it he could wrest control of the golden half from whoever or whatever opposed him. Strength began to flow back into his arms, his legs. He took a deep lungful of air and tested the threads of energy that sprouted from his astral body like spines on a sea urchin. *Yes,* he thought, *I am still here.*

He got out of the car and looked around him, turning slowly in a circle until he spotted it—the white steeple of a church. It was an omen, standing tall and proud in sharp relief against the black sky. White against black. Silver against gold. His was the winning hand.

*

"Did you see it?"

William's question filtered through the Circle to Ellen. "Yes," she replied. "I've seen it, and I know who is within that darkness."

Ellen knew then that her supposition was correct. This was an old and poisonous evil so tightly woven into the fabric of the past by those who had used it to commit innumerable atrocities and unspeakable cruelty that its insidious attachment to human destiny could not be dissolved without the greatest risk to those who opposed it. Though Ellen had always been aware of the dangers of their work, never had she been so compelled to consider death, both physical and psychic, as a likely outcome. Much more daunting was the very real possibility that even their very souls might be cast adrift for time out of mind, reassembling only after a thousand turns of the universal spiral of consciousness. It was quite literally a fate worse than death for the Circle, and the ramifications for the earth plane were even more repugnant to them. A change so profound as the loss of the Light workers could derail the destiny of the planet, shift its reality, and send it off on a path of violence and conflict never before seen. The balance would be lost, and so, quite likely, would humankind. Even without this immanent evil, the linking of minds, hearts, and souls the world over had barely been sufficient to maintain a fragile and sometimes briefly interrupted peace in the world. Now the stakes were very high indeed.

"His strength faded briefly." Her thoughts reached William and the others easily. "I believe he may have encountered the Wainwright half of the Goddess of Avebury pendant. And I'm quite sure Connor is wearing it. Somehow, without being aware, she is drawing on our strength to create a field of protective energy."

"Gwendolyn?" asked one of the others.

"Let us pray she is with Connor now," said Ellen. "Otherwise, I don't think we can protect her or ourselves."

Ellen slipped into yet a higher field of vibration, and felt the others shift to stay with her. Gradually she ramped up the energy, and the globe revolved more quickly.

*

Connor knew she was in a car, and that Laura was no longer nearby. That thought gave her some pain, but it was somehow distant from her, as if she'd had a small injection of anesthetic to block not only pain, but fear.

"You still haven't stretched yourself much," Gwendolyn.

"How? You always act as if I'm supposed to know things by sheer osmosis. But I don't know how to be somewhere else. I'm not in my body anymore, though."

"Actually, part of your old awareness is very much in your body. But a much more powerful and real version of you has settled in as well. You're in the process of marrying the two together."

"*Marrying?*"

"*Joining, fusing, uniting. Whatever words suits you, child. But we need to accelerate the process. Ellen and the others can't hold the high ground without you. Only as thirteen can you take the conflict to the doorstep of our greatest enemy.*"

"*You're beginning to sound like an old war movie, Grandmother.*"

"*I was in an old war, and you're being impertinent.*"

"*Sorry.*"

"*You're forgiven. Do you know where your physical body is now?*"

"*Yes, I'm fairly clear on that.*"

"*Then you must also realize that if the one known as Friedrich obtains the silver half, and you have not yet opened yourself to the truth of who you are, and what you can do, then he will most certainly take control of that object and use it for the greatest evils you can imagine.*"

"*Why must I bear so much responsibility? Aren't there others, the ones who know about this magical stuff? Why can't they do this?*"

"*Since when did I raise you to avoid your duty? Everyone has a destiny, every single being a path they've chosen, lifetime after lifetime. There have been other crises of the spiritual and physical realms that have been met by others. This one happens to be yours. And it is particularly dreadful in some ways.*"

"*What, I couldn't get a beginner's test?*"

"*You haven't been a beginner for several thousand years—something you seem to have forgotten to remember.*"

"*I don't think that makes sense.*"

"*If you think about it, child. But for now I suggest you do as I instruct you. Time may be entirely irrelevant on this and higher planes, but in your reality on Earth, time is something of which we have very little left.*"

"*All right.*"

"*I shall repeat to you a series of sounds. They may be likened*" *to words, yet they are not words such as you might use in your third-dimensional world. They are sounds that vibrate at the frequency of creation. That passage you've read, "In the beginning was the word…"*

"Yes, from the Bible."

"Quite. Let's just say that the authors had only a tiny idea of what that meant. You're about to find out a great deal more."

*

"Benjamin's not far behind us," said Malcolm, snapping the phone shut. "The tracking program shows the phone has stopped moving. It's in Hingham, right about the town square."

"Check the map," she said, as they turned onto Main Street. "It'll show where there's a cemetery near there. And there's a spare weapon in the glove box."

He almost smiled. "I'm not authorized."

"Now you are," she said. "Exigent circumstances."

He opened the compartment and slipped a cold, sleek 9-mm from its holster.

"Thanks."

Within a few minutes, they saw a grassy area ahead of them. Cars flowed around them as Ayalla pulled to the curb. They scanned the scene carefully, each one experienced in identifying anomalies in an otherwise everyday scene.

"Doesn't it seem awfully dark out?" said Ayalla.

"I think that's what nighttime means," Malcolm muttered, still surveying the street and the square.

"Don't be a jerk," she snapped. "It should be more like twilight, but the sky is pitch-black."

Malcolm craned his neck to look at the sky through the windshield, then shook his head. "Maybe it's gonna rain again. I don't know." He shook his head in frustration. This was like the old needle in a haystack. Even one small town would take time to search. "Wait, look over there."

On the other side of the square, a car moved away from the curb. It had been almost hidden behind a fat oak tree and an ornate park bench.

"That's it," said Ayalla, dropping the gearshift into drive. "That's got to be Devin's car."

"But what about the van?"

She paused and followed his pointing finger. The rear door of a gray panel van swung shut. "You don't suppose..." she murmured, straining to see whether there was anyone in the driver's seat.

"Don't have to suppose," said Malcolm. "I know."

And, oddly enough, he did know. The instant his gaze settled on the van, he heard it. Well, he heard something. But it called to him, demanded his immediate attention. And the focus of that attention was something in the van, something that... called him. He wasn't about to take the time to try and explain this to Ayalla.

"You know what?" she asked, but he was already out of the car and walking fast down the sidewalk. She put the gearshift in Park and flung her door open. "Hey, slow down."

But Malcolm was being pulled forward. He barely heard Ayalla. Some part of his mind considered that this felt a lot like the night, years ago, when he'd wandered in the desert alone and confused, but determined to find Connor Hawthorne.

His vision had narrowed to a square tunnel that contained only the van and nothing else. He felt Ayalla tug at his arm. "Hang on a minute, for God's sake. You can't just go up and roust somebody without a reason."

"I have a reason," he said, not slowing down.

"Well for God's sake, let's at least sneak up on them. You're acting like Dirty Harry."

"More like Shaft," said Malcolm, as he broke into a trot.

*

Inside the van, Laura had maintained her psychic focus on staying firmly in a vibration of peace and strength. Any small contribution she could make to help Connor and the others might give them an edge. Thus she no longer called for help. Instead she sent her inner strength to where it might do the most good. She'd already concluded that she was of no use to these people, whatever their agenda, and she hoped she'd die with reasonable dignity when the time came. So intent was she on the task at hand, she barely felt the surge of righteous fury and fierce determination that preceded Malcolm Jefferson's assault on the van.

A door slammed open with a screech of metal on metal. A sudden scrambling press of bodies around her. Someone kicked her in the side.

Then the sound of a dearly familiar voice: "Don't fucking move or I'll blow your fucking heads off! Now get the fuck out of the van."

That's my Malcolm, she thought with a grin. A minute later, gentle hands pulled her up into a sitting position, and the mask was finally removed. She looked at him, his eyes troubled, his brow creased with worry, as he quickly unlocked her cuffs.

"Thank you, God," she whispered before throwing her arms around his neck. "So, good buddy, what kept you?"

Within a few minutes, local police responded to Ayalla's call for backup, and five men were handcuffed and sitting on the curb. She ran down the list of potential charges. The stash of weapons inside the van was in itself enough to guarantee long prison sentences in the Commonwealth of Massachusetts. Then there was kidnapping, and whatever else might come out of finally breaking the back of the Supreme Aryan Brotherhood. Laura quickly informed them that Grace Wainwright had been taken elsewhere.

Upon hearing this, Malcolm strode over to where the prisoners were sitting and picked up one of them as if he weighed absolutely nothing and dragged him into the back of the van. While the local cops pretended not to notice the sound of thuds, Malcolm conducted a brief but productive "interview." When he emerged a few minutes later, minus some bits of skin from his knuckles, he gave Ayalla the location of the S.A.B. headquarters. "Guy swears you won't be able to find it, though I have a feeling you will. But he really doesn't know where this guy Friedrich took Connor."

Ayalla looked at him, her expression a mixture of bewilderment and admiration. "How did you know Laura was in that van? And don't tell me it was just a hunch. For all we knew, there could have been two teenagers necking in the back."

Malcolm looked at the ground. Laura, standing a few feet away, didn't interrupt. She thought she could explain it, but this time it was up to Malcolm to figure it out.

He sighed. "You won't like the answer, any more than I liked the idea when I had to deal with it back in New Mexico. But I'm never going to deny it again. Human beings have more senses than the ones most people believe in. I don't know where it is in the brain, but I do know there's a whole lot of our brains we don't use. When I saw that car pull away and then my attention was pulled completely off the car, and onto the van, I just *knew*. It was like the van was the only lit-up thing in the whole scene of the town square and the shops and the other cars. It stood out from the background like everything else was flat and two-dimensional and it was the only real thing."

Ayalla stared at him. "You're right, I don't like it. But at least for once you're telling me what you're really thinking." She turned to look at Laura. "You didn't hear anything about this Friedrich character or why he took Connor?"

Laura shook her head. "I just heard him come for her. And he talked about the pendant."

They all turned at the sound of hard braking. Benjamin jumped out of a car that had pulled up behind the police cruisers. One of the cops tried to restrain him, but he produced some sort of identification, and they immediately stepped aside.

He almost ran to join them. "Thank God you're all right," he said to Laura, but they saw the excitement in his eyes fade when he realized his daughter was nowhere in sight.

"Connor?" he asked, his eyes on Laura.

"Friedrich took her," she said. "I'm so sorry. There wasn't anything I could do."

He shook his head and put a hand on her shoulder. "Don't go there," he said, his voice thick and husky. "Don't start assigning blame."

Ayalla interrupted. "I'm betting on the cemetery where Billy Dagle is buried." She turned to Laura. "Which one is it?"

"What?!" said Laura, grabbing Ayalla's arm without even thinking. "What about a cemetery?"

"Billy Dagle's partner found the silver half of the pendant and might have taken it to Dagle's grave."

Laura stared at the steeple of the church only a few short blocks away. "He's buried right there," she said. "That's the one."

✳

"You're with us, Connor. You're fully within the circle. But now it's time to step into your rightful place." Ellen's voice was musical: gentle, but insistent.

"Not yet. It's too soon."

"Perhaps, my friend. But fear cannot rule you."

"I can help right here, where I am."

"Yes, but it is not simply the power of thirteen together that opens the gateways, but twelve led by one. You are that one."

"The evil is strong in him. It is frightening where I am," said Connor.

"That's not where you truly are. That is but one tiny fractal image."

"This is real then? Where we are together right now?"

"It's still a reflection, but a very great step closer to Reality."

"What shall I do then?"

"Move to the center of the Circle, the center of the sphere. Open your heart to receive us all. The time is not yet right for you to act. But it is coming, my dear. It is coming."

Chapter Eighteen

And now I see with eye serene
The very pulse of the machine;
A being breathing thoughtful breath,
A traveler betwixt life and death;
The reason firm, the temperate will,
Endurance, foresight, strength and skill;
A perfect woman, nobly planned,
To warn, to comfort, and command;
And yet a spirit still, and bright
With something of angelic light.
—William Wordsworth, "She Was a Phantom of Delight"

Friedrich shone the flashlight on the gravel path. With his right hand, he gripped the Luger as well as the back of Connor's jacket. He still did not dare touch the pendant, but he'd have no compunction about taking it off her dead body if necessary. Ahead he saw a dim light at ground level, presumably a marker to guide him toward Arthur Raley, though what the man thought he could extract from Friedrich out here in the damp, cold darkness remained a mystery.

The woman beside him showed no signs of fear or curiosity. Instead she walked confidently, never looking at the ground in front of her, or from side to side at the tombstones that loomed out of the night on either side of them. He'd never seen anyone so unconcerned with death. He would admire her warrior spirit, were it not for her gender and the fact that she stood between him and his ultimate prize.

"Raley," he called out in English. "Where are you?"

There was no answer. He kept walking. Finally, the light was only a few feet away, and he saw that its glow emanated from the front of a mausoleum, the door of which was slightly ajar. "Raley," he called out again.

"In here," came the reply from the interior of the mausoleum, the voice echoing against the stone. "Bring the woman with you, but leave the gun outside."

Friedrich scowled, wondering if Raley could see his gun. Then the obvious thought occurred: Raley assumed he had a gun. In that case, he could just assume that Friedrich had tossed it away.

"Hurry up, old man. We have business."

Friedrich tightened his grip on both the gun and Connor and turned off his flashlight so as not to be an easy target. Still, he wasn't unduly afraid. Raley was a greedy, lying coward who wanted only money, who had no understanding of the bigger picture. Such a man could not defeat destiny.

Friedrich walked into the mausoleum and stared. The ten-by-twenty interior was brightly lit by two camping lanterns perched atop a granite sarcophagus. There was no one there, and nowhere to hide. He started to turn, but not quickly enough. The barrel of a gun pressed into his left ear, and a hand snatched away the Luger. "You're easily fooled, old man," said the familiar guttural voice of Arthur Raley. "Sleight of hand." He pointed at the little speaker sitting next to the camp lanterns. "I've often found it's better to be somewhere other than the place people are looking for you. Now go stand in that corner over there. You, too," he snapped, giving Connor a shove. She walked straight ahead, and stopped when she got to the edge of the sarcophagus.

"What's with her?" growled Raley, waving the barrel of his gun in her direction. "Doesn't talk much."

"I don't know," Friedrich lied. No sense in Raley knowing any more about the pendant. He rather hoped the man knew very little, other than that Friedrich wanted it.

"So, we're going to conclude our business here very quickly. That computer is logged on to your banking system. You'll be making a transfer."

"A transfer?"

"Don't pretend to be stupid, Herr Doktor."

Friedrich felt a wave of nausea at being addressed by his old title. It should have made him feel important. It didn't. On the other hand, at least his body felt even stronger than when he'd arrived the cemetery. His mind was sharp, clear. Something good was going to happen for him this day. That much he knew.

"I'm not. But what makes you think I would carry my account numbers and authorization passwords around with me?"

"You wouldn't," grinned Raley. "But you certainly would have them memorized. I seem to recall reading somewhere that you were quite the brilliant little researcher. Lots of brainpower. So why don't you use that brain to weigh your choices."

"I don't even know that you have the...that you have it."

"Oh, you mean this?" The silver pendant appeared in Raley's other hand as if he had materialized it out of thin air. Friedrich realized he'd been holding it all along. But why had he not sensed its presence? What stood between him and his rightful possession? For in Friedrich's mind, the desire to steal the pendant had been transmuted into a righteous retrieval of what was clearly meant to be his. And once he reunited the halves, if he himself could not harness the power of *le voleur d'âmes*, he still had Grace Wainwright. She, as a legitimate heir to the pendant, could control it, and he would certainly control her and her considerable fortune.

He stared at the silver object dangling from Raley's clenched fist. At that moment, Connor Hawthorne stepped back, out of the space between Friedrich and Raley, and the force of the von Adler pendant hit Friedrich with such momentum, he barely kept himself from falling.

"What's the matter, Doktor? Feeling the ravages of time? Or is it the cancer? You know, I can almost smell it on you—the scent of death. I suggest you stop wasting any more time There's the computer. Get to work. You will be transferring twenty million dollars to the account listed on the left side of the screen."

"Twenty million dollars! You must be insane."

"No, the fact is, I've decided I must be rich. I feel retirement coming on."

Friedrich rose to his full height, entertaining the fleeting wish he'd worn his uniform. "You would steal from the Fatherland, from the Reich?"

Arthur Raley's face darkened. "There is no Reich. And you're nothing but a sick, deluded old man, as twisted as all the paranoid little psychos Hitler called a general staff."

Friedrich trembled with a rage he could barely contain. "But you were sworn to our cause."

Raley lips twisted into a half-sneer, half-smile. "That's the thing about causes, Friedrich. In the end they're just the delusions of half-witted optimists and sore losers. Now start typing, or I'll take both halves of the pendant and leave you here to think about your failures."

Friedrich started at Raley for a good ten seconds. His eyes expressed no emotion at all. His hands were no longer clenched. "Very well, then," he said. "I see I have no alternative."

Raley watched him narrowly, looking for signs of dissimulation. But Friedrich turned to the laptop computer and peered at the screen. His left hand reached into his jacket pocket and Raley raised his pistol. "What are you doing?"

Out of Friedrich's pocket came a pair of spectacles. "I can't see what I'm doing without these," he said.

"Hurry up."

Within two minutes, Friedrich, long accustomed to shifting money from one bank to another, had done precisely what Raley wanted. But it was a small price to pay.

"Back away," said Raley. "Get in the corner." Raley gave Connor barely a glance as he moved close enough to the computer to confirm the transfer.

"The pendant," said Friedrich.

Raley tossed it through the air. It hit the wall first, then clattered to the stone floor at Friedrich's feet. He bent down and snatched it up, his heart beating wildly. Here it was, in his own hands, the von Adler pendant! Only the sound of laughter diverted him from placing it around his neck.

"You find this amusing, Herr Raley," said Friedrich coldly, the pendant firmly encased in his clenched fist. "Perhaps you won't laugh tomorrow, or the next day."

"Ah, but I will. You see, your little protégé wasn't the only one who could do research, and there's quite a lot he didn't tell you anyway."

Friedrich experienced a minor spasm of doubt, but refused to indulge it. "He doesn't matter. He was a fool."

"I'd have to agree. But he wasn't as foolish you think."

"Don't play games with me. He didn't know anything."

"He knew that the von Adler pendant was here in Massa-chusetts."

"That's absurd."

"Not really. You see, it seems his grandfather—Karl, I believe it was—hated your guts. I mean, really hated your guts."

"You're lying. He was my friend and a loyal officer."

"Wrong again. He wrote a whole bunch of letters over the years. Devin ended up with them. And it seems Karl found out all about where von Adler went—and all that gold and jewelry he took with him. He found out years ago. He just never told *you*. I can only imagine he thought you as pathetic as I do."

"How dare you?"

"What? You're going to zap me with all that magical power? Even if I believed in the pendant, the legends say only the right-ful heirs can use it. Since you had me snuff out poor Billy Dagle, you pretty much shot yourself in the foot."

Friedrich smiled. "I only need one heir, one blood relation who can harness its powers. And Grace Wainwright is safely tucked away. I'll get to her soon enough."

Raley laughed again. This time it was all Friedrich could do to keep from lunging at him. Instead, he dropped his glasses on the floor. Raley, distracted by the sound, did not notice Friedrich's hand brush against his trouser cuff as he bent to pick up the spectacles. Friedrich came up firing, two bullets from a small snub-nosed automatic catching Raley in the upper chest.

Raley looked down at his own chest, an expression of sur-prise pasted on his features. It was Friedrich's turn to smile. The ankle gun had been his ace in the hole, and his timing had been impeccable.

"Not so amused now, are you?" he said, walking toward Raley, gun pointed at the man's forehead.

The pistol fell from Raley's hand onto the granite blocks of the flooring. He looked up at Friedrich. "Actually, I am," he said, a trace of defiance hardening his jaw. "Because I still get to have the last laugh, and I've heard that's the best one."

"Hardly."

"Oh, yes. You see, Grace Wainwright isn't the one."

"What are you talking about?" snarled Friedrich, ignoring the frisson of anxiety that arced through his chest.

"Just that. You were so sure you had it all figured out. But after I had a chat or two with Mr. Underwood, I did my own checking. Everyone thought Claire Wainwright was the oldest sister."

"The oldest—"

"Isn't that how it works? Oldest daughter, oldest son?" Raley coughed and tiny flecks of blood appeared on his lips.

"Yes, but—"

"It was Florence Gardner. She was the oldest sister by almost twenty minutes."

"You're deluded," snarled Friedrich, his whole body trembling with anger and fear. "Florence didn't even have a daughter."

"So what? The fact is, you assumed it must be Claire Wainwright because she did have a daughter. You really are a fool."

Friedrich's mind was spinning. He'd never imagined that anything could spoil his ultimate success. Then he had another thought. "Dagle had a sister. I'll find *her*."

"Dead, too," said Raley, coughing up more blood. "Car accident in Arizona four years ago."

"You're lying! And you're insane."

"No, I'm prepared. You see?" Raley held up a tiny metal tube that he'd been concealing in his left hand. Another bit of deception. He pressed a button and the tip of the tube began to blink. Raley put out his right hand to steady himself against the sarcophagus. "Check out the door, Friedrich. It's another surprise."

His hand went to his chest. "And kind of ironic. You killed all the people you needed to carry out your ridiculous little plot to rule the world. And now you're going to join them."

Raley slumped to the floor unconscious.

Friedrich ran to the door. Above the lintel he saw another blinking light illuminating a pair of contacts glued to the door frame and top of the door. He instantly recognized it for what it was—and what would probably happen if the connection were broken…He cast his eyes around the interior of the mausoleum and quickly spotted the wired charges in the corners. No, it couldn't be. There had to be a way to disarm it. Raley wouldn't have trapped himself. But that was just it. He hadn't planned to trap himself, only Friedrich.

He stood there panting, wondering how much time he had. Then he looked at the pendant in his hand. Of course! What was he thinking. There was no need to panic. He'd seen the black magicians do amazing and terrible things with von Adler and his pendant. Now he had both halves! He needed them both! *That* was why the heirs were all dead. Friedrich had merely been the instrument of Fate, the same Fate that had brought him *le voleur d'âmes*, and filled him with strength and conviction. He was ready to take the Fitzhugh pendant from Connor Hawthorne.

He went to where she stood, her back against the wall of the mausoleum, her eyes fixed on him in a way that made his skin crawl. He focused on the pendant. Its light grew brighter, and Friedrich stopped. First, he would put the von Adler pendant around his own neck. Then he would claim the rest. He unfastened his collar button, then another, and slipped the chain over his head. The glittering silver slid down his chest with the cold sting of frigid metal. He closed his eyes for a moment, breathing it in, feeling renewed strength flowing into his once-faltering limbs. When he opened his eyes, the mausoleum had disappeared. All that remained was Connor Hawthorne and the pendant, and she didn't look at all like the woman who'd stood in front of him only seconds before.

*

"It's down this way," Laura called to the others as they piled out of the two cars. "We need flashlights."

Benjamin was already opening the trunk of his car. Ayalla did the same. Between them they had four powerful lights. The police officers pulling up behind would no doubt have their own. Either way, Laura wasn't going to wait, and the rest of them were right behind her as she flung open the gate and rushed down the gravel path. They ran, feet crunching on the stones, lights swinging wildly. Laura's feet flew over the ground and she outdistanced the others within seconds. In less than a minute she reached a point where the pathway split. She shone the light ahead as the others came up to join her.

"Which way?" said Malcolm, panting hard.

"To the right…I think. It looks a lot different in the dark."

"You and Malcolm go that way," said Benjamin. "Ayalla and I will take the left, just in case. The cemetery can't be that big. We can see your lights from wherever we are. If you find it first, holler for us."

With this divide and conquer strategy established, the four-some raced away. Seconds later, Laura's toe caught on a brick and she went sprawling. Malcolm skidded to a halt and ran back to pick her up. "You okay?"

"I'm fine, just clumsy. Go, go!"

They rounded a curve in the path and there it was, right in front of them—the Dagle mausoleum. But everything was dark…or was it?

"Look," said Laura. "There's a light."

They stepped quietly along the side of the small building and saw the source of the illumination: a tiny vent cut high in the back wall. Through it, a soft yellow light glimmered. They stood for a moment listening. But all they could hear was a low thrumming sound, as if the building itself were vibrating. Laura put her hand to the stone. It was vibrating. They moved swiftly back to the front.

"What do you want to do?" asked Malcolm, gun at the ready, his hand laid gently against the metal door.

"Let's signal the others," replied Laura, waving her flashlight back and forth to attract Ayalla and Benjamin who, as it turned out, were less than fifty yards away, having abandoned the path that had dead-ended at a fence. In the distance, at the front of the cemetery, they could see a bouquet of flashlight beams wavering toward them—the police contingent.

"Connor's in there," said Laura. "I'm sure of it."

"With only one entrance, it's risky to rush through the door," said Benjamin. "We could wait until they come out and take them."

Laura turned to Benjamin. "I don't think Friedrich is planning on bringing Connor out of there." Her dark eyes bored into his, and he saw the truth of what she said. Connor's abductor would think nothing of killing her and leaving her in the mausoleum.

"Then we go in," he said.

"And I go first," said Malcolm. "I make a great shield."

"No," interrupted Ayalla. "I'll take the point."

"But—"

"I'm the only one wearing a vest," she said, pulling back her raincoat. "Strangely enough, us Feebs have a habit of being prepared." She shoved in front of them and began to push on the door, her service weapon at high port.

I bet it's gonna creak. Maybe I'd better just do it fast, she thought, steeling herself against the rush of adrenaline. She pushed hard. The door didn't stick, and it didn't creak, but Ayalla felt herself sailing through the air backward, and she heard Laura scream, "No!" right before the lights went out.

★

"Who are you?" Friedrich hissed. "You don't belong here. The pendant isn't yours."

"No," replied Connor. "Nor is it yours."

They stood in a vast arena, so enormous indeed that the sides were only dim shadows among lighter ones. Connor could not see the Circle, but she believed they were as close as they were able to be. With a new flood of awareness, she knew this was how it had been for her grandmother and the warrior priestesses who had come before them. In the final hour, when the balance of light and dark was threatened by the most baneful evil, there must be one who could call on the heart of the universe, on all that was good and kind and loving, to face down the ultimate fear.

"I claim this power," said Friedrich, his voice growing more powerful, more resonant with each word. "I feel it moving inside me."

"It is not yours to claim. It's a reflection of rage and fear that attached itself to the family of Wilhelm von Adler when his ancestor, Genevieve Fitzhugh, was nearly beaten to death and her child later taken from her as she died. In that moment of passing, she abandoned the Light and gave over her power to the darkness. Your black magicians used that power for great evil. They used it to torment, to spy, to turn brother and sister. They interfered with the souls of humanity. They challenged the natural order."

"How would you know this? You are nothing."

"I am Lydia Connor Hawthorne, daughter of Amanda Joan Hawthorne, and granddaughter of Gwendolyn Katherine Broadhurst, once priestess of the Circle of Light. I wear her mantle of authority, and I refuse to permit you access to this plane of existence."

Friedrich, now more powerful than he'd ever felt, even in the glorious days of the Third Reich, laughed. The sound echoed through the arena—a horrible dissonance of human screams and panicked wails.

Connor almost shrank back from the wall of noise. It assaulted her from every side and she felt Friedrich's presence coming closer. He was so much taller than she, so much more powerful. His arms were spread wide, as if to engulf her entire astral body, and from his arms shadows draped like the wing feathers of a black crow. His facial features ran together, shifting from one person to another, as if he held within him a thousand souls as evil as himself. But the same few were repeated, then again. Connor knew they were the black magicians, the ones who had almost brought Adolf Hitler to the pinnacle of world domination. These were the men and women who had opposed her grandmother and the Circle. This was the force that had almost rendered Gwendolyn insane, and it was abroad once more, fed by fifty years of the Doktor's simmering rage and resentment.

He was almost upon her now, and she stood rooted to the spot, unable to hear, unable to see anything but the menace before her. In the whirl of shadows, the two halves of the pendant burned like fire, one cold and silvery, the other molten gold. Closer they came, these two parts of one whole, halves of one creation, seeking each other with inexorable purpose. She reached out with her heart and mind, trying to connect with Gwendolyn. *"Help me, Grandmother, please. I need you."*

The shadow figure of Friedrich's astral projection laughed once more. "Begging for a rescuer? Your grandmother can't help you. The old witch defeated us once, but only by sheer luck. Only because my servants failed me at the moment I most needed them. She was stronger than you, much stronger. You shall fare much worse," came the rasping words, as if spoken by a dozen voices not quite in sync with each other. "You I will consume slowly, until every shred of your soul is part of me. You will serve me."

"Never."

"Never is a very long time here. And now I have all the time that exists."

"Only if you actually defeat the Circle."

She saw rather than heard the snarl from lips drawn back over sharp teeth. "There is no Circle. If they were ever with you at all, they've gone."

"No," said Connor, not as certain as before. She couldn't feel them, couldn't sense their presence.

The mask of her enemy shifted into a sneer. "I hear your thoughts, and you're right. They are not here. You are alone. You don't have the knowledge or the power to withstand me." He drifted still closer, the outstretched wings of a predatory bird growing larger with each passing second. "Die, Witch of Light, die now!"

In that tiny space of an instant before he struck, Connor understood. Genevieve Fitzhugh had been willing to die for her daughter. She could have fought back, but she had chosen not to do so because she was determined to buy time for her child. She had taken the horrible beating and had not cried out. Her voice had been stilled, her spirit broken. And now Connor saw it all, that she would be the voice of Genevieve, the spirit that would remain unbowed even in death. Connor's would be the hand that meted out justice at long last, even if she must die here and now. Her fear melted away, and then, as if a veil had been lifted, she could *see* them, the members of the Circle, no, *her* Circle, in the distance yet clearly visible, their hearts and souls still linked together. They'd been there all along.

Above them glowed an evening star so iridescent, so infinite…with a surge of elation, she felt something hard and cold in her right hand, as well as something in her left. With neither enmity nor fear, but only a clear understanding of the price of eternal justice, Connor swung her right arm high as his black wings rushed down to enfold her, to crush her astral body into cosmic dust.

He/it screamed in rage and terror—a horrible, grinding, searing noise. It was the voices of those lost in the darkness, screaming out the pain of untold lives wasted in suffering. He saw her arm swing toward him again, and a thousand beams of light exploded all around him, their jagged shards piercing through his astral body from every direction. He could not fathom what had happened. Clearly, the witch had been alone, without a weapon, and then something had cut into him like fire, disintegrating his gathered form as only an object shaped from pure energy could. It was as if she wielded the Sword of…but no, it wasn't possible. No woman had ever touched it.

Connor staggered backward as wave upon wave of fragmented yet deadly energy surged in all directions. She was sent reeling away from the epicenter, still clutching in her left hand the glistening star crystal, its facets pulsating and smoking. Her right hand was now empty. She closed her eyes as the impact waves reached the edges of the Circle itself. Now was the moment of truth. The evil would die, but so might the Circle of Light.

*

In Boston, high above the city, Ellen Carlisle gasped and her body shuddered. From deep within her came a single exhortation that resounded through the astral plane: "Hold fast to the Light!"

*

Ayalla looked up into Malcolm's scowling face. "Well, that's something not to wake up to every morning," she said. He didn't answer.

She scrambled to get up off the ground. "What the hell happened?"

"There were explosives in the mausoleum."

"But what about Connor?"

That's when she finally realized that Malcolm's jaw was working hard, the muscles rippling back and forth. She saw his clothes were covered in dust, his hands bleeding. He swallowed several times. "They found a skid steer with a front-loader scoop. Before that, we were digging by hand. I wanted to check on how you were doing."

Ayalla gaped at the scene before them. The walls of the mausoleum still stood, but much of the roof had collapsed. Thirty flashlights were focused on the little machine dragging pieces of granite away from the rubble. Benjamin stood atop one of the walls, Laura on another, directing the machine's operator.

"Do we know for sure she was in there?" asked Ayalla.

"Laura says she was…is." His voice broke, and tears coursed down his cheeks. He didn't even try to wipe them away. "I couldn't stand being there, in case…in case they find her…" The pain in his eyes made her stomach clench. She had this sudden and horrible image of Malcolm breaking into a million pieces, and she was scared to death of the possibility. Without even thinking, she grabbed his hand. "She's okay. Either she's not in there at all, or somehow she's…I don't know…but she's okay. Connor's a survivor, you know that."

He finally focused on her face. "You really believe that?" It was said with all the hope and fear of a child wondering if there really is a God.

She didn't hesitate for an instant. "Yes…I do."

He wrapped his arms around her…and she let him.

*

"That was the quite the adventure. I must say you handled it rather well, considering."

"Considering I didn't have any idea what I was doing."

"Quite."

"But how did I get those weapons?"

"You were ready to wield the star crystal. But as for the other, well, I must say I didn't actually expect such active intervention from our archangel friend."

"So that was his?"

"Indeed. He must have believed you worthy of such a weapon of light, if only for the briefest instant. You should thank him sometime."

Connor floated in the void, thinking. Finally, she said, "Grandmother?"

"What child?"

"Am I dead? I mean, you know, physically dead?

Gwendolyn's delightfully mellow laughter drifted through Connor's mind. "Not unless you want to be, my dear. And I can't imagine that you wouldn't prefer to get back to that lovely young woman of yours—and your father and your friends. They wouldn't do very well without you, you know."

"I have a choice?"

"Well, of course. The only unknown was whether you would truly understand what created this unfortunate dissonance that grew into such a powerful darkness. And whether you would understand it in time to save yourself and your Circle. Had you not, I'm afraid the question of physical death would have been the least of your concerns."

"Then I can go back."

"Naturally. You've restored the equilibrium, at least for now."

"You'll still come to me, won't you? Don't leave me entirely?"

"I told you once, a very long time ago, that I would never abandon you, my darling granddaughter. You are me, and I am you. Such a bond is never broken. Sleep now, and when you wake, the colors of the earth plane will be visible once more."

*

"Ellen, darling, wake up. It's over, and we're still in one piece." William gently helped his wife to stand, took her to be nearest bed, and laid her down on it. "Sleep, my love. The danger has passed." He knelt beside the bed and said a prayer.

*

"Hold it!" shouted Benjamin over the rumble of the machine's engine. "I see something!"

He and Laura scrambled down over the rubble. Malcolm and Ayalla came running.

"What is it?" Malcolm tried to shout, but the question stuck in his throat.

Laura and Benjamin were frantically tossing aside pieces of granite and concrete and mortar. Bit by bit, they uncovered Connor's legs, then her torso, then her arms and shoulders. Laura shoved a thin slab of granite and realized it had been propped up against two other pieces, all of them forming an almost perfect triangle, protecting Connor's face and head.

"Look," said Ayalla. "What is that?"

Benjamin leaned closer. There, in the hollow of Connor's throat, gleaming like fire in the shadow of the stones, lay the Goddess of Avebury pendant, not silver, not gold, but both. The two halves had been reunited.

Laura hunkered down next to her lover. "Connor... honey...sweetheart," she crooned, stroking the pale cheeks. "Please be okay, please!" Laura waited, holding her breath, every fiber of her being focused on just one prayer.

And those amazing green eyes flickered open. "I am, I think," said Connor. "But that was one helluva dream."

Laura burst into tears and shouted at the top of her lungs. "She's alive! She's okay!"

A roar went up from the assembled crowd—the police, the neighbors, the workmen. Cheers and whistles pierced the cold night air as Laura and Benjamin helped Connor slowly rise from her would-be tomb and removed her handcuffs.

Ayalla, still holding onto Malcolm's hand, said, "I told you so."

"You *would* say that," he replied as he cleared his throat one more time. "But this is one time I don't mind."

Epilogue

Doubt thou the stars are fire;
Doubt that the sun doth move;
Doubt truth to be a liar;
But never doubt I love.
—William Shakespeare, *Hamlet,* act II scene 2

As if intent on discrediting the late Amanda Hawthorne's dim views on the capricious nature of the weather in England, sun poured down on the tidy little cemetery of St. Dunstan's Anglican Church in the equally tidy village of St. Giles on Wyndle, a place Gwendolyn Broadhurst had called home for most of her life. Her daughter, Amanda, had never cared for the village or its motley assortment of "characters," of which Gwendolyn was decidedly a member.

Philip Janks, the vicar of St. Dunstan's, awaited the arrival of the family at the postern near the lane rather than the main entry closer the front of the church. He was aware of Connor Hawthorne's desire to maintain a low profile, as she put it. He was pleased to oblige, not being of that subset of vicars who tend to spread gossip without considering that their listeners are not as charitable as members of the clergy.

The casket containing the deceased had already been put in

place by four of the church's deacons, who stood by, willingly though uncomfortably clad in morning coats because formality was expected. Gwendolyn Broadhurst, whose husband, Richard, had been knighted for service to Her Majesty the Queen, had been St. Giles's only claim to landed gentry. Sir Richard hadn't taken himself or the role of "squire" too seriously, and in gratitude the villagers had treated the old couple with unfailing respect and deference. Amanda on the other hand, had always been accorded a sort of strained civility that only added to her disdain for the St. Giles folk during her infrequent visits. Today marked her final trip home.

Two cars arrived, one hired in London, the other an old but elegant Jaguar. From the latter emerged Lord and Lady Carlisle and Connor's daughter, Katy. From the former, a rental estate wagon, came Connor, then Jessica, Gwendolyn's sister and Amanda's aunt, followed by Laura, Benjamin, and Malcolm. The vicar greeted each of them in turn, and when the party had assembled, led the way toward the grave site. He was a trifle disappointed that he would not be presiding over a funeral service. They did very fine funeral services at St. Dunstan's. But Miss Hawthorne had said the church part had taken place in the States and she only wanted a graveside observance.

The mourners took their places around the grave, in the shadow of an elegantly carved angel cenotaph, as the four deacons stepped back. Mr. Janks opened his little prayer book. "O God of grace and glory," he recited in his most resonant and funereal tone, "we remember before you this day our sister Amanda. We thank you for giving her to us, to know and to love as a companion on our earthly pilgrimage. In your boundless compassion, console us who mourn. Give us faith to see in death the gate of eternal life, so that in quiet confidence we may continue our course on earth until, by your call, we are reunited with those who have gone before. Amen."

He waited a moment before asking if anyone wished to speak. For a few seconds, no one spoke, and the vicar was about to close when Connor stepped forward. "She was my mother, and I don't suppose I ever really knew her, or gave her the love she needed so very much. I didn't often try to pierce the outer illusion she presented to the world so that I might see her true heart. She taught me an important lesson, and maybe I'll be the richer for it. Maybe even a better mother." Katy, standing very close, reached for her mother's hand. Connor swiped away a tear, and took a deep breath. "I know Amanda is in good hands now, very good hands." The others, who knew full well of what Connor spoke, all smiled a little. Gwendolyn and Amanda were finally getting some quality time between mother and daughter.

Sensing that the moment had come, the vicar indicated with a nod of his head that the deacons could leave. "If there is anything at all you need," said Reverend Janks, as he shook Benjamin's hand. "Anything at all."

None of them wished to stay behind to see the casket placed in the ground. Instead, they drove directly to the house Gwendolyn had bequeathed to Connor. The old sign on the front gate still bore the name ROSEWOOD HOUSE. Once they'd all found comfortable chairs in the study, Connor's Aunt Jessica bustled around in the kitchen and soon emerged with a tray of tea things, then made another trip for the warm scones. Like many a traditional Brit, Jessica considered tea a basic staple of life.

After pouring out, she sat on the comfortable settee with Laura and said, "Now, you will bring us to date on all that's happened."

Little by little, with everyone in the American contingent contributing various pieces of the story, Katy and Jessica learned all there was to know about what had transpired on the other side of the Atlantic. By turns, Connor's aunt and daughter were shocked, concerned, relieved, and then finally thankful that she had survived it all. Connor did not share quite all of the details of her encounter with Friedrich, or more precisely, with what Friedrich had become, if only because she wasn't sure that Katy was quite ready to hear it. After all, she was the next woman in the Broadhurst line.

"Your friend Grace. She was found all right?" asked Katy.

"Within a couple of hours. She was none the worse for wear and a lot more like her old self. I hear she's planning on selling the Beacon Hill house and moving back to the Hingham cottage."

"So this Raley character died as well?" inquired Jessica. "And all for what?"

"That's one of the real ironies in all this," said Benjamin. "What he wanted was money, and he died surrounded by it. The search teams must have recovered more than twenty metal boxes filled with gold bars, valuable jewelry, even cash."

"So poor Billy's grandfather really was the Frenchman turned Nazi?"

"Absolutely. He changed his name from Guillaume de L'Aigle to William Dagle when he arrived in America. Soon after that, he bought the mausoleum from the family who'd owned it. They were desperate for money, and he sweetened the deal by offering to have their family members interred somewhere else in the cemetery. Then he used all the crypts to hide his wealth. He was smart enough to disperse bits and pieces of it gradually so as not to arouse anyone else's suspicions. He invested in real estate and later in the funeral home that his son, and eventually his grandson managed."

"And this necklace everyone wanted? What's become of it."

Benjamin turned to the Carlisles. "You want to take that one?"

"The Goddess of Avebury pendant is safe now."

"Ah," said Jessica. "I understand. The less said, the better. But what of this terrible man, the old Nazi? You found his body in the tomb, I take it."

Benjamin, noting Connor's reluctance to discuss her foe, answered the question. "We found him several feet away, twisted and broken. From the looks of his body, I can't imagine how he ever managed to travel from Germany to the United States. His skin was deathly white, and his muscles seemed horribly wasted away. The autopsy showed he was riddled with cancer. He would have died soon enough anyway."

"Not necessarily. He was…" said Connor, then she shook her head. "Never mind. It's not important."

Jessica nodded. "Exactly dear. I've asked enough questions, silly old woman that I am. You must be exhausted."

Connor almost yawned. "I could use a short nap. Katy, would you mind? We can talk more later."

"Sure, Mom. I think I'll take a walk. She glanced at Ellen. "Would you and William like to come along?"

"Yes," she replied after an affirmative nod from her husband. "That would be lovely."

An hour later, Connor awoke, refreshed and alert, even with the effects of jet lag and so little sleep. She'd been dreaming, but couldn't quite recall the images or the words. Beside her, Laura opened her eyes. "You up already?" she murmured, shifting herself to put her head on Connor's shoulder.

"Hmm. Seems like it."

"You really okay?" said Laura. "About your mom, and well, everything?"

"I really am."

"You sound surprised."

"Well, I guess I am surprised."

"Why?"

Connor rested her chin on Laura's forehead. "All this astral plane stuff—the Circle, all of it—well, for so long I ran away from it because it frightened me. And you know what?"

"It wasn't as bad as you thought?"

"No. Actually, it turned out to be a lot worse than even I could have imagined."

"Oh."

"But I'm okay with it. And I'm okay with my deceased grandmother dropping in on me when I least expect it. And I'm not scared anymore."

Laura curled her arm over Connor's stomach and hugged her. "I'm just glad you came back, and you're right here where I can hold you."

"You know, I've been thinking."

"About what?"

"Would you mind if we stayed here a while?"

"You mean here in England? Of course not."

"I want to spend more time with Katy, not intrude on her life, but get to know her better. Sometimes I worry that we're almost strangers."

"That might be overstating it a bit, but I understand. Besides, you'll have a chance to work with William and Ellen, to get to know all those things you never let Gwendolyn teach you."

"Does that bother you?" asked Connor.

"Does what bother me?"

"That this Circle doesn't include you?"

"No, should it?"

"It sort of bothers me because I like us doing things together."

"We will, sweetheart. But there will always be some things we do apart. That's how it is."

"Did you know I love you?" whispered Connor.

"I'd sort of gotten that impression."

"Good."

Connor lay there for several minutes before realizing Laura had drifted off to sleep once more. She gently kissed Laura's forehead. "Enjoy the Dreamtime, my love. I'll be right here when you come home."